Praise for the *New York Times* Bestseller *Donnie Brasco*

"Courageous and extraordinary."
—*New York Times Book Review*

"Thoroughly absorbing true-life adventure."
—*Newsday*

"The tension builds with the machine-gun rapidity . . . the suspense of a fictional mystery yarn but the chilling ring of reality."
—*Virginian Pilot*

"Excellent . . . for a view of how the Mafia operates, none can match Joe Pistone!"
—*Seattle Post-Intelligencer*

"Unprecedented. . . . A chilling chronicle of Pistone's undercover work in the Mafia."
—*UPI*

"Truly exciting . . . so skillfully written it's worth your time."

—*Palm Springs Desert Sun*

"Oozes with names . . . and plenty of behind-the-social-club-door gossip."

—*New York Daily News*

"A penetrating look into the Mafia inner circle . . . frightening . . . daring."

—*Fort Worth Evening Telegram*

"Compelling, gripping, revealing . . . raw, hard-hitting nonfiction at its best!"

—*Toronto Star*

"Immensely satisfying!"

—*Oakland Press*

DONNIE BRASCO
DEEP COVER

Joseph D. Pistone

AN ONYX BOOK

ONYX
Published by the Penguin Group
Penguin Putnam Inc., 375 Hudson Street,
New York, New York 10014, U.S.A.
Penguin Books Ltd, 27 Wrights Lane,
London W8 5TZ, England
Penguin Books Australia Ltd, Ringwood,
Victoria, Australia
Penguin Books Canada Ltd, 10 Alcorn Avenue,
Toronto, Ontario, Canada M4V 3B2
Penguin Books (N.Z.) Ltd, 182–190 Wairau Road,
Auckland 10, New Zealand

Penguin Books Ltd, Registered Offices:
Harmondsworth, Middlesex, England

First published by Onyx, an imprint of Dutton NAL,
a member of Penguin Putnam Inc.

First Printing, April, 1999
10 9 8 7 6 5 4 3 2 1

REGISTERED TRADEMARK—MARCA REGISTRADA

Printed in the United States of America

PUBLISHER'S NOTE
This is a work of fiction. Names, characters, places, and incidents either
are the product of the author's imagination or are used fictitiously,
and any resemblance to actual persons, living or dead, events, or locales
is entirely coincidental.

BOOKS ARE AVAILABLE AT QUANTITY DISCOUNTS WHEN USED TO PROMOTE
PRODUCTS OR SERVICES. FOR INFORMATION PLEASE WRITE TO PREMIUM
MARKETING DIVISION, PENGUIN PUTNAM INC., 375 HUDSON STREET, NEW YORK,
NEW YORK 10014.

To my dad, Samuel, my mom, Rose, and wife, Peggy,
for all their help and understanding.

ACKNOWLEDGMENT

To my editor, Michaela Hamilton, and my agent, Carmen LaVia, without whose guiding hands none of this would have been possible.

*And after all, what is a lie? 'Tis but
The truth in masquerade.*

—Byron, *Don Juan*

PROLOGUE

The FBI agent known as Donnie Brasco was staying at the Sheraton Towers Hotel on Seventh Avenue, up in the VIP section where there was security and you needed a guest key to operate the elevators. He strode through the cool, bustling lobby in a hurry, glancing left and right. Outside, he paused for a moment before taking the shallow steps to the sidewalk, using the high ground to survey the street in both directions.

Everything seemed normal—insofar as midtown Manhattan could appear normal—except for a middle-aged guy across the street wearing shorts, white socks, clunky black dress shoes, and a camera slung around his neck. He sure looked harmless enough, but Donnie's world had become one where middle-aged guys in white socks and black wing tips could be the most dangerous.

He swept down the steps, a tall, graceful man with broad shoulders beneath a two-button gray summer blazer. His legs were long and his stride was easy and fluid. The breeze rolling down Seventh with the cab-yellowed traffic ruffled his thick black hair. His alert blue eyes never stopped moving as he walked confidently through the throng of pedestrians to the Metropolitan Garage.

Within a few minutes, the pimply faced kid with the Lyle Lovette hair who'd taken his ticket drove up in the dark blue Bureau rental car.

As the boy climbed out from behind the steering wheel and Donnie tipped him, a big Buick rocked to a halt behind the car and the driver honked the horn.

Jerk-off oughta calm down, Donnie thought. But despite his irritation, he lowered himself into the rental a little more hurriedly than usual and drove down the ramp and out of the garage to join the stream of traffic.

When the man straightened up in the backseat, grinned at Donnie, and said he had a gun aimed at him through the seat back, Donnie realized he should have paid more attention to the fact that the Buick in the garage had distracted him for a second. He was sure now it hadn't been coincidental. It had been to rush him so he wouldn't glance at the floor in back and see the man now leaning forward and smiling at him in the rearview mirror.

The gunman was blond and had a deep tan, like he'd just flown in from Florida or California. Dressed California, with a half-buttoned silk shirt and a gold chain flashing. Handsome smile, handsome guy, not much older than the garage attendant. But he had an outdoorsy look to go along with California, like he was some kind of movie cowboy. Donnie could see his nervousness peeking through the smile. A cowboy, Donnie thought. He didn't doubt the man really did have a gun aimed at his back through the driver's seat. Just like a real cowboy with a six-shooter, but this one might as well have had "dude" stamped on his forehead.

"You ever wear a ten-gallon hat?" Donnie asked.

"The fuck's that s'pose to mean?"

"Never mind. Doesn't matter."

"Better know it don't."

Donnie glanced beyond the man's reflection in the mirror, then checked the left outside mirror. No Buick. If the big car and its driver had been a deliberate diversion, they were no longer part of the plan. Just Donnie and the young cowpoke. Donnie almost smiled back at him in the mirror.

"Cut down to First Avenue and head uptown," the cowboy said, trying to sound tough.

He sounded tough enough. Donnie made a right turn in front of a cab and attracted an angry horn blast.

"Don't try and get nobody's attention," the blond man said. "Just drive to the Queensboro Bridge and be a good boy all the way."

Traffic was stop and go on First Avenue.

"I could cut over to Third and make better time going uptown," Donnie offered.

"Shut the fuck up," the blond man said.

Traffic opened and Donnie began to drive. Shielded by his body, his left hand edged over and touched the button that adjusted the left outside mirror. The tiny electric motor that moved the mirror didn't make enough noise to be heard above the din of traffic. Fine. Young gun wouldn't realize Donnie was inching the mirror to aim in toward the car.

Within a few blocks the mirror reflected the head and shoulders of the man in the backseat. The slope of his shoulders indicated he'd relaxed with the gun and had it lowered, knowing Donnie couldn't see it anyway. A high-caliber handgun was heavy; the arm tended to drop after a while. Donnie tried not to think about the gun and watched the cowboy's eyes in the outside mirror. They were trained on the back of Donnie's head. The man was being careful, playing by the rules. That could be fatal. Donnie played outside the rules.

At a stop sign, a professional dogwalker with half

a dozen assorted breeds on leashes made his way across the intersection. An attractive woman in shorts and jogging shoes was waiting to cross in the other direction, and holding a leash that led to a large dalmatian. It was easy to see she was worried about what was going to happen when the dogwalker and his charges got to her side of the street.

The light changed, and the dogwalker picked up the pace, tugging on the leashes bunched in each hand.

As Donnie started to accelerate, the cowboy glanced sideways to see what was going to happen at the corner.

Donnie pivoted in the seat, lashing back with the point of his elbow and slamming it into the cowboy's temple so his head bounced off the window. At the same time, he stamped on the brake pedal, yanked back on the door handle, and tumbled sideways out of the car and onto hot concrete. The cowboy's gun must have had a silencer. Donnie heard nothing but saw stuffing fly from the middle of the seat's upholstery. In a low crouch, he pumped with his legs and got around the side of the car, then stayed low behind the back bumper.

It had all taken only a few seconds. Cowboy had been surprised.

He was still in the car and couldn't see Donnie, but he had to figure Donnie was carrying.

He was right. Donnie reached behind him and beneath his blazer, and his hand came out with the stubby 9mm he'd had tucked in his belt in the small of his back.

Traffic was stopped and didn't look as if it would ever move again. Horns blared. Drivers shouted above and between their blasts of protest. Donnie could feel heat rolling out from the grill of the cab that was stopped only a few feet behind him.

But it was cowboy who had the problem. He couldn't see Donnie to get a shot at him, couldn't even be sure where Donnie was, and if he left the car and made a run for it, he had to guess right or he'd be an easy target.

He guessed wrong, but it didn't make any difference, because Donnie had his hand on the car, felt it lean almost imperceptibly to the left.

Cowboy broke from the driver-side door. Donnie shifted his body slightly so he could see the fleeing man. Cowboy must have caught him in the corner of his vision, because he whirled and aimed a gun with a long silencer at him. A bullet *thunked* into the car's steel near Donnie as he got off a return shot and put a bullet in the man's chest, where he was meaty and would stop the hollow-point slug.

Amazingly, the cowboy kept running, limping slightly as he began weaving between cars. Donnie couldn't get another shot away without possibly hitting a civilian.

He started to pursue, but his right leg gave way and he stumbled and leaned against the car. He'd banged his knee on the pavement and hadn't realized it until he'd straightened up.

Sirens were yodeling along Second Avenue now, but Donnie knew that with his head start and all the cover New York provided, the cowboy wouldn't be caught.

And he wasn't, exactly.

He was found dead on the sidewalk in front of a building on East Fifty-ninth.

Donnie almost felt sorry for the man who'd tried to kill him to collect on the half-million-dollar open contract the Mafia had put out on his life. He wouldn't have worried much if the cowboy had made his escape. It wasn't the young hotbloods or ambitious amateurs trying for an express ticket to riches and reputation who concerned him.

He knew that sooner or later someone would come for him who knew the work.

1

―――――――――

"**I** was just informed they had another go at you," Donnie's Bureau supervisor Jules Donavon said on the phone.

The time for violence and bravery was past. Donnie was sitting on the bed in his room in the Hotel Amington on the Upper West Side, waiting for the Bureau to send his things over from the Sheraton. He'd spent the past ten minutes trembling, even had a brief spell of uncontrollable sobbing. He was still coming down from the stress and adrenaline rush of fighting for his life. Somehow death seemed closer now than it had a few hours ago in the rental car.

This wasn't the way to deal with his situation, he told himself. It was a normal reaction, he knew, but one he couldn't afford. It was unacceptable. Definitely not the way to talk with Jules.

"Donnie?"

He breathed in and out evenly and found in himself what he needed, who he needed to be. Tough guy.

"Another cowboy," he said into the receiver. "He didn't get the job done."

"Obviously."

Donnie Brasco had lived for six extraordinary years as an undercover agent in the Mafia. Actually,

Donnie Brasco wasn't even his real name; it was a false identity he had adopted during his "wiseguy" years. But he had trained himself to answer to that name as a matter of life and death, and even after his undercover role had ended, the name continued to feel right. Now only his family and childhood friends called him by the name that appeared on his birth certificate—Joseph D. Pistone. Even his colleagues in the Bureau knew him as Donnie Brasco.

While walking the thin line between pretending to be a "stand-up guy" for the Bonanno family, and reporting everything he saw to his FBI contact, he had attained a surrogate father-son relationship with Mafia soldier Lefty Ruggiero, and he had worked his way up in the mob until he had gotten the evidence to bring about the arrests and convictions of several made members of the Mafia and then two Mafia dons themselves. Almost single-handedly he'd brought about the ruin, then extinction, of much of the East Coast Mafia. When the lengthy legal process was finally over, Donnie had become a very special kind of special agent.

The problem was that he still loved Lefty, even though he'd done what both men knew he'd had to do. And Lefty had warned Donnie about what would happen. After the trials and convictions, the Mafia had put a half-million-dollar price on Donnie's life, an open contract with the amount payable to whoever killed him. It meant Donnie would have to spend the rest of his life sneaking glances behind him, using aliases, living with danger almost as if he were a criminal himself. It meant his marriage to Elana had deteriorated to a legal separation after she'd cracked under the strain and moved out to become herself again. She'd wanted him to become a vanilla agent again, tracing leads, doing desk work as well as fieldwork, to get out of undercover work and the risk that went with it. Donnie hadn't been ready, couldn't do it, and she couldn't understand why. He couldn't explain it to her because he didn't have many of the answers himself. Then his Mafia exploits had been made into a major movie that even the critics had loved. That didn't exactly help him fade safely into society.

Donnie had adapted to the constant apprehension. His intelligent blue eyes were always scanning, his mind calculating. His powerful body had a perfect stillness in repose, and a surprising quickness and smoothness when he did decide to move. He'd grown up street-smart in a rough section of Paterson, New Jersey, and despite his education and sophistication, it still showed. You didn't have to listen closely to hear a rough New Jersey flatness in his voice, especially when he was angry.

So he still worked undercover for the Bureau, and sometimes it seemed his only identity was the one he was feigning at the time. The job could create a loneliness that was pure pain. He missed Elana and his daughters, Maureen and Daisy, with a fierceness that ate like a predator at his gut. He saw them only occasionally. There was always the danger someone would try to get to him through them. He didn't want them to feel the same fear that haunted him, that had become his life. Learning to live with the danger the Mafia had jacketed him with was itself a death sentence for anything like a normal life. The only way to survive the dread and constant wariness was to learn to love it in the perverse way masochists loved pain. Now he fed on the fear, because that was all there was. And it fed on him.

"You still there, Donnie?"

"Here," Donnie said, okay now, no longer having the shakes. "Still among the living."

"You sure you're all right?"

"Yeah."

"Why I called was because I need you here," Donavon said. "In Florida."

Donnie was surprised. He'd assumed Donavon was calling from across town in New York. But he didn't consider the request unusual. He'd gotten used to receiving unexpected phone calls from Donavon, packing a change of clothes, and catching planes all in the same day. Because of Donnie's unique status in the Bureau, and the need to stay undercover and reduce the possibility of assassination even when not on a case, Donavon was always his direct supervisor regardless of geography. Donnie drifted from role to role, danger to danger, with Donavon one of the few constants in his shifting, lonely world.

"You should get out of New York for a while, anyway, after what happened today," Donavon told him.

"I don't think it much matters where I am."

"Maybe not," Donavon said, "but I already had an airline reservation made for you. I need you here, Donnie. South."

2

The Atlantic had a nasty look, like roiled, dirty bath-water. As Donnie drove his rented red Ford Taurus north on A1A along Florida's east coast, he occasionally glanced out the window at the looming swells that rushed toward shore and became white-capped waves as they met the resistance of the land. The sky was a moving maze of clouds, and down low was the same dirty gray-green of the ocean, so there was no horizon line. And there was no rain yet, but gusts of wind with muscle were blustering in from the sea and occasionally rocking the Taurus.

The National Hurricane Center had announced there was a slight chance the second hurricane of the season, Blaze, would make landfall early tomorrow north of the small coastal town of Palmville, toward which Donnie was driving. He supposed the weather he was passing through now was the southwestern edge of Blaze's leading storm line.

A particularly hard gust of wind rocked the Taurus, causing him to tighten his grip on the steering wheel and pay more attention to his driving.

Donnie had arrived in Florida only yesterday morning. His face-to-face conversation with Jules Donavon had been the same afternoon, in a hotel restaurant in

Fort Lauderdale. Donnie had eaten lunch on the plane, so he ordered only a draft dark beer. Donavon, also not lunching, sipped a more genteel single-malt scotch. He was a solidly built man in his fifties, a dedicated jogger with a flat stomach, barrel chest, and salt-and-pepper hair. Always impeccably dressed, he had a calm, confident air, looking as if he were the CEO of General Motors and had the job by the ass. Often his aging, handsome face wore a faint look of amusement.

Like Donnie, Donavon had grown up tough on city streets, but in Jersey City, New Jersey. He'd served in the Green Berets in Vietnam and graduated from Seton Hall University before joining the Bureau. He and Donnie had entered the Bureau at about the same time, gone through training and initial assignment together. Donavon had finished third in his class. Donnie had been first. The distinction had disappeared when Donavon saved Donnie's life in a shootout in New York's Chinatown. A quiet, thoughtful man with a sardonic sense of humor, Donavon was married with two children, a boy and a girl. He and Donnie liked and trusted each other and could talk freely in the knowledge that nothing they said would go further.

The two men ate pretzels and worked on their drinks in silence for a few minutes, watching a group of businesswomen at the bar laughing and drinking, their eyes glued to a Marlins baseball game with the St. Louis Cardinals.

"You never used to see so many women sports fans," Donavon said, around a mouthful of pretzels. He had the same tough flatness in his voice as Donnie's, only it wasn't as evident.

"Or serial killers," Donnie said.

"You got a point," Donavon agreed, lifting his glass. "Though I don't know what it is."

Donnie didn't explain it to him, only waited.

"There's a woman down here in Florida," Donavon said after a while, "Marcia Graham, writes for the *National Ethical Chronicle*. She's here to cover possible political corruption."

"Possible, hell," Donnie said. "If it's political, it's corrupt."

"We agree again. I only arrived here in Florida yesterday, after Marcia Graham phoned me in D.C. She wanted me to send someone from the Bureau to talk to her."

"Why wouldn't she talk over the phone?" Donnie asked.

"She was too smart for that."

"She think somebody's gonna steal her scoop?"

"Not really," Donavon said. "You see, there is no *National Ethical Chronicle* and she's not really a journalist. Who she happens to be is FBI Special Agent Marcia Dunn, working for a nonexistent magazine invented by the Bureau. I've worked with her before, and I recently refreshed myself on her record. She's good at what we do, Donnie."

Donnie knew Donavon didn't toss compliments around like souvenir gumballs. "What prompted the Bureau to assign her to Florida?" he asked.

"We got a reliable but anonymous tip that a lot of money was collecting in Swiss bank accounts and in banks in the Caribbean Islands, and that it was the result of corruption in Florida politics."

"If the tip was anonymous, what makes you think it's reliable?"

"It was accompanied by information only an insider would know."

"You think Dunn found the tipster?"

"Maybe. She's obviously developed a source, but probably one who assumes he or she is merely talking to a journalist and not an FBI agent."

"You talk to Dunn yet in person?" Donnie asked.

"No, and I'm not going to. I had to come to Florida on other Bureau business, and I wanted to meet with you before you go to see her. I want to know as soon as possible what she's mixed up in. Maybe you can help."

"She probably stumbled over the corruption she was looking for and wants to talk about it personally to somebody she can trust. Now you want her to open up to my honest face and reassuring manner."

Donavon smiled without humor. "Something like that. Whatever she's got, it can't be something small."

"How do you know, if she wouldn't talk on the phone."

Donavon chewed the inside of his cheek for a moment, staring out the window at the gently swaying masts of pleasure boats moored at the hotel dock. "She was scared shitless. I could hear it in her voice, almost feel it coming through the phone."

"It can be scary sometimes, this business we're in."

"She wouldn't trust anyone in Florida, Donnie, not even her own people in the Bureau."

"Who's her contact agent?"

"Wisowski. He's top-drawer. An honest agent."

"But she isn't so sure, or she would have gone to him with her story."

"That's how scared she is. She decided to go over him, to me."

"Should I be scared, Jules?" Donnie asked. He pronounced the name *Joo-ools* in his Jersey accent.

Donavon smiled thinly. "You're never scared."

"You're wrong," Donnie said. "I survived in the Mafia for six years by always being at least a little bit scared. Fear keeps your eyes open wide and sharpens your judgment." He sipped his beer from its iced mug. "Why's Dunn pretending to be a journalist? Nobody wants to feed those folks any kinda information that isn't self-serving."

"That's exactly what the Bureau figures the bad

guys will think," Donavon said. "And Dunn-Graham has spent time making it clear she has her own low standards and is open for bribery. The theory is, with all the money involved, when she gets close to whatever's causing the odor, someone connected to said odor will come forward and try to buy her off."

"Dangerous theory." But Donnie knew the crooked journalist scam had worked before.

Donavon glanced at his watch. It had lots of little dials on it and looked as if it might reveal times, dates, and various measurements on other planets as well as earth. "I've gotta fly back to Washington tonight. I want you to talk with Agent Dunn tomorrow, then phone immediately afterward and report on what she told you."

"Maybe she won't talk to me, somebody she doesn't even know."

"She knows you by reputation. That's why I called you."

"She didn't want to give out the information over the phone. Maybe when I learn what it is, I won't, either."

"She's badly scared," Donavon said, standing up. "You're only a little bit scared." He unbuckled his briefcase, reached inside, and brought out a small gray plastic device that looked like a high-tech toy, which in a way it was. "To be on the safe side, use this scrambler when you call, so no one can eavesdrop on us. Before you depart Florida, leave it with Agent Dunn. She obviously wasn't supplied with one."

That didn't seem unusual to Donnie. The presence of a scrambler in an undercover agent's apartment or house could be more dangerous than a risky phone call. Owning a scrambler didn't automatically make you an informer, but it could definitely put you in a spot where you'd need a plausible story to avoid a bullet behind the ear.

Donavon fished in his briefcase again and laid a

ten-by-twelve brown envelope on the table. "That's a partial file on Agent Dunn," he said. "Destroy it when you've finished reading it. We wouldn't want a real journalist to somehow come across it after you'd misplaced it or put it in the trash."

"There's no chance that would happen."

Donavon picked up the edge in Donnie's voice and stared down at him with a neutral expression, making sure Donnie wasn't kidding.

"No, there isn't," Donavon said. "Sorry."

After watching Donavon walk from the bar, Donnie removed a yellow file folder from the envelope and studied its contents. There were only a few pages inside, but they were informative. Marcia Dunn, a.k.a. Marcia Graham, had graduated from FBI training facilities at Quantico near the top of her class nine years ago. After seven years as a field agent, she was promoted and transferred to the New York Field Office. During the past five years she'd gained the confidence of and exposed a child pornography ring that operated throughout New England, a gang of car thieves that stole and stripped newer model cars and left what remained of them in remote wooded areas, and an Asia-connected network that sold counterfeit designer clothes.

Donnie studied her Bureau snapshot. She was an attractive yet nondescript woman with dark hair and a wide, friendly smile. Her file said she was forty-six, five-foot-eight, and highly trained in communications and surveillance. She'd worked in a criminal division in the New York Field Office for three years, assigned to a white-collar crime squad. For one of those years she'd posed as a bond salesman for a fraudulent brokerage firm.

Donnie was impressed. And curious.

What could frighten to the bone a woman like Marcia Dunn?

*   *   *

A burst of wind from the sea almost blew the Taurus out of its lane and into the path of an oncoming car, bringing him back to the present. While the southbound traffic on the coast highway was thin, Donnie noticed that the northbound traffic, of which he was a part, was becoming heavier. When he stole a look to his right, he saw that the sky had darkened off the coast and the clouds seemed lower.

Without taking his eyes off the road, he reached over, switched on the radio, and used the scan button.

He didn't have to search long for information on Hurricane Blaze. An announcer with a quaver in his voice said the National Hurricane Center was revising its forecast. Blaze was expected to make landfall south of its original course, and sooner than expected. Not only that: a fast-moving weather front from the northwest, combined with warm water off the coast, had caused the hurricane to strengthen. It had been upgraded from a Category One hurricane, with winds of approximately seventy-five miles per hour. Now it was a Category Two, with winds approaching ninety.

Donnie considered turning west and driving inland. But Blaze was still five or six hours from landfall. He'd be at Agent Dunn's rented beach cottage within an hour, if traffic didn't bog down on the coast highway. He decided to continue driving north.

It didn't take him long to skirt the eastern edge of Palmville. Beyond the businesses, public marina, and expensive beachfront homes, traffic thinned. People fleeing from the storm's path were cutting west, most of them to get onto Interstate 95 or the Florida Turnpike, to make better time driving north.

As he passed the Sand Crab restaurant on his left, Donnie followed directions and began looking for the

sign marking the turnoff to the beach and Agent
Dunn's cottage. A seagull crossed his line of vision
only about ten feet in front of the windshield. It
wasn't flying as a gull should. Instead it was skewed
sideways, tumbling and flapping its wings defen-
sively against a wind that had captured its fate.

There was the crude wooden sign lettered BEACH
LANE, canted to the west in the fierce weather.

Donnie braked the Taurus and veered onto Beach
Lane, looking out at the vast ocean as he did so. He
was shocked by the height and force of the waves
breaking on the beach. In fact, there wasn't much
beach visible now. The surging white surf, with its
reaching fingers of foam, seemed to retreat reluc-
tantly against the wind after splaying out on the
sand.

The nervous announcer on the radio was now saying Blaze had fooled the weather forecasters. Its eye
was only twenty miles off the coast and its winds
were battering Florida from Pompano Beach to beyond Fort Pierce.

Something was very wrong here, Donnie decided,
stopping the car. Beach Lane disappeared into the
ocean. Obviously the surf was reaching even farther
onto the shore than he'd imagined.

He looked ahead and to his right and saw a low,
flat-roofed cottage with its windows shuttered. One
of its metal awnings was hanging crooked and banging around in the wind. The cottage was white with
red shutters and had a plank porch that ran the
length of its front. Though he couldn't see anything
resembling an address, Donnie was fairly sure it was
Agent Dunn's cottage.

He decided to drive the car off the road and park
as far from the water as possible, then walk to the
cottage.

Less than ten yards off the road's packed gravel

surface, the Taurus's front wheels were buried and spinning in wet, sandy soil.

Donnie adroitly used the transmission lever and accelerator to rock the car back and forth, trying to get the tires to jump from their ruts. But the vehicle was stuck firm. He decided to use brute force and gave a final try with more throttle, spinning the wheels and hearing mud and rocks bounce off the insides of the fenders. A last resort.

It didn't work. When he let up on the accelerator he could smell hot rubber as the car settled deeper into its ruts.

Donnie forced himself to be calm. So the car was stuck. No major deal. He'd known the weather was going to be lousy when he'd begun his drive north.

But when he got out of the car he was astounded by the wind's force and by needles of water and sand striking his face. An object he recognized as an old jogging shoe bounced past, then an empty plastic bottle. A second glance revealed that the bottle wasn't plastic, but glass.

He turned his face away from the driving wind and saw tall palm trees bent with Blaze's force so that their shimmying fronds almost touched the ground, looking like graceful women leaning low and shaking their heads after washing their hair. Whenever the roaring surf subsided, he could see dark debris and driftwood scattered along the north-ward curve of the beach.

Donnie's suit and shirt were already soaked, his coat unbuttoned and whipping in the wind.

Wondering if Agent Dunn had been one of the smart ones who'd fled inland in the face of the hurri-cane, he hunkered down and began making his way toward the cottage.

3

Donnie had to lean into the wind and move at an angle toward the cottage. Rain and blown sand continued to blast him, and something large struck the side of his left thigh painfully, then bounced past. He didn't bother turning and opening his squinted eyes wide enough to see what it was. Crouching low, he fought the storm to keep if from blowing him off course on his way to the cottage.

He saw shingles rise and scatter like startled birds from the cottage's roof as the wind increased to an even higher pitch and began to howl. Then thick sheets of rain began blowing in from the sea, obscuring his vision. He clutched what appeared to be an old fence post jutting from the ground and held on, feeling wet splinters penetrating his hands.

Then through the almost horizontal sheets of rain he thought he saw two figures on the cottage's porch, standing near the door. They looked tall and were dressed in what appeared to be long, dark raincoats. In unison they ducked low against the wind and moved along the front wall of the cottage, edging toward the south end of the porch.

Donnie loosened his grip with one hand and used his knuckles to rub moisture from both eyes, then peered again through the wind-driven rain and sand.

The figures were no longer visible.

He felt a coolness about his feet and ankles and realized the pounding surf was reaching him. Staying where he was wouldn't work for very long. Between blasts of wind he began again to make his way toward the cottage, sometimes being shoved several yards across the sandy ground by powerful gusts before finding a handhold on a jutting stone or stubborn, tangled plant growth.

Finally he wrapped his arms around one of the cottage's porch posts, then gathered strength and pulled himself up beneath the rail and onto the plank floor. He could hear the metal awning crashing violently against the wall as if sounding a frantic alarm.

The cottage's door was open. Half crawling, half rolling in the wind, he managed to reach the door and get inside. Rain was still crashing into him. His groping fingers found the door's wooden edge, and with great effort he managed to close it.

Though the wind still howled and the rain beat at the cottage, it seemed almost silent inside. And dry.

Not that it was either. It was only dry and quiet by comparison.

Donnie blinked and looked around. The place was a mess, probably from the wind that had rocketed in through the wide-open door and ricocheted all over the interior. A blue lamp shade lay on its side in a corner. Furniture was toppled. Framed pictures had been blown from the walls and lay broken and scattered.

Donnie became aware of about an inch of water on the floor and saw a steady stream falling from the roof where the shingles had been blown away.

That was when he saw something else. A large brown dog, a German shepherd, lying on its side. It appeared to be sleeping but had to be dead to lie so still in the surrounding havoc.

A window suddenly broke with a shattering of glass and the entrance of what looked like part of a tree trunk, taking the wall beneath the sill with it. The wind and rain were back inside in full force. A curtain that had been over the window came detached from the jagged end of the splintered wooden frame and flew across the room like a tattered battle flag.

Donnie moved toward the window, thinking he might be able to push the jutting chunk of tree outside and shove something against the opening to keep out at least some of the hurricane's force.

And he realized the water on the floor had become deeper. Its level was above his ankles now.

Movement caught his eye and he turned. A dark tennis shoe, then its mate, floated from behind what looked like a breakfast bar. Unbelievingly at first, he saw that there were ankles protruding from the shoes. A woman's calves appeared, her knees, her thighs, the edges of a pair of red shorts. Her flesh had the pale, waxy cast of the dead.

Then light and sound burst into the cottage. Donnie slipped and fell backward into the sloshing water. He was staring up at open sky.

It took several seconds for reality to take hold in his mind. The roof had been blown off!

He knew he had to get out, and fast. Pushing through water that he realized was now up to his knees, he waded to the door and yanked it open.

And was terrified to see nothing but angry ocean. *Blaze had moved the sea onto the land!*

A vast swell rose from churning, whitecapped water and rushed ponderously toward him. He froze, not knowing which direction to run, wondering if it made a difference anyway.

The swell became a wave that rose higher and higher and curled and loomed over him . . . then dropped with a clap like thunder and knocked him backward, taking out the front wall of the cottage. Pain exploded in his head, and when he stopped choking and spitting out salt water, he found himself slumped against the back wall, near a floating upside-down table.

He saw that the front of the cottage had disappeared. And another giant swell was rising like a mountain in the ocean.

Donnie got to his feet, gripping the wall, and shoved himself sideways, toward a gaping hole that had been a back door.

Water struck him from behind, pinning him against the wall, then lifting him, whirling him. He swallowed salt water and began to choke. For an instant he caught sight of land, and he struggled in that direction, flailing his arms and legs.

He was dropped hard into about two feet of water, feeling muddy ground beneath. Fighting to regain his breath, he got to his feet and ran in what he thought was the direction of the highway, letting irresistible forces shove him along. He was lifted, spinning and tumbling, and dropped again by an incoming wave, but this time more gently. He scrambled upright immediately and continued running. The wind was his ally now, hastening his flight from the sea. He could feel firmer footing, see water splashing at his feet with each panicky step.

Suddenly he was on what felt like hard pavement beneath several inches of water. The highway? He saw cars resting on their sides as a gust of wind took him and he lost his footing. He didn't try to rise, instead letting the wind roll him, and he dropped heavily into what might have been a ditch along the opposite side of the road. There was debris and water in it, but the water wasn't deep and was running swiftly. The ocean-side edge of the depression was reinforced with concrete and did provide some shelter from the wind. And maybe Donnie had run far enough inland to avoid the terrible vastness of the sea.

Maybe.

Maybe would have to be good enough. He was exhausted and couldn't go any farther, and he didn't have the will to rise again into the fierceness of wind and rain and try to find better shelter. Besides that, he realized the right side of his head still ached from when it had struck the back wall of the cottage.

The hell with it, he thought, clenching his eyes shut and tasting the salt of the sea on his lips. And he said aloud and unheard over the wind, "The hell with it."

He wedged his body against something hard, maybe part of the Dunn cottage or some other broken structure, and dragged himself up slightly so that only his lower legs trailed in the water. If the water didn't rise, he wouldn't drown, and the ditch that had become a creek provided a windbreak.

Then he opened his eyes to slits and looked around. He extended his arms over his head as far as they would stretch and gripped with both hands what looked like roots sticking out of the soil between two stones or slabs of concrete near the upper lip of the ditch.

Closing his eyes again, he turned his head and pressed his cheek into the mud as if it were a comforting pillow.

Blaze's wind and rain roared above him but became fainter as he lost consciousness.

4

Donnie thought it was some show. The Rockettes were wearing black plastic raincoats, kicking high with their long, pale legs and grinning wide and bright. Beside him sat a woman wearing red shorts and black tennis shoes. He couldn't quite make out her face in the dark theater, but he knew she was smiling like the Rockettes.

"It's fun being with a gent like you," she said over the music. A gent . . . a gent . . . agent.

It began raining heavily inside the theater, and Donnie understood why the Rockettes were wearing raincoats.

"It's part of the show," he explained to the woman beside him.

The music, a cacophonous, howling thunder Donnie had never heard before, got even louder.

"For you!" the woman next to Donnie was screaming.

He didn't understand what she meant.

"For you!" she repeated. She reached into her purse on her dark lap and drew out a cell phone, holding it out for Donnie. "*I* can't talk on the phone."

As he accepted the phone, she floated away from him into the darkness. Donnie was a bit unnerved to notice that all the Rockettes were staring directly at him as they danced.

"H'lo," Donnie said into the phone. "Hello!"

"Hello," said the nurse.

Nurse?

She was leaning over Donnie, her curious moon face close to his nose and left cheek. He could smell garlic on her warm breath. "Can you hear me?"

He nodded.

The nurse straightened up. "Tell doctor he's awake," she said to someone else in the room.

Donnie looked around. The Rockettes were gone. It was quiet. It was dry. He was lying on his back in a bed, covered to his neck with a thin white sheet. The walls of the room he was in were pale green. There was a small table near his bed, and on it were a green plastic glass, a matching plastic pitcher beaded with moisture, and a cellophane-clad box with a white tissue protruding from it like a tiny emerging cloud stuck in its progress.

Donnie remembered pieces of this afternoon—if it had been this afternoon—and started to sit up. His head exploded like a grenade and he let himself drop back on the bed.

"Have you got pain?" a man's voice asked.

Donnie looked up at a tall, thin man in his fifties. He had a cadaverous face and inquisitive brown eyes. There were deep horizontal lines in his forehead. He was wearing a dark suit with a white shirt and striped red and blue tie. Several pens, and something that was like a pen but wasn't, were sticking up out of his breast pocket.

"My head hurts," Donnie said. "From when I hit it on the wall."

"You might have a slight concussion," the man said. "I'm Dr. Constantis. Blaze was rough with you yesterday, I'm afraid. But you're better off than some."

"Yesterday?"

"Yes. A rescue crew found you unconscious and brought you here. The hurricane had tossed you around among debris and rough concrete, so the pockets were torn from your clothes. You had no identification."

"Where's here?" Donnie asked, putting off the question of identification.

"Bailey Memorial Hospital in Palmville."

Donnie thought about exploring his body with his hands, searching for other injuries, then decided he didn't want to do that. It might be quicker and less painful to ask. "Anything other than my head wrong with me?"

Dr. Constantis smiled kindly, caving in his lean cheeks so he looked even more like a cadaver that had escaped from the research wing of the hospital. "Only minor cuts and contusions."

"Then I can leave?"

The doctor's thin, dark eyebrows rose. "I wouldn't advise it, considering you have a possible concussion. We should keep you another day for observation."

"I feel dandy."

Dr. Constantis smiled again. "Oh, I can tell."

Donnie sat up in bed, not changing expression, this time ignoring the little man working inside his skull with a jackhammer. The pain was intense but bearable. Donnie wasn't being brave; he'd endured head injuries before and thought he could sense how seriously he was hurt this time. He figured all he had to contend with was temporary pain.

"See," he said to the doctor, "I'm okay. I promise I'll call 911 if I get drowsy, or if my pupils aren't the same size."

The doctor cocked his head and stared at Donnie.

"You've either had medical training or previous concussions."

"The latter," Donnie said.

"Do you remember much about the hurricane?"

"A lot, but not everything. Isn't that normal in a case like this?"

Dr. Constantis didn't answer. He leaned close to Donnie, as the round-faced nurse had, and peered intently into his eyes. Then he placed a lighted mirror on his deeply lined forehead and looked again. He raised a forefinger, told Donnie to fix his gaze on its tip, and moved the finger left to right.

"I seem okay?" Donnie asked, when the finger was lowered.

"So far. But as you no doubt know, sometimes complications develop."

"I know what to watch for and I'll be careful. You said I was luckier than most. There have to be lots of serious injuries from Blaze, so you must need this bed."

"You happen to be one of those injuries, only you don't want to admit it."

Donnie swiveled on the mattress and placed his bare feet on the cool tile floor. "I'm checking out," he said firmly.

"I don't consider your condition *that* serious," Dr. Constantis said.

"You know what I mean—checking out of the hospital."

"We haven't really checked you in yet. We don't know your name."

Donnie stood up. Oops! The floor tilted and he was hit by a wave of dizziness and nausea. Walking was out of the question. He sat back down.

Dr. Constantis gently gripped his shoulders and forced him to return to a lying position.

"Feeling better?" the doctor asked after a while.

Donnie's head no longer ached so much, but his stomach was still queasy. "I think I swallowed some salt water."

"Possibly half the ocean. You're going to stay here for observation, or I won't be responsible."

Donnie didn't argue with him this time. "For one more day," he said. He considered telling the doctor he was FBI but decided against it. He might want to spend time in Palmville under another identity, so why take chances? The fewer people who knew who he really was, the better. The hospital staff might get pushy trying to discover his identity, but Donavon could fix things, and Donnie wasn't going to be here that long anyway.

"Now that you're conscious and have at least some of your bearings," Dr. Constantis said, "a nurse will come in with the requisite paperwork and take down information."

"I can pay the bill," Donnie said.

"That's not what I meant, Mr. . . . .?"

"Is there a phone in this room?" Donnie asked.

"You don't have to put a strain on yourself. The nurse will be glad to notify anyone you name as to your whereabouts and condition." He smiled. "That is, once you're identified."

Donnie merely stared at him. He couldn't reveal his whereabouts to Elana or the girls. It would put them in danger as well as himself.

Dr. Constantis sighed, moved to his left, then placed a green plastic telephone on the table near the green plastic pitcher. He shook his head at Donnie. "You are one stubborn man."

"That's true," Donnie said. "You've identified me."

5

"**Y**ou're right about the dead woman in the cottage," Donavon said that evening, after Donnie had told him about yesterday and the hurricane. "The local police found Marcia Dunn's body in the wreckage. They have her down as one of Blaze's victims, battered to death when her cottage collapsed around her."

"She was dead before that," Donnie said. He was sitting up in his hospital bed, trying to keep his head level to hold sudden pain at bay. "I saw her floating out from behind the breakfast bar."

Donavon took a sip of ice water from the green plastic glass. "The doctor says you're likely to be a little bit addled from your ordeal. The fog hangs on for a while, after the kind of thing that happened to you."

A pang of irritation made Donnie's head hurt even though he'd kept it still. "Dammit, Jules! I'm sure about seeing her down before the cottage collapsed. And the inside of my skull's not so foggy that I can't remember."

"But it might not be as significant as you think," Donavon said. "She might have been knocked out by something blown by the wind when the door flew open. I mean, we're talking about a major hurricane here."

Donnie didn't answer. What Jules suggested was possible, he supposed, but he wasn't buying it. Someone had murdered Marcia Dunn almost under his nose, and he had to find out who and why.

Donavon was staring dubiously at him. "What about the two men you saw on the cottage porch? Were they real?"

"Probably."

"Uh-huh."

Donnie glared at him, though the truth was he couldn't be sure himself if the two figures he thought he'd seen on the porch had actually been there. It hadn't been like inside the cabin, where distance and driving rain hadn't been factors. Though he wouldn't admit it to Donavon, he knew that the storm, his memory, his injury, could play tricks. "I think they were real, and I'm assuming they were men and not women. They looked tall."

Donavon still appeared skeptical. "Far as the hospital's concerned, we better leave you as Mr. Anonymous," he said. "I'll fix it with the administration. I don't know yet where all this is taking us, or what you might need to do when you get out of here." He leaned down in his chair and held up a red and white TWA carry-on bag he'd brought with him. He unzipped the bag and reached into it. "We recovered this near where you were found," he said, holding up Donnie's 9mm Sig Sauer handgun. Placing it back in the bag, he added, "There are fresh clothes in here for you, too. I understand the ones you were wearing look like they were played with by gorillas."

Donnie thanked him.

"And we'll let Agent Dunn remain a journalist named Marcia Graham," Donavon said. "That way the investigation can still be ongoing. If she was taken out, whoever hit her might have seen you in or near the cottage. We'll have to explain who you are. I'll think on that one. When you get out of here, you need to play it straight, go to the local law and tell them you're suspicious because you saw two men leaving Graham's cottage and you found her unconscious inside. That's what a legitimate visitor would do, and whoever did the hit on her—if she *was* hit—might be watching to find out who and what you are, and whether you're any kind of threat."

"I doubt that. With all the weather last night, I don't think they saw me."

"Why not? *You* saw *them*."

"You had to be there," Donnie said.

Donavon sucked in his lips and looked worried and thoughtful. "Whether or not Agent Dunn was murdered, we've gotta find out what she was onto. It's almost surely political, since that was what she was in Florida to investigate, and it's gotta be something big that might blindside us if we don't figure it out."

"Mafia, maybe," Donnie said.

"Could be, or it could be you've still got Mafia on your mind after what happened in New York."

"You said politics," Donnie reminded him. "Politics means Mafia in parts of Florida. Political corruption is Mafia corruption."

"Usually," Donavon said, still looking contemplative and concerned. "Reason I think this is big, Donnie, is that there's unbelievable pressure on me from above to get it figured out. Somebody senses this is important."

"Pressure, huh?"

"You of all people oughta understand pressure, with what you've been through. People on high have inside knowledge and pressure of their own, pass it on down. And we both know some of the suits in the Bureau resent somebody like you anyway. They figure you undercover guys are too much ego, playing it all out, maybe you're working on another movie."

"Tell me about it," Donnie said. Pain started moving around inside his skull again, like something with claws and sharp teeth trying desperately to get out. Pressure.

Donavon stood up from his chair, still holding the carry-on. "Where do you want this?"

"Closet over there." Donnie motioned with his hand.

Donavon placed the bag on the closet shelf. For some reason whoever had hung up Donnie's ruined clothes had slipped a plastic cleaners bag over them. Maybe they thought they were preserving evidence, just in case Mr. Anonymous turned out to be a wanted criminal.

After shutting the closet door, Donavon stood at the foot of the bed, his suit coat unbuttoned, his hands jammed in his pockets. Donnie knew the hard look on his face. Donavon was capable of almost anything at crunch time, and this was it. "We've gotta learn what Agent Dunn wanted to talk about. That's top priority, you understand?"

"We're clear on that, Jules."

Donavon slowly removed his hands from his pockets and crossed his arms, kinking his tie. A certain gleam went out of his eyes. Reasonable guy again. "You need anything else here, Donnie?"

"No, I'm okay."

"Anybody you want me to notify about this?"

Donnie thought again about Elana, living her new life in St. Louis. He'd heard she was dating a stockbroker. He had an expensive house, a luxury car, a stable life. The things Donnie could never give her. Predictability was what Elana had longed for most. It wasn't part of Donnie's life, and he didn't want it to be. Not usually, anyway.

"Nobody," he said.

6

The next day, after his release from the hospital, Donnie took a cab to an office of the agency where he'd rented his car. He reported what had happened. He didn't have any doubt that for at least a brief period, the car had been underwater. The insurance he'd signed for covered the situation, and he was even provided with another car. It was the first time he'd seen a car rental agent seem glum because a customer had paid for the optional insurance.

After leaving the agency, he drove to Palmville police headquarters. His head still ached, but pain pills from the hospital pharmacy kept the throbbing discomfort to a minimum. His new identity, complete with social security number, Missouri driver's license, and credit cards, had been couriered to him at the hospital that morning. He was now Donnie Blaine.

As he drove through Palmville, Donnie was surprised by the extent of the damage Blaze had inflicted. Some streets were still blocked by trees that had fallen across them, phone and electric lines were still down, and about half the buildings had blown-out windows. Often their roofs were missing or stripped of tiles or shingles, and pink insulation bulged out where siding had been ripped away by the force of the wind. Donnie had to make several detours away from streets near the ocean that were still flooded. Police, fire department, and municipal repair crews were toiling in the wreckage, along with civilian volunteers wearing luminous orange vests over T-shirts or bare torsos. The faces of the workers were grim; they were constantly afraid of what they might find, and their own homes and businesses probably hadn't escaped damage. Blaze had been a bitch from hell.

Palmville police headquarters was a low, rectangular structure of beige brick with a flat tile roof. Two of the tall palm trees alongside the parking lot were down, and a crew with chain saws was cutting the wood and loading it into trucks.

Donnie parked the new rental car well out of the way.

When he used his cover name and showed his fake ID, then explained what he wanted, a bored-looking desk sergeant instructed him to take a seat near the booking desk.

Ten minutes later, Donnie was escorted by a uniformed policewoman into an office with a light oak door lettered LT. WARD KOZNER. It was a large but sparsely furnished room with a battered gray steel desk, matching file cabinets, and an obsolete computer and printer on a table near the single window that looked out over police cars parked in the lot alongside the building. Through dirty glass, Donnie caught a glimpse of one of the trucks being loaded with fallen palm trees and heard faintly the persistent snarling of chain saws. There was a small potted plant on the windowsill, dead. Sand crunched beneath Donnie's soles on the threadbare green carpet. Lieutenants in the Palmville PD didn't live like royalty.

Kozner stood up behind his desk and introduced

himself. He was average height but broad, with a wide jaw and thick neck. He had the bushy black hair, dark eyebrows, and piercing brown eyes of a guy who fit the terrorist profile at airport security checkpoints. His blue uniform shirt fit too tight, and muscles rippled beneath strained short sleeves as he waved an arm to motion Donnie into a wooden chair with black vinyl padding on its back and arms.

"Sergeant Aims said you mentioned a possible homicide," he said. He didn't seem pleased to be talking with Donnie, who knew that all the detectives were probably on call in the aftermath of Blaze, which was why he rated a lieutenant.

Donnie used his cover story again. He was the cousin of Marcia Graham, the journalist who'd died in the hurricane, and had come to Palmville to visit her while he was in the area on vacation. The rest he told as it had actually happened.

Kozner sat rubbing his darkly whiskered jaw all the while Donnie was talking, stopping only when Donnie was finished. Donnie looked for a sore spot but saw none.

"Where'd you say you were from, Mr. Blaine?" Kozner asked.

"St. Charles, Missouri," Donnie answered. "Just outside St. Louis."

Kozner leaned back in his chair and began playing with a bulky silver and turquoise ring on his left index finger. "You sure you actually saw those two men on the cottage porch?"

"I'm sure," Donnie lied.

"But even if you did, way I heard it, you didn't see either of 'em lay a hand on your cousin."

"True," Donnie admitted.

Kozner sat forward. "What exactly is it you think happened, Mr. Blaine?"

"I'm not sure. You're the police, so I thought you needed to know about this."

"We got your cousin listed as an accidental death, one of over a dozen hurricane victims. Medical examiner didn't find any stab or gunshot wounds, nothing at all suspicious, or he'd have notified this department."

"But she was on the floor when I got to her cottage, after the two men left."

"*Mighta* left, you mean. 'Cause we don't know for sure they were actually there. Kind of weather we had that night, it was the devil just to see three feet in front of you."

"True enough," Donnie said, "but I saw her on the floor. And there was a dead dog there."

"You also said there was water on the floor, deep and getting deeper, and the front door was blown open. Blaze had been in there, Mr. Blaine, roaring around like only folks who live down here on the Florida coast understand. Things fly every which way under those circumstances. Heavy, sharp objects. Lots of broken glass, usually, as well as other things blown in by the hurricane. Being in that cottage mighta been like trying to find cover in a blender. It might not have lasted long, but it wouldn't need to in order to kill or knock unconscious a woman and a dog."

Donnie knew what was going on here. The Palmville police had more problems than they could handle, and here was Donnie trying to get them interested in a might-have-been homicide. Marcia Graham was going to stay an accident victim as long as Lieutenant Kozner had anything to say about it.

Kozner glanced pointedly at his watch—silver, with a silver and turquoise band to match the ring—then stood up behind his desk.

His voice took on a friendlier yet deeper tone and there was a perfunctory smile on his broad, tan face.

"You were right to tell us about this, Mr. Blaine, and though it doesn't look like anything other'n accidental death, we sure will look into it. Meantime, if I was you I'd get outa this mess, go back to Missouri, and be glad you don't live down here during hurricane season."

Donnie stood also. "I'll do that, Lieutenant, but first I want to see if I can sort through what's left of Marcia's effects. For the family."

"Understandable," Kozner said. "You better watch out for looters, though, and make sure you're not mistaken for one yourself. We do what we can about those jackals, but there's too many of 'em to cope with at times like this. It's like they pop right up outa the ground after any sorta disaster."

"I'll be careful."

"You gonna claim the body?"

"I can," Donnie said, figuring Donavon could handle that one. "Marcia was from Chicago. I'm sure her folks will want her remains shipped back there for burial."

"Course, course," Kozner muttered. He seemed to realize suddenly that he'd been remiss in expressing his sympathy. "We are sorry about your cousin. Truly. Thing is, we got so much trouble, so much work here in Palmville and environs . . . well, we forget everything but that work sometimes."

"I understand how it is," Donnie assured him. "Wouldn't want to be in your shoes."

Kozner gave a grim smile. "Sometimes they don't fit me too good, either." He went with Donnie to the door. "Whatever you saw or think you saw that night, Mr. Blaine, you can just stop worrying about it. Leave it to us."

"I'll do that," Donnie lied smoothly, opening the door. "And thanks, Lieutenant."

He wondered how certain Kozner would be about

that accidental death finding if he knew Marcia Graham had been an undercover FBI agent.

When he pushed open the tinted glass door and stepped back outside, heat hit him like a soft hammer and caused his headache to flare up again.

He stood at the base of the steps and took another pain pill, glancing around at the debris left by Hurricane Blaze. Palmville now lay beneath a calm and cloudless sky of such a delicate blue it looked like the curved interior of a fine china bowl. The glaring sunlight found every colorful or reflective surface and made even the damaged cars and buildings look fresh and clean. Despite the heat, it was a beautiful day, Mother Nature trying to make up after the quarrel.

Not accepting her apology, Donnie climbed behind the wheel of his new ride from the rental agency and drove toward the ruined beach cottage.

7

The beach was still littered with flotsam and jetsam washed up by the hurricane, but now the surf lapped gently at the sand. Blaze had passed like a spasm in paradise, leaving a restored calm, and the incongruity of massive destruction along with beauty and blue sky.

Donnie could drive only to within a quarter of a mile of the cottage's ruins. Beach Lane had been washed completely away at that point, and water still stood behind police barricades with flashing yellow lights.

He pulled to the road shoulder and parked behind a muddy Ford pickup truck that might have been abandoned. Mud coated all its windows, making it impossible to see in.

Anticipating these conditions, Donnie was wearing jeans and boots, a knit pullover shirt with a pocket for his sunglasses. He also had a gray windbreaker, tied by its arms around his waist. Though it was early evening, the sun was still hot and bright.

He put on the sunglasses before leaving the car and setting out to walk along the littered beach. A large pleasure boat, listing sharply and high in the bow, drifted far offshore. Gulls circled above the beach, crying to each other as if lamenting the mess below.

There were half a dozen other people wandering the beach, but no one near Donnie. The variety of washed-up debris interested him. There was a jumble of deck and jogging shoes, bound together by their tangled laces. Nearby was the splintered half of a wooden dinghy, complete with one oar. Alongside it rested an upside-down foam cooler and a tattered, pin-striped suit coat with a red tie dangling from a pocket. There was part of a surfboard, what looked like a one-piece swimming suit, a cluster of caved-in cardboard boxes labeled "Barbados," a mud-caked fur jacket—

Wait!

Not a fur jacket.

Donnie's stomach tightened and his heart picked up a beat.

Hearing the sucking sounds of his boots in the wet sand, he strode toward the brown fur.

When he got close he caught the odor and heard the droning of flies and he was sure. It was the dog. The German shepherd he'd seen in the cottage just before the hurricane had hit full force. He held his breath and bent over its corpse.

What he hadn't noticed that day in the cottage was now obvious. The dog's throat had been slashed. Apparently its blood had run and been diluted in the water on the cottage's floor and Donnie hadn't seen it.

He knew exactly what a knife wound looked like. The gaping injury in the dog's neck wasn't caused by any other sharp object, including flying glass. Probably Marcia Dunn had used the animal as a watchdog. It had been killed to stop it from attacking or to silence it. Either way, Hurricane Blaze hadn't killed it.

Which meant the hurricane also hadn't killed Agent Dunn. She'd definitely been murdered.

Standing up straight and moving away so he could breathe without taking in so much of the stench, Donnie continued staring at the dog. While the evidence was good enough for him, he knew the dog's body wouldn't be enough for Kozner and the overworked Palmville police. Kozner would say the fatal injury might not be a knife wound, that something sharp propelled by the hurricane had killed the dog. Or maybe the wound had even been inflicted after death; the ocean had taken the dog, then washed it back up onto the beach, whirling and tumbling it with other wreckage from the hurricane. Donnie had run into that kind of local bureaucratic obstruction before and knew how frustrating it could be.

But maybe in this instance it would be wiser not to try to interest the local law. A bona fide homicide investigation would surely reveal "Marcia Graham's" true identity and make any further inquiries into whatever it was she'd been afraid to talk about on the phone difficult if not impossible. Donnie would fill in Donavon, and he was sure the decision would be to let Agent Dunn continue to be journalist Marcia Graham in death, a death that would remain listed as accidental—at least for the time being.

Glad to be getting away from what was left of the dog, Donnie continued his walk along the beach. The odor, the steady droning of flies, the perfect stillness of violent death's aftermath, seemed to cling to him, as he knew it would. Some sights played over and over in the mind, and some smells were strong enough to become taste. He spat off to the side and walked faster.

There was little left of the cottage. Only one wall was still standing. Half the plank floor had been

pried up by the wind, then washed away. The structure had been piered, supported by wood stilts sunk
deep and set in concrete, like everything built so
close to the sea, and its crawl space enclosed by
wood latticework. Because of its porosity, the lattice
rectangle had withstood wind and sea and served as
a kind of basket that still contained some of the cottage's contents. Stepping carefully across exposed
joists and what was left of the floor, Donnie began
picking through the basket's contents.

He found a glass coffeepot from the brewer, amazingly sitting upright and unbroken and still with coffee in it only slightly diluted with rain or seawater.
An upside-down dresser yielded little when he rummaged through its remaining contents. Six feet from
the dresser was what looked like part of a desk, but
its drawers were missing or empty, everything in
them washed away. Beneath a smashed kitchen cabinet and lots of broken glass, he found a muddy
Smith & Wesson .38 revolver. Every chamber in the
cylinder contained a bullet, indicating it hadn't been
fired. It was a small gun, probably Agent Dunn's.
Undercover agents often carried guns other than
standard FBI issue. Still, the revolver should be
checked out. Donnie untied the windbreaker's arms
from around his waist, slipped into the thin jacket,
then lifted the revolver with a splinter of wood and
deposited it in a pocket.

Then he continued rummaging through the wreckage. He was sure that to an untrained eye there'd be
nothing other than the gun that might suggest the
cottage's occupant had been more than a working
journalist; undercover agents never carried or even
had hidden near them their FBI identification. And
Agent Dunn would have had her contact phone
number memorized.

He found a couple of three-and-a-half-inch computer disks first. It took him almost another hour to find the thin, charcoal-gray notebook computer. It was half-submerged in water and its plastic case was cracked. The lid with its screen had been torn from it, leaving the muddy keyboard exposed. Danny didn't hold out much hope that any information on its hard disk could be recovered, but he knew the computer whizzes at the Bureau could sometimes work miracles.

"Can I help you?" a woman's voice said suddenly above the murmur of the surf.

Donnie looked up to see a stocky, middle-aged woman wearing a white nylon windbreaker and baggy shorts. His gaze fixed on her hands. Always now when someone surprised him, he looked first at their hands. Hers were empty. Her jowly face was wearing a frown.

Donnie smiled at her. "Who are you?" he asked pleasantly.

She didn't return his smile. "I'm Mrs. Grotowski. My husband and I own the cottage south of this one."

"I just came from that direction. I didn't see a cottage."

"The hurricane took it." She crossed her arms. "Now, who are *you*? Why are you here?"

Donnie understood now. She thought he might be a trespasser or looter.

"I'm Donnie Blaine, Marcia's cousin."

For an instant Mrs. Grotowski's expression softened, then again became guarded. "I didn't know Marcia had a cousin."

Donnie put on a perplexed look. "Almost everybody has a cousin. I'm from Missouri, where Marcia's family lived before they moved to Chicago." He tossed down a broken lamp he'd lifted from the debris. "Look, Mrs. Grotowski. When I saw you, I figured you might be someone here to see what you could find of value to take away with you. You probably thought the same of me. I think now we can believe we're both who we say we are."

Mrs. Grotowski smiled, embarrassed, and nodded. "I'm sorry about Marcia. My husband and I didn't get to know her well, but she seemed like a pleasant young woman. And a hard worker . . . curious, always asking about things. That's why she became a journalist, I suppose."

"She was curious even as a little girl," Donnie said. "And she liked to tell stories." He glanced to the south, at a beach barren of everything but wreckage. "Too bad about your cottage."

She shrugged. "We've got insurance, thank God. But my husband and I are getting out of here, leaving to drive back up to Iowa tomorrow. It won't take us long to pack, since we've got nothing left."

"Just about everything on this stretch of beach was wiped out, I guess," Donnie said.

"That's how it looks. This cottage, the Perez cottage to the north, and ours got hit hard because we were close to the shoreline. Blaze was a surprise. We didn't have time to prepare for it. Not that any preparation would have helped much."

"Did Marcia ever talk to you or your husband about her job?" Donnie asked. "I mean, what she was working on here in Florida?"

Mrs. Grotowski ignored his question and her gaze moved to the damaged computer Donnie was holding. "Is that why you came here? For that?"

"Partly. Marcia's editor asked me to see if I could find it while I was looking for anything the family might want."

"Well, she never talked about her writing to us. We knew she was doing some sort of a piece on politics, but we never discussed any details. Mostly we talked about the best local restaurants, the heat, the mosquitoes. Polite small talk. She was curious and asked her own questions about our lives and the people around here, but now that I think on it, she never revealed much about herself."

"Writers are naturally very private people," Donnie said.

"Really? I wouldn't have thought it." Mrs. Grotowski hunched her shoulders and stuffed her hands in her windbreaker's pockets, though it was still warm even in the ocean breeze. "I'll leave you to your task, Mr. Blaine. I want to continue my walk and take one last look around before we drive north. Maybe we'll use our insurance settlement to get a place over on the Gulf side. There aren't as many hurricanes over there."

Donnie wished her luck, then watched her walk away. Graceful for such a stocky woman, she stayed as close as possible to the reaching fingers of foamy surf while picking her way through the debris on the beach.

He wasn't so intent on observing Mrs. Grotowski that he didn't notice the approach of a small, round man with an obvious white toupee. He was about fifty, not much taller than five feet, with a puffy red face and blue eyes. As he walked he swung his short arms in exaggerated arcs, as if getting around was hard work. He didn't look healthy.

He stopped and stood still about ten feet from the splintered wood lattice.

"I couldn't help overhearing you mention you were Marcia Graham's cousin," he said to Donnie.

"That's right."

The man looked at him with timid indecisiveness. "Did you and your cousin know each other well? I mean, did you talk much?"

"Some," Donnie said noncommittally, trying not to stare at the preposterous white toupee.

"She possessed dangerous knowledge," the little man said.

"Dangerous how?"

"Several ways."

Donnie knew he had to play this exactly right. He didn't ask the identity of the man. Instead he said, "Marcia always had a strong interest in politics."

The man glanced at the cottage's wreckage and nodded. "It's a shame she's dead."

"Were you and my cousin . . . working together on something?" Donnie asked.

"No," the man said. He was obviously uneasy. Ready to bolt. "No, I wouldn't say that." He smiled and backed away. "Politics . . ." He shook his round head vigorously, causing double chins to jiggle. The badly fitted toupee threatened to fly off.

"Politics and money," Donnie said, trying to draw the man out.

"Ham and eggs, nitro and glycerin," the man said. He clamped his mouth shut, then took several backward steps, stumbling and almost falling over a beer can protruding from the sand.

"I'll probably be around here from time to time," Donnie told him, letting him know they could talk in the future. "Getting this mess straightened up."

"Good luck," the man said. Then he turned and walked quickly up the beach in the direction Mrs. Grotowski had gone. Every six or seven steps, he glanced behind him, making it impossible for Donnie to follow unobserved.

Watching him, Donnie wondered if he'd just met Marcia Graham's source.

Donnie searched through the cottage's wreckage for another hour without finding anything of interest.

Then he noticed that the sky had become dimmer and the faint breeze was somewhat cooler. Dusk would be closing in soon. While there was still adequate light, he made his way over to where a closet must have been and began sorting through a jumble of clothes, some of them twisted by wind and water around their wire hangers.

In the pocket of a light nylon jacket he found a folded slip of paper. A note. Fortunately it was in pencil and hadn't dissolved and run like ink. Though the writing was faded, it was still legible. A man's name: Luis Perez. Beneath the name was a phone number.

Mrs. Grotowski had mentioned a Perez cottage, the neighboring cottage to the north.

Donnie remembered finding Agent Dunn's tennis bag an hour ago and examining its contents. It had contained shoes, a change of clothes, and a can of new tennis balls. He located the bag again and emptied it, then put the revolver, diskettes, and the note inside it. In the outside pocket made for the head of a tennis racket, he placed the notebook computer.

Dusk had dimmed the beach when he climbed from the ruins of the cottage and started walking north. Like Mrs. Grotowski, he stayed near the surf line, where the sand was wet and packed and walking was easier. But he had to watch where he stepped. There were a lot of objects partly buried in the sand, including broken boards with nails protruding from them.

When Donnie got within sight of the Perez cottage he saw that it hadn't been completely destroyed. There were three walls still standing and under roof. The place might even be salvageable. There was a narrow wooden pier, crooked and broken now, extending out into the sea, probably where a boat had been docked. There was no boat there now.

Donnie heard a screech that he at first thought was the cry of a gull.

Then in the fading light he saw motion near what had been a far corner of the Perez cottage. Two— no, three—people, on their feet and punching and grappling with each other as if locked in a bizarre dance.

The cry came again.

Not a gull.

The scream of a woman.

Donnie dropped the tennis bag and began running toward the three struggling figures. He veered up the beach slightly to gain an angle so his approach wouldn't be seen, then picked up speed, pumping his legs hard, throwing up rooster tails of sand at his heels. Every fourth or fifth stride he stepped on something hard or uneven and had to fight to keep his balance. The butt of his 9mm tucked into his belt was digging into the small of his back as he ran, but he decided not to draw the gun. He had no idea yet what was going on and didn't want to blow his cover so soon.

His headache was back and his lungs began to burn. He could hear himself gasping over the whisper of the surf.

The woman screamed again.

He ran faster.

8

One of the men was shoving the woman backward so she tripped and fell over a length of board. The other was surprised to see Donnie round the corner of the cottage. He stood with his hands at his sides, his mouth slack, and his eyes open wide.

Even as he lowered his left shoulder and slammed it into the man's midsection, Donnie knew these weren't the figures he'd glimpsed on Agent Dunn's porch the night of the hurricane. They were both too short, and one of them was forty pounds overweight. It was the fat one Donnie hit. Air *whooshed!* from the man and he staggered backward a few steps and fell to an awkward sitting position with his legs straight out in front of him.

The other man had turned away from the woman on the ground and was moving toward Donnie. As he got closer he hunkered down into some kind of martial arts fighting position Donnie had never seen. Donnie wasn't impressed. As the man screamed and hacked at him with the edge of his hand, he clutched the wrist and twisted it, letting the momentum of his assailant's charge carry him past, exerting tremendous pressure on the man's arm. Through his grip on the sweaty wrist, Donnie could feel the arm slip from its shoulder socket. The man screamed again, this time in pain.

Something collided hard with Donnie and his shoulder bounced off the cottage wall. Here was a surprise. The fat one was game and back for more. Nothing fancy about him, though. He came at Donnie with his fists balled and carried low, like a barroom fighter with a buzz on. He wasn't much past his teens, but his chubby face was clenched in determination and his eyes held no fear. Donnie kind of admired the kid as he stepped inside the wide arc of his swing and hit him with a straight right hand to the nose. He didn't want to do anything fancy here and show his skills; he was still the cousin from Missouri.

The kid staggered backward, clutching the broken nose that was gushing blood down the front of his T-shirt. The guy with the dislocated arm was hunched over and hugging it close to his body with his good arm. Donnie saw the woman, who'd risen from the wreckage, run at the man with the arm and bring what looked like a bent brass table lamp down toward his head. It missed his head but hit the bad shoulder. He yelped in pain and grabbed the woman by her shirt, whirling her around and away from him.

"Fuck this, Eddie!" he yelled. "Let's go! Let's go!"

As the moonlight glanced off his pain-distorted features, Donnie saw that he was much older than the fat kid, maybe in his thirties. Leaner and more physically capable than the kid, but he lacked the balls.

"In a minute," the heavy one said, spitting blood. He came at Donnie again.

Donnie realized by now that these two were simply looters interrupted by the woman when she'd seen them on her property sorting through her possessions. He didn't want the police in on this, didn't want to explain he was FBI. What he wanted was for these two lunkheads to run, to get away.

He spun away from the kid this time, giving him a shove as he went past so he'd fall and have some time to gain a little sense.

But he was agile for his size and didn't drop. Instead he dug in the side of his foot like a football running back making a sharp cut as he swiveled all that weight and charged again.

Donnie chopped the side of his neck, not too hard, then grabbed a handful of sweaty or bloody T-shirt and yanked him back toward him.

"Wise up, asshole!" he whispered in his ear so the woman wouldn't overhear. "Get out before I kill you."

He released his grip and shoved the kid toward the open beach and his accomplice, who was already running away, lugging what looked like a large duffel bag at the end of his good arm.

Finally the kid decided to break it off. He backed away, continuing to spit blood in regular little puffs and bubbles. He was staring at Donnie, still without fear, as if wondering why he hadn't solved him.

"Go steal something somewhere else," Donnie said.

The kid spat a red arc in his direction. "You ain't such a badass. Not nearly so tough as you think."

"Not as tough as you. Or as dumb."

The kid backed another couple of steps, then nodded at Donnie, turned away from him, and broke into an easy jog in the direction the lean one had gone. There was something still defiant in his short but surprisingly fluid stride, as if he were a bull who hadn't given in to the matador and had been spared.

"Scum!" the woman said, behind Donnie. She picked something and threw it at the fat kid, grunting slightly with the effort. But whatever it was, it dropped to the sand twenty feet behind him.

Donnie turned around and looked closely at her. She was in her thirties, short and slim with a fine figure, wearing jeans and a cropped white T-shirt. When she turned away from staring after the fleeing looters and he got a good look at her face he was stunned by her beauty. She was Latin, with chiseled features, thick dark hair that tumbled in black waves to her shoulders. Her eyes were large and dark, and somber even in their anger.

She returned Donnie's frank stare. "Thank you for helping me run them off," she said. She had only a trace of Spanish accent.

Donnie smiled.

She was still too mad to smile back. Her breasts were rising and falling as she breathed with contained fury. "They are everywhere, stripping people's possessions like vultures worrying carcasses."

"Disasters always bring out those sorts of men," Donnie agreed.

"If only Luis—" She bit off her words and looked again at Donnie, as if just now seeing him clearly. "I'm sorry. I'm Grace Perez. This is—was my cottage. Are you with the police or sheriff's department?"

"No, I'm Donnie Blaine. Your neighbor down the beach, Marcia Graham, was my cousin. I'm here in Florida for the family, making arrangements for her body to be returned to Chicago. I was going through what was left of the cottage she rented, seeing if there was anything of hers worth saving, things with sentimental value the family might want."

"I'm sorry about your cousin," Grace Perez said.

"I hardly knew her. She hadn't lived here long, and we only saw each other a few times."

"She was only planning on being here a month or so. She was a journalist working on a story."

"Yes, that's what someone said. It was horrible, the hurricane. I—" She broke off her speech again with a tiny choking sound, as if the words had inflated and were suddenly too large for her throat.

"I understand you lost your husband," Donnie said. "I'm sorry."

She nodded, still unable to speak. In the fading light, tears glinted in her dark eyes.

"It's gonna be completely dark soon," Donnie said. "You must have been planning on leaving anyway. You got a car parked nearby?"

"Up near the highway. But it isn't running. I'm in a motel now, but I intend to put things together here enough so that I can come back and stay."

"You mean move back in?"

"Yes. Luis and I lived here, Mr. Blaine. It wasn't our vacation home. I have no place else to go."

Donnie stared at the damaged cottage. It didn't look inhabitable. Still, this was the kind of climate that didn't require much shelter other than protection from the rain. And quite a bit of the cottage's roof was intact.

She knew what he was thinking. "I've already restored running water, and there's a dry place to sleep. I can cook with a kerosene stove. It will only be until I can bring contractors in to make real repairs."

"The honest and reliable contractors are gonna be busy. They might take a long time getting around to you."

She shrugged. "After a disaster, we can expect delay. I won't be the only one living with inconvenience."

"I've got a car parked a short walk from here," Donnie said. "Why don't you have something to eat with me at a restaurant? Then I'll drive you to your motel or back here, wherever you want."

"Thanks, but the motel's within easy walking distance, Mr. Blaine."

He grinned at her. "Less than a mile?"

"Less than two."

"I think after running off the bad guys, we deserve hamburgers and coffee. And two miles is a long walk in the dark. You might even meet up with our two friends again," he added, as a clincher.

She snorted in disdain. "They won't stay around here. The looters are mostly from nearby towns or cities, drawn by others' misfortune. But I'll join you for coffee, Mr. Blaine."

He waited a few minutes while she put some things in order and found a light sweater. He saw now that the cottage was considerably larger than Agent Dunn's had been, and what furniture hadn't been washed away or ruined looked more expensive.

Pretending to be killing time while he waited, Donnie paced around the cottage, making his way over to a mud-smeared white desk phone perched on top of some rubble. He saw that the number printed beneath the plastic tab above its keypad matched the number next to Luis Perez's name on the paper he'd found in the pocket of Marcia Dunn's jacket.

The dead man's widow stood still and gave a final glance around. Instead of putting on the sweater, she slung it over her shoulder. She looked at Donnie to let him know she was ready, but she didn't smile.

On the walk back along the moonlit beach, he picked up the club bag he'd dropped.

"Some of my cousin's things," he explained to Grace Perez.

9

The Lookout Inn had a wide, curved window that usually provided a panoramic view of the Atlantic. Now every frame in the window was boarded over with rough plywood, some of it battered and splintered by flying debris during Blaze's recent onslaught.

But the restaurant was open for business. As Donnie parked the Taurus next to a minivan in the muddy parking lot, Grace told him the Lookout Inn was where she'd been taking her meals since the hurricane.

He was struck by the loneliness of her grief. "Don't you have family in Florida?" he asked. "Anyone you can stay with?"

She shook her head. "The few that are left are in Cuba. I don't have friends who are close enough I'd ask them to let me live with them. Do you have such friends?"

"I don't know," Donnie said. He didn't pursue the subject.

The Lookout Inn was a modest restaurant. A fresh menu tacked up near the door boasted of jumbo hamburgers and Cajun-style seafood dishes. The building's interior had been cleaned up, though Donnie could feel a residual sogginess to the carpet as a hostess led them to a table that a few days ago had been one with a view. There were only three other customers, a man and woman together at a far table, and a man sitting alone near the center of the restaurant. It was as if the hostess wanted to keep customers as separated from each other as possible, perhaps sensing that people were unpredictable after a disaster, or might want to be left alone to reassemble their interior lives.

The restaurant was dim despite lots of track lighting and what looked like temporary floor fixtures whose beams were being bounced off the ceiling. It was far enough from shore not to have been invaded by the ocean, but rain blown in through the broken windows had done enough damage. There were water stains on the walls, along with rectangular lighter areas where pictures had hung before being taken by the hurricane. Near the salad bar, the powerful wind apparently had peeled wallpaper away from the plaster, leaving it dangling in water-stained strips.

"What's good here?" Donnie asked Grace, picking up one of the menus the hostess had left on the table. "Other than the ambience."

She didn't smile. Not in the mood for humor. "Everything and nothing," she said.

Donnie thought he understood what she meant. In her grief, she wasn't thinking about food. He shouldn't be, either, though he was only claiming that Marcia Graham-Agent Dunn had been his cousin, and wasn't a woman he'd never met until after her death. And then only briefly.

"What did your husband do?" he asked, while the mood was somber.

Grace stared at him with her huge, sad eyes. "Do? Oh, you mean his work. He was a real estate broker. He had his own agency, with a small office in Palmville. It was a one-person operation. He handled mostly industrial properties."

"I'm sorry," Donnie said. "Maybe you don't want to talk about him."

"Not much, I'm afraid." She lowered her head.

A waitress came over and said she was Louella and would be there to attend their every need, then reeled off a list of specials. Grace took literally what Donnie had said on the beach and asked only for a hamburger and coffee. Donnie ordered the same.

Louella bustled away, then returned a few minutes later with their coffees on a tray, as well as a small glass globe with a removable top. She placed everything on the table, the globe in the center. Then she removed the globe's top. She touched the flame of a cigarette lighter to the wick of a thick white candle in the globe. Around the base of the candle was about an inch of water, still unsettled by its trip to the table. The resultant shimmering, soft yellow light made Grace Perez even more beautiful and somehow intensified the sadness in her face.

Donnie took only a sip of his coffee, then excused himself to make a phone call while the burgers were being grilled.

The pay phone was in a small, paneled foyer near the door Donnie and Grace had used to enter. Donnie inserted his coin and punched out a number he'd memorized, then he leaned near the phone and stared across the restaurant at Grace Perez sitting quietly in the oasis of candlelight and staring into her coffee cup.

Donavon was on the other end of the line within seconds.

"Something for me?" he asked when Donnie had identified himself.

"And something *from* you," Donnie said. "I need

to know about a Luis Perez, real estate broker here in the Palmville area. Also his wife Grace, probably Cuban."

"How do they figure in this?"

"Agent Dunn had Luis's name and phone number on a slip of paper in a pocket of one of her jackets. The Perezes lived in a cottage up the beach from Dunn's. It was pretty much destroyed and Luis was killed in the hurricane. His widow is stubborn and intends to stay and rebuild."

"Admirable," Donavon said.

"She's an admirable woman in a lot of ways."

"You've met her?"

"We're about to have dinner together."

"My, my."

"We're both grieving," Donnie reminded Donavon.

"Yeah. Now, what do you have *for* me?"

"I found the dog."

"Dog?"

"The one whose dead body I saw in Agent Dunn's cottage. I came across it washed back up on the beach. Its throat was slashed."

"Could it have happened during the hurricane? Or afterward when the dog's body was being blown or tossed around in the waves?"

"Come on, Jules!"

Donavon's sigh came loud and long over the phone. "So you were right, Donnie. It looks like Dunn was killed after the dog was silenced by whoever hit her."

"The other news," Donnie said, "is I found her revolver in the wreckage of the cottage. It hadn't been fired."

"Okay. Send it in, though. We'll need to examine it for prints and whatever."

"I also found some computer disks and her notebook computer. The disks look okay. The computer took some heavy damage."

"The lab can still probably get something off the hard disk," Donavon said. "They won't need much. You know how those folks are—give 'em a couple of nails and they can reconstruct a house."

"The computer's been through a hurricane," Donnie reminded him. "There might not even be a couple of nails left to work with."

"Have faith in the lab," Donavon said. "Don't believe everything you read in the papers."

"I had an interesting visitor on the beach," Donnie said. "A pudgy little guy with a bad white toupee. He told me my cousin Marcia had some dangerous knowledge, then he mentioned political corruption and left without leaving his name."

"Her source, maybe."

"That's how I see it. But he sure wasn't in the mood to open up to me."

"If he's in Florida politics, we can find out about him." Donavon was silent for a while. Then: "Pressure's still building to solve this one, Donnie. An undercover agent inside the Mafia, somebody like you were, says there's probably Family involvement. We might be getting to the point where we activate your E.O. Squad."

He meant the Extraordinary Operations Squad that Donnie headed in especially sensitive or demanding cases. Donnie had been given the squad since he'd accomplished what no other agent found possible, and he possessed the skills and could command the respect needed to run it. The agents he called on as its members were very special people, highly individual operatives yet with the savvy and resourcefulness to adapt and thrive in a bureaucracy as well as in almost any outside situation. Above all, like Donnie, they'd been forged in the fire and were proven. The

few other agents who knew of or suspected the
squad's existence sometimes jokingly referred to it as
the "A-team," after the old television series. Donnie
thought of it more as "Mission Impossible."

"I don't think we're quite there yet," he said, "but
I'm getting the same feeling Marcia Dunn must have
had. Something deep and wide is out there, and I'm
on the edge of it."

"Dunn apparently fell into it," Donavon said
grimly.

"She was pushed," Donnie corrected.

"What about the widow you're about to break
bread with? Do you think she might be involved?"

"It doesn't look that way. But she might know
something if her late husband was a player."

"We'll run him through the computers," Donavon
said. "It won't take long."

The burgers hadn't taken long, either. Donnie saw
Louella the waitress return to the table with their
order. She was placing Donnie's food before his
empty chair. Grace was looking over at him.

He said good-bye to Donavon and returned to
the table.

"Good hamburger," he said, taking a sample bite
after Louella had smiled at him and left.

Grace nodded agreement, chewing her second generous bite. Donnie wasn't surprised to see she was
plenty hungry.

"What kind of industrial real estate did your husband sell?" he asked casually, dousing his french
fries with ketchup.

"All kinds. Factories, hotels, raw land, shopping
malls."

"Sounds profitable."

"We were doing fine." She stopped eating and
took a sip of coffee, grimacing as if it burned her

tongue. She didn't swallow right away, holding the hot liquid in her mouth as if she wanted to punish herself, as if the hurricane, everything that had happened, was in some way her fault.

"I'm sorry," Donnie said. "We can talk about something else."

"Do the people who own your cousin's cottage intend to rebuild it?" she asked.

"I haven't talked to them about it. There isn't much to rebuild. They'd probably have to start from scratch."

A look almost of terror crossed her face. "Blaze was awful. The wind and rain found their way into our cottage, then the ocean, the waves. Everything . . . Luis . . . everything was gone in seconds. Only seconds! The water was there with such force! I was washed outside. I found something to hold on to and lost consciousness. When I came around and regained my senses, Luis was nowhere. A few hours later they found his body. His head was injured where something had struck it. He must have lost consciousness before he could save himself." She bowed her head and stared into her coffee cup as Donnie had seen her do when he was at the phone, as if there might be answers in its steaming depths. "Luis drowned," she said in a soft voice he barely heard. Her account of the hurricane had burst out in a flurry; now she was spent.

"I'm sorry," Donnie told her again. Though she seemed strong and put on a brave front, he was sensing now the potency of the grief that gripped her heart. It could create its own internal storm, every bit as destructive as Blaze.

"Who would have thought the hurricane would be so sudden and violent?"

"Not the weather bureau," Donnie said.

"It was such a surprise, its brute strength. People

were trying to get away—the radio said the high-
ways were clogged with traffic. But there were others
who decided to ride out the hurricane. Even people
out on the beach acting as if nothing was wrong."

"What people?" Donnie asked, sipping his coffee.
It was too hot to drink and he put it back down.

"When I glanced out the window, I saw two men
standing around not far from our cottage. I don't
know what they were doing there. They were wearing raincoats."

"Long, black plastic coats?"

She raised her eyes and took him in with their
dark sadness. "Yes. How did you know?"

"I think that's the kind of raincoat the police wear.
The two men were probably cops."

She shook her head. "I don't think so."

"Exactly when did you see them?"

"I'm not sure. My memory's not totally clear about
that night. But I know it was around the time Blaze
hit."

"Before or after?"

"I can't say positively. Not about much of anything
that night except for Luis. Can you understand that?"

Donnie could understand. She didn't know he'd
been on the beach himself, then in Marcia Dunn's
cottage, during the worst of Blaze.

"They weren't the two looters we ran off," she
said. "They were much taller, not like those worthless ones. Vultures!"

"There was something to the fat one," Donnie said.

She stared harder at him. "Because he could
fight?"

"Because something made him fight instead of
run."

"Men! . . ."

"Okay," Donnie said, "they were both worthless."

"Why do you ask about the raincoated ones?" she said, still staring at him.

He shrugged. "I don't know. Just feeling around for something to talk about, I guess. I keep bringing up the wrong subjects." He gave her a slow smile. "I apologize. You want some ketchup?"

She smiled back sadly to let him know he was forgiven, then said no to the ketchup. It was the first time he'd seen her smile and it was worth the wait.

When they'd finished eating he paid the check despite her insistence to cover half of it. Then he drove her to her motel, a drab, Spanish-style place called the Seahorse, about a mile from the restaurant. Before they parted, he jotted down the phone number at the Leeward Motel, where he was staying, and told her to call him if she needed anything. She thanked him but didn't offer her number in return.

Donnie waited until she'd disappeared inside her room and its lights came on, then another few minutes, before driving away.

Near the Leeward, he bought a large, padded brown envelope at a drugstore, then went to his room and prepared a package of Agent Dunn's revolver, notebook computer, and disks. Also the slip of paper with Luis Perez's name and number written on it in faded pencil. He knew it might be surprising, what information the lab could glean from the simple, water-damaged memo.

In the morning he'd courier the envelope to Donavon. With Donnie working undercover, they would talk by phone frequently, but they'd meet personally only when it was necessary.

The Leeward had a small gym, where Donnie used the free weights to get his regular workout, doing bench presses, curls, shrugs, then sets of squats with 350 pounds on the bar. Two other men, using the Nautilus equipment and the treadmill, looked over at him in awe. One of them, a potbellied guy who said he was an insurance claims adjuster down from Jacksonville to appraise hurricane damage, offered to spot for Donnie. Donnie took him up on it for an extra set of squats.

He didn't stop working out until he'd exhausted himself, which had been part of his purpose.

Back in his room, Donnie got undressed and took a long shower. Then he stretched out on his back on the bed. He studied the ceiling, its fine pattern of thin cracks in the textured plaster, its sprinkler head clinging like an unmoving tarantula near a corner. A tiny red light on the smoke detector above the foot of the bed winked at him at the edge of his vision.

He tried to relax by thinking about fair, blue-eyed Elana, not the dark and troubled woman he'd met and counseled over dinner. Elana, still his wife though they were legally separated. His children's mother and his very life until he'd been caught in the pull of another world . . .

He fell asleep with the lamp on and dreamed of the sea, vast and ominous with deep whirlpools like knowing dark eyes. A mystery.

Another mystery.

10

The phone woke Donnie at nine the next morning. He groped for it, found it, and mumbled a thick hello into the receiver.

"Had your coffee yet?"

"I know this isn't room service," Donnie muttered.

"It's Jules, Donnie. We're scrambled from this end, so you can talk."

"I haven't even breathed yet this morning. You talk first while I wake up all the way."

"The Bureau's been busy while you've slept," Donavon said. "Luis Perez was indeed a real estate broker specializing in commercial property. His mother was a naturalized citizen from Argentina, father unknown. Grew up and went to school here in Florida, sold residential real estate for an agency in Miami for ten years, got into the commercial end of the game, then went in business for himself seven years ago. Apparently he was doing okay. He was fifty when he was drowned by Blaze."

"What about his widow?"

"I thought you'd ask. Grace's maiden name was Carerra. She's second-generation Cuban, born in Miami, worked as a sales clerk and an office temp before marrying Luis five years ago. Neither of these two has ever been in trouble with the law, Donnie. They're straight citizens."

"That doesn't surprise me."

"Looks like they had a happy enough marriage. They bought the beach cottage outside Palmville for quarter of a million three years ago."

"Some cottage," Donnie said.

"Lots of those places on that stretch of beach were fairly expensive homes. Until Blaze."

"I've got a package for you, Jules. That stuff we talked about last night. Give me an address for the courier."

"You're not even up and around yet. How about I send somebody to pick it up. I think we need to move fast on this, Donnie."

"Okay. After I get rid of the package, I'll go back to Dunn's cottage and see what else I can come up with. And there's something else, Jules. Grace Perez told me last night she looked out her window around the time of the hurricane and saw two men in long plastic raincoats hanging around outside."

"Cops, maybe," Donavon suggested.

"She didn't think so."

"What about the two looters you chased away?"

"They were too short to be the same men. And one of them was overweight. The men Grace Perez saw must be the two figures I saw on Dunn's cottage porch when the hurricane hit."

"Let's keep it in mind," Donavon said noncommittally.

Donnie smiled. Everything had to be nailed down at all four corners before Donavon counted it in the fact column. He'd chosen the road of the bureaucrat and had to think that way. Donnie was glad—not for the first time—that he'd built his career in the streets, where acting on a hunch sometimes meant survival.

Where, in a way, you were more free even if you were in more danger.

"One way or the other," Donavon said, "we've got a dead agent and no perpetrator. That's intolerable. Whitten wants results. That's why he's mentioned activating the E.O. Squad." Whitten was Special Agent in Charge Victor Whitten, a twenty-year veteran who understood the occasional necessity of overstepping the boundaries of bureaucracy. Like Donnie, he was fiercely loyal to the FBI but loathed some of its constraints. It was with his blessing and protection that the E.O. Squad operated. Donnie the noncomformist was just the agent to command it. "I think it's time, too," Donavon added.

"Political corruption's not usually E.O.'s beat," Donnie reminded him.

"Maybe Agent Dunn was onto something more than that. You said yourself the Mafia's probably in on whatever's going down. People who can hire a battery of slick lawyers to fight kickback or illegal campaign contribution charges don't usually kill to try getting out of trouble."

Donnie admitted Donavon had a point.

"I'm sending someone around to talk to you about the Mafia," Donavon said. "That undercover agent I mentioned who's doing much the same thing here in Florida that you did back in New York. She might have something to add."

"We got a meet set up?"

"She'd rather contact you. She's cautious, like you were. Keeps her alive. She'll use my name so you can be sure she's who she says."

"The Family plays baseball with hand grenades down here," Donnie said. "She better be extra careful."

"Which means you better be extra careful, too, Donnie."

"But not so careful it keeps me from being curious."

"That's the job, old buddy."

"Marcia Graham's cousin will keep nosing around," Donnie assured him before hanging up.

Donnie had finished showering and was dressed except for his shirt when Donavon's runner arrived for the package of items from the cottage's ruins.

He opened the door to a young woman in shorts and a faded blue workshirt. Nothing like most people's idea of an FBI agent. She smiled at Donnie, and he watched her eyes as she noted every aspect of his appearance, a pro making sure he was the man she was supposed to see. Then she showed him her ID and he handed her the brown padded envelope. He wondered for a moment if she might be the undercover agent Donavon had mentioned. But it didn't seem so. Not a word had been exchanged. He watched her walk to a plain blue Chevy sedan, climb in, and drive away without looking back at him. FBI experts would be poring over the envelope's contents before noon.

Donnie finished getting dressed, slipping a red polo shirt on over his head but not tucking it into his chinos. The shirt was cut generously enough to conceal his gun stuck inside his belt in back. He was wearing the boots he'd had on yesterday and was ready for another romp through the wreckage.

But before driving back to the ruined beach cottage, he had a breakfast of eggs, toast, and bacon, washed down with black coffee, at the Leeward's attached restaurant.

He was walking to his car when a small, wiry woman with long blond braids approached him. She looked seventeen, moved with the grace and easy confidence of a dancer, and was smiling. What looked like a small, glittering diamond was set in one of her front teeth.

"Donavon sent me to see you," she said. "It's a Family matter. Why don't we go back inside the restaurant, and you can have another cup of coffee."

"You don't waste any time," he told her.

Still smiling, she said, "It's fleeting, don't you think?"

Donnie thought.

11

Donnie found himself sitting again at the same small table with its wilted flower-in-a-vase centerpiece. The waiter had already cleared the dishes and set out new place mats on the red and white checked tablecloth.

The young-looking undercover agent ordered coffee, and Donnie did the same, though it would be his third cup of the morning.

While they were waiting for their order, the woman placed her elbows on the table and gazed over at him. He knew that to be an undercover agent she had to be at least in her late twenties and was probably in her thirties. She was one of those women who would look youthful most of their lives. She said, "My name's Blondi, spelled without the *e*."

"That's what Hitler called his dog. It the only name you got?"

"Only one you'll get," she said. She flashed him her jaunty diamond-lit smile, no doubt a hit with the rough crowd she must be running with. "You got quite the reputation."

"You must know how I earned it."

"Six years!" she said, "Jesus!"

"He bailed me out a few times, I'm sure."

"I don't know if I could do this for six years,"

she said, with the slightest quaver of uneasiness in her voice.

"It happens a day at a time," Donnie told her. "Like growing old before you know it, or being married twenty years."

"I wouldn't know about the married part."

"Me, either."

When they had their coffees, she added cream and sugar to hers, then sipped. "I been down here in Florida seven months," she said. "I'm not nearly as far in as you were, but I'm in. I know things."

"Do you know the big thing?"

"Oh, we never know that, do we? But what's your notion of the big thing?"

"What did Agent Dunn know?"

"That I don't know, either. But you can be sure the Florida Mafia was involved in some way. I overheard talk to that effect."

"Who did the hit?"

"Don't know. Wish I did. It might tell us why."

Donnie looked at his coffee, then pushed it away. He didn't know quite what to think of Blondi. "Donavon said you needed to talk to me."

"It's about pornography," Blondi said with a wink.

Donnie wondered if her playfulness was an act that helped keep her alive. "Still early in the day for that," he said.

She shrugged as if to question his judgment. "There's a struggle going on over who controls pornography production and distribution on the East Coast. The Italian Mafia's still got the biggest piece of cake. The Russian Mafia wants some and is going about taking it."

Donnie knew about the war waging over pornography control. The Russian Mafia, centered in New York's Brighton Beach, so mobbed up now it was sometimes called Little Odessa, had moved into the power vacuum he'd helped to create when the Italian New York mob had been all but destroyed. Its kingpin, Vyacheslav Ivankov, had been taken out of circulation by the FBI, but the "Organizatsya" still thrived. When the Iron Curtain had fallen and travel restrictions from the former Soviet Republic were made lax, some of Russia's most hardened criminals had gone to the U.S., much in the way Cuba's worst criminals had entered Florida during the 1980s *Mariel* boat lift. The old order of the Russian mob had been ousted by newer, harder, and smarter criminals. Its members were at least as vicious as the Italian Mafia's. Several deaths had already occurred, casualties in the battle over vast potential wealth, just like war in the outside world.

"The news is, there's been a marriage between the Italian and Russian Mafias," Blondi said.

He understood that by "marriage" she meant an agreement, a pledge to live together for better or worse rather than die separately.

"They've decided to cut their mutual losses and call a truce," she continued. "They'll divide control of the East Coast porn industry. The Russians put up some money to buy peace. The Italians wanted something more. You became part of the negotiations. A condition's to be met. You're it. The Russians do the hit on you for free. That way the Italians get the job done and save the half-million price they put on you. There's a Russian Mafia hit man on your trail. His name's Yesa Marishov, and he's the best they have."

Donnie felt a cold rush of fear despite himself, but he didn't let it show. Blondi was looking at him, studying.

"Got his description?" he asked.

"No. Nobody seems to know what he looks like. I only know him by reputation. He's a displaced KGB assassin, trained in the Soviet Union before it was dissolved, and he's got notches on his gun. He was part of a secret program to avoid suspicion by using teenage assassins. He's been working at his trade for a long time, but no one knows how old he is. He might still be a young man, or have one of those faces that age slowly. That's why the trainees were chosen, so they could use their youth to charm people and gain access so they could kill."

"He'll have plenty of help here in South Florida," Donnie said. He knew that along with the Italian Mafia, the Russian Mafia was influential from Miami up to around Fort Lauderdale, mainly involved in smuggling drugs in from Cuba and Haiti and shipping them north. "You have any kind of in with the Russian mob?" he asked Blondi.

"Only through their dealings with the Italians."

"They at war over drugs the way they are over pornography?"

"No. Here in Florida the Russians control most of the drug-running. The Italians are satisfied to collect a percentage and stay out of the way."

"Can you use that connection to find out more about Marishov?"

"It's chancy, maybe impossible, but I'll try. Should I let you know through Donavon if I learn anything?"

"That'll soon be the only way to reach me," Donnie said.

She didn't ask him to elaborate.

"I've put out some feelers about Agent Dunn's death," she said. "Nobody talks about it. That's why I'm sure they're involved."

"Maybe Marishov was one of the men who hit her," Donnie said.

"I don't think so. This latest development is recent. Not much more than hours old. Anyway, it's said he's a solitary worker."

"You got to me fast," Donnie said. "I appreciate it."

"I reported what I'd heard to Donavon, and he got me to you," Blondi said. "At this point, the Florida family might not even be aware you're in the area, but they'll find out."

"Eventually," Donnie said.

"Marishov will find out."

"Eventually."

"Eventually is what we live for, people like us, even while we worry about the next few minutes." She winked and stood up. "I better run, but we'll meet again, I'm sure."

He didn't ask when.

Instead, he waited for her to get well clear of the restaurant, a slight figure who looked like an innocent high school girl rather than what she was. Not so unlike Marishov, probably, if he'd begun his lethal career as a teenage KGB trainee. It was something, what this kind of life did to people, how it twisted their priorities and rearranged their lives while they were looking the other way. It turned them into someone different from who they'd been. Elana knew.

Donnie asked the waiter for a glass of ice water and drank some to wash away the aftertaste of too much coffee. He sat for a while pondering the big question: What had Marcia Dunn known that got her killed?

Then he went back outside to the now blistering-hot parking lot.

This time he made it to his car.

12

For the next several hours, Donnie picked and sorted through the sun-warmed wreckage of Agent Dunn's cottage.

He came up with nothing more that seemed it would be of any value. Reflecting on how much more productive it might be if the Bureau could turn loose its experts in the ruins, he leaned back against a section of wall that hadn't collapsed and felt the hot Florida sun beat down on his face and chest. It was important to maintain the cousin facade, he knew, so for now he would remain the solitary searcher. And maybe he'd already found what was important. Maybe the contents of the envelope he'd gotten to Donavon would open some doors in the investigation.

At least the sun had pretty much dried the mud in the cottage. He looked out at a pelican flapping low over the surface of the sea, searching for a glimmer of a meal. Everything was calm and picturesque this morning. It might be years before the ocean ever reached this far up on land again. He hoped that would hold true, if Grace Perez was rebuilding her home not far from where he stood.

Donnie raised a sunburned arm and glanced at his watch. Eleven-fifteen. Too early for lunch, and after the big breakfast he'd eaten, then more coffee with

Blondi, he wasn't hungry anyway. He wondered if Grace was at her cottage.

With a final look around the damage and disorder, he made his way out through the Dunn cottage's broken latticework and began striding up the beach. On his right, the ocean was trying to whisper something to him in a language not his own.

Ten minutes later he was close enough to get a good look at the Perez cottage. Nothing seemed to have changed since yesterday. The bright sun made the three standing walls and the roof tiles seem new and clean, in contrast to the surrounding debris on the beach.

Donnie went up three steps onto what recently had been a wide plank porch and called Grace's name. Got no answer.

If there had been a door, he would have knocked. Instead, he stepped inside, took a look around, and called again.

She wasn't home, if "home" was the appropriate word. It would take a lot of work and time to restore this ruined house to a home. He looked more closely at the thick, stained carpet, the broken furniture that obviously had at one time been expensive. Even the shattered crystal and pieces of smashed china had a different look from Agent Dunn's. Quality shone through the dirt and debris. Luis Perez hadn't necessarily been wealthy, but the couple's possessions bore out Grace's comment that her husband had been doing okay in his business.

Donnie had turned to go when he noticed the small metal coffeepot on a portable gas burner. The burner's element was glowing red. On an upright lamp table near it was a white coffee mug. Beside the mug was a folded piece of paper with a yellow pencil lying across it.

A lump of dread grew in Donnie's stomach as he

went to the table and felt the mug. It was warm. There were even faint traces of steam rising from its contents. He unfolded the paper. The writing on it was compact and elegant—four words: *To whom it may*

Someone had begun writing a note, then changed their mind and left it incomplete.

He turned in a full circle, looking all around him. "Grace!"

No answer.

He switched off the burner under the coffeepot, then walked back out onto the porch, listening to his boot heels clomping in the quiet morning.

That was when he saw Grace Perez standing facing away from him, knee-deep in the foaming surf, her rich dark hair catching the sunlight and blowing gently in the breeze off the sea.

She was fully clothed in white slacks and a green blouse.

Because of the rushing and ebbing surf, Donnie didn't realize at first that she was moving.

That she was walking at a ninety-degree angle away from the beach.

Into the ocean.

13

"Grace!"

She didn't turn around. She was ignoring him. Or the wind had snatched his cry and carried it in the opposite direction.

Donnie leaped down from the porch and began running across the beach.

Grace was now waist-deep in the sea and still facing away from him. He lengthened his stride, his heels digging deeper. Glancing up and down the beach, he saw that there was no one in sight, no one closer to Grace who might help. The inexorable slide of the sea onto the shore made her seem to be moving away from land faster than he was running. The sand was like sleep, putting him in one of those nightmares where the dreamer struggles desperately to run in a slow, thick world and can't make progress.

He saw Grace lean forward, then extend her arms for a few lazy breaststrokes as she gave up perhaps forever her tenuous connection to the earth. She let herself float free for a moment, then began a steady, determined crawl stroke out to sea.

Keeping his gaze fixed on her, Donnie felt cool surf around his ankles as he slowed in the drag of the surging water. The surf withdrew and he picked up speed, but was slowed again as another breaker dashed onto the beach and rose to his thighs. Lifting his knees high, he plowed ahead. The surf was louder now, slapping and crashing onto the beach. When he was waist-deep he threw himself forward and swam after Grace.

His boots made swimming difficult, slowing him down. And as his body rose and fell with the sun-shot swells, it was impossible to keep Grace in sight.

But she didn't know he was there and she was swimming almost languidly now, not in any rush to get far enough out, winded enough, so she couldn't possibly return.

He was gaining on her.

Then something did make her turn her head, and she noticed him. Her eyes widened and she began stretching her arms to reach farther ahead with each stroke, swimming faster away from him.

Donnie stroked harder himself, feeling the strain in his lungs. A stitch developed in his right side, but he swam on, glancing ahead every three or four strokes to see if he was gaining on Grace, to make sure he was in line with her path toward the sea and eternity.

She was a strong swimmer with her heart set on oblivion, and he could barely keep up. His legs were weakening from forcing the heavy leather boots through the water, and he was weary enough to be sucking in ocean now and then, causing him to gasp and spit when he should be breathing smoothly. He was aware that he might be following Grace into death, that he'd soon be too far out himself and too weary to return to land. He craned his neck and peered ahead as a swell lifted him.

Grace was pulling away from him.

The boots! The goddam boots! They were making this impossible!

He thought for a moment about stopping and treading water, working to loosen the laces and slip the boots from his feet.

But he knew it wouldn't work. There'd be no way to make up the time.

He continued his struggle, feeling the drain on his endurance. His coordination was leaving him along with his strength. Instead of making forward progress in the face of the next incoming wave, he was lifted high, flailing feebly with his arms, then tossed backward.

Spitting salt water, he raised his arms and twisted his body to turn again into the swells roaring toward shore. The next wave hoisted him even higher and hurled him tumbling in the opposite direction.

When he came to the surface he tried treading water, buying time to think. That didn't work. It was as if there were weights strapped to his ankles, dragging him down.

Water closed over the top of his head.

He was sinking.

He stroked toward what he hoped was the surface, broke into light and air, and sucked in oxygen. Rolling onto his back, he attempted to float so he could get his bearings, regain his strength. His soaked clothes, the leadlike saturated boots, wouldn't permit it. His feet and legs dropped, rotated, and he was trying frantically to tread water again. The sun was bright and hot on his face and shoulders, then it was gone and he was in cool darkness.

Now he did attempt to unlace and slip off the boots, bending his body severely, fumbling with numbed fingers.

The laces had swollen and felt as if they were knotted and cemented to the leather.

Giving up, he stroked again toward the surface.

But he'd used most of his strength struggling with the laces.

He felt himself sinking, faster this time, passing through layers of coolness.

And he knew he was drowning.

Fingernails dug into his neck, cut deep, were gone.

Then he felt blunt knuckles, a fist, at the nape of his neck. Someone had hold of his shirt, pulling him upward.

His face was in air and sunlight again. An arm was crooked around his throat. Too tight. He gagged, coughed, spat.

And finally began to breathe again, his mouth and nose only inches above the tilting, rushing planes of glittering water.

"We can make it back," Grace said calmly.

Her face was near his, strands of her long dark hair twined across his cheek, stuck in a corner of his lips. He felt the powerful, metronomic movement of her body stroking and kicking toward shore.

"When we get close, the sea will help us," she told him.

He started to answer but coughed up more water. Better not waste energy talking, he thought, and began kicking in time with Grace. It was a help. He cupped his hands and stroked awkwardly with his arms toward shore, getting some of his strength back, some coordination. He was facing toward open ocean, seeing only unmoving horizon as the sea lifted and lowered them, but he sensed they were making progress. Locked together, they were like a single struggling sea creature, a primal thing in a timeless sea, making its way unsteadily toward land and a metamorphosis to human.

After a while the incoming waves seemed to be moving more beneath them, carrying them and no longer rising and bearing down on them. And the rush of water around them was faster.

Donnie could hear breakers crashing on the beach. A wave hoisted them, spun them. Grace kept her arm locked firmly around his neck, momentarily choking him.

With his help they regained their balance and direction, and he felt a different, familiar rhythm in the movement of Grace's body.

Her feet had made contact with the ocean floor near the beach. She was walking!

He lowered a leg and felt his heel drag on pebbles and sand. Then he contorted his body and tried to stand up so he could walk.

Another wave slammed into them from behind, separating them and sending Donnie sprawling. He got to his feet, felt the backwash trying to pull him out to sea, and struggled toward shore. There was Grace, fighting to remain standing. He gripped her elbow and helped her accomplish three or four wobbly steps.

Another wave roared in and knocked them forward. They crawled for a few feet, then stood. The water was only knee-deep now, then suddenly waist-deep, pushing them forward.

This time they kept their balance until they were only a short distance from where the surf splayed out and withdrew foaming on the sand. They crawled the final distance onto the beach and safety, then rolled onto their backs.

Unmoving, they lay exhausted beside each other.

The surf continued rolling in, sometimes reaching far enough so that there were a few inches of cool, swirling water around their bodies. Donnie was gradually getting his breath back, listening to Grace gasping and choking beside him, as if she'd almost devolved and had to reaccustom herself to land.

After a while, he simply lay in the baking sun and listened to their bellowslike breathing gradually lessen and even out. Life again, taking them over. Wonderful! Sun, air, heat. Life again!

Grace's fingers brushed the back of his arm, then rested there.

"You saved my life," she said. "I was crazy with grief and you saved my life. You and your bullheadedness and your watersoaked boots and all."

Donnie stared up at the brilliant blue sky.

"Somebody saved somebody," he said.

14

Donnie drove her to the Leeward, where she waited in the car while he grabbed some dry clothes. He didn't want Grace to be by herself for long, so he hurried back outside still wet and climbed in again behind the steering wheel. Neither of them said much while he drove to her motel.

While she showered, Donnie changed into the clothes he'd brought. Dry socks and his dry Nike jogging shoes finally made the ocean seem far away.

Five minutes after the hissing of the shower stopped, Grace emerged from the bathroom wearing blue shorts and a baggy gray Florida Marlins' T-shirt. Her hair was still wet and glistening, combed straight back and starting to curl again where it was beginning to dry.

"Feeling better?" Donnie asked.

She smiled and nodded. Water dripped from her hair onto the carpet. Donnie caught the scent of perfumed shampoo. "I got depressed," she said, "sitting there in the middle of what's left of my life with Luis. The unfairness, the utter hopelessness . . . it all came over me like something dark and heavy and I almost couldn't breathe. Christ! I didn't want to live."

"But you do now?"

She gave him an upward look, her chin tucked in, as if she was ashamed. "Yeah. I think I can make it okay. I *will* make it."

Donnie didn't say anything, thinking she felt that way now, but would it last? She hadn't gone to her beach cottage this morning planning on suicide—then there they were, swimming in the sea.

Grace ducked back into the bathroom and came out with a wadded white towel, which she used to dry her hair. Drops of water flew as she rubbed vigorously with the rough terry cloth. The action left her thick hair wildly tangled, in an odd way making her more beautiful.

"You seem like a strong woman," Donnie said. "And you're young and obviously smart."

"Well, I don't go swimming with my boots on," she said. She was smiling, but only slightly.

"It was a special occasion," he told her.

She stood before the dresser and plugged in a hair dryer. It was tiny and pink but powerful. It began to whir with a fury and he watched her play the flow of hot air over her hair, using her free hand to undo tangles and rake her fingers through the dark, damp strands.

Donnie used his thumb and little finger to represent a phone and held them to the side of his head. He mouthed that he had to use the phone.

Grace was watching him in the mirror, still moving the dryer around and fluffing her curls.

Then she switched off the dryer so he could hear to make his call. "Sure. Go ahead."

"No, you keep drying your hair. I'll use the phone outside."

Without taking her eyes off him, she nodded, and the dryer started whirring again.

*   *   *

The pay phone was on the edge of the motel's parking lot, near the highway. Donnie fed in his coin, punched out Donavon's number, and stood with the receiver held to his right ear, the tip of his left forefinger plugging his left to block out traffic noise. The sun sure was hot out here, like somebody's feverish hand on the back of his neck.

Donavon answered on the second ring.

"You scrambling?" he asked, when he knew it was Donnie.

"No. Public phone."

"Maybe that's why it sounds like you're calling from a NASCAR race."

"I called to check. Anything?"

"Info for you, Donnie: Agent Dunn's revolver hadn't been fired, and hers were the only prints on it. The slip of paper with Luis Perez's name and phone number is a grocery receipt. Writing was on the back in pencil. It'd faded a bit, but the cash register ink washed away almost completely. The lab brought it back enough to learn that the store it's from is Quick-Check Market."

Donnie remembered seeing such a store on A1A, not far from Agent Dunn's cottage. It was a small convenience store connected to a gas station. Mostly brick and glass, its door and windows had been boarded up with plywood, but it and the service station were still open.

"Quick-Check's not far from where Dunn was living," Donavon said, as if reading Donnie's mind.

"What about the disks and Dunn's computer?" Donnie asked.

"The computer's hard disk is a mess. Lab's still working on it. The individual diskettes are something else. One of them, anyway. One contains the phony text Dunn was using to maintain her journalist identity. Not much useful on it. But the other disk was the jackpot. The information's cryptic and incomplete because of water and salt damage, but it shows Dunn was onto something much larger than your run-of-the-mill election fraud. It makes reference to a man named Munz, and some sort of illegal tie-in that involves a place called Belle Maurita."

"Belle Maurita?"

"I never heard of it before either. Had to use a magnifying glass to find it on the map. It's a small town at the edge of the Everglades, on the Gulf Coast. Across the state and south from where you are and from where Dunn was operating."

"What about this guy Munz?"

"I've got the Bureau working on him. We'll know more about him before long."

"Was there mention of this in any of Dunn's reports?"

"No. I'm sure it was what she wanted to talk to me about in person. And it was probably why she was hit."

"Then you agree with me that she *was* hit?"

"I've always agreed with you, Joe."

Donnie knew better. The use of Donnie's nearly forgotten real name was Jules's way of apologizing. Well, admitting he was wrong, anyway. The relationship between the two men wasn't one that required actual apologies.

"I've talked to Whitten," Donavon said. "We're activating your E.O. Squad. They're on the way to Florida now. Code name of the operation will be Blaze."

FBI operations were usually coded after something pertinent to a case. The hurricane appellation seemed apropos to Donnie. But there was something else about the situation that irritated him.

"Thanks for letting me in on what's happening," Donnie said. "But when I'm on a case, I'm the one who decides when the team's needed."

"Usually. This time it's Whitten. Those are the rules, that there are no rules. Sometimes you've gotta live with that like the rest of us."

Donnie knew he was right. Didn't like it, though. He didn't need Jules to tell him there were times when he had to dance, that because of his reputation as a rogue agent he was looked on with disdain and envy by some of the gray suits in the Bureau. The ones who did the dull, necessary jobs that didn't entail somebody's idea of glamour. That was what Elana wanted, for him to draw back from the seduction of danger and be one of the suits again, doing safer, saner work. At times Donnie wavered, thinking she might have a point. At times he wanted more than anything to be back with her in her ordered and secure world where he wouldn't go to sleep and wake up with fear. At times.

"I've got you Logan, Acuna, and Lily Maloney. If you need anyone else, let me know."

"That seems like enough for now," Donnie said. He'd worked with all three agents before and knew they were among the best.

Rafael Acuna was thirty-two, of Cuban descent. He was bilingual, a former carpenter who'd become a trained economist and whose specialties as an agent were narcotics and bank fraud cases.

C. J. Logan was African-American, former Green Beret, and a weapons expert. Everything from Molotov cocktails to guided missiles. He was cool, resourceful, and reliable as sunrise.

Lily Maloney, a fit, attractive redhead in her late twenties, was a former dancer and acting student who was an expert in computers, explosives, and had taught hand-to-hand combat at Quantico.

They would be enough, Donnie thought again.

"I'll let you know when they arrive so you can link up," Donavon said. "You got anything for me?"

"I swam out into the ocean this morning and stopped Luis Perez's widow from committing suicide. In a manner of speaking."

"The suicide attempt was in a manner of speaking?"

"No, the rescue."

"Am I right in assuming the lady's still alive?"

"Yeah. She's fine now."

"In a manner of speaking, I'll bet. Do you think there was a reason for the suicide attempt other than grief?"

"I doubt it," Donnie said. "She's the kind of woman who mourns hard."

"What's her status now?"

"Still a widow."

"Don't fuck with me today, Donnie."

Too far, Donnie thought. Time to back away. "There's no way to know her status for sure, but I think she's gonna be okay."

"She could be a source of information."

"It's possible. If Luis Perez was involved in whatever's going on."

"It oughta be looked into."

"It will be. But so far my conversations with her suggest that if he was involved, she knew nothing about it."

"And maybe Luis is innocent of everything but original sin. Only we can't ignore that slip of paper in Marcia Dunn's pocket with his name and phone number on it."

"Maybe Dunn was seeing Luis for . . . you know, some reason of her own. His wife might not know about that."

"Jesus! Don't even think it, Donnie. Dunn was a seasoned agent on a case."

"Okay. I'll figure out a way to cover this angle along with everything else," Donnie assured him.

"We got murder, a widening case, and two locations now," Donavon said. "And there's something else, something that comes through between the lines. What scared Agent Dunn so much was Munz."

"Then she became dead," Donnie said.

"How did the meet with Blondi go?"

"She thinks the Mafia might be involved in whatever's happening in Florida."

"Almost goes without saying. She also tell you about Marishov?"

"What she knew."

"Nobody knows much about him except that he's out there and he's deadly and he's assigned to home in on you like a smart bomb. Be careful with yourself, Donnie."

"I always am."

"And I'm J. Edgar Hoover." Donavon hung up.

"No, you're not," Donnie said into the dead phone.

He couldn't imagine Donavon in anything other than one of his pin-striped suits.

When he knocked and reentered the motel room, Donnie found Grace wearing dark blue slacks instead of the shorts, and the same loose-fitting gray T-shirt. She had brown leather sandals on her suntanned feet and her hair was combed and pinned back. He thought she looked like someone who wanted to live. But then to her, he looked like Marcia Graham's cousin.

"I'm going shopping for some things I need," she said, "then I'm going back to the cottage."

"You sure you want to go back there today?"

"Yeah. It'll be okay."

"I'll go with you. Help you shop."

"No, I can be alone."

"Listen, Grace—"

"I'll be fine." She sounded determined. He was

pleased to note she was also still talking to him in a less formal way, as she had been since the rescue, as if her suicide attempt had created a comfortable familiarity. "I have to do this alone, don't you understand?"

"No."

"Somebody can't always be there. I have to be by myself sometime. I have to get used to it."

Donnie didn't like this but knew he could do nothing about it. Something told him Grace was a woman who couldn't be pushed.

"Okay," he said, "I'll drive you back to your car."

"I don't have a car. Mine's still not running, and there's a shortage of rentals all over Florida. I don't see how you managed to get one."

"If your car's not running, I'll have to go with you to shop. You can't schlepp everything you need between the store and your cottage unless you make a lot of trips."

She stood thinking about that, and maybe about the tropical sun searing the world outside the cool room.

Then she nodded. "You're right again. Let's go." She picked up a small black leather purse, then left the motel room with him, locking the door carefully behind them.

They walked across the sunbaked lot to where his Taurus was parked. Donnie could see heat vapor wavering and rising from the lot's surface—and from the hood and roof of his car.

They sat with the windows down and the air conditioner on high for a few minutes before driving out onto the highway.

Grace was silent beside him.

When they'd picked up speed, he drove with his wrist draped over the top of the steering wheel. "Did

you or Luis happen to know a man named Munz?"
he asked.

"Not that I can remember." There was nothing in
her voice to suggest she was lying or that he'd surprised her. Or that she was frightened of Munz.
"Why do you ask?"

"Munz mentioned over in Belle Maurita that he
used to be in real estate in this part of Florida. I
thought he and Luis might have run into one another, maybe done some business together."

"Belle Maurita?"

"It's a little town on the Gulf Coast."

"I was never on the Gulf Coast. I don't think Luis
was, either."

Donnie pulled into the lot of the Quick-Check Market and parked near the boarded-up glass door to
the store.

Grace looked over at him. "How did you know I
wanted to come here?"

"I didn't. I remembered it was nearby, and I need
to buy gas."

True to his word—more or less—he moved the
Taurus over to one of the pumps and filled it with
89-octane while she shopped inside for whatever it
was she needed.

When Donnie went in and paid for the gas, he
found her in an aisle that was stocked with cleaning
supplies. She was already carrying a push-broom, a
box of cleanser, and a green rubber bucket.

He took the items from her to hold. She resisted
for a few seconds, then smiled and gave in.

"Your place needs hammers and nails more than
this stuff," he said.

"I know. I'm doing this for me as well as for the
cottage. At least *something* will be getting done."

He understood how she felt. If a problem seemed

overwhelming, it helped to be making progress by inches even if miles were required.

That was, in fact, how he felt right now. There was something big out there. Big enough that an undercover agent had been murdered in order to continue its concealment. And Donnie was exploring only the contours of its edges.

He found himself impatient for the squad's arrival.

15

The directions Donavon later gave Donnie by phone took him to a large, deserted-looking building outside Palmville. It was constructed of gray cinder block and had a corrugated steel roof painted white to reflect the sun. A section of the roof was raw metal, however, probably replaced after Hurricane Blaze had blustered through.

Donnie entered an unlocked side door, as instructed, and found himself in a well-lighted interior filled with rows of steel racks on which were stored various kinds of boats. Most of them were runabouts, but there were a few sailboats and even cabin cruisers. It was cooler in the warehouse than outside and didn't seem as humid. Controlled conditions to keep the boats from deteriorating in the racks, Donnie guessed. There was a sharp, acrid scent in the air that tickled the nose, like freshly applied varnish. Wide concrete aisles ran between the racks. The concrete had a gloss on it from what Donnie assumed was some kind of moisture proofing.

At the end of one of the aisles, Donavon appeared. He looked spiffy. He was wearing a tie and blue or black suspenders and had the sleeves of his white shirt neatly rolled to just below his elbows.

"Donnie boy!" he called, waving an arm. "Come

on back here!'' There was a hollow echo in the vast warehouse.

Donnie listened to the sound of his footsteps reverberate as he walked toward the broad-shouldered figure at the end of the aisle. Donavon was waiting for him in a casual stance, with one hand in a pants pocket, the other on a hip. Donnie thought he looked like a men's fashion model with muscles.

"Everybody here?" Donnie asked when he was near enough.

"All but C.J. He's winding up a case in New Jersey and will fly down early tomorrow." Donavon removed his hand from his pocket and turned to lead the way. "C'mon. The building's ours. Confiscated narcotics largesse. It's empty except for us, and it's clean of devices. We can talk freely. Even dance if we want."

Donavon led Donnie toward a partitioned-off space with an unpainted door. There was a window in one of the wallboard partitions, and Donnie could see a couple of desks with phones and computers on them, a large cork bulletin board cluttered with memos and notices. Obviously the warehouse office. But they didn't go inside. The E.O. Squad members who were present, Lily Maloney and Rafael Acuna, were lounging outside the office, seated on crates of boat parts or accessories.

When they saw Donnie they stopped talking and stood.

He shook hands with them, grinning. These were people he liked and respected, who'd had his life in their hands before and probably would again. What E.O. Squad members knew was that they'd protect each other's backs under *any* circumstance. It was the primary reason they'd been chosen. Few people fit into that category.

Lily was wearing a businesslike light tan skirt and

blazer, low-heeled white pumps. Her red hair was cut short and brushed sideways above keen green eyes. She looked her freckled and fit self, though paler than when Donnie had last seen her over a year ago. She had a square Irish jaw and a ready, white smile. *Lovely* didn't quite describe her; *beautiful* might. *Lovely* didn't fit her fearless attitude or the eager, good-humored challenge in her direct gaze.

Rafael—or "Rafe," as he was called in the Bureau—had on pleated gray slacks and a white Izod polo shirt with the requisite alligator logo over the pocket. He was medium height and very muscular, handsome but for a nose that had been broken one time more than it had been set. Donnie knew that Rafe's father, a former Cuban Olympic team boxer, had given him lessons from an early age. Rafe might have been a contending middleweight, only his Mexican mother had squelched the idea and steered him toward higher education and masters degrees instead of contusions and possible brain damage. Like in the movie, it still sometimes bothered Rafe that he coulda been a contender.

Donnie saw the familiar expressions on their faces, subtle but noticeable if you knew what to look for. He'd seen it in his own face in the mirror. They were about to go undercover and part of their minds and souls loved it, loved the danger and being someone else for an extended period of time, creating a new person in broad and minute detail and making him or her real even to themselves. Donnie wasn't sure why they felt that way. Maybe it was something left over from childhood that could be made good use of as an adult. Whatever it was, he knew it was a necessary component of every skilled undercover agent, needed in order to be convincing. If they were playing a game that was rooted in childhood, it had become grown-up and deadly.

"We heard about your close call in New York," Rafe said. "Glad the right guy took the bullet."

"It's good to be working with you again, Donnie," Lily said. "I was getting bored punching computer keys."

"I'm afraid there might be a few more for you to punch here in Florida."

"I figured that, only I'll bet it won't be all I do here."

"Sounds like you're into something major," Rafe said. He hadn't a trace of Spanish accent. Donnie knew that when speaking Spanish, Rafe also had no trace of an American accent. "La Cosa Nostra again," he added.

"I wouldn't speculate," Donnie cautioned, though he figured Rafe was right.

"Where you find corruption and murder, you find the Mafia," Lily said.

"I've briefed everyone," Donavon explained to Donnie. "But there's one thing I waited to say until you got here. The computer nerds have been working on Agent Dunn's damaged laptop. They got tired of trying to figure out partial information and got into the Paintbrush feature of Windows, the one kids like to use to create lines, shapes, and colors. There were files there that looked like Dunn's five-year-old niece had played with the computer. But when the nerds started deleting colors one by one, they discovered that if they left only the underlying pale yellow lines, the name Jake was readable. There was also some kind of personal code Dunn must have used."

"Jake . . ." Rafe said. "Must have been her source."

"And probably my visitor when I was at Agent Dunn's cottage," Donnie said. "The little guy with the ridiculous white toupee."

"Maybe," Donavon said. "But keep in mind 'Jake' is probably a code name. Dunn wouldn't leave the real name of an informer on her hard drive." He smiled and moved back a few feet, leaning against a gray fiberglass hull. "Now it's your turn to run the show, Donnie."

Here was the thing Donnie liked most about having Donavon for his control agent; he had the guts to delegate authority completely.

Donnie didn't waste time. "C.J. is going to play free safety and act as liaison. Lily will be a journalist sent here by her magazine to start over at square one and take the place of Agent Dunn's identity, Marcia Graham. We'll assume Graham was killed because she was a journalist who learned too much, not because she was FBI, but we can't be positive." He glanced at Donavon.

"We can set her up with an ID and a liberal bias in a matter of hours," Donavon said. "She'll be all set to take on Jake if he turns up again as a source."

"I'll be watching for that toupee," Lily said.

Donnie looked at Rafe. "Remember how to swing your carpenter's hammer?"

"Sure. It's something you never forget. Like riding a bicycle only you hit yourself in the thumb now and then."

Donnie said to Lily, "You settle in and get set up with your journalist's persona." To Rafe: "You checked in at a hotel?"

"Sure. Holiday Inn on A1A."

"Good. You can come with me as soon as possible. Jules can get some ID for you, too. Same name, different occupation, should be okay. You're an out-of-work carpenter from Nashville, down here to make fast money repairing hurricane damage."

"I can fix him up easy with everything he needs," Donavon said, "but maybe not Nashville. Not on such short notice."

"Wherever," Donnie said. "But I've gotta know now."

"Houston," Donavon said. "Makes more sense anyway."

Donnie didn't ask why. Donavon always had his reasons.

"There's no building code in Houston," Rafe explained to Donnie. "More free-lance contractors there."

"I know I don't have to stress secrecy to either of you," Donnie said. "A slip of the lip and we all go down with the ship."

As if suddenly uncomfortable, Donavon pushed himself away from the hull he'd been leaning against. "From now on I won't meet with any of you personally unless it becomes imperative," he said. "C.J. will carry the mail."

"Since C.J.'s not here yet," Donnie said, "the thing to know is that I'm going to be in Belle Maurita, leaving tomorrow. I'll be Donnie Banner, government field agent with the EPA. Can you swing that ID by tonight, Jules?"

"Sure," Donavon said. "Federal ID's no problem. I'll get it to you this evening. What about a plain four-wheel-drive vehicle for the EPA field agent? Cheap. Efficient model. Very government."

"Great," Donnie said.

"Whatever Dunn was onto in her identity as Marcia Graham," Donavon said, "she learned enough about it to get her killed. All of you be extra careful, especially Lily at this point." He gave Lily a concerned look. "Whoever hit Agent Dunn might figure you, her replacement, should be next in line. All three of you stick close to your motels tonight, and whatever you need in goods and information will be delivered to you." He glanced at his wristwatch, as if they were talking about minutes instead of hours.

"Everyone involved here has worked with everyone else on previous cases. We should have this operation up and running smoothly in no time." He looked at Donnie. "Any questions, before I fade away and play guardian angel?"

Donnie glanced at the squad.

"We might need to contact each other before we see C.J.," Lily said. "Wouldn't it be better if we did that directly and not through you?"

Donavon agreed, and the squad members filled each other in on where they were staying and how to get in touch. Already registered under assumed names at motels outside Palmville, they'd be moving tomorrow to register somewhere else under their new identities.

"That's it then," Donavon said. "Remember, the object is to discover what it was that got Agent Dunn killed. And don't let all that sunshine and natural beauty outside fool you. As of now, we're on the alert in enemy territory."

"Let's roll," Donnie said to Rafe. "There's somebody I want you to meet."

"The enemy?" Rafe asked.

Donnie hesitated before answering. "I'm not sure. That's part of what I want you to find out."

16

"The deal is," Donnie said, steering the car onto now barely passable Beach Lane, "the lady needs help in several ways."

Rafe stared at him from the passenger's seat as they bounced over the ruts. They'd stopped at a hardware store for some props, and Rafe had a blue chalk marker sticking out of his shirt pocket, a metal tape measure clipped to his belt. He'd even dirtied his fingernails and wrapped a bandage around the tip of his left little finger. Donnie thought the bandage was an effective touch.

"She needs to have her beach home rebuilt," Donnie said, "which will be kind of like rebuilding her life. And she recently tried to commit suicide. Part of your job's to make sure that doesn't happen again—successfully, anyway."

"Tall order."

"You're a tall man, Rafe."

Rafe smiled. Though five-foot-ten, he was sensitive about his height. "Always been tall enough." His voice was amiable but tight, warning away any possible sarcasm.

Donnie had gotten the reaction he'd sought. This job might not be as easy as Rafe anticipated. Donnie wanted him into it all the way, alert to anything.

"The other part of your assignment is to make sure she isn't involved in whatever it is that's wrong here in Florida. Except for bad toupee, a woman who's gone back to Iowa, and a couple of looters who didn't get a good look at me in the dark, she's the only one who might reveal that Donnie Banner, the EPA environmentalist, is the same man as Donnie Blaine, the cousin of Marcia the journalist."

"Ah, I understand. I thought for a moment your heart had melted."

"Only a little," Donnie said.

Rafe stared at him again.

"Not everything about this assignment's unpleasant," Donnie said.

When they reached the beach cottage, Rafe studied it through the windshield.

"Major work needed here," he pronounced. "Hurricane raised some hell."

"Nobody expects you to rebuild the whole thing," Donnie said. "You might even wanna hire a crew when things get to be too much for you."

Donnie parked in front of what was left of Grace's cottage. He and Rafe got out of the car and strode toward the front porch. Two pretenders.

Grace had heard them drive up and walked out onto the porch, letting the screen door slam behind her. She came down the damaged steps to greet them.

Rafe stood taller and visibly brightened when he saw Grace Perez. She had her thick dark hair skinned back and tied at the nape of her neck and was wearing work clothes, tight threadbare jeans with gloves tucked halfway into a pocket, and a T-shirt lettered BASEBALL CARES. Donnie remembered the women at the restaurant who were cheering the televised ball game when he and Donavon had drinks and first discussed the case.

"This is Rafe," Donnie said. "I thought you two oughta meet. He's a carpenter down here from Houston."

"How do you know each other?" Grace asked, looking dubiously at Rafe, then at Donnie.

"I saw him repairing a house in Palmville," Donnie said, "and the work was solid. Carpenters are hard to hire right now, with all the repairs needed after Blaze. But when I asked him if he might know somebody who'd work on your cottage, he said he was almost done with the job he was on, and he'd be glad to drive out with me and give you an estimate."

"I don't know . . ."

"It's not bad as it looks," Rafe said, starting to amble around and get a closer look at the cottage. "I got some impressions walking up to it. The main structure's still firmly fixed on the piering. That's what's important. Some of these places on the beach blew clear away."

"My husband knew construction," Grace said in a tight voice. Her eyes misted.

Rafe glanced at Donnie. "Is he—"

"He was killed by Blaze," Donnie said.

Rafe looked sympathetic. Donnie knew it wasn't all an act. "I'm sorry."

"I'm not looking for favors," Grace said.

Rafe smiled. "Oh, I don't work free, ma'am."

He walked around some more, did more assessing, even used his tape measure. Then he returned to the car, got the clipboard and tablet he and Donnie had bought at the hardware store, and jotted down some notes.

"I can't say much for sure until I work up the figures," he said, when he was finished. "I can get a solid estimate to you tomorrow."

"That's fast," Grace said.

Rafe shrugged. "Time being money, I don't have

much choice. Guys like me, who do quality work with good materials, are in short supply right now in this part of the state. If you don't hire me, I'll move on and find other work. But I've gotta keep busy or I might as well have stayed home in Houston."

Grace looked at Donnie, who nodded almost imperceptibly.

"All right," she said. "Let's see what kind of figures you come up with."

Donnie and Rafe were confident as they returned to the car.

Rafe had quite an advantage when bidding this job.

After dropping Rafe off at his motel, Donnie drove to the Leeward and packed. Then he went to the bar off the lobby and had a beer while he watched a program featuring half a dozen attorneys sitting around a table and arguing about race and sex discrimination suits and murder trails around the country. He soon decided it was all show business, lost interest, and returned to his room.

There he found himself thinking about Elana and their girls. Grace's BASEBALL CARES T-shirt had reminded him of his daughter Daisy's first organized ball game. He'd only seen a photograph, an image of a tiny girl in a uniform too large for her, her cap somehow making her almost unrecognizable. He'd been present when his oldest daughter Maureen had played softball, after he'd taken a chance that day and sneaked across the bridge from Manhattan to Jersey, into his other, real or unreal, life. He remembered her hitting a fly ball over the left fielder's head, how her eyes had found him and she'd smiled at him out of breath from where she'd stopped at second base. The evening had been warm, the infield

grass freshly mowed. He'd had a beer from the
cooler of some guy who was the father of another
girl on Maureen's team. Donnie could almost taste it
now, feel the warm breeze, smell the grass. Elana
was next to him, in a webbed lawn chair, talking
with a woman who was the wife of the umpire. For
a moment Elana's hand had drifted over and touched
the perspiring back of Donnie's wrist, as if trying to
make contact with the past, to keep him from slipping completely away from nights like that one.
Then, without looking at him, she'd withdrawn her
hand.

What was he doing here alone in a motel instead
of with his family in St. Louis? Baseball cared. Did
Daddy care?

Enough?

He didn't wait until morning. As soon as the courier from Donavon had delivered his Daniel Banner
EPA identification and cover story, Donnie checked
out at the office, then loaded the drab gray Jeep Cherokee parked nearby.

The courier had left the vehicle before driving
away in Donnie's rental car. The Cherokee was three
years old, liberally dented, and even had a chipped
and scraped "U.S. Govt." decal on the driver's side
door. Very authentic, Donnie thought, already beginning to feel like an EPA inspector.

The fishing and water-testing equipment that came
with the Cherokee rattled around in back as he drove
from the Leeward's lot, no longer the cousin from
Missouri, no longer Donnie Brasco, slipping deeper
into character and away from who he really was.
Elana and the girls were from another life in another
universe. The universe Donnie moved in now was
lonely, cold, and vast, peopled by the doomed and
disappeared. Even time was different here, more crit-
ical and limited, for a man who was someone else

who had been someone else. His identity was in fragmented images, like pieces of a shattered mirror. How could the hit man Marishov find him if Donnie couldn't find himself?

The Jeep's engine kept up a steady, lusty growl, a glutton for the road. Donnie took the Florida Turnpike to Alligator Alley and cut west across the state to Highway 29, where he turned south toward the Ten Thousand Islands, the deep Everglades, and the town of Belle Maurita.

There he'd find the mysterious and dangerous Munz.

And if he was good at his job, lucky, or both, more answers than questions.

17

Donnie reached Belle Maurita just after sunrise. But even at that brightening, optimistic time of day, the town seemed as gloom-ridden as the surrounding swamp.

Belle Maurita's main street, Cypress Avenue, was lined with weathered and canted clapboard buildings that were slowly losing their battle with the elements. Here and there a brick building stood out among the darkly decrepit frame ones, but the bricks were mottled and mossy from the looming swamp's heat and humidity.

There were a few side streets intersecting Cypress, but they couldn't run very far without meeting foliage as thick as an Amazon rain forest. Only gray, sad buildings, similar to the ones on Cypress, were occasionally visible as Donnie glanced up and down the streets at each corner.

The swamp was crowding the town. It was close behind the buildings on each side of the main street, tall cypress and mangrove trees towering and leaning as if about to fall upon and devour the helpless structures and people beneath. Even with the Cherokee's windows up and the air conditioner on high, Donnie could smell the fetid stench of the swamp, the teeming life and death and decay. It seemed to underscore the danger of what he was getting into; he was soon to be part of the primitive, endless struggle that included the town and its people as well as the surrounding swamp.

He made a mental note of the businesses lining Cypress. There was the Keen Kut barbershop, Floyd's Bait and Tackle, the White Flame Restaurant, Norton's Automotive Service and Small Motor Repair, Hoppy's Happy Bar, First Solidarity Insurance, Second Chance Used Clothing . . . Prosperity was nowhere in sight. Near the end of the block was the combination city hall and police headquarters, a low, beige brick building with darkly tinted windows. Kudzu vines were growing up the south and east walls, making measurable progress in their effort to cover the windows entirely even as Donnie watched.

He made a U-turn and drove the length of the town again, seeing if there was anything of interest he might have missed. Anything of interest at all.

Only a few people were on the streets, beaten-down women in jeans or cheap dresses, along with men in work boots and overalls. There was a lazy resignation in the way they moved and the lack of animation in their faces, as if the gloom of the swamp had infected their souls. Some of them did make the effort to glance curiously at Donnie as he drove past, maybe noticing the U.S. government seal on the Jeep's door. There was a flicker of resentment and open hostility in most of the glances, as if a stranger displaying an interest in the town didn't bode well.

This might seem a strange place for the Mafia to be operating, but only to someone unfamiliar with the tightly knotted crime families. Donnie knew they might be found anywhere, and would turn a profit even from desolation and small dollars. Seemingly insignificant amounts added up, and the Mafia knew how to calculate.

He pulled the Jeep into an angled parking slot in front of Handy's Hardware, but only to turn around. Then he drove through town again and continued driving to see what was on the other side of Belle Maurita.

What was on the other side was swamp. Thick saw grass and mangroves, vines and elegantly draped Spanish moss. There were small, dark birds of a type Donnie had never seen before, as well as herons doing their balancing act on stalklike legs.

A shrill sound caught Donnie's attention. The Jeep's water pump about to break down? He switched off the air conditioner to make sure the battered vehicle's engine wasn't making the noise, and he realized he was hearing the collective scream of insects. A tire hissed as it passed through water. The narrow road was only slightly elevated, and rancid puddles lay here and there like dull, reflecting mirrors on the cracked pavement.

Donnie was driving slower, looking for a place to turn around, when he saw the old neon sign. Not that any of the curved and broken glass tubes were glowing, or had glowed in years. But he could make out what they would have said if they'd been lit: HUTCH'S DROP INN. Beneath the long-dead neon lettering was a small VACANCY sign. Donnie didn't doubt it for a second.

He braked the Jeep and made a right turn into the motel's parking lot.

Hutch's was comprised of a two-story brick and cinder-block structure built in a *U* around a swimming pool. There were no vehicles parked near any of the units. Next to the office was a rusty black Volkswagen Beetle with a faded and tattered Confederate flag on its aerial.

The place was a mess. The brick walls were stained from long-time gutter leaks. The iron steps and catwalk that gave access to the second-floor units were rusted and badly in need of paint. Doors and shutters were weathered and cracked, and some of the venetian blinds visible in the units' dirty windows were hanging crookedly, their metal slats twisted as if by fierce winds.

Listening to the tires crunch over the muddy gravel of the parking lot, Donnie let the Cherokee coast to a stop, then climbed out.

Now he got a close look at the swimming pool. Its surface was coated with algae and leaves. Something alive plopped and made the water ripple. The pool was like a miniature version of the surrounding swamp. Donnie didn't regret not bringing his trunks.

He walked toward the end unit with the OFFICE sign in its window, pushed open a screen door that needed patching, and stepped inside.

There was an old mahogany counter that looked as if it was half of a saloon bar. The walls were paneled in dark wood and the floor was black and gray checkered tiles that made Donnie dizzy until he looked up and away from them. Though there were no chairs in the area in front of the registration desk, there was a low table with years-old magazines fanned out on it. The *Popular Science* on top promised plans to build a hi-fi record player.

Donnie stepped forward and rang the bell on the counter, noticing as he did so that everything in the room was fuzzy with dust.

He'd expected someone to come through the door behind the desk. Instead, at the bell's tone, newspaper rattled, a voice said "Goddammit!" and a man stood up from a recliner adjusted so low on the other side of the desk that Donnie hadn't noticed it when he'd rung.

He was a small, wiry man in his seventies and had one of those faces whose halves didn't seem to match. One of his eyes was oddly brighter than the other, as if somehow illuminated from behind. There was an overpowering stale odor about him, suggesting he'd worn his crusty jeans and wrinkled plaid shirt for days, maybe weeks. His shaggily cut gray hair stuck out in tufts, like detonators on an ocean mine ready to explode at a touch, and his grizzled, contorted face scrunched up like a crushed paper sack as he stared at Donnie.

"Who the fuck are you?" he asked in his phlegmy, crackly voice.

"Customer?" Donnie ventured. "You know. The guy who's always right?"

The old man glared at him.

"This is a motel, right?" Donnie said, trying not to breathe too deeply. The man's rank odor permeated the tiny office.

Parchment skin suddenly wrinkled into a wicked smile. "Oh, it's that, all right Thing is, we don't get many guests this time of year."

"What time of year do they come?" Donnie asked.

"Other times." No longer smiling, the old man advanced on the opposite side of the desk. "You fuckin' serious? You *really* want a room here?"

"You sold me," Donnie said.

"Why?"

"To sleep in. Hang up my stuff. The usual thing."

"I mean, why are you here?"

"I told you—"

"I mean *here*, dammit! In Belle Maurita!"

"Oh. Business. I work for the government."

The old man backed away a step and glared at him as if Donnie had declared himself a leper. "What the fuck kinda government?"

"Ours. You know, the U.S. Where we are."

"Federal, you mean? *Federal* government?"

"That's right."

Donnie had apparently confirmed the man's worst fears. His left eye began to glow eerily like the right. Both sides of the old, mismatched face twitched violently.

"I'm with the Environmental Protection Agency," Donnie explained. "Here to check the fish and water for pollutants. It's part of a national program, though we're concentrating on the southeast for now."

"I don't fuckin' trust the federal fuckin' government," the old man said.

"Neither do I. But jobs are hard to find, and with this one I get to work outside."

"Bastards with their taxes an' their black helicopters!"

"Not me," Donnie said. "I'm driving a Jeep."

"Fuckin' hate 'em!"

"I don't give a shit," Donnie said. "I'm not in love with them myself. I only work for them. Do I get a room?"

"I guess so. You bein' a sorta outdoors type an' not a fuckin' bureau-cat. Jesus, I hate bureau-cats!"

"Me, too," Donnie said. "That's why I was sent here. I didn't keep quiet when I should have. So somebody else was assigned to Kentucky Lake, and here I am with you, Mr. . . . ?"

"Banjo Hutchinson. But ever'body calls me Hutch."

"Why not Banjo?"

" 'Cause my name ain't Banjo—it's a fuckin' nickname! You ever met anybody actually named Banjo?"

"Well—"

"Fuckin' right you ain't!" Hutch hurriedly interrupted, not taking any chances. He bent low and groped beneath the counter, then straightened up and slapped a registration card down in front of Donnie. "Cash or charge?"

"Charge," Donnie said, grateful for the Visa card Donavon had supplied with the rest of his Donnie Banner ID.

"We only take cash," Hutch said.

"Cash, then," Donnie said. He peeled enough money off his cash reserve to stay at the motel for a month.

"This'll do you for two weeks," Hutch said, pocketing the money.

Donnie shrugged. "Well . . . you're the only motel in town."

"Tha's why our rates are high. 'Specially this time of year."

"I thought—"

"There's an ice bucket in every room," Hutch practically screamed at him. "Machine's right near your room, number 107." He tossed a brass key with a large red plastic tag onto the registration desk. "Sody pop machine's right close to you, next to the steel stairs. Cookies an' 'tater chips in a vending machine, too, but they're always soggy in this weather an' it was a mistake to put that machine in, I say." He leaned with both withered hands on the desk, hunching his bony shoulders beneath the filthy shirt. "We don't serve breakfast."

Thank God, Donnie thought.

He picked up the key, nodded to Hutch, and went to the door. "Is the pool heated?" he asked as he went out.

Hutch sneered at him with both sides of his face.

Donnie found room 107 as depressing as the rest of the motel. The walls were once white but had over time taken on a yellow hue, not brightened by what seemed to be twenty-five-watt lightbulbs behind yellowed shades. The threadbare carpet was blue but appeared green in the yellow light.

When Donnie opened the dusty, flowered drapes that matched the bedspread, sunlight burst in as if eager to do a good turn. He found himself looking at cheap motel furniture, a long dresser with half its plastic drawer pulls missing, a small TV propped on a table near the foot of the bed, a desk with its veneer peeling so badly it might be impossible to write on its surface. The headboard was imitation wood and obviously bolted to the wall. Above it was mounted a framed print of an alligator sitting in a rocking chair and wearing a cowboy hat. Near the chair was a human skull and rib cage. The alligator was grinning and picking its teeth with what appeared to be a bone.

Donnie tossed his suitcase up on the bed, watching dust motes rise and swirl in a yellow sunbeam, and looked around for the air conditioner. There it was, jutting from the wall near another framed print, this one of half a dozen alligators sitting around a poker table, secretly passing aces and winking at each other over a generous pot. The alligator whose hand was visible was smiling conspiratorially and holding five aces. The decor was consistent, anyway, Donnie thought. A dust-and-alligator motif.

He switched on the air conditioner. There was a *thunk* and a low hum that grew steadily louder. Then a growl and a lot of clanking ensued. After a while, cool air began flowing from the unit's plastic vent, and the clanking quieted down.

Sweat streamed down Donnie's face as he walked over to the window and looked out across the parking lot at the oppressive lush swamp across the road. He moved his gaze to the left, and he could see about half of the swimming pool. Its green-coated water was as motionless as asphalt. There was a broken and rusted chaise lounge. Nobody but a bullfrog was taking advantage of the motel's amenities.

He went into the bathroom and switched on the light. It was a cheerless place of cracked gray and pink tile. Water was dripping with metronome precision into the tub. A black palmetto bug as fat as Donnie's thumb scurried to a crack behind the toilet and somehow managed to flatten itself enough to squeeze through and escape the light. Donnie tested the washbasin faucets. The water was brown and came out of the spigots in trickles. He glanced at the shower with its age-stiffened plastic curtain. Mold grew on what was left of the grout between the gray tiles, and a ceramic towel rack was broken in half. But the water leaking from the tub faucet was relatively clear. Here was hope.

Donnie ran the washbasin water until it, too, was clear. Then he rinsed his face, put on a fresh shirt, and decided to drive into town for breakfast. While he was gone, the room would have a chance to cool down under the spell of the clattering air conditioner.

Before leaving, he rummaged in his suitcase and came up with the roll of duct tape he'd brought. He used some of it to fasten the .38 Smith & Wesson Special revolver Donavon had supplied him with to the back of one of the dresser drawers.

Like most agents, Donnie seldom carried a gun that was standard FBI issue, or registered to the Bureau, when working undercover. Donavon was aware of Donnie's preferences in firearms and had chosen well. Donnie like the old revolver with its cracked, checked-wood grip; it was just the sort of gun an EPA agent might carry for shooting small game or plinking. But he didn't want to carry it into town, or leave it where it might be found in the room, so for now a hiding place would be best.

He locked the door behind him carefully, knowing Hutch would have a duplicate key and might be snooping around in the room minutes after he drove away. Not that the old man was necessarily involved in whatever was going on in Belle Maurita. It was just that there probably wasn't much other than nosiness to provide any amusement around town.

Hutch was standing outside the office, leaning with both hands on the wood handle of a worn-out broom, as Donnie drove the Cherokee from the motel lot.

When he heard the growl of the motor and the crunching of tires on gravel, the crusty old man looked over and nodded to Donnie, grinning exactly like one of the alligators in the poker game painting in Donnie's room.

The one with five aces.

18

The White Flame restaurant was a clapboard building next to Handy Hardware. Years ago it had been diligently primed with gray paint before a coat of white was applied. Now the building was mostly gray but with grainy white streaks. If flames had ever been painted on it, they'd long since worn away. A huge black and white cat with one ear lounged near the door and wore the same bored, hostile look as the townspeople. Donnie nodded good morning to it. It yawned.

When Donnie entered the restaurant, there was no lull in the conversation because there was no conversation.

The restaurant had a counter on the right, with wooden stools with gray vinyl seats that had been patched with electricians' tape. To the left and beyond the counter were tables with mismatched chairs. There were two booths near a front window that looked out on Cypress Avenue as if there were something to see. On each table sat a steel dispenser of napkins surrounded by salt and pepper shakers and bottles of condiments, and a narrow-necked glass vase containing an obviously plastic rose. An air conditioner was humming away ineffectually somewhere. Large paddle fans mounted on the old tin ceiling were lazily rotating and moving the warm air around, but not so much that anyone would notice.

Two men in jeans and sleeveless T-shirts sat at the counter, forking in eggs and potatoes and staring at the waitress, an attractive woman in her thirties with short blond hair, pouty lips, and a bored expression not unlike the cat's. An elderly man and woman sat at one of the tables, she in a flower-print dress that reminded Donnie of the drapes in his motel room, he in well-worn but clean overalls. At another table sat a man in a greasy khaki uniform and with grease smudges on his face and hands. Everyone was concentrating on eating or on the waitress behind the counter. Nobody paid much attention to Donnie as he sat down at one of the tables and pretended to study the menu.

"Coffee?" the waitress with the bee-stung lips asked. She'd walked over to stand by him. Beyond her he could see the two men at the counter still chewing their food like automatons and studying her reflection in the mirror behind the coffee urn.

Donnie said he'd like coffee and looked in earnest at the typed menu while she went back behind the counter.

"What's good here?" he asked when she returned and placed a white mug of steaming coffee in front of him.

"Eggs."

"What kind of eggs?"

"Chicken. They're all chicken eggs. Sometimes they're from the same chicken."

He looked at her to see if she was kidding. She looked away, way beyond him, her mind somewhere else entirely. This was a woman who was obviously in the wrong place. He wondered why.

Glancing again at the menu, he said, "I'll have the Sun-Up Special." Though it didn't seem so special to him, merely eggs, toast, and bacon.

The waitress jotted something on her green order pad, then went back behind the counter, opened a small serving door to the kitchen, and stuck the order on a prickly steel rack that held captive another green slip of paper.

"Gimme some more of your hot wet stuff, Ida," one of the men at the counter said with a leer, and held up his coffee mug.

The waitress dutifully took the mug and topped it off at the big steel urn. The two guys at the counter exchanged knowing glances, as if progress of some sort had been made. Ida the waitress continued to appear bored. Donnie figured it must be a problem, to be a looker like Ida in a place like Belle Maurita.

The door from the kitchen opened and a heavyset woman wearing a white apron over her blue work-shirt and jeans strode toward Donnie. She was in her fifties, had a beefy face, a loose hair net over graying black hair, and a distinct dark mustache. She was perspiring heavily as she demanded to know if Donnie was the one who'd ordered the Sun-Up Special.

He confirmed that he was.

"I'm Blanche Dumain," she said. "Own this place. Call it the White Flame 'cause that was my stage name when I was a striptease artist. I'm also the cook today, as my regular man's got time off to take care of a family matter. Thing is, I gotta apologize to you this mornin' 'cause we're outa eggs, all but one small brown one. How about you settle for pancakes, on the house?"

"Fair enough," Donnie said.

"Off the beaten path as we are," Blanche said, "not many people come through town."

"The time of year, maybe."

She smiled. "Don't matter much what time of year it is. Or what year."

"I'm gonna be here a few weeks," Donnie said. "Running tests on the fish and water."

Blanche raised her dark eyebrows with interest. "You some kinda scientist?"

"Environmentalist. I work for the EPA."

"The government?" Blanche asked.

Everyone turned to stare at him.

He smiled uneasily. "Yeah, the federal government. Is that okay? I mean, I don't like the bureaucracy any more than you do, but it's not like I'm employed by a foreign power. And I'm only here to make sure nothing's wrong with the environment."

"Hell, yes, it's okay," Blanche said. "We don't want nobody to come down sick eatin' the local-caught fish. 'Specially if they eat it here."

Everyone turned back to their food.

"You're welcome here anytime," Blanche said, "which is a good thing, us bein' the only restaurant in town. Hey, I gotta get back to the kitchen and whip up them pancakes."

She gave him an offhand wave and trudged back toward the swinging door. Before the door swung closed behind her, Donnie caught a glimpse of an industrial refrigerator, a corner of an oven with a steel door with a blackened window in it.

Ten minutes later Ida the waitress walked over with Donnie's pancakes and a glass coffeepot. She set his plate on the table, then warmed up his coffee.

"Welcome to Belle Maurita," she said, smiling down at him. "Don't worry, you won't get food poisoning here. In fact, the food's good."

She spoke with no discernible accent and her gray-green eyes were now alert and interested. Her pouty lips parted to say more, but the bell over the door tinkled and she glanced in that direction, then returned to the counter. Watching her slender body move and lend class even to her cheap yellow uniform, Donnie could better understand the interest of the two men at the counter.

She was right about the food. The pancakes were delicious.

Donnie had poured more maple syrup on them and was ready to take a second bite when the chair beside him groaned and a portly man in a sweat-stained blue police uniform sat down across from him. The incredibly ornate badge on his shirt read CHIEF OF POLICE in black letters on a gold background.

The chief didn't look as good in uniform as Ida. It wasn't just the uniform. He was an average-height man who had never been muscular and had probably been just this side of obese all his life. His shoulders were narrow and his stomach bulged to stretch the blue uniform shirt at the buttons. He wore a thick black leather belt laden with gear—handcuffs, night-stick, notepad with pen, walkie-talkie, and a blue steel 9mm semiautomatic in a black leather holster.

Smiling sweatily, he said, "I'm Belle Maurita Chief of Police Billy Lattimer, an' you would be . . . ?"

"Johnny Depp, if I could." Donnie extended his hand and shook the chief's warm, damp one.

The chief looked blank.

"He's a movie star," Donnie explained. "Always wins, gets the girl. Anyway, I'm Donnie Banner, with the EPA. Here to run tests on the environment for the U.S. Government."

The chief was the only one Donnie had met in Belle Maurita who didn't seem taken aback by mention of the federal government. "What kinda tests?"

"Mercury content in the fish, pollutants in the water. The Florida wetlands are in trouble, being drained, polluted. But Florida's not the only state with a problem. There are—"

"Okay, okay," Chief Lattimer interrupted. "I think you done answered my question."

"I wouldn't think there'd be much crime in a place

like Belle Maurita," Donnie said, then forked in a bite of pancake.

"There ain't. Domestic disturbance now and again, minor burglary or some kid smokin' a joint. But I more or less keep busy."

"How about poaching?"

Chief Lattimer gave him a sly smile. "Why, Mr. Banner, you wouldn't really be an undercover man with the Fish an' Game Department, would you?"

Donnie laughed. "No, I was only making conversation. If I see any alligator poachers while I'm out fishing or testing, you can count on me to turn around and go the other way."

"That'd be wise. There's some real bad people in this part of the country."

"I thought you said there wasn't much here in the way of crime."

"An' so there ain't. The bad ones I'm talkin' about don't foul their own nest. But we got some folks spent hard time in the Florida State Prison over in Raiford. An' they're hard men for it, Mr. Banner. Don't usually take well to strangers, either. They're naturally suspicious."

"Maybe you oughta say who they are," Donnie said. "That way I can avoid them. I only want to do my work, then go back to Washington."

"Healthy attitude," the chief said as Ida the waitress dropped by the table to top off Donnie's coffee again. But she didn't pour right away.

"You want a cup, Chief?" she asked.

"Thank you, no, Ida. I gotta go shuffle some papers back at the office."

"I overheard you say you were going to do some fishing here as part of your work," Ida said to Donnie. "I recommend you buy your bait down the street at Floyd's."

"You part owner?" Donnie asked with a smile.

"Nope." She grinned at him. "It's just that I figure you for a guy who really wants to catch fish, and Floyd's worms do everything but reach out and grab them when they swim close."

"Do you fish?" Donnie asked her.

"Nope. Rather eat them than catch them. And I definitely don't like to clean them."

Chief Lattimer laughed without mirth and stood up. "Enjoy your stay in Belle Maurita," he told Donnie. "An' you let me know if you have any trouble."

"Why would he have trouble?" Ida asked.

The chief hitched his thumbs in his thick leather belt, as if he'd watched too many *Dukes of Hazard* reruns. "The man jus' told me if he saw any poachers he'd turn right around and go the other way," he said, looking down at Donnie. "Somethin' about him, though. He strikes me more as the sort who'd drift toward trouble 'stead of away from it."

"You don't know me very well," Donnie said, sipping coffee.

Staying in his stereotype southern police chief mode, Lattimer merely gave Donnie a smile and a half salute, then sauntered out of the restaurant, swinging his arms wide to avoid all the paraphernalia hitched to his belt. Leather creaked and gear clinked and rattled as he walked. Donnie suspected the chief liked it that way.

"Know what?" Ida said to Donnie when Chief Lattimer was gone. "For some reason you strike me that same way, the sort trouble'd attract like a magnet."

Donnie smiled and extended his coffee mug. "How about some more of your hot wet stuff, Ida?"

She returned his smile as she poured.

The two cretins at the counter stared hard at Donnie in the mirror.

Green-eyed monsters, Donnie thought, and turned his attention back to his pancakes.

19

Donnie bought worms and a fishing lure at Floyd's Bait and Tackle, as Ida had advised. The lure was called the Hopeful Hooker and was a brightly feathered, many-barbed menace to fish and in the water was supposed to look and act exactly like a struggling insect.

As part of his fishing outfit, Donavon had provided Donnie with a brown slouch hat adorned with lures. Donnie added the Hopeful Hooker to the rest of the colorful array before putting the hat on his head gingerly, so as not to snag a finger, and driving back to Hutch's motel.

In his room, he changed to older clothes and his boots, then returned to his Jeep. Knowing Hutch was probably observing him out a window, he made a five-minute project of inspecting his fishing gear and green rubber waders, along with some sample bottles for swamp water. Then he replaced his lure-laden slouch hat on his head, carefully adjusted the brim to block the sun, and climbed behind the wheel of the Cherokee.

He drove along the road back toward town, then turned off onto a firm area he'd noticed. Using the

Jeep's four-wheel drive, he made his way into the swamp until he saw a clear area of still water ahead.

After making sure the Jeep wasn't stuck, he killed the engine, then reached into the back for the rubber waders. He struggled into the waders so he could walk in hip-deep water without getting wet, then slogged around to the back of the jeep and got out his fly rod. For the first time, he noticed the droning of insects was incredibly loud here. Something that had to be larger than a fish or frog made a splashing sound in the nearby foliage. Birds screeched and nattered. The swamp was a busy place.

Donnie knew only the rudiments of fishing, but he had to make a show of it. He still had no idea what was happening in and around Belle Maurita and never knew if he was being observed. Simple mention of the federal government as his employer seemed to have been enough for people to mistrust him. Maybe there was an active paramilitary unit in the area, with members who seriously suspected the government of spying on them with silent black helicopters and setting up road signs with double meanings for secret contingents of troops that moved by night. This was an isolated and twisted part of the country, a swamp in more ways than one, where organized paranoia as well as almost anything else might grow in the fetid warm atmosphere so humid you could almost swim in it.

For over an hour Donnie alternated between getting his line tangled and feeding Floyd's premier worms to the fish. When the worms were gone he tried the Hopeful Hooker, careful to cast where the water was clear of weeds and saw grass. Though the day had heated up he was fairly comfortable in the shade of the moss-draped trees. Except for the ever-present scream of insects, it was now quiet in the swamp, as if his presence had been grudgingly accepted. Mosquitoes were something of a problem, but the insect repellent Donnie had sprayed on himself back at the motel worked well enough to discourage most of them. They seemed content to circle him like planes in a perpetual landing pattern.

The Hopeful Hooker worked. Within half an hour Donnie had caught two small carp. He beheaded and gutted then, placing their entrails in plastic bags. He guessed that was what an EPA agent might do so he could run tests.

Though he continued fishing, he was glad not to catch anything else. Like Ida the waitress, he much preferred eating fish to catching and cleaning them.

Donnie's luck held for hours. He caught nothing. It was as if the Hopeful Hooker had lost its allure.

After eating a candy bar and drinking a warm canned Pepsi for lunch, he tried another fishing spot, with equally welcome bad luck, then drove back to the motel. His plan was to establish a pattern, make it appear that he did his fishing and sample-taking in the morning, then later at night, and his analysis in the afternoons. He wanted people to get used to seeing his Cherokee parked off the road, knowing he was in the swamp for presumably innocent purposes. Donnie would soon be confident nosing around in almost any area. Choosing this kind of cover had been a wise move. An environmentalist's world was a wide one.

That evening Donnie decided to drive back into town and see what he might learn at the local watering hole, Hoppy's Bar.

The interior of Hoppy's was narrow, but so long that the tables and booths in back were barely visible in the dimness. Most of the light was from illuminated beer signs on the walls. Some of the brands no longer existed.

It was warm in Hoppy's, and the requisite paddle fans were stirring up the haze of tobacco smoke pressing against the ceiling. The bar was long but with only a few stools. Most of the drinkers were leaning against it, feet propped on the brass foot rail that ran its length. There were about a dozen people at the bar. Another dozen at the tables and booths. The men wore work clothes or Levi's and T-shirts. The women wore slacks or cutoff Levi's with T-shirts or wrinkled blouses. Large speakers were mounted in the corners and along the walls near the ceiling, tilted down at a sharp angle the better to spew sound on the customers. A country-western singer with a deep voice was crooning about how love always went wrong for him and he drank too much and went crazy one night and that was how he wound up in prison listening to the lonely wail of train whistles. It could happen, Donnie knew.

The bartender was a stocky, curly-haired man wearing a crinkly red vest but no shirt. Donnie didn't think it was the kind of place where you should order a martini. He bellied up to the bar and asked for a draft beer.

Surprisingly, the beer came in a frosted mug. Donnie tilted back his head and took a long pull of the cold liquid. It felt all the better going down because of the heat and smoke and tobacco smell in the place. The singer was moaning now about solitary confinement and how the prison guards couldn't tame his wild soul.

"You ain't worth frog shit as a fisherman," said a deep, gravelly voice beside him.

Donnie turned and saw a man several inches taller than his own six-one, lean-waisted and bull-necked, bare arms corded with weight lifter's muscle and marked with tattoos. Many of the tattoos were the crude blue kind acquired in prison with needles or ballpoint pens. The man had a seamed, thick-featured face, a jaw like a brick, and unruly black hair growing low on his forehead above bushy black eyebrows that thinned only where they merged above the bridge of his curiously flat nose. He was grinning at Donnie with tiny, crooked teeth, but his dark eyes were as friendly and piercing as laser beams.

"How would you know how I fish?" Donnie asked.

"Seen you back in the swamp."

"I didn't see you. You shoulda said hello."

"Sayin' it now. I hear you work for the U.S. Government."

"What you hear is true," Donnie said. It felt good not to lie.

"Us taxpayers dishin' out your salary just so's you can fish?"

"Not exactly. I'm with the EPA, testing—"

"I heard all that shit," the man rumbled. He lifted a glass of scotch or bourbon, made miniature by his huge hand, and tossed the liquor down his throat with a violent motion of his head and entire upper body. "There's gators in that swamp."

"I know," Donnie said. "Part of my job's to see to it they'll still have a swamp to live in after the building and polluting in Florida's all finished. If it ever gets finished."

"Wally," the big man said to the bartender, "tell this cocksucker to stop preachin' to me. Next he'll be leanin' on me to recycle."

"Better stop like you're told," the curly-haired bartender told Donnie. He seemed serious.

"Recycle, my ass!" the big man said.

"I wasn't—"

"Things even more dangerous than gators where you been fishin'," the giant cut in. "There's sinkholes, poisonous snakes . . . other things."

Donnie adjusted his body sideways so he could face the man. "You concerned about my safety?" he asked.

"In a way, I surely am."

"Is that why we're having this conversation, for you to warn me about the swamp?"

"The swamp an' what's in it an' near it. Things 'round here that'd make a snack outa you if you gave 'em a third of a chance."

"I don't plan on—"

But the big man had turned away from Donnie in dismissal. He'd been doing the talking, and now he was finished. Conversation over. "Six-pack to go, Wally," he said.

The bartender hurriedly handed him a six-pack of Budweiser.

The giant dropped a twenty-dollar bill on the bar, pocketed his change, then ambled out the door. He didn't look left or right, and no one looked at him.

When the door had closed behind him, the mood in Hoppy's lightened. Conversation picked up, more drinks were called for from one of the tables, and the country-western singer on the sound system had somehow found salvation, a governor's pardon and a good woman.

"Who was that asshole?" Donnie asked.

"That was Pinscher," the bartender said in a soft voice, as if the man might reappear and find himself being talked about. "You best walk careful around him."

"Why's that?" Donnie asked.

"He ain't just acting. He's a rough man who likes to hurt folks."

Donnie sipped his beer. "Is everybody in this rat-hole town afraid of him?"

"Everybody with good sense."

"How'd he know I was fishing this morning?"

"He makes it his business to know. 'Cause of that guy he works for."

"Guy?"

"Munz." Now the bartender's voice was even more hushed. It was obvious that Munz was the real reason for the kind of deep fear inspired by Pinscher.

"Do Munz and Pinscher have first names?" Donnie asked.

"Mr. Munz, his first name's Curt. Pinscher's just Pinscher."

"Like the Doberman dog?"

"Yeah, though I sure wouldn't mention that to his face. Wouldn't call him an asshole again, either, even behind his back."

"How come either the asshole or Munz would be so interested in my fishing?"

The bartender took a worried look around. "I dunno. Maybe you was fishing near where Munz has his place."

"He live in the swamp?"

"Yeah. Out off the old state road that winds through it."

"What kinda place has he got?"

"Nobody knows for sure."

Or will say, Donnie thought. If Hoppy's was any indication, it was obvious that Munz and Pinscher had Belle Maurita terrorized and under tight control.

The table over by the window called for another round, and the bartender nodded nervously to Donnie, then hurried away.

Donnie finished his beer, letting himself relax, listening to another country-western song. This one was about a decent man who drank too much and got crazy one night and did something that landed him in prison, where he refused to be broken. He stayed until he was redeemed by God and a good woman and was pardoned. Hmm, Donnie thought.

He finished his beer, said good-bye to the bartender, and headed for the door.

Though it was early evening, it was still mercilessly hot and bright outside, and so humid the moss on the north sides of the buildings glistened with moisture. As he started across the gravel parking area alongside Hoppy's, Donnie blinked several times to adjust his eyes after the dimness inside.

And there was Pinscher, leaning back casually against the Cherokee's front fender with his leg-sized, tattooed arms crossed.

Waiting for him.

20

When Donnie got closer, he took another look at the tattoos on Pinscher's arms. They weren't as crude as they'd appeared in the dim light of Hoppy's. Some of them were simply faded. Like the skull with the snake twined through the eye sockets, just below Pinscher's left elbow. Farther down the arm, near the wrist, was a more recent tattoo of an evil-looking green and yellow lizard. On Pinscher's other forearm was a tattoo of a nude woman hanging from a gallows. As his forearm muscle flexed, she appeared to be writhing at the end of the rope around her neck. There was a spiderweb tattooed over the elbow above the woman, an often-used symbol to identify those who had killed another human being. Donnie figured Pinscher had earned his spiderweb tattoo.

"This Jeep of yours don't look like it'd have the power to pull your hat off," he said to Donnie.

Donnie stopped walking and stood quietly in front of Pinscher. "They're assigned to us. I'd rather have a Rolls-Royce."

Pinscher smiled. "It's good that you got a sense of humor even scared."

"Have I got a reason to be scared?" Donnie asked. He knew he should play this a little frightened. An EPA field agent would be spooked by this guy. Donnie consciously shuffled his feet, realizing it wasn't at all difficult to act afraid of the huge and ominous Pinscher. There was a power about the man that went beyond mere physical size and strength. A kind of enthusiastic evil emanated from him. He might do anything to anyone anytime for any reason.

"Any stranger who's gonna stay awhile in Belle Maurita oughta be scared. This is a place don't take to folks we don't know nothin' about."

Donnie made a point of swallowing hard. "Not much to know about me. I'm a simple government employee here to—"

"Sure, sure," Pinscher waved a plate-sized hand as a signal for Donnie to be quiet. "I'm not interested in your story, even if it's true. Maybe you really are a government fuckhead here to count fish or whatever. I don't give a healthy shit." Pinscher stepped away from the Jeep, toward Donnie. "Tell you the truth, there's just somethin' I don't like about you personally. I mean, I wouldn't like you no matter when or where we met."

Donnie flashed an obviously forced smile, backing away a step. "Maybe if you got to know me better you'd see I wasn't such a bad guy."

Pinscher smiled confidently, a bully who knew he had his prey helpless and paralyzed with fear. Donnie understood how jerk-offs like this thought. In Pinscher's mind, the battle was already won. There was nothing left now but the fun part.

Donnie didn't like this a bit. He knew why Pinscher was forcing this encounter. He wanted to see if Donnie fought like a DEA or FBI agent, or a cop. Anything other than an EPA field agent.

Pinscher moved with amazing fluid quickness for such a huge man. In a blink, he had Donnie's shirt-front knotted in his massive fist. Donnie could smell beer on Pinscher's breath as he grinned.

Pinscher shoved hard, and Donnie let himself fall backward onto the gravel surface of the parking lot. In the corner of his vision he was aware of several people who'd wandered out of Hoppy's and were watching him. Pinscher wasn't the only one who wanted to know how he'd react to this kind of pressure.

Donnie got up slowly, brushed his hands together where gravel had dug into them, then lowered his head and charged Pinscher.

Pinscher laughed. "Well, ain't you a surprise!" He sidestepped neatly, and Donnie slammed into the Jeep. Donnie took a wild swing at Pinscher and missed. He felt Pinscher's fist plow into his stomach, and he was on the ground again.

For a moment he thought Pinscher might kick him. Donnie could let this go only so far; if Pinscher really started to work on him, he might have to fight back in earnest, maybe even kill the giant.

If it was possible.

But Pinscher didn't kick. He was cool for hired muscle. His glittering dark eyes studied Donnie, wondering if the EPA employee had gotten his fill.

Donnie stood up and took another swing at him, this time with his eyes closed.

Astoundingly, the punch landed.

Donnie felt the shock of it up his arm as Pinscher grunted and stepped back.

Then the big man smiled. "Say, you're a tough little cocksucker."

Quick as a heavyweight contender, he threw a left jab, then a right cross that snapped Donnie's head around.

Donnie dropped, actually losing consciousness for a few seconds.

This time he stayed down. The peaceable environmentalist would have had more than enough violence by now.

He rose only to a sitting position and leaned his back against one of the Cherokee's muddy tires.

"Fuck!" he said. "You cut the inside of my mouth!"

"That sorta thing's what a man aims to do when he throws a punch."

"So what'd you prove?" he asked Pinscher, tasting salt, realizing the cut on the inside of his cheek was bleeding badly. He turned his head to the side and spat blood.

"More'n you might think," Pinscher said, staring down at Donnie curiously. "You ever been in a fight before?"

"Not in a long time," Donnie said.

Pinscher gave a deep, rumbling laugh. "Well, you still ain't been in one." He squatted low and peered closely at Donnie. "But I gotta say, the raw material is there. You got some balls."

"Thanks for the compliment and the sore jaw," Donnie said.

Pinscher shrugged. "Coulda been lots worse, an' you know it." He straightened up and turned his back on Donnie.

Donnie didn't move from where he sat on the gravel, watching Pinscher stride to a black Ford Bronco on jacked-up suspension and oversized tires, then swing himself up and in behind the steering wheel.

"Hey! Fuck you!" Donnie yelled at him.

Pinscher looked over at him and grinned. Gravel flew as he gunned the Bronco's engine and roared out of the lot and down Cypress. He apparently figured he had nothing to fear about getting a speeding ticket from Chief Lattimer.

People were gathering around Donnie. He strug-

gled to his feet and leaned with a hand against one
of the Jeep's fenders, noticing the metal was still hot
from the sun. He was dizzy and his head blazed with
pain. He couldn't be sure if it was from the punch
that had snapped it around, or if Pinscher had re-
vived the old pain from the hurricane.

"You done right well," a man's voice said, not
very convincingly.

Somebody handed Donnie a bottle of beer. He
used it to rinse out his mouth, then turned away and
spat a rust-colored mixture of blood and beer onto
the lot's gravel surface.

"You gonna need stitches?" the same man asked.

"No," Donnie said. "A cut inside the mouth
heals fast."

"Sure as hell ain't gonna leave a scar that'll show,"
another man said. "But I was you, I'd go see Doc
Whithers, right down the street. You got yourself a
cut on the side of your head, too."

Donnie raised his hand to his forehead, then lowered it. There was blood on his fingertips. He looked
down and saw that his shirt was splattered with
blood. He was still dizzy, and he knew he wasn't
thinking clearly. He tried hard to focus. He didn't
want to find himself in a hospital emergency room
or a doctor's office where he might have to fill out
forms and answer questions. He'd had enough of
that back in Palmville.

"I'm okay," he said. "I don't need a doctor." He
wiped away blood that was dribbling down his chin.

A hand clutched his elbow. "That cut's bleeding
bad," a woman's voice said. "You better come with
me."

"I told you," Donnie said, "no doctor."

She led him away from the knot of people, a few
unsteady steps.

"I didn't say anything about a doctor."

He glanced over and saw that the woman who had his elbow was Ida, the waitress from the White Flame.

Donnie let himself be led.

"Have you ever been a man's salvation after he got himself drunk and went crazy and wound up in prison and then got pardoned?" he asked. Blood bubbled at the corner of his mouth.

She laughed. "Sounds like a country-western song."

"Don't it, though?" Donnie said, feeling her strong right hand lighten its grip on his elbow, now that he was going with her so willingly.

21

Ida lived in a house trailer near the edge of town. It was furnished and decorated so it felt more cozy than cramped, and its interior seemed surprisingly upscale compared to the rusting metal and stained fiberglass of its exterior. The carpeting and drapes were blue, the walls off-white, and the furniture light oak and functional.

Lots of lamps had winked on the instant Ida flipped a wall switch, so everything was bright, adding to the illusion of generous space. The dampness of the swamp had permeated everything, but at the same time there was no oppressive odor. Everything looked and smelled clean.

"You're a neat housekeeper," Donnie remarked.

"I've got the time."

She led him into the small bathroom—rather *to* it. There wasn't room in it for both of them. After rummaging through the medicine cabinet, she handed him a bottle of pale blue liquid.

"Rinse your mouth out with this," she said, stepping out of the way so he could enter and stand before the washbasin. "It'll fix you so you won't have to keep swallowing or spitting blood."

Donnie was for that. He did as she instructed, feeling the cut on the inside of his cheek sting and his mouth pucker as he swished around the oddly minty liquid.

"What is it?" he asked, after straightening up from the washbasin.

"An astringent. Like sucking on a lemon, but it stops the bleeding. I used it after a slight accident I had last year."

"Car accident?"

"Not exactly."

Donnie figured he'd better let the subject drop— for now.

"Here," Ida said, somehow squeezing into the tiny bathroom with him. She ran water, gently dabbed a cool washcloth to the cut on his head, then handed him a folded white towel. "Hold that on the cut. I'll put a bandage over it later."

He followed her into the tiny living room that was a step down so it could be described as "sunken" by mobile home salesmen. Donnie sat in a corner of a small gray sofa and used his left hand to hold the towel in place against his forehead. The cut didn't hurt much, but it was throbbing. The bleeding inside his mouth had almost completely stopped.

Ida sat in a chair across from him with her legs tucked beneath her. There was a cool, assessing calmness about her, as if she didn't expect much and whatever it might be, she could live with it.

"Pinscher was testing you," she said. "My guess is you passed."

"It wasn't much of a fight," Donnie pointed out.

"But it was a fight. Most of time when Pinscher shoves or hits somebody they stay down, because they can't or won't get up. You not only got up, you went at him a couple of times."

"So now I've got the prize," Donnie said, using his free hand to point to his head. "Does Pinscher test everybody who comes through town?"

"No, just the ones who interest him and who for one reason or another plan to stay awhile. And we don't get many of those."

"Back at Hoppy's, somebody mentioned a man named Munz. Know anything about him?"

"He's rich—for around here, anyway. And eccentric. Lives in a kind of compound out at the edge of the swamp. It's off an unmarked road that cuts into the highway out near Hutch's Drop Inn, where you're staying."

Donnie didn't have to ask how she knew where he was staying. Belle Maurita offered no alternative to Hutch's.

"How about someone named Jake?"

"Him I never heard of."

"I was told Pinscher works for Munz."

"He does. Sort of his right-hand man. Two other goons do things for Munz, too. Carl and Pedro. But after Munz, Pinscher's in charge. You can find the three of them—Pinscher, Carl, and Pedro—playing poker in Hoppy's some nights. Not much else to do in this town."

"Does Munz ever play cards with them?"

"No, but he's in Hoppy's sometimes, too."

"Munz have a lot to say about what goes on in Belle Maurita?"

"Sure. I said he was rich. And everybody's afraid of him."

"Why afraid? He backed by some kinda mob?"

"Mob?"

"You know. Organized crime. Like the Mafia."

"I don't know anything about any Mafia. Folks around here are afraid partly because of Pinscher, partly because nobody really knows a lot about Munz or what goes on out there at his place that's surrounded by all that security."

"Security?"

"They carry guns sometimes, there and in town. And the place is surrounded by razor wire."

"Think they might be into drugs?"

"Maybe," Ida said. "You know how it is—drugs and Florida. And running drugs in from Mexico or some ship in the Gulf wouldn't be that hard with the coastline near here, the maze of small islands, and the swamp for cover."

"Drugs and organized crime," Donnie said. "That's why I asked about the Mafia."

Ida was staring at him. She seemed to be sizing him up the way Pinscher had earlier but without the menace. His string of questions had made her curious.

Donnie smiled and looked back at her. She was beautiful in the lamplight, with her soft blond hair that curled at her temples, her gray eyes that tipped up slightly at the corners and gave her an intent expression probably when she wasn't even concentrating. He noticed for the first time that there was a tiny dent in the tip of her nose, and the lamplight emphasized her cupid's-bow lips and a cleft chin.

"We're studying each other, Ida."

"Uh-hm. Did I hear you say your last name's Banner?"

Donnie nodded.

"Mine's Clayton. Know what I'm wondering, Donnie?"

"Probably whether I'm going to spit or swallow."

She didn't smile. "I'm wondering if you're really an EPA field agent."

"What else would I be?"

"A reporter, maybe."

"Is there a story here?" Donnie asked.

"There are eight million stories in the naked city, Donnie. A few hundred in and around Belle Maurita."

"I'm not a journalist," Donnie said. "I fish and test water. Can't even type except with one finger on a computer keyboard." He swallowed some blood, not much. Whatever the blue liquid was, it worked well. Ida had been inquisitive; he thought he had a question coming. "Why hasn't a woman like you left Belle Maurita long ago?"

"I did leave. Was born near here, went away to college, found a job in Miami, got married. Then, two years ago, my folks died within a few months of each other, first Mom, then Dad. Not long after my dad's funeral, I came back with my husband Rod. He was a writer, and we saw Belle Maurita as a cheap place to live and a quiet place to write."

"I'm not sure how quiet it is," Donnie said, refolding the towel and pressing it again to the cut on his head. "You mentioned your husband in the past tense."

"A little over a year ago, he died in the swamp. When his body was found, it was mostly . . . well, the alligators had gotten to it."

"I'm sorry."

"I'm more than sorry," Ida said. "I'm suspicious. Rod left Hoppy's one night after telling somebody he was going home—here—only he never showed up. It was never explained how or why he wound up deep in the swamp. The coroner said as far as he could tell, the death was accidental. An alligator got him, and that was it."

"Are alligators really a danger around here?"

"Sure. There are plenty of them. If you do run across one, usually they leave you alone. But not always."

"Do you believe one killed your husband?"

"Not entirely. I do have to admit there's no way to know for sure, considering the condition of the body. Chief Lattimer believes Rod's death was accidental because he'd like it to be."

Donnie knew how that worked. He found himself wondering about the relationship between Lattimer and Munz. "Did Lattimer offer an explanation as to why your husband went into the swamp alone at night?"

"Only that he was a writer, and writers do odd things sometimes. Several people suggested Rod was doing research. Or that he'd had too much to drink at Hoppy's and simply acted irrationally and paid for it with his life."

"*Did* he have too much to drink that night?"

"No one knows for sure. That loss of memory's something else that makes me suspicious. I do know Rod would never have ventured into that swamp alone in daylight much less darkness. He wasn't a sportsman or any kind of outdoorsman. He hated the insects and the heat and the smell of the swamp. All he liked was the privacy we had here."

"And you," Donnie said.

Now she did smile, but it turned sad within seconds as reality overwhelmed memory. She'd lost a great deal. Her husband had lost even more.

"I stayed here after Rod's death because I couldn't turn loose of the past. And I still can't. I have to know for sure what happened to him and why. Belle Maurita isn't the most pleasant place to live, but I don't want to leave. I can't leave. Not yet." She leaned forward in her chair. "Whoever you are—even if you're exactly who you say you are—you're an outsider and an objective observer. I'm asking you to let me know if you hear or find anything that suggests Rod . . ." She bowed her head as her voice trailed off. Her hair concealed her face and Donnie couldn't see if she was crying.

"Was murdered," he finished for her.

"Yes." She unfolded her legs from beneath her and stood up, brushing back her hair with her fingers. Her eyes were red but there were no tears. She was past tears and was burning with curiosity, maybe vengeance. Beyond where Grace Perez was in her loss. The difference a year could make.

"I'll do as you ask," Donnie told her, getting up from the sofa so they were both standing. His headache ran wild for a moment, then settled down.

She thanked him and led him to the trailer door.

"And I'm really who I say I am," he said, smiling down at her.

Lies could save lives.

"Not many people are that," she told him without expression.

He opened the screen door and saw a rolled-up newspaper lying on the top steel step.

When he picked it up and turned to hand it to Ida, she said, "You keep it. In a couple of hours it's gonna be yesterday's news."

Donnie nodded. He stepped out into the black, sultry night, hearing the shrill and constant cry of insects coming from every direction in the dark.

Rod Clayton, who hated the heat and insects, must have heard that same ongoing, frantic scream the night he went into the swamp.

Went or was taken.

Old news or not, Donnie decided to take the newspaper back with him for something to read in his motel room. Belle Maurita didn't have its own paper, so this one was probably from somewhere that had more people than alligators.

Only he didn't read it in his room. When he laid the paper on the front seat of the Cherokee, he saw a familiar face staring up at him. A black and white photograph of the chubby little man who'd talked to him at Agent Dunn's beach cottage, the one with the preposterous white toupee.

Donnie switched on the Cherokee's dome light and slipped the string from the paper. It was a *Miami Herald*, and the news item was front page because it was about a fire that had destroyed half a block of homes in a Miami suburb. The fire had started in the home of the white-haired man, who lived alone and had died in the fire.

His name had been Iver LaBoyan, and he was described as a state employee. Investigators said the cause of the fire had been faulty wiring in a television set. It had shorted out and ignited nearby drapes. LaBoyan and an elderly woman two houses down who'd suffered a stroke were the only casualties.

Donnie switched off the interior light and sat thinking. LaBoyan was probably the Jake in Agent Dunn's computer, an informer to a woman he assumed was a journalist but who was really an FBI agent. If he'd been implicated in a crime and had lived, he would have been surprised to learn he wasn't in much of a position to cut a deal with prosecutors after all.

A fire in Miami. Did it have something to do with whatever was going on here, in Belle Maurita? It was hard to believe. But then so had been LaBoyan's toupee.

22

An instant before Donnie flipped the light switch as he entered his room at Hutch's motel, he was startled by a man's voice.

"You gotta be more careful."

The light came on to reveal the compact, muscular form and wide grin of Special Agent C. J. Logan. He was seated casually with his legs crossed in the room's only chair.

Donnie stepped all the way inside and closed the door. It was like C.J. to try to best him, show he could get into the room without Donnie being aware of his presence. Donnie didn't like it, but he admired C.J.'s skill.

"I checked the paper match," Donnie said, referring to the match he usually placed between door and frame when he was out. "It was still in place." If the match had fallen in his absence, it meant the door had opened and closed. An ancient trick made a cliché by a hundred old books and movies, but it continued to work. For inside doors where the air was still, like hotel doors, Donnie used an almost invisible hair from his head. He wondered if C.J. would have noticed that.

"Found that match," C.J. said. "Used some of my

chewing gum to glue it right back up where you had it, then I came on in and made myself comfortable."

"Where's your vehicle?"

"Swamp." C.J. was still grinning. He was a handsome black man in his mid-thirties, with mischievous eyes and one of those pencil-thin mustaches like dashing movie stars wore in the thirties and forties. Donnie thought C.J. strongly resembled Errol Flynn, but he never mentioned it to C.J., figuring C.J. probably knew it.

"I hope your vehicle's stuck," Donnie said.

"You can bet it's not."

"I'm sure." Donnie sat down on the edge of the mattress, making the ancient bedsprings squeal. He didn't have to ask if anyone had seen C.J. enter. Even the watchful Hutch was no match for C.J.'s stealth.

C.J. glanced around. "Place is much better in the dark. Shine some light on it, and it looks like a Kmart exploded in here long time ago."

"Still," Donnie said, "it's Belle Maurita's best."

"And only, far as I could see. I'm glad you're here and not me. I got a Coke outa the machine around the corner. Damned can's even hotter than outside. Liked to burned my fingers. Machine must heat them up."

"I wouldn't bother complaining to the management," Donnie said.

"Ha! Management's got no idea I'm here. No idea I'm this operation's message man."

"So what are the messages?" Donnie asked.

"Rafe says the Perez woman still looks like a straight citizen. Says that so far it seems her late husband, Luis, was too. Also says work on the beach cottage is coming along fine. He's hired more men with Bureau money. Having a grand time, from what I could see. The Perez woman is a bit of something, eh?"

"The way she looks, how she is, do you think it might be clouding Rafe's judgment?"

"I don't know. Did it cloud yours?"

Donnie shook his head. "Who can know for sure, with a woman like that?"

"Speaking of women, Lily's settled in as the replacement journalist for the late Marcia Graham, staying in Palmville and trying to learn more about whatever it was Agent Dunn stirred up. 'Specially *salvaje*."

"Which is what?"

"Something else the Bureau turned up on Dunn's computer hard disk. At first it was a puzzler, but turns out it's a new designer drug manufactured in Cuba. It's dangerous stuff, has some unpleasant long-term effects on brain tissue, and it's just beginning to find its way into the U.S."

"So Donavon thinks it was Agent Dunn uncovering something about *salvaje*, and not political corruption, that got her killed?"

"Don't know. Donavon doesn't tell me what he thinks unless he figures I need to learn it."

Donnie knew C.J. was right. Need-to-know basis might as well be Donavon's middle name. Compartmentalization was a philosophy that not only protected the agents under Donavon's control, it also served well as bureaucratic cover.

"Lab have any more luck breaking the Windows Paintbrush code on Dunn's computer?" Donnie asked.

"No. Why?"

Donnie tossed the front section of the *Miami Herald* on C.J.'s lap.

C.J. stared down at it. "Another Washington scandal?"

"No," Donnie said. "The white-haired guy who died in the fire, I think he was Jake."

C.J. looked again at the paper. "*Our* Jake?"

"Look at his toupee," Donnie said.

"I see what you mean. Well, if he was Jake and Agent Dunn's source, that source is gone."

"Inform Donavon about it," Donnie said. "I want to learn more about LaBoyan."

"Right. How's this paper say the fire started?"

"Bad TV wiring, caught the drapes."

"Hmph. That's easy enough to arrange, fool the local arson investigators."

"Did the name Jake turn up anywhere else on Dunn's computer?"

"Nope. Far as we know, it only appears on the Paintbrush program, and we don't know why yet."

"No mention of Jake here in Belle Maurita, either," Donnie said.

He told C.J. about his stay in Belle Maurita, including his run-in with Pinscher, and the rest of the evening's activities.

"I guess you want this Pinscher run through NCIC and the other files."

"I want to know more about him, and about Munz, Pedro, and Carl. Tell Donavon I'll get more preliminary information on all of them to him as soon as I can." He shifted his weight on the mattress and the springs squealed again. "Better see if there's anything on Ida's late husband, Rod Clayton."

C.J. added the name to the list he was making on the back of an envelope. He wrote with a kind of shorthand only he could read. "Can't help noticing there are lots of 'lates' that keep popping up in this case."

"We need to try to limit that," Donnie told him.

"Munz sounds like the dangerous one," C.J. said. "Hired thugs like Pinscher are no problem."

"Not usually," Donnie said, "but there's something about this one that doesn't set quite level. I was holding back in the fight we had, and I got the impression he was doing the same, figuring I might be forming an opinion about him just like he was about me. I think there are times he'd rather be underestimated than feared.''

"Then he doesn't run true to type," C.J. agreed.

"Since you're here," Donnie said, "I won't check in with Donavon again for a while. I've gotta drive somewhere and use a pay phone, don't want to call from this dump even using a scrambler unless it's a must."

"Makes sense. There's lots of high tech out there for the bad guys, too. They might have an *un*scrambler." C.J. reached into his pocket and pulled out a scrap of paper, then handed it to Donnie. "That's where you can reach me if you can't contact Donavon for some reason and want news to get to him fast as possible."

Donnie glanced at the number on the paper, then folded it and stuck it in his shirt pocket.

"Another thing," C.J. said. "Bureau's had somebody on Wisowski, the control agent Dunn didn't want to call. He seems clean as anybody with a badge. It could be Dunn simply didn't feel she could absolutely trust *anyone* with a Florida connection."

"Which means she was into something that wasn't only local, something big. Probably Family business."

"I thought Mafia too, till I saw Belle Maurita." C.J. glanced around the room, then toward the window with its closed drapes. "You really think anything that big could be happening in this place?"

"How big it is, I don't know. But guys like Munz and Pinscher are here for more than the ambience."

"That I have to believe."

"*Salvaje*, huh? What's it mean in Spanish?"

"Means 'savage,' 'wild.' But the more direct translation is 'trouble.' " C.J. stood up from his chair.

"Anything else you want me to carry back to the others?"

"No. Just make sure to get any new information to me as fast as possible. You starting back to Palmville now?"

"I'm sure as hell not gonna hang around here," C.J. said. He moved toward the door. "You can have that soda, boss." He pointed to the warm can on the desk corner.

"Thanks so much," Donnie said. "Be extra sure you don't have car trouble in the swamp."

"Why? You afraid something might eat me up?"

"That's right. Alligators."

C.J. stared at him. "You serious?"

"It's a swamp," Donnie said. "Ida Clayton's husband found that out. It's where alligators live and we don't belong."

"Hey, you're really into this EPA environmental thing."

"I just wouldn't want to test the water and find you."

C.J. tried to look unconcerned but couldn't quite make it.

He placed his hand on the doorknob. "Listen, Donnie, things get bad here, you put in the call to us right away, you hear?"

"That time will come," Donnie said confidently.

"Alligators," C.J. said softly, shaking his head. The door opened and closed noiselessly, and he was gone into darkness.

Donnie undressed and stretched out on the bed, but he slept little that night.

The slightest of sounds woke him, and when he did doze off again he dreamed lonely dreams of Elana and their old life together, or of Grace Perez or Ida and the sea or swamp, or of alligators that he somehow knew were Russian.

23

Early the next morning, Donnie extended his fishing territory. He found the dirt-and-gravel cutoff Ida had described and walked along it toward Munz's compound. He had on his boots and not his waders and was carrying his fly rod with the Hopeful Hooker already attached to the leader line. At a rakish angle on his head sat his tan slouch hat adorned with colorful lures. In the hand not holding the rod was a small black tackle box. Every inch the fisherman.

It was peaceful striding along the muddy gravel road. The morning hadn't yet heated up, and warm sunlight found its way through the trees to lie dappled on the ground. The crunching rhythm of Donnie's footsteps, along with the ever-present drone of insects, was oddly peaceful.

Until he heard the rumbling sound of a vehicle approaching behind him.

Donnie quickly left the road and waded into concealing foliage. He felt water, still warm from yesterday, soak into his pants almost to his knees, then begin working its way down inside his boots, saturating his socks.

The engine was louder. Donnie could hear the thunking sound of a suspension bottoming out, and the crunching of tires on the gravel- shot, rutted road.

Pinscher's black Bronco jounced into view. Pinscher was driving. A man with deadpan Latin features, wearing a red bandana tied around his head and with a cigarette dangling from his lower lip, rode in the passenger seat.

It was movement and not image that gave away people trying not to be noticed. Donnie remained motionless as the Bronco growled and bounced past. Neither man in the dusty black vehicle glanced his way.

He listened until the sound of the Bronco almost ceased, not very far down the road from where he stood.

After about a minute the engine noise grew louder. Apparently the Bronco had stopped for a while, then continued. Probably the Latin man had gotten out of the vehicle and removed a barrier or opened a gate.

Donnie counted to himself slowly until the sound of the Bronco stopped altogether. Calculating distance from sound wasn't always easy in lush terrain, but he figured the vehicle had stopped about two hundred yards down the road.

He returned to the road to make walking faster and easier, but when he thought he might be getting close to where the Bronco had stopped the first time, he waded back into the swamp and proceeded more slowly.

Swarms of infinitely tiny gnats found him this time and circled him, some of them flying into his eyes or flitting into his nostrils. He could see them like overactive dust motes wherever sunbeams penetrated the thick overhead growth. Every second or third step, he had to tuck his tackle box beneath the arm carrying the rod and use his free hand to brush the minute insects away from his face.

Knowing he had to move more silently as he got closer, he slowed down so his strides wouldn't stir the water so much and cause spreading ripples and lapping sounds. As he moved into complete and cooler shade beneath towering, ancient trees strung with Spanish moss, the gnats thinned out. But those remaining seemed to think they had to be extra pesky to make up for the sunseekers.

He spotted the gate on his left at the same time he snagged his pants on the razor wire concealed in the water and in the swamp's thick green foliage. If he hadn't felt the pressure and stopped immediately, his flesh would have been torn.

The sharp wire was almost as persistent as the Hopeful Hooker. It took Donnie a few minutes to detach its barbs from the material of his pants leg a few inches above his right boot top.

Instead of going back to the road, he moved parallel to the loosely coiled wire. Sweat was stinging the corners of his eyes, and each move he made seemed to generate enough noise to be heard by every ear in the swamp, human or otherwise. Through the thick foliage he could make out a shingled roof, a dull gray clapboard wall with windows.

Donnie moved farther along the perimeter of the razor-wire barrier, until he saw the rotted trunk of a fallen tree half submerged in the algae-coated water.

Trying to make as little noise as possible, he reached into the water and lifted one end of the trunk, ignoring something that swam and glimmered away as he disturbed it. He walked the log around, swiveling it on its submerged end, then stooped low with it and dropped it across the razor wire.

The splash was louder than he'd anticipated. He stood very still for a long time, as if by intensifying the following silence, the sound of the splash could be made not to have happened. The childhood riddle ran through his mind: *If a tree falls . . .*

Then he decided that if anyone in Munz's compound had heard the splash, they'd probably contribute it to the movement of something with bulk that lived in the swamp.

An alligator.

Donnie didn't like the thought. He felt the icy vacuum of fear in the pit of his stomach and couldn't help looking around.

Nothing he could see was looking back at him.

Using the insect-riddled log as a bridge across the razor wire, he moved in the direction of the gray clapboard building.

As he drew nearer he was surprised by the size of the structure. Though it was low and with a gently sloping roof, it was wide and long. Thick wooden pillars supported it five feet above the damp ground. There were two other, smaller buildings, also with clapboard siding painted the same dull gray as the house. Donnie guessed one of them was a three-car garage, and the other, smallest one, was for storage. The black Bronco was parked next to the house, and beyond it and to the left, the driveway ran until it met a razor-wire-topped iron gate. The rest of the razor wire was concealed by the swamp. The compound didn't look as tightly secured as it was.

A reverberating clap of a shot made Donnie's body jerk in reflex action and he ducked down.

Another shot, then a man's high laughter.

Donnie pushed through the thick saw grass so he could see beyond a corner of the house.

A tall, shirtless man with a whipcord-thin body was standing with a shotgun. A hundred feet away, an alligator about three feet long was dangling from a rope tied to a tree limb. The rope was tightly knotted around the alligator's snout.

"Missed both shots clean!" said another man's voice. He was concealed by the house.

The lean, shirtless man raised the shotgun to his

shoulder again and took careful aim at the writhing alligator. The big gun roared and the alligator jumped and swung on the rope. Though there was a hole in its midsection the size of a fist, it wasn't dead. It was making high-pitched, muffled noises, almost like an injured dog, and thrashing around on the rope that was still swinging from the force of the impact. Donnie knew the gun hadn't fired shotgun pellets. Probably the man was shooting the single lead slugs that alligator poachers sometimes used in the area.

"Didn't kill him," said the man Donnie couldn't see. "You don't shoot worth a fuck, Carl!" Donnie detected a slight Latin accent.

Carl had a lean face to go with his body, a bushy brown mustache too large for his head. His complexion was pale and his hairless torso was tattooed with images Donnie couldn't make out at this distance, but unlike Pinscher, his arms were unmarked.

He didn't rile. Instead he only smiled at the other man's remarks.

Then, with an easy, casual motion, he placed the stock of the gun against his shoulder once more and immediately squeezed off a shot.

The slug hit within inches of the first and the alligator was blown almost in half. It swayed motionless now at the end of its rope. "That one put him outa his misery," he said in a slow southern drawl.

The other man suddenly swaggered into sight. He was the Latino who'd been in the Bronco with Pinscher. Probably Pedro, Donnie thought. What looked like a deep, curved knife scar on his right cheek gave him his impassive expression. Pedro walked to the dead alligator, drew a switchblade or gravity knife from his pocket, and flipped out a long blade. He was wearing what had once been a pale blue dress shirt with a white collar. The collar was yellow now and the sleeves had been cut roughly from the shirt.

Though Pedro was powerfully built, he wasn't tall, and he had to stand on his toes and stretch to cut the rope a few feet above the alligator's bound snout. Deftly, he caught the severed rope as the alligator fell, then smoothly swung the dead reptile around twice and released it in a high arc so it soared into the swamp and out of sight.

"Damn thing gonna smell soon in the heat," he said to Carl. He got a pack of cigarettes from his shirt pocket and lit one with a paper match.

A screen door slammed and reverberated like another gunshot.

Donnie shifted position and peered through the saw grass and lushly leaved trees at a tall, obese man who'd stepped out onto the porch. Despite the dampness and increasing heat, he was wearing a neatly pressed cream-colored suit with a yellow shirt and dark bow tie. The other two men walked toward him, their attitude changing as they got closer, becoming more subservient in their facial expressions and the way they carried themselves. They seemed to shrink a fraction of an inch with each step. The man on the porch must be Munz.

A few seconds later Donnie's assumption was confirmed when he heard Pedro address the heavy man as "Mr. Munz."

The three men stood in the shade of the porch and carried on a conversation, but Donnie couldn't make out what they were saying. Munz had straight, thinning blond hair that had receded drastically. That and unusually sharp features in a flesh-padded face made him look like a fat man who actually did contain a thin man yearning to escape. He was doing most of the talking.

Pinscher emerged from the storage building and

walked toward the house, then joined the others on the porch. Everyone listened to what he had to say for a while, then Munz began talking again.

As Donnie watched, Pinscher and Pedro got back into the Bronco, and Pinscher drove it to the iron gate. The gate swung open automatically, then closed behind the Bronco as soon as it had driven clear. It seemed to be controlled like an ordinary garage-door opener, from a transmitter inside the car.

Then the screen door slammed again, and another man stepped out onto the porch. He was tall and good-looking, wearing well-cut brown slacks and glossy dress shoes, a white shirt open at the collar. His carefully styled black hair was long on the sides so it half covered his ears, and blow-dried and fluffed high on top to make him appear even taller than his six-one or -two. His handsome, jut-jawed face reminded Donnie vaguely of the old TV cartoon hero, Dudley Doolittle.

The man took a swig from the beer can in his right hand, then stared in the direction the Bronco had driven. At that moment Donnie wished he had a camera. He could have gotten a good shot of the man, then had the Bureau enlarge and enhance it so he could be identified.

Carl hopped down off the porch, strode to the storage shed, and flipped his cigarette away and went inside. Then Munz and the dark-haired, handsome man went back into the house. As they entered, a large, brindled dog that looked like a rottweiler emerged and scrambled down the porch steps.

Donnie watched the dog trot down to the gate, then move away as if patrolling the property's boundaries.

More security. Which meant there was something here to hide and protect.

If the dog was going to follow the property line,

it would soon make its way around to where Donnie stood.

Slowly and with almost no sound, Donnie backed away into the swamp.

When he thought he'd gone far enough, he turned around and moved more quickly through the shallow water and thick grass. He set as straight a course as possible toward the road.

The clouds of gnats found him again and went after him with what seemed like a special malice, as if they recognized the scent and sweat of fear. Tangled underwater growth snagged his ankles and slowed him down, making him think of razor wire and tense for the jolt of pain when steel sliced flesh.

Behind him the dog barked twice. It didn't seem to be close, but it was difficult to be sure of that, the way the swamp muffled and distorted sound.

Donnie was relieved to reach the road, and even more relieved to get back to where he'd parked the Cherokee. Though it was only six feet off the shoulder, it was completely concealed in the dense swamp.

But he wasn't as relieved as he might have been.

He knew what had to be done next.

Whatever the danger, he'd have to return to Munz's compound after dark.

24

After returning to the motel and stowing his fishing gear, Donnie showered and changed clothes, then drove into Belle Maurita for lunch at the White Flame.

It was past one o'clock when he slid into one of the booths along the wall. Only three customers remained of the lunchtime diners. A young bearded man sat on the last stool at the counter, and two elderly women with severe gray hairdos were in another of the booths. Though it was warm, as usual, in the restaurant, it wasn't uncomfortably so. Where Donnie sat, the air was stirred slightly by an overhead fan. He had a view of the street, but he might as well have been looking at a painting, since nothing was moving out there in the heat.

Ida emerged from the kitchen with a glass of milk and a sandwich for the man at the counter. When she saw Donnie she smiled and used her free hand to give him a tentative little wave. It must have been plenty hot in the kitchen. Her blond hair was mussed and damp, a few strands lying plastered to her forehead. There was a weariness around her eyes, and a sheen of perspiration glistened above her upper lip. Donnie wondered why none of it detracted from her beauty.

As soon as she'd placed the plate and glass on the counter in front of the bearded man, she walked over to Donnie's booth with a round glass coffeepot. He righted his upside-down mug and she poured.

"I forgot to give you that bandage for the cut on your forehead," she said.

"That's okay," Donnie told her. "Better for it to get some air anyway."

"It looks ugly, like it needs more doctoring."

"And you look like you need to relax and have a nice cool drink."

Ida used the sleeve of her blouse to dab perspiration from her cheeks. "Guess I do. It's just me and the cook here today. Blanche had some business up in Ochopee."

Donnie lowered his voice enough so he wouldn't be overheard by the other customers. Above him the paddle fan hummed and ticked as it rotated, further obscuring his words even if their volume would happen to reach someone. "I visited Munz's place this morning, only he didn't know it."

She gave what he'd just said some thought. She didn't seem to know quite what to make of it. This was dangerous territory. "Why'd you do that, Mr. EPA?"

"Curiosity." Mr. FBI added cream to his coffee and stirred. "I want to confirm something: Is Munz a fat man, taken with light-colored suits?"

"That's him. Dresses like some kind of colonial Englishman in the jungle."

"I think I saw Pedro and Carl, too." He described the two men for her.

"That'd be them. Ugly and mean, but not that way as much as Pinscher."

"There was another man there, tall, darkly handsome, well dressed. Might be able to play James Bond in the movies."

Ida gnawed her lower lip for a few seconds, think-ing. "I'm not—no, wait a minute. He comb his hair real high on top, have a kind of long jaw?"

"Sounds like him."

"I don't know his name," Ida said, "but he comes into town every once in a great while and talks with Pinscher. They've even had lunch in here, and I've seen them at Hoppy's drinking together."

"Even seen him with Munz?"

She placed the coffeepot, which was getting heavy, on the table. "I think so, but usually he's been with Pinscher."

"Those two don't look like they'd have much in common," Donnie said.

"Maybe they're business associates."

"That's my thought, too."

Ida stared at him for a while without speaking, then said, "You oughta come by my place sometime, and I'll give you that bandage."

"It'd make me less ugly."

She grinned. "I said the cut on your head was ugly, not you. Fact is, you look pretty good consider-ing just recently you were used for a pinata."

The two elderly women were staring at Ida. One of them smiled and waved for her to come to their booth.

"Want to order before I go over there?" Ida asked Donnie.

"I'll have whatever you recommend," he told her. "I trust you."

"Everybody's gotta trust somebody," Ida said, lift-ing the coffeepot. "I guess we have to trust each other."

He watched her walk across the restaurant toward the two women in the booth. It was something to see.

That night Donnie took some extra equipment when he left for his evening fishing session. In his tackle box were wire-cutters he'd gotten from the Cherokee's FBI-modified tool kit. In the Jeep's locked glove compartment was a small 35mm camera with an infrared telephoto lens. It had been stored in the hidden compartment in the seat cushion of the driver-side bucket seat. Stuck beneath Donnie's belt, in the small of his back, was his .38 revolver concealed by his untucked shirt.

He drove the rutted road toward Munz's compound without headlights and parked the Cherokee where he'd left it concealed that morning.

This time Donnie was more prepared and had brought his rubberized waders. After struggling into them, he got the camera with its infrared lens from the glove compartment and slung it by its strap over his shoulder. Then he picked up his tackle box, rod and reel, and entered the swamp.

In the dark, it took him more than fifteen minutes to find where he'd left the log lying across the razor wire. Without giving himself time to be afraid, he hopped onto the slippery fallen tree trunk and walked clumsily across the wire, barely keeping his balance in the heavy rubber waders, and found himself inside the boundaries of Munz's compound.

He stood still for a moment, listening to and observing the swamp. Night insects were screaming now, and everything other than the rippling water he'd disturbed seemed motionless. The thick trees and dense saw grass were dark obstacles. Spanish moss draped from overhead limbs formed eerie black forms in the yellow moonlight. Quietly, Donnie moved toward the lights glowing faintly through the foliage. The windows of the rambling clapboard house.

It felt better to be wearing dry clothes, unlike this morning, but the heat remained in the swamp. Donnie was sweating profusely, his lower body beginning to itch inside the thick, rubber-coated waders. The camera swung and bumped against his arm and ribs with each step. He was uncomfortable and afraid, and there were plenty of places he'd rather be, yet in a way he'd rather be no place else.

But he didn't have time to contemplate what made him and people like him tick. He kept a watchful eye in the moonlight, and stayed alert for any sound of the rottweiler that had earlier been running loose.

When he heard an abrupt, low snarling noise, he thought at first it was the dog.

Then he realized it was the motor of a distant airboat, one of the flat-bottomed crafts powered by airplane propellers mounted high on their sterns. They were well suited for traveling in shallow water and even skimming over flat, wet ground surfaces.

Far away though the snarl of the engine seemed to be, Donnie stood motionless until it had faded and only the shrill cacophony of the swamp remained.

The camera lens was compact and only a 60-to-90-millimeter zoom, so he had to be closer to the house than he'd been this morning. And if he worked in near enough, maybe even to where he could peer through a window, he might be able to see what was happening as well as hear what was being said.

The water became more shallow, the saw grass thinner, and he was soon walking on damp but solid ground. He ducked into a low crouch and made his way toward the rear of the house, and a window with a partly lowered shade.

Because the ground sloped slightly, the pillars supporting the house above the swamp were shorter along the back wall. Holding the camera at the ready, Donnie moved in against the clapboard wall and raised his head cautiously to look in the window.

The light was coming from a room beyond the one he was peering into. There was what appeared to be a short hall that led to a large room in the front of the house. Donnie could see a corner of a sofa, an ornate brass floor lamp with a tilted shade, the edge of a television showing something on its flickering screen.

Then a figure crossed the doorway, huge in a fluffy white bathrobe. It was Munz, gesticulating with both hands as he talked. He was pacing, Donnie realized, as Munz walked back and forth across the doorway, his stomach bulging beneath the robe.

Then two men crossed the doorway. Munz and the tall, dark-haired man Donnie had seen that morning. The tall man was wearing the same clothes he'd had on earlier, but he carried his sport coat folded neatly over his arm. Dapper as James Bond as played by Dudley Doolittle.

He was obviously leaving.

As the two men paused for a moment in the doorway, still talking, Donnie raised the camera and took two quick shots, listening to the almost silent autowinder advance the light-sensitive film.

Then he left the window and crept to a corner of the house where he could view the tall man as he left.

One of the big garage's overhead doors was raised to reveal only darkness, and a red Range Rover was parked near the house. Donnie heard voices, then watched as the tall man came into view and walked toward the Rover. The rottweiler trotted along at his heels.

As the man opened the Range Rover's door, then turned to glance back at the house, Donnie raised the camera and risked another shot.

The man gave no sign he suspected his photo had been snapped, but the big dog grew rigid and stared in Donnie's direction.

Donnie froze and stayed that way, holding his

breath. Fear tasted like copper at the edges of his tongue.

It must have been the faint whirring of the winder that had caught the dog's attention. The animal resisted slightly as the man clutched its collar and forced it into the hulking vehicle. It moved over quickly onto the passenger side, but it continued staring in Donnie's direction.

The tall man climbed into the Range Rover, and the powerful engine turned over. Donnie tried to get a look at the license plate as the Rover maneuvered around so its hood was aimed at the driveway, but it appeared that the plate was missing or somehow concealed.

He used the sound of the big four-wheel-drive vehicle rolling along the driveway toward the gate to cover his own noise as he withdrew along the side of the house.

Donnie was satisfied. He'd gotten what he'd come here for. He was sure he'd obtained at least one clear photo of the man who'd driven away in the Range Rover.

When he reached the back of the house, he retraced his steps toward the surrounding swamp.

He didn't breathe easier until he was across the razor wire and slogging through knee-deep water toward the road. Though he was still sweating hard, he was cool in a breeze that had sprung up and was evaporating his perspiration. His night was almost over, and it had gone well.

"Hold up there, hoss," a man's voice drawled.

An instant later a gun roared and bits of leaf and shattered wood fell on and around Donnie from where the bullet or shotgun pellets had passed through the trees overhead.

Donnie's heart was hammering but he kept his head. Though his hand twitched to drop the fly rod and reach around behind him, he realized the gunfire had been a warning shot, and he didn't go for the revolver tucked into the back of his belt. Unobtrusively—he hoped—he slipped the camera's leather strap from his shoulder so the camera dropped into the water at his hip.

Holding the rod in his right hand, the tackle box in his left, he raised his hands above shoulder level. Then he turned in the direction the shot had come from, at the same time placing his right foot on the camera and grinding it down into the muck of the swamp floor.

At first he saw nothing but total blackness and moonshadow. Then water swished, ripples spread through the dark saw grass, and lanky Carl approached, grinning beneath his overgrown mustache. For a moment his eyes caught the moonlight. They didn't look like part of his smile.

Carl's long body swayed with each step as he forced his way through the water and tall grass. Though the shotgun he carried loosely and expertly with both hands swung widely from side to side, the maw of the gun's big barrel remained fixed and steady as a dark star.

Aimed at Donnie.

25

"**Y**ou better stand real still, just a statue of the way you are," Carl drawled.

He stopped advancing about twenty feet from Donnie. The black water he'd pushed ahead of him continued to ripple out in the moonlight. He unclipped a walkie-talkie from his belt and nuzzled it intimately, speaking into it softly enough so Donnie couldn't hear what he was saying.

Carl replaced the instrument on his belt and stood loosely with the shotgun still aimed at Donnie's midsection.

"You're making a major mistake here," Donnie said. "I'm a government employee doing my job."

"Just which job is that, hoss?"

"I'm fishing so I can analyze the catch and determine if there's—"

"Oh, yeah. You must be that dude I heard about. One got his clock cleaned by Pinscher."

"I guess I'm the one," Donnie said. "At least now you know who I am and what I'm doing here."

He started to lower his arms. The shotgun barrel rose and he put them back up as they'd been.

Carl gave him a slow smile beneath the awning of bushy mustache.

"The question is, who the hell are you and what

right do you have to do this?" Donnie asked, putting on a show of anger. Not completely a show.

"Answer is, I'm the man with the gun."

"Answer is, you're gonna be in a shitpot fulla trouble if you don't back off from messing with a federal employee!"

"That a fact?" Carl waved the barrel of the shotgun a few inches up and down. "Tell it to the gun, see if it'll talk back to you."

"Piss on the gun—"

There was a noise behind Donnie. He turned and saw the dark figures of Pinscher and Pedro. They were standing about fifty feet away and they both held shotguns like the one in Carl's capable grasp.

Pinscher laughed and shook his head. "Looka who we got here. The handsome stranger that rode into town. One day you're all beat up and gotta be nursed back to health by the Clayton bitch, an' the next day here you are all well an' fishin' up a storm. Ain't you jus' the one!"

"She musta nursed him some special way," Carl said.

"That I don't doubt, him bein' a special fella. Mr. Banner, here, he's got a way with the ladies, is what I bet."

"Wonder if he's got a way with the fish?" Pedro asked. He and Pinscher still hadn't moved. Pedro's gun was supported in the crook of his arm, pointing at shallow swamp water.

Pinscher's was resting on his shoulder.

"I haven't had time to catch anything," Donnie said. "My instructions are to test for—"

"Shut the fuck up," Pinscher said, no longer in his amused mood. "We ain't scientists and we don't wanna hear all that technical bullshit you got memorized." He nodded at Carl, unshouldering his shotgun. "See if this bad boy's got anything on him he shouldn't."

Water swished and flowed as Carl eased up to Donnie and expertly ran his hand over him in a search. He found the revolver tucked in Donnie's belt immediately and yanked it out with a little bark of triumph.

"Looka here!" He held the gun high for the others to see in the faint moonlight.

"We ain't fuckin' owls," Pinscher said. "What is it?"

"Revolver. Had it in his belt at the small of his back. Lucky he didn't shoot his ass off."

"Thought you was fishin', not huntin'," Pinscher said.

"I was. Don't talk stupid. The gun's for alligators. It's an old one that used to belong to my father, but it still works. After what you said about alligators being thick in the swamp, and after what Ida Clayton told me happened to her husband, I figured it'd be wise to carry it."

"He got his hook baited?" Pinscher asked.

Carl examined the line on Donnie's fly rod. "Got him one of them Hopeful Hookers that Floyd sells."

"Can't catch shit with those things," Pedro said, causing the ember of the cigarette stuck to his lower lip to wag red-orange in the night.

"I'm doing okay with it," Donnie said.

"Not tonight, you ain't," Pinscher said.

"This rod and tackle box are getting damned heavy," Donnie said, feeling the strain in his shoulders. "I gotta put down my arms."

"You jus' do that," Pinscher said.

Donnie lowered his arms, watching Carl back away out of reach, still with the shotgun trained on him.

"Now come on over here," Pinscher said. "Like right now."

Donnie knew the concealed and partly submerged razor wire was between him and Pinscher. Pinscher wanted to know if he was aware of the danger. Another test.

If Donnie knew where the wire was, it meant he'd probably been on the other side, roaming Munz's compound.

Carrying rod and tackle box at his sides, Donnie slogged directly toward Pinscher. He kept a steady pace and the same frightened, angry expression on his face as he walked.

The wire scraped his rubber-coated waders, then penetrated and sliced through his pants and into his thigh. Another of the sharp barbs dug into the back of his wrist.

"Holy Christ!" Donnie dropped his tackle box and pretended to be losing his balance as he sloshed around. Pulling back, he felt the wire tear loose, ripping his flesh and then his pants. But he was free. He flailed with his arms and legs and shouted.

"Shut up! You ain't gonna die," Pinscher said.

"Sometime he is," Pedro said. "Maybe tonight."

Donnie was quiet. He looked down at his bleeding wrist and the blood on his right thigh. The cut on his leg was on fire and throbbing.

"What the hell happened?" he asked in an amazed voice.

"Must be that razor wire," Carl drawled. "Guess somebody shoulda warned you about it."

"Razor wire? Are you guys nuts? Jesus! I thought a gator had me."

The other three men laughed.

"You'd know the difference," Pedro said.

"Now Ida's gonna have to patch him up again," Carl said. "Bright side to everything, I s'pose."

"What the hell is razor wire doing out here in the swamp?"

"You take a little walk with Carl an' you'll find out," Pinscher said. He turned abruptly and strode into the darkness.

With a parting glance at Donnie, Pedro followed.

"Let's go, hoss," Carl said, motioning with the shotgun.

Donnie carefully felt underwater for his tackle box, curled his fingers around its familiar plastic handle, and raised it. "Didn't do this any good," he complained, holding the dripping box up and examining it. "Some of this is my own equipment. The government doesn't furnish everything."

"Gonna furnish you a funeral if you don't walk," Carl said, waving the shotgun more vigorously.

Donnie walked.

26

When they reached the road, they trudged along it toward the iron gate to Munz's compound. Donnie was having trouble walking in the heavy rubber waders, and he could feel blood running from his thigh down into his boot, warming his lower right leg. Carl plodded along a few feet behind him, shotgun at the ready, seemingly oblivious to Donnie's injury or difficulty in maintaining the pace. Donnie remembered the alligator Carl had shot almost in half. Compassion wasn't in his makeup.

Carl must have carried a transmitter, because when they were about twenty feet from the gate, it glided open. They walked through, and Donnie heard the faint whir of an electric motor as the gate closed.

Flanked by Pinscher and Pedro, Munz was standing on the house's porch, waiting for them. He was as tall as Pinscher and looked immense in his bulky white robe. Donnie saw that he was wearing huge paisley house slippers.

Pinscher and Pedro appeared impassive, but Munz's fleshy face was creased in a wide smile, as if Donnie were an invited guest he was immensely pleased to see. There was plenty of moonlight, and the men on the porch were backlighted by illumination spilling from the windows. Perfect targets for any other would-be prowlers, they were serene in their security and arrogant in their power. Weaknesses not lost on Donnie.

When they were a few feet from the porch, Carl nudged Donnie's ribs with the shotgun barrel and both men stopped and stood still. Donnie had to look up at Munz, who peered down at him like a benevolent uncle.

"I've been hearing and hearing about you, Mr. Banner," he said. "I'm glad finally to meet you. I'm Curt Munz." His voice was surprisingly high for such a large man; it had a faint vibrato, as if he'd once sung opera. Donnie doubted if he had.

"I've only heard slight mention of you," Donnie said. "I didn't know you lived here. What's the deal? I mean, what am I supposed to be guilty of? Was I fishing on your property?"

"That's something I'd like to know," Munz said. "My associate Mr. Pinscher explained the circumstances of how and where you were—"

"Captured," Donnie interrupted.

"You were almost trespassin'," Pinscher said, grinning down at Donnie.

"An' he had this on him," Carl said, holding up Donnie's revolver.

"His pistol," Pinscher said. "Donnie Pistol. Ain't he jus' the one?"

"Oh, he does seem to be," Munz said. "Do you have an explanation, Mr. Banner, other than that you work for the government and were gathering samples?"

"That's what I *was* doing," Donnie said. "And it's the *federal* government."

"Yes, the EPA, I was told. I thought you people were concerned mostly with automobile exhaust fumes and toxic waste disposal, those sorts of problems."

"Also the quality of wildlife and water, and the health of citizens who eat the fi—"

"Yes, yes . . ." Munz waved a bloated hand as a signal for silence.

"We don't like the federal government even a little bit," Pedro said in a sullen tone.

"Why not?" Donnie asked as innocently as possible. His right leg was beginning to ache and he wished he could sit down.

"Tax and spend," Pedro said, "tax and spend."

"Usually people who live in rural areas such as this are here because they want to be left alone, Mr. Banner," Munz explained. "And that's the case in this instance. We're a suspicious lot, but not without reason."

"Bilateral Commission," Pedro said somberly.

No one spoke for several seconds.

"Pedro don't like that commission," Pinscher said. "The way they secretly run the world an' all."

"He means the Trilateral Commission," Donnie said. "I know about it, and I'm not wild about it myself. And I'm not crazy about the federal government. If I could find another employer who'd pay me more, I would. But I've got a job to do, and I was here doing it, trying to catch fish to use for mercury content analysis."

"At night?"

"Fishing's better in the early morning and at night," Donnie said.

"Huntin's better, too," Pinscher said. "For the gators."

"I wasn't hunting alligators," Donnie said.

"He meant it the other way around, hoss," Carl explained, and jabbed Donnie's ribs with the shotgun. "Some big, ornery gator mighta been huntin' *you* out there tonight."

"Oh. Well, that's why I was carrying my father's old gun."

"Donnie Pistol, Senior," Pinscher said, grinning wider.

"His name's Joe," Donnie said.

"Whatever anyone's name is, and regardless of his employer, we're not inhospitable," Munz said. "And you're certainly not a captive, Mr. Banner. It's just that we don't like interference. That's why we've strung razor wire along the property's boundaries."

"Interference with what?" Donnie asked, displaying what he thought would be taken as natural curiosity.

"With our private business," Munz said simply. "The Constitution does guarantee citizens the right to privacy."

Still aware of the bleeding into his right boot, Donnie fought a faintness. He wiped his arm across his forehead, then took a deep breath to steady himself. "It sounds to me like you might be some kinda private militia organization," he said. "If you are, I don't give a damn. I'd probably agree with your philosophy. But you shouldn't put down razor wire all over the place without posting signs." He glared angrily at Pinscher and Pedro. "And these dick-heads shouldn't stand grinning and let somebody walk square into it."

"Hey, he's got himself a temper," Pinscher said. "You think maybe there's a side to him we ain't seen yet?"

"Maybe I should shoot him someplace that spins him around, so's we could see all his sides," Carl drawled behind Donnie.

"Johnny Pistol shooting off his mouth," Pedro said, giving Donnie a mean stare. "He don't talk like no scientist."

"I'm not a scientist; I'm just a technician. And I

grew up on the streets in New Jersey. Sometimes I talk that way."

"Growin' up in the streets don't make you no bad-ass," Carl said. "Where I grew up we didn't have many streets, mostly jus' dirt roads."

"And you're a badass?" Donnie asked.

"You best s'pose so."

Munz rubbed his three chins with a thick forefinger, as if musing on all of this. "Well, you have something of a point about letting you walk into the razor wire," he said to Donnie. "But understand that was the only way we'd know if you'd been trespassing, to test you and see if you knew about the wire. We had to find out if you'd encountered it before and had actually been on the property."

"Kind of a harsh test," Donnie said, gritting his teeth against the pain.

"But one you should be pleased you passed," Munz said, his smile unchanging. "You're obviously in extreme discomfort. Would you like to take care of that unfortunate injury to your leg? And do I see a gash on your wrist?"

"I'd rather get back to my motel and take care of both problems," Donnie said.

"He's got himself a little private nurse," Pinscher said. "Tends to all his needs free of cost."

"Like a damned government health plan with a cunt," Pedro said.

"Whatever you wish," Munz said, "but I suggest that when you get the chance, you see the doctor in town. He's a competent man. You'll be driven back to your vehicle, then your firearm will be returned."

Munz started to go inside, then suddenly turned back and looked at Donnie with obviously feigned sincerity. "I'm genuinely sorry this happened, Mr. Banner. I hope it doesn't happen again."

"It won't," Donnie assured him. "This isn't the only area where the fish are biting."

After Munz went into the house, letting the screen door slam behind him, Carl poked again with the shotgun, forcing Donnie off to the side.

Pinscher stayed on the porch, staring down at them, as Pedro descended the wooden steps, then swaggered to the garage.

A few minutes later the black Bronco backed from the shadowed doorway and maneuvered around to point toward the gate.

"Le's go, hoss," Carl said, nudging Donnie toward the vehicle.

Donnie climbed into the passenger seat, next to Pedro, who smelled strongly of peppermint gum he was slowly munching with his mouth open. Wadded on the dashboard was a wrapper from a brand of nicotine chewing gum that helped wean people away from cigarettes. Donnie had seen drug dealers before who wouldn't touch marijuana or cocaine and were hooked on nicotine.

Carl sat in back, directly behind Donnie, keeping the shotgun barrel touching the back of Donnie's neck. Pinscher got in and sat next to Carl. No one had spoken since Carl's instruction to Donnie.

Pedro moved his foot from brake pedal to accelerator and the Bronco rolled toward the gate.

"My Jeep's parked—"

"We know where it's parked," Pinscher said. "Kinda hidden by the trees, wouldn't you say?"

"Not really," Donnie said. "This is a swamp. You pull off the road and park most anywhere and you're gonna be behind some trees."

"Federal man's got another point," Carl said. "Also got them other sides we ain't seen yet. We oughta keep in mind he might not be a hunert percent stupid."

"Fuckin' Bilateral Commission," Pedro muttered. "He knows about that."

"I've only heard of it," Donnie said in an exasperated voice. "I'm not a member."

When they were opposite where the Jeep was parked, the Bronco slowed and stopped. Carl prodded the nape of Donnie's neck painfully with the shotgun.

"Get out slow, hoss."

Donnie found the door handle and did as he'd been told, standing unsteadily on the muddy gravel road. Carl had climbed out the back as Donnie had emerged from the Bronco. He held the shotgun with one hand, its stock tucked beneath his arm, and handed Donnie's revolver to him butt-first, barrel-down. Donnie didn't glance at the gun as he slid it into his pants pocket.

"You take care of that leg, now," Carl said as he climbed back inside the Bronco, this time in the passenger seat where Donnie had been sitting.

Pinscher had slid over in back. He grinned out the rolled-down window at Donnie. "You are really fulla shit, Donnie Pistol. That's why I kinda like you."

"I can't say I'm even a little fond of you guys right now," Donnie said.

"Had a dog once," Pinscher told him. "Kept chewin' the furniture no matter what I did to him. Had to kinda admire the poor, dumb bastard. That's you, Pistol, you just keep chewin' furniture no matter what."

"Still got the dog?" Donnie asked.

"Nope. Had to kill the little fucker. It was him or the furniture."

Pinscher leaned forward and said something to Pedro, and the Bronco growled away in reverse, its tires slinging gravel. It passed from sight around a curve in the road, and Donnie listened to its engine change tone and watched the play of its headlights in the trees as it found a spot to turn around for the return drive to the compound.

Donnie struggled out of the heavy waders, then hoisted himself up into the Jeep and drove with difficulty, keeping his right hand pressed to the gash in his leg. The flow of blood had slowed, but it was still a nasty wound. He reflected that razor wire was an invention right up there with the machine gun.

When he reached Hutch's Drop Inn, he parked the Jeep near the office, then limped inside.

Hutch seemed to be nowhere around. Donnie rang the desk bell but got no response.

He was about to go knock on the door behind the desk when the outside door opened and Hutch ambled in with his peculiar stooped gait. One side of his face was scrunched up as if in agony, the other impassive.

"Lose your key?" he asked.

"No. Got myself hurt when I was out fishing. I need some antiseptic. And something to use for a bandage."

Hutch glared down at the bleeding leg, the cut in Donnie's wrist. "What happened, you hook yourself like a fish?"

"Something like that. If you don't mind looking for those two things . . ."

"Sure, seein' as you're bleedin' all over the fuckin' floor. Mind steppin' outside?"

Donnie kept his temper and limped out to stand a few feet off the concrete stoop.

A few minutes later, Hutch came out holding a wad of yellowed gauze and a rusty aerosol can. "Got these outa the company first aid kit."

"That gauze hasn't been used, has it?"

"Not as I know of." He handed the gauze and

spray can to Donnie. The can was so rusty the label
was illegible.

"What is this stuff?" Donnie asked, staring at the
can.

"I dunno. Nobody ever learned me fuckin' Latin.
It's some kinda anti-speptic made from this South
American plant. Doc Whithers give it to me some
time ago when one of the guests got bit—got hurt in
the swimming pool."

"How long ago?"

"Some months, years maybe. I tested her, she still
sprays. Some of them fuckin' cans last forever. I had
a can of spray-on hair oil long time ago, that thing
never ran out. Had to throw it away, then it exploded
like a grenade sittin' there in the hot sun. Killed a
fuckin' cat that was rootin' around in the trash."

Donnie looked to see if Hutch was serious. Hutch's
eerily glowing right eye glared back fiercely.

Donnie could only nod and thank him for the medical supplies.

When Hutch started back into the office, Donnie
stopped him.

"I thought I heard an airboat in the swamp when
I was out fishing tonight. Is there someplace around
here I could rent one?"

Hutch stared at him with his luminous eye. "You
couldn't have heard no airboat. Swamp's too thick
around here to use one of them things. Too thick for
miles. You drive up north, fella named Roy Orthwein
rents swamp boats, takes tourists for rides, lets 'em
pet drugged gators, that kinda pussy stuff."

"I was interested in using one around here," Donnie said.

"You're outa fuckin' luck, son. You can see for
yourself the way this part of the county's overgrown.
You'd need some kinda fuckin' military equipment
to get through that swamp. Course you bein' a fed-

eral man, maybe the government'll borrow one from the fuckin' army, lend it to you so's you can fish from it." Hutch stared at him expectantly, waiting for a response.

"Excuse me," Donnie said, "while I go stop my bleeding."

He left the Cherokee where it was parked and limped toward his room. The night suddenly seemed hotter, the shrill scream of insects louder.

"You make sure you use that anti-speptic spray on your leg," Hutch said behind him. "You don't want no fuckin' gan-jereen to set in."

"That's for fuckin' sure," Donnie called back, thinking that as nurses went, Hutch was a sorry substitute for Ida Clayton.

27

Donnie slept until ten the next morning. When he got up and examined his wounds from the night before, he found that the bleeding from his thigh had been reduced to seepage into the questionable gauze. His wrist wasn't bleeding at all. Amazingly, whatever was in the rusty aerosol can had been effective.

He showered in the steamy, fetid bathroom, then started to spray his leg again with the antiseptic. But as he stared at the condition of the can, something stopped him. Probably it was the flakes of rust adhering to his damp hand. He put down the can, then wrapped his thigh with what was left of the yellow gauze.

After getting dressed, he'd drive into Belle Maurita and buy some actual bandages and an antiseptic that had an expiration date in the present decade.

Before leaving the motel room, he stood on his toes and retrieved his wallet from where he'd hidden it on the back of the closet shelf while he showered. Probably it would have been safe on the dresser, but he couldn't be sure. Hutch had a pass key.

As he withdrew his hand, the knuckle of his little finger scraped something metal over the rough wood. He groped and found what felt like a half-dollar-size coin, only it was thinner. He managed to work the object on its edge, gripped it, and brought it down where he could examine it.

Instead of a coin, it was a bronze Aztec calendar. It didn't look valuable, more like something bought at a souvenir shop. There was a small round hole drilled in it off center, probably to accommodate a chain or strip of rawhide so it could be worn as a necklace. The side opposite the calendar was smooth except for what felt like engraving.

Donnie carried the bronze trinket over to the window and examined it in brighter light. The engraving was worn almost off and was in Spanish: *De buena suerte.*

Donnie had seen the phrase before, engraved on the back of a wristwatch given to Rafe by his father, and could interpret it: "In good luck."

He stared at the trinket. It probably meant nothing, might have been left by a motel guest years ago. At a motel like Hutch's Drop Inn, the closet shelves might never be cleaned or examined.

He slipped the object into his pocket, thinking he could use some good luck.

Before driving into Belle Maurita, he left the aerosol can in the motel's empty office, where Hutch would be sure to find it for use on the next guest injured in the pool.

He thought he'd find Ida at the White Flame, but there was only Blanche Dumain and apparently the cook, who Donnie had never glimpsed. Blanche told him Ida had the day off.

Since it was the slow time between breakfast and lunch, Donnie was the only customer. He made up for it by ordering the White Flame Whopper, not a hamburger but a generous breakfast of scrambled eggs, biscuits, and fried potatoes.

He left none of it on his plate.

Feeling well fed, lazy, and glad not to be bleeding, he left the White Flame and strolled down sunny Cypress Avenue to where Ida's house trailer sat in the shade of a grouping of palm trees.

She answered his knock immediately and smiled out at him from behind her screen door. "Lose your way?"

"Found it," he said. "I need to talk to you."

She opened the door and stood back to let him in. She was wearing what must have been her kick-back-and-relax outfit, a loose-fitting red pullover shirt, baggy denim shorts that came to just below her knees, brown leather sandals with flat heels and with soles that extended too far beyond her toes. She still looked good.

He climbed the three mesh steel steps and entered. The air conditioner was working hard. The trailer's interior was surprisingly and pleasantly cool.

"You hurt your wrist," she said.

"Pinscher made sure I did," he told her. "Another of his tests."

She lifted his hand and held it lightly, looking at the cut on his arm. He thought about what Pinscher had said on Munz's porch, how Donnie had his own private nurse.

"Did you put anything on this?" she asked.

"Sure, but I don't know what. It was in a rusty spray can and came from somewhere in South America. It helped."

She raised an eyebrow at him, then turned and walked into the tiny bathroom. He sat on the gray sofa and listened to her rattle things around in the medicine cabinet.

When she came out she was carrying a box of bandages and a darkly tinted small bottle.

"What is it?" Donnie asked, pointing at the bottle.

"Old-fashioned iodine," she said. "It hasn't been improved on as an antiseptic."

She sat down next to him and used a dropper to apply some of the orange liquid to the cut on his arm.

Donnie winced. "That stings like hell."

"Make you a well boy, though." She searched through the box for an adhesive bandage the appropriate size. When she found one she placed it neatly over the cut. Then she smiled at him. "There. You can't see it, so it doesn't hurt anymore."

He said, "I've got another owie on my leg."

"Oh?" She grinned up at him. "Should we take care of that one, too?"

"Why not?" he said. He wasn't shy, and he really was concerned that the leg might become infected. He unbuckled his belt and slipped his pants down to his knees, then removed the gauze wrapping.

"How did *that* happen?" she asked, looking down at his right thigh with a horrified expression.

"I cut it on some razor wire."

"You went to Munz's place last night."

"That's right." He told her what had happened, still playing the EPA field agent, leaving out the part about the camera.

"Those bastards have got some gall!" she said, sounding angry and protective.

"Something to hide, too."

"Drugs, maybe. Or they might actually be Mafia, like you were wondering."

"They might be, the way they act like they're not afraid of the law. Maybe it's drugs *and* Mafia out there in the swamp. Know anything about drug use here in Belle Maurita?"

"There's some," she said, "but nothing you wouldn't expect if you hadn't spent your life with your eyes closed."

"Did you ever hear mention of *salvaje*?"

"No. What is it?"

"Designer drug from Cuba. I hear it's finding its way into the U.S."

"It's not here in Belle Maurita, far as I know."

"This might only be the staging area, where they ship from," Donnie said, recalling the bartender at Hoppy's saying the bad guys in Belle Maurita didn't foul their own nest.

Ida was quiet for a while. Then she said, "Well, this *is* Florida. We've got white sand and white powder." She looked again at the injured leg, then at Donnie's face. "Jason . . ." she said.

"Huh?" He tried to remember, was that the name of her late husband? No. He was Rod. Rodney, probably.

"Jason," she said again. "It came to me after you left the other night. Once when the tall, dark-haired man was playing cards at Hoppy's with Pinscher and those other two goons who work for Munz, one of them—not Pinscher—called the man by name. Jason."

Donnie leaned over and kissed her cheek.

"What was that for?" she asked.

"Gratitude."

"Now show yours," she said, "by not going near Munz's again."

"I thought you were curious," he said.

She didn't answer.

"Since you recalled the name Jason," he said, "let me try another one on you. Iver LaBoyan."

"No," Ida said. "And that one I wouldn't forget."

"I don't think it matters anyway," Donnie said. "He's dead."

"Yet you asked."

He watched her walk gracefully from the room, then returned a minute later with adhesive tape and a roll of gauze white enough to make Hutch's gauze appear unmistakably brown.

"I'm getting tired of patching you up," she said, sitting next to him. "God! This is far worse than the one on your arm." She picked up the iodine bottle, removed its glass dropper, and began placing the cool liquid on the gash in his leg.

Donnie blotted the stinging sensation from his mind and sat quietly, watching the solemn, pensive expression on her face as she tended to him. Her husband had lost so much more than his life that night in the swamp.

When she was finished, she screwed the cap back on the bottle and used adhesive tape to fasten a gauze dressing to his leg. She stood up, then leaned down and kissed him lightly on the lips.

"Better?" she asked.

"Better."

"Promise to be more careful?"

"Promise."

"Pull your pants up," she said.

He did.

He didn't tell her he was planning on returning to Munz's compound that night to try to retrieve his camera.

28

It was two o'clock when Donnie left Ida's house trailer. The sun was out full force, reminding everyone as painfully as possible that this was the tropics and not a hospitable place for humans.

He was about to get into his Jeep to drive to a public phone and call Donavon when he heard footfalls behind him and turned to see Chief Lattimer.

Lattimer's uniform looked crisp. His shoes, black beltwork, brass buttons, even his handcuffs, gleamed. The gear dangling from his belt was bouncing and jingling. Only the gap where his shirt strained against his belly spoiled the intended effect of brusque competence and officialdom.

Donnie shut the Jeep door and leaned against it, keeping most of his weight on his good leg. The warm sun that made his eyes ache was soothing on his bandaged thigh.

Lattimer raised a hand and tapped the shiny black bill of his cap. "Good to see you're makin' friends here in Belle Maurita," he said, glancing lewdly in the direction of Ida's trailer.

Donnie said nothing, imagining what must be playing on the screen of Lattimer's mind. Let him wonder.

Lattimer licked his lips. "That Ida, she's got some funny ideas about her husband's death."

"She mentioned them."

"Well, you best not take 'em too serious. She's still a woman in mournin', even though considerable time's passed since that gator got her hubby. You gotta understand she's kinda biased on the subject."

"How do *you* think he died?" Donnie asked.

Lattimer appeared surprised by the question. "Why, jus' the way the coroner said. Death by misadventure. Big ol' gator upped an' got him. It's happened before. Young widows go into deep denial real frequently, too. Poor Ida jus' can't accept the fact her husband's really gone, an' that's why she can't accept the way he went."

"It works that way sometimes," Donnie said, wondering where Lattimer had heard such bullshit.

Lattimer grinned. "You might say, from time to time she looks for substitutes." The grin disappeared. "Not that you can blame the poor woman, to see in her grief her dear departed in other men that comes through town."

"I wouldn't blame her," Donnie said.

"No," Lattimer said thoughtfully, "I s'pose you wouldn't. 'Tween you an' me, I think hubby coulda went 'cause of a heart attack or some such thing. One of them big reptiles gets to gnawin' on a body, 'specially in this heat, how you gonna tell after a while the cause of the original demise?"

"Then you think he might have been murdered?" Donnie doing some fishing in town.

"Holy Christ, no! I mean, there's no earthly reason to believe that. I'm jus' speculatin' it mighta been natural causes. That it was his time an' the Good Lord took him, then along come that gator."

"You're kind of a fatalist," Donnie said.

"Gotta be, in this business. You think you're gonna

understand everything people do, you'll jus' go nutti-er'n a bag of cashews in no time." Lattimer put on an official face, stood taller, and hitched his thumbs in his belt. Barney Fife in need of Jenny Craig. "What I actually wanted to talk to you about, Mr. Banner, is I hear you been trespassin'."

"At the point of a gun," Donnie said, not surprised news of last night had found its way to Lattimer.

"Well, that Mr. Munz, he's particular about his pri-vacy, and the way I hear it, you *were* on his property."

"The way you're hearing it now is, I was abducted."

"Invited, did you say?"

Donnie got the point and remained silent.

"Mr. Munz is one of our most influential citizens," Lattimer said.

"That's been driven home to me."

"He ain't a bad sort, really. He's not even gonna file an official complaint."

"Hell of a guy."

"I sense sarcasm," Lattimer said. "You should sense you damn near got your ass in big league trou-ble." He moved his right hand over to rest on the butt of his holstered gun, emphasizing his words. "I hope you *do* get my intended message, which is for you to keep the hell away from Mr. Munz's place."

"I thought that might be what you were hinting at."

Lattimer smiled and nodded.

"You ever hear of *salvaje*?" Donnie asked.

Lattimer appeared puzzled. "Ain't that the Spanish dance where people stand in one spot an' wave their arms around a lot?"

"That's it," Donnie said. He opened the Cherokee's door and prepared to climb in. "I'll keep what you said in mind, Chief."

" 'Preciate it," Lattimer said, tapping the gleaming bill of his cap again in a gesture aimed to convey official helpfulness. This guy was really something.

Donnie glanced in the rearview mirror as he drove down Cypress and saw the chief standing in the street with his fists propped on his hips, staring after him. *Get out of town*, said the chief's look. And that's what Donnie was doing, at least for a while.

On Highway 29 was a combination gas station and grocery store that had a public phone in the corner of its parking lot.

Instead of driving close to the scoop-shaped metal sound deadener so he could stay in the Cherokee and use the phone, Donnie parked and walked over to stand and talk. He didn't think the Jeep was bugged, but it was always possible.

There wasn't much traffic on 29, so noise wouldn't be a problem. With a glance at a guy pumping gas into a pickup truck, and a family pulling out of the lot in a van, Donnie stood feeling the heat radiate up through the soles of his shoes and fed coins to the phone. He punched out the number he'd memorized that would get him through to Donavon.

"What've you got?" Donavon asked.

Donnie told him about last night.

"You gonna be okay?"

"I think so," Donnie said. "In fact, I think what happened might have been helpful. Another test passed. But what I wanted to do was grab one of the shotguns and blow those bastards away."

"You sound emotionally involved." There was a hint of amusement in Donavon's voice.

"It isn't hard to get emotional when you're standing there bleeding and those smug assholes are grinning down at you."

"Maybe you need an EPA assistant," Donavon said.

"No, I'm making progress here."

"I hear you," Donavon said. "But what I'm hearing in my other ear is more bullshit. The higher-ups are being themselves only more so, pushing hard to get this case wrapped."

"It's not something we can rush," Donnie said. "You know that. Can't Whitten hold them off?"

"Not much longer, Donnie. Neither can I on my level. There's a faction in the Bureau that wants the glorified maverick agent off this case."

"Glory I don't want. Don't the assholes know that? Anonymity's what keeps me alive."

"Some don't see it that way. Because of the movie, maybe. We don't show results soon and you're sure to get plenty of help. Suits and badges everywhere. A major, visible effort in Belle Maurita."

"That won't work. This one's gotta be done undercover, Jules."

"So we both know. You mentioned progress."

"Yeah. This morning Ida Clayton told me she overheard one of Munz's goons call the dark-haired man Jason when they were playing cards."

"Not Jake?"

"Uh-uh. But Jake might have been Agent Dunn's code word for Jason, in case somebody broke into her computer files."

"Possible," Donavon said. "But I still favor the late Iver LaBoyan to be Dunn's source Jake. We found out more about his employment. Turns out he worked for a state-financed agency called Immigration Placement Center until six months ago. That's when he left to work for his party's Finance and Funding office."

"Sounds like an outfit that keeps records on a lot of money flowing through."

"It is," Donavon said. "But unfortunately, any kind of personal records LaBoyan kept would have been destroyed in the fire that killed him. We're checking now to see if he had a safety deposit box or some other place where he might have kept documents."

"He have any Mafia connections?"

"Not any we know of so far. Blondi's working on that one."

Donnie was sweating so heavily the receiver was getting slippery against his ear. He wiped the wet plastic on his sleeve and switched the phone to his other ear before continuing the conversation. "I'm going back tonight and try to recover the camera."

"Doesn't seem smart, Donnie."

"Seems necessary, though."

"Yeah, you're right. You want some cover this time? If they find you there again tonight, they might not be so nice as to only make you walk into razor wire."

"If there's somebody with me, it'll make being noticed twice as likely."

Donavon didn't speak for a few seconds. Then: "Okay, it's your call. Now I've got something else for you, though not much. Ida Clayton's husband apparently was a solid citizen, struggling writer type. So far the computer data bases show nothing on Munz, Pinscher, or Pedro. Carl is probably Carl Franklin Sandival, thirty-six years old from Atlanta. He did ten years at Marion for helping rob a bank in Nashville, and he's got a long record for rape, assault, and robbery. One conviction for possession of a controlled substance. Cocaine."

"There must be something on Pinscher. Some of his tattoos tell me he's been behind the walls."

"There could be something on him. Maybe he's

not using his real name. We don't have much to conduct a search. Maybe you could get his fingerprints."

"They might be on the Cherokee," Donnie said, "but it would attract attention if we dusted it." It occurred to him that he could take Ida further into his confidence. She could set aside whatever glasses or silverware Munz, Pinscher, and Pedro used the next time they ate at the White Flame. Maybe even Jason-Jake would have a meal there when he was in town. "I think I know a way."

"I had faith you'd find one."

"There's something peculiar in the relationship between Pinscher and Munz," Donnie said.

"Well, you said Pinscher's probably done time. Maybe a lot of years without women."

"I don't mean that. Munz is the kind of guy who's resigned himself to hell and isn't afraid of anything, but he seems a little scared of Pinscher. There's nothing in his words or actions that says so, but now and then it's in his eyes."

"From what you say, Pinscher's a scary guy."

"Munz'd be afraid of brain, not brawn."

"Maybe he knows Pinscher's insane and unpredictable. Sometimes an amateur can whip the ass of a champion chess player because there's no way to use strategy on that kind of opponent. Ignorance can be a fortress." Donavon cleared his throat. "Something else you oughta know, Donnie. Lefty Ruggiero died in prison last night."

Donnie stood stunned. He'd let himself get too fond of Lefty, Lefty's overwrought wife, his poor fucked-up son, his miserable life. Lefty, who'd shown him the ropes that sometimes led to people's necks.

Lefty, the man he'd betrayed and helped place in prison where he'd died.

Jesus, Lefty!

"How'd he go?" he asked, keeping his voice level.

Goddamn Donavon didn't have to know how he felt, how he grieved.

"Classic Cosa Nostra. Knifed while he was in the shower. Nobody knows who did it. Nobody's talking."

"It was quick, then," Donnie said. This time his voice broke.

"Quicker than for most, Donnie. I know how you felt about Lefty, but remember who and what he was."

"Not now with that shit, Jules!"

"Okay," Donavon sighed. "I'm sorry."

"There were more sides to him than you knew. There are more sides to everybody. That's why I'm standing here in the fucking sun being somebody else."

"It's not exactly the same thing, Donnie."

The guy who'd been pumping gas into his pickup had paid and was now striding toward the phone.

"I better sign off," Donnie said. "Got a stranger coming this way."

"You gonna be okay?"

"Yeah. Don't worry, I'll do the job."

"That's not what I meant. Hell, Donnie!"

"I know. I'm sorry, Jules."

"Check in within the next few days."

"Don't worry," Donnie repeated.

He hung up.

The pickup's driver wasn't more than nineteen, with a wide smile and a tall, gangly body made to look even thinner by a skintight T-shirt and Levi's.

Squinting into the sun, he nodded at Donnie as he took over the phone. "Sorry. Didn't mean to hurry you."

"You didn't," Donnie assured him, and walked back toward the Cherokee. His legs felt rubbery and he knew he probably looked like he was drunk.

He glanced back, and the kid wasn't paying any attention to him. Probably a nice, ordinary kid calling his girlfriend or his young wife, Donnie thought as he drove from the lot onto 29 and tapped the accelerator.

This work could sure make a man suspicious.

Then with a chill he remembered Marishov. Blondi had said he might appear young, even as a teenager.

Donnie had been standing by the phone thinking about Lefty, not Marishov. Both hoodlums. Donavon was right. Lefty was still dangerous even in death, could still get him killed.

Donnie made up his mind not to think about Lefty again. It was ended for Lefty and for Donnie. He'd been somebody else in another time and place. Lefty was dead. Over. He couldn't afford to think any other way. Not for a while, anyway.

Furious with himself for lowering his guard, Donnie realized he was squeezing the steering wheel so hard it was affecting his control of the Jeep. He relaxed his grip, flexing his fingers. It was doubtful Marishov had already traced him here, to Belle Maurita, but an unguarded moment could still be fatal. He should have been suspicious of the kid and his phone call, not standing flat-footed being sentimental about Lefty.

Suspicion might keep him alive. Sentimentality would surely kill him.

Lefty would understand.

29

That night Donnie parked the Cherokee farther away from Munz's razor-wired property line than he had the last time he'd visited. Then he sloshed in his waders in a wide circle in the swamp, so he could approach at a different angle toward the spot where he'd dropped the camera.

Approximate spot, rather. In the dark swamp it was difficult to recall where he'd been standing last night when he'd let the camera fall, then used his foot to shove it down into the mud beneath the surface of the black water.

There was less moonlight tonight. Dark clouds were scudding across the starless sky in a threat of rain. Donnie swallowed the burr of apprehension caught in his throat and wished it would rain. That would make it less likely Pinscher and his goons would be out patrolling the swamp around Munz's compound. He wondered if they'd discovered the fallen tree he'd laid across the razor wire. And if they had, did they assume it had dropped there of its own accord?

He waved his hand before his face to shoo away pesky night insects, then gazed about at the still, dark water, the overhead limbs adorned with dangling moss, the irregular shadows of the thick saw grass that might conceal anything. Except for the shrill, ratcheting cry of cicadas, there was no sound in the sultry, enveloping swamp. And no movement.

Donnie thought he was at or near the place where he'd let the camera drop. Certainly he was in the vicinity.

He detached the thin end section of his fly rod, about half the diameter of his little finger and three feet long, then snipped the line to free it entirely. Mentally dividing the immediate area into quadrants, he began moving slowly and deliberately, probing the soft underwater floor of the swamp with the thin end of the rod.

Over an hour passed and he hadn't found the camera. His injured leg was beginning to ache, and perspiration was causing the cut on his arm to sting.

Then rain began to fall, pattering on the leaves at first, then making tiny splashes and circles of ripples in the dark water. Some of the raindrops that had made their way through the trees were falling on Donnie and working beneath his collar to trickle down his back and the sides of his neck.

The rain did nothing to cool the swamp, and he couldn't be sure if it was the steady drizzle or his perspiration that was blurring his vision and had his shirt plastered to his body.

A low roll of thunder cascaded over the swamp, and the rain began falling harder, in larger drops that created widening ripples that merged in soft circular patterns and kept the shimmering water alive with motion.

Figuring it was time to give up, Donnie reassembled the fishing rod and began sloshing back toward where he'd left the Cherokee. Other than his skin crawling, there was nothing to indicate he was being watched or followed.

Still, he was glad to get into the Jeep's dry interior.

It provided an illusion of shelter from more than the rain.

He got the vehicle started and drove with its lights out and its windshield wipers flailing. It took all his concentration to stay on the road.

Almost half an hour of painstaking driving had passed before Donnie peered through the fogged and rain-streaked windshield and saw Hutch's Drop Inn. He realized with amazement that the squalid motel was beginning to feel like home.

He was fitting his key in the door when he noticed movement in the dark near the corner of the stairwell.

This time C.J. was waiting for him in the shadows instead of inside the room.

"Message from the man," C.J. said.

"Quit talking like an aging radical and come on in," Donnie said, opening the door.

The wary FBI agent glanced around before entering the motel room ahead of Donnie.

Inside, he slouched in the chair he'd occupied during his previous visit. Donnie sat again on the bed, not worrying about the mattress getting wet.

"First off," C.J. said, "Donavon wants a meet with you tomorrow morning early at the Wayside Motel, on Highway 846 just east of Immokalee."

"Long drive," Donnie said.

"Not for Donavon, I guess."

"What's happening in Palmville?" Donnie asked.

"Rafe's still being a carpenter, watching, and watching *out* for, the beautiful Grace Perez. I think he's got the best of this gig, Donnie."

"What about Lily?"

"That's one reason I came here. She's been poking around, doing her journalist thing, and she followed the few leads gleaned from Agent Dunn's mixed-up computer. Dunn had her teeth into some political corruption, all right. Looks like there was a serious diversion of campaign funds a few months before the last elections."

"State or federal?"

"State and local," C.J. said. "Both political parties are riddled with Mafia cancer, if you can believe it."

"I can."

"Looks like vouchers listed as unpaid actually had been paid, and the funds were deposited in offshore banks."

"Where offshore?"

"Cayman Islands we know about, but that one's only a small account. Little pissant, high-five-figure thing. The Bureau's still trying to track the rest of the money. And they will."

Donnie knew he was right. Money always left a trail, and nobody was better at following it than the Bureau. It was a good bet that the political largesse was used as seed money to finance even more grandiose, Mafia-infected operations. Governments within governments, economies within economies. The world was like a series of those Chinese boxes, each containing another smaller than itself.

"Did Iver LaBoyan's name come up in the investigation?"

"Not that I know of," C.J. said.

"Does Lily think the misuse of political funds is what Agent Dunn was investigating that got her killed?"

"No. This is a lot of money, apparently, but it's not the kind of thing that usually becomes murder. These are white-collar criminals, after all."

"With the Mafia in the mix, some of those white collars could have blood on them."

"I get your meaning. But it's still white-collar crime, money big enough to get wired from place to place rather than changing human hands. Everybody involved likes to keep murder and what it attracts far away from an operation like that."

Donnie thought Lily and C.J. were probably right. And what would the Mafia, big-time political corruption, and misappropriation of funds have to do with anything in Belle Maurita?

C.J. might have been wondering the same thing, but he gave a dismissive little movement of his shoulders, not exactly a shrug. He obviously thought the subject was exhausted until they had more information.

"Donavon said you might have some undeveloped film for me," he told Donnie.

"I don't have it," Donnie said. "Tell him I couldn't recover the camera."

"Might not matter." C.J. reached into the pocket of his blue windbreaker. "Turns out he's got a photo for you to look at. Said to tell you he put together 'Jake, Jason, red Range Rovers registered in Florida, dark-haired handsome guy with jutting jaw,' and came up with this."

C.J. leaned forward in his chair and handed a copy of a newspaper photo to Donnie.

It was a grainy black-and-white shot. A man in a dark suit was standing near a palm tree, smiling and talking to someone outside camera range. The breeze had mussed his dark hair and blown his tie up over his shoulder. He was undoubtedly the man Donnie had seen with Munz and Pinscher.

"It's Jason," he said.

C.J. said, "Uh-huh. He's also Jake, according to Lily. And she sees him as a suspect, not Agent Dunn's source. She's been busy. The hard proof's not there yet, but he's up to his ass in the campaign funds diversion case."

"Don't forget *salvaje*," Donnie said. "Maybe some

of that campaign money went to one or more of the drug cartels as well as to offshore bank accounts."

"Lots of possibilities," C.J. agreed.

"What do we know about Jason other than he's a crooked pol?"

"Last name's Cohan. He's not an elected official himself," C.J. said, "though he might have ambitions along that line. His job now is being a top aide to Alan Merchant."

It took a few seconds for Donnie to realize what C.J. had just said.

"*Governor* Alan Merchant?"

"The same," C.J. said.

"Is Florida law looking into any of this?"

"Not so's you can tell. Agent Dunn musta thought if the governor might be involved, there was no one in state government she could trust to clue in on what she'd tumbled to."

Donnie thought about Chief Lattimer's relationship with Curt Munz and figured Marcia Dunn had been right to be cautious. She hadn't even completely trusted her Bureau superiors in Florida. Yet obviously she hadn't been cautious enough. Donnie wondered where she'd slipped up.

"So you see," C.J. said, "this political thing might not be as small as we thought, even if it is state, and not federal except for the banks. But I stress 'might.' And I still don't see it as the reason Agent Dunn was taken out. Money and murder are two different things."

"And politics, money, and murder are three different things," Donnie said, "but don't they sound natural together when you say them fast?"

30

The Wayside Motel seemed to squat uneasily in the slanted morning light. Its drab brick facade absorbed the sun, and its rows of reflecting windows somehow resembled the blank eyes of the blind. It was two stories, with jackknifed steel stairs to the upper rooms, and was built in a U-shape that embraced a tiny swimming pool. The architect who'd designed Hutch's Drop Inn might have later designed this motel to show he hadn't yet gotten all the venom out of his system.

Donnie parked the Jeep next to a cheap-model gray Chevy, climbed out, and stretched his muscles. He glanced around at the dozen or so cars and vans parked between faded yellow lines, at the green canvas awning drooped above the office door, the ratty-looking palm trees huddled beyond a canted stockade fence bordering the parking lot. None of it cheered him up.

A sound from above made him look up to see Jules Donavon leaning over the second-floor railing looking down at him.

Donavon waited until Donnie had climbed the stairs before going back into the motel room, so Donnie could see which door he'd entered. He'd left the door unlatched, with the thrown deadbolt up against the striker to keep it from closing all the way. Donnie pushed the door open and stepped inside.

A beefy, crew-cut man in a gray suit sat sideways at the room's small desk. Another man, in a darker gray suit, stood near a window with the light to his back. Jules stood near the center of the room. He'd removed his suit coat and had his sleeves rolled up, his arms crossed. He was as conservatively dressed as the other two men only his suspenders were a bright red plaid.

"This is Agent Charles Andreska," he said, motioning with his head toward the silhouette at the window. "Agent Bert Clover." A nod in the direction of buzz-cut at the desk. "Donnie Brasco," he said, with a nod toward Donnie.

The three men nodded slightly to each other. Lotta nodding, Donnie thought. None of it very friendly.

"Wisowski sent them," Donavon said.

Marcia Dunn's control agent. Donnie wondered if Wisowski and not Donavon had set up this meeting.

No one said anything for a while. A prop-driven plane went over, flying low. Lost? Crop dusting?

"Seeing as you're running around Florida acting like Sam Spade," Clover at the desk said, "our office figured we had an interest in knowing what's going on."

"Donavon briefed us," Andreska said. He hadn't moved from in front of the window.

"Then why did you need to see me?" Donnie asked.

"We wanted to hear it from you," Clover said. "We were wondering, are you really making any headway down there in Belle Maurita, or are you spending your time jacking around at taxpayer expense?"

Donnie stared at Clover, then looked inquisitively at Donavon. "He's real, Jules?"

"Real enough, Donnie. But he should watch his tongue."

"So he doesn't choke on it," Donnie said.

Andreska stepped forward now. "Let's ease up, huh?" In the softer light Donnie saw that he was a dark man with a pointy chin, pointy ears, and shoulders or shoulder pads wide enough to make his head seem small. "We only wanted to meet you, impress on you we were around, size you up, sorta, what with all the reputation you come with."

"Earned reputation," Donavon said. "Let's all be civil now." This last with a sharp glance at Donnie.

"Have there been any developments since you last reported to Donavon?" Clover asked.

"Only you putting on a few more ugly pounds," Donnie said.

Donavon shook his head. "Dammit, Donnie—"

"Let the fucker talk," Clover said.

"Talk, but see if you can get serious," Andreska said to Donnie. "Or is your reputation as a hotshit justified?"

Donnie smiled at Andreska. "I've got nothing to say to these jerk-offs," he said to Donavon.

That caused Clover to stand up from the desk chair. He was tall as well as beefy, but he had an oversized gut.

"Don't let him frighten me, Jules," Donnie said flatly.

Clover's face was puffy and red. "You think you scare me?" he asked in a throaty, mean voice. "You only think you wanna mix it up with me, pretty boy."

"You couldn't win a fight with me, Clover, only a round."

Donavon raised both hands. "Dammit now, take it calm, everyone."

"These undercover pricks," Clover said, "why

don't you come back into the real Bureau, follow leads, do some honest work like a genuine agent? 'Stead you run around in fancy cars, got money to spend, dress like pimps."

"That's what it's like, all right," Donnie said. "I been going fishing every day in my mink topcoat and Gucci loafers."

Clover moved toward him and Donnie got ready.

Clover saw he was ready and stopped and stood still.

"Keep coming," Donnie said. "I'll tighten that little tie knot for you till you choke."

Andreska laughed and shook his head. "Couple of rough guys, all right." He pointed at Clover. "Why don't you sit back down, Bert." It wasn't a question.

Clover sat back in the desk chair, sideways again, and rested his forearm on the desk. He was breathing hard but he kept his silence.

"Let's all settle down and keep this in the family," Donavon said. Meaning, let's not tell Dad in Washington.

"Good idea," Andreska agreed. To Donnie: "So talk to your family. We want a verbal report from your lips on what's going on in Belle Maurita."

"I think not," Donnie said.

"Donnie, come on!" Donavon pleaded.

Donnie stood silently.

Clover stood up again. "He ain't gonna share. He figures he's too important. I hope that guy Marishov finds him then—"

"That's enough of that kinda talk!" Donavon said.

Clover knew he'd gone too far. He clamped his lips tight enough to whiten them and glared.

"I don't think I can trust you," Donnie said. "You look too much like that stooge, Curly, and you're a hothead with a loose mouth."

Clover fumed and moved toward him, then realized he was further proving Donnie's point and settled back and smiled.

Andreska looked at Donnie. "Gonna talk to your family?"

"Only family you remind me of is my crazy uncle," Donnie said.

Andreska lifted his shoulders, then his dark eyebrows. "That's it?" he asked.

"It," Donnie said.

"Have a good day, gentleman," Andreska said with a nod to Donavon, and he went out the door. Clover followed, breathing hard and still smiling sweatily.

When the sounds of their footsteps on the steel stairs had faded, Donavon looked glumly at Donnie.

"I think that went pretty well," he said. "You sure are a people person."

"Only way it could go," Donnie told him. "That fat one was pissed to the gills when I got here."

"You kept him—us—waiting."

"You got me—me—out of bed at six-thirty to get dressed and drive here."

"Do you realize how much shit this is gonna bring down on me?" Donavon asked, more sorrowful than angry.

"I'm sorry, Jules."

"Of course, of course," Donavon said. "You know it rolls downhill."

"Come on, Jules. I really am sorry. I'll pay for breakfast."

"Of course, of course."

31

It was still early when Donnie left Donavon and drove south. He thought it might be a good idea to put in something like a normal day as an EPA field agent. On the way back to Hutch's, he bought a new Hopeful Hooker at Floyd's Bait and Tackle to replace the one he pretended to have lost when his line got hopelessly tangled in saw grass.

After changing into his environmentalist's clothes and getting his gear together at the motel, he went into the swamp and fished for several hours. He was casting into still water when he heard movement behind him, turned, and was amazed to see Blondi step from the tall grass.

She was wearing a red bandana, denim shirt, black windbreaker, and jeans tucked into bright green rubber boots. A short-handled net was attached to her waist, and in her right hand was a small fly rod. Everything looked brand-new, even Blondi.

"I thought this'd be the best way for us to talk," she said, grinning. Direct sunlight somehow pierced the overhead foliage, found her face, and made her look almost ready for her high school graduation. Donnie reminded himself not to be misled by appearances.

"Maybe it is," he said, wondering what had

brought about this odd and unexpected visit. "But it might not be good for either of us if we are seen together here."

"When I phoned Donavon a few hours ago about this," she said, "he told me it'd be best if you got word as soon as possible. Turns out I was the fastest way."

"And the word is what?"

She stopped smiling, looking suddenly older. Maybe twenty. "My backup crew learned from a taped conversation in a restaurant that Marishov's in Florida. You're the reason."

"Do we know that for sure?"

"If I were you, I'd be sure enough."

Donnie relegated his fear to isolated places in his mind and gut where it wouldn't interfere with what he had to do. "You're right," he told Blondi, "we have to assume I'm his reason." He looked at her holding her gleaming new fishing equipment and baking in the heat in her layers of denim. "There was some risk for you in coming here, wasn't there?"

"Some," she said. "It's part of what we do. You know that."

"Yeah, but I still appreciate you letting me know. You're starting to sweat. Why don't you take off that jacket?"

"I only put on this outfit in case somebody came along and wondered what I was doing in the swamp. I had no idea it was so damp back in here along with the heat. I bet even the alligators sweat."

"You got a way to get back okay to wherever you came from?"

"Sure. Don't underestimate me because I'm small."

He laughed. "That I wouldn't do."

"Don't underestimate Marishov, either. As hit men go, he's a legend. You know how it is, these guys come in through Canada, the Bureau doesn't even have prints on them, or any other kind of identifiers. Nobody even knows exactly what Marishov looks like." She gave him her cheerleader smile. "Course, you're a legend, too."

"Legends bleed," Donnie said.

She looked serious and stared at him with a compassion that made him uneasy, as if she already knew his fate and probably her own. He wondered exactly what she was into with the Florida Mafia, but he knew better than to ask. "Bleeding's the worst part of the job, I guess," she said.

"Inside and out, slow and fast." Now he smiled at her. "Don't stay undercover too long. The life has a way of getting a grip on you."

"Love-hate relationship," she said. "The bad guys you deal with and try to become one of, some of them seem like the most normal, dull people in the world. It's not so hard to develop the knack of moving among them. A lot of them are likable. But now and then you glimpse the void in them that makes them what they are, and it's scary."

"Part of the knack is to stay scared." *The knack of staying alive.*

She nodded and glanced around, hugging herself as if cold in the sweltering heat. "Donavon can shove this swamp up his ass," she said. "You won't see me in it again."

Donnie wondered about her rough way of talking, the diamond set in her front tooth. What kind of people was she running with, and what was it doing to her? Was it only the South Florida Mafia, or was she mixed up with Cuban Marielitos, former inhabitants of that country's maximum prisons and mental institutions?

"It's not so bad here once you get used to the alligators, snakes, and disease," Donnie said.

"Well, you be careful even though you're happy."

"You, too."

She began moving away from him through the tall grass. She was small enough so that she'd soon be concealed by it and the taller ferns and saplings.

"I never in my life had the slightest desire to go fishing," she said, and disappeared.

32

After Blondi had left him, Donnie fished for a while but was uneasy. Blondi was good enough at her job not to have been followed, but nothing was a hundred percent. He decided the smart thing might be to move to another spot.

He drove the Cherokee out to an area of the swamp far from Munz's compound and fished until almost two o'clock. Then he showered and changed clothes at Hutch's Drop Inn and drove into Belle Maurita. He planned on eating a light, late lunch or early supper, nothing more than a beer and one of the microwaved sandwiches served at Hoppy's.

It was past three when Donnie walked into the narrow, dim bar, and at first he thought that was why the place was almost deserted. Noontime drinkers and eaters would be gone, and it wasn't yet time for the serious drinkers to arrive for the late afternoon and evening. It wasn't as warm as usual in Hoppy's, and the ceiling fans were actually rotating at a fast enough clip to stir the air.

When he moved toward the bar, Donnie glanced to his left and saw why people had places to be other than Hoppy's. It was the company they would have had to keep.

In the gloomy recesses at the back of the long

room, Pinscher, Carl, and Pedro sat playing cards at one of the round tables.

Pedro looked in Donnie's direction as he laid aside three cards from his hand. "It's the bilateral fucker," he said.

Carl, who was dealing, snapped three replacement cards off the deck for Pedro.

"Donnie Pistol!" Pinscher said, as if made gleeful by Donnie's arrival. "We're playin' five-card draw here, an' poker's lots more fun with four than with three."

"Only if the fourth player's got him some money to lose," Carl added.

"No, thanks," Donnie said tersely. "I just stopped in for a beer and some microwaved lunch."

Nothing in the cardplayers' faces suggested anything other than amiability. Except for Pedro, whose features suggested no emotion at all. There was also nothing to suggest that only a few nights ago these three goons had stood by and let Donnie walk into razor wire, then escorted him around the swamp at gunpoint.

"It's too late for lunch," Pedro observed.

"That's why I'm hungry and I'd rather eat than play cards."

"Bring Donnie Pistol a beer and one of them spoiled meat sandwiches here to the table," Pinscher said to Wally, the curly-haired, apprehensive bartender.

"Yes, sir!" Turning to draw the beer, Wally looked quickly at Donnie and whispered, "You best play cards." Donnie wondered if the man spent his entire life afraid of imminent disaster.

Actually, playing poker with these three was fine with Donnie. They wanted to amuse themselves with him some more, find out more about him. Maybe *he* could use the opportunity to find out more about them. Maybe he could walk away with one or more of the glasses they were drinking from and wouldn't have to enlist Ida's help at the White Flame to obtain fingerprints. Maybe he'd even win some money.

"I've only got a few bucks on me," he explained, striding toward the table.

"Shit, that don't matter," Pinscher said with a toothy grin. "We're not playin' for high stakes, an' we know your credit's good."

"Tha's 'cause we know where to find him," Carl drawled.

"Also lose him," Pedro said. "Down deep in the swamp."

They scooted around to make room at the table, and Donnie dragged a chair over and sat down between Pedro and Carl, directly across from Pinscher. Pinscher had the most chips, stacked next to his half-empty Budweiser bottle and beer mug. The pot in the center of the table was a small one, about a dozen chips, mostly white.

Donnie watched silently while Pedro won it with a pair of jacks and somberly used his cupped hands to gather and drag the chips to him.

Nervous Wally delivered Donnie's beer to the table, along with fresh drinks for the other three men. Donnie told him to skip the sandwich. He wasn't hungry anymore.

Pinscher gave Donnie a hundred dollars' worth of chips on credit, then dealt another hand of five-card draw. "Guts to open," he said.

"There oughta be enough of that here to go around," Donnie said.

"After the way we had to treat you the other night, we didn't want you to think we was in any way personally hostile toward you," Pinscher said.

The players examined their cards. Donnie had a pair of sixes, then junk.

"What's a little spilled blood between friends?"
he said.

On his left, Pedro opened for a dollar. When it was
his turn, Donnie called.

"You guys don't like the federal government, I
don't give a fuck," he said, looking at his cards.
"And you can play any games you want out there
where Munz lives. Shoot yourselves with paint-ball
guns, whatever. Far as I'm concerned, personal free-
dom's what it's all about."

"Donnie Pistol's got himself a nice, easy attitude,"
Carl drawled.

"Fuckin' terrible altitude, you ask me," Pedro said,
staring hard at his cards.

" '*At*titude,' I said." Carl looked disgusted. "Not
'*al*titude.' "

Pedro picked up a cigarette he had propped in an
ashtray and drew on it, then exhaled and narrowed
his eyes in the smoke. "I meant '*al*titude,' just like I
said. I think he acts all high and mighty, way above
everybody else. Got himself an altitude's gonna get
him in trouble."

Everyone had called Pedro's opening bet. He asked
for one card, Pinscher took one, and Carl and Donnie
each asked for three.

Holding his cards in close to his body, Donnie
moved them around in his hand without looking at
them, then peered down and saw that he had three
sixes, a queen, and a nine. A strong hand for five-
card poker.

Pedro bet five dollars.

"That all you're gonna goddam risk?" Pinscher
said. He raised five dollars. "Missed your little
straight or flush, didn't you, an' now you're tryin'
to bluff."

Carl called the raise. So did Donnie, figuring
Pinscher probably had two pairs, or maybe had gone

for a straight or flush himself. Maybe even hit one or had a full house. There were no guarantees. Poker was about risk, making it the ideal game for Belle Maurita.

"Show 'em," Pinscher growled.

Pedro laid down two pairs, jacks and tens. Pinscher had pairs, too: aces and threes. Carl showed three deuces. Donnie's sixes took the pot.

"Why'd we invite this bilateral asshole?" Pedro asked.

"We want his money," Carl said.

Donnie knew it wasn't as simple as that.

"An' his sparklin' conversation," Pinscher added.

Or that.

Pedro dealt.

The cards continued running Donnie's way for the next several hours, obligating him to observe poker protocol and not leave the table while a big winner. By six o'clock he was five hundred dollars ahead.

A few more customers had wandered into Hoppy's and become aware of the poker game. Pinscher sent one of the men down to the White Flame for some carryout dinner, then sat out a hand to go to the bar and buy a round of drinks with some of Donnie's money.

"Donnie Pistol, he's plenty lucky," Pedro said glumly as he munched a roast beef sandwich and watched another pot slide to Donnie's side of the table.

"We knew that about him," Carl said slowly. He was staring intently at Donnie, as if wondering if he might be cheating.

Donnie watched the muscles flex in Pinscher's forearm as he shuffled the cards, the tattoo of the hanged woman dancing on the rope.

By eight o'clock, Donnie was getting tired. He noticed the others didn't seem tired, only irritated at losing. It was as if they'd slept most of the day in anticipation of this game.

By nine, Donnie's exhaustion was affecting his play and beginning to cost him money. He was soon less than a hundred dollars ahead.

"Gotta get my line in the water early tomorrow morning," he said. He slid his chair back as if about to leave. "I better cash in and get back to the motel."

But Carl had just returned to the table with another round of drinks. He placed a beer in front of Donnie. His fifth of the night, Donnie calculated.

"We'll play around the table one more time," Pinscher said. "That way we'll have a chance to win back our money, an' you'll have a chance to walk away a big winner 'stead of a little one."

Though he was tired almost to the point of slumping over the table, Donnie didn't see how he could refuse and not get some ribs broken.

He lost three out of the next four hands.

The final pot was his, leaving him slightly ahead for the night—afternoon and night.

He'd drunk only half of his last mug of beer. He wanted to be able to walk a straight line out of Hoppy's, then drive back to the motel without running the Cherokee off the road and into the swamp.

Maybe that was the idea of getting him into this game, he realized. Get him to drink enough to be over the legal limit to drive, then follow him and force him off the road. And tomorrow someone would find his wrecked Jeep, upside down or submerged in the swamp, with Donnie still in it. He would have joined Ida Clayton's late husband.

He was aware that he'd stood up, but he couldn't remember having done so. Pinscher and the other two men were still seated, staring up at him amused and mildly curious.

"You okay, hoss?" Carl drawled at what seemed like one-tenth speed.

"He don't look okay," Pedro said.

"Never did, though, really," Pinscher remarked.

Donnie was dizzy, nauseated. He'd sat too long in one spot, drunk too much. He was afraid now of losing consciousness altogether, knowing that no one would stop his fellow poker players from leaving with him to drive him back to the motel. If he passed out here in Hoppy's, he might wake up nose-to-nose with an alligator.

If he woke up.

He tried to nod, let everyone know he was fine. He could manage even if the floor was moving around beneath him, swaying to music he could barely hear. Some country-western song about a man who'd gone to prison and got himself tattooed. Donnie wished he could hear the song clearly, or remember how it went.

God, he was tired!

He began the long walk toward the door.

And stepped off into blackness.

He did wake up the next morning. And not next to an alligator in the swamp.

Donnie was lying on his side on Ida Clayton's sofa in her house trailer. The drapes were open, and the morning sun was blasting like white-hot fire through the slanted blinds.

He clenched his eyes shut, but the light still got inside his skull and bounced around, creating a painful kaleidoscope that might have been brilliant reflections of shattered glass.

This was no ordinary hangover. Someone had slipped something into one of his drinks. Donnie was sure of that.

As sure as he was that his head ached.

Ida was suddenly standing beside him, looking down at him in a way that narrowed her eyes but softened her face.

"Me again," he said.

"I know." She smiled. "You think this is some kind of hospital emergency room?"

"Isn't it?"

"Nope," she said, bending down and kissing him lightly on the forehead. "This is Intensive Care."

33

"**H**ow'd I get here?" Donnie asked. The sofa was unsteady, as if rocking on gentle waves, and there was an odd, tight feeling in the pit of his stomach.

"You really don't remember?"

"No. I think I was drugged."

She stared at him. "You were drunk and passed out, that was for sure. They brought you here to me, I guess because they were too lazy to drive you all the way out to the motel."

This was all news to Donnie. The last thing he remembered about last night was standing and swaying in Hoppy's, then stepping off a cliff into darkness.

And the worry . . . the fear that Munz's three henchmen were going to kill him and leave his body in the swamp. Instead they'd done him a favor, brought him here.

"Why?" Donnie said aloud.

Ida smiled faintly at him. "Why what?"

"Would they bring me to you? These aren't guys whose blood runs warm with charity."

"It is out of character," Ida agreed. "But there was a knock on my door and there you all were. Pinscher and Carl had you propped up between them, and they were all apologetic about waking me up and

sticking me with you, as they put it. Just good ol'
boys, all of you, into harmless mischief and needing
a little help. How could I refuse?"

"By saying no," Donnie said. He sat up slowly.
The effort made him dizzy. Something more than
alcohol had worked on him last night and was still
in his system. Probably Pinscher had slipped something into his drink after folding his poker hand and
walking over to the bar to buy a round. They might
have even gotten Wally the bartender to cooperate
in drugging him.

"I wonder what the hell they gave me," Donnie
said.

"Me, for one thing," Ida told him. "At least that's
what I'm sure they thought."

"That's their turn of mind, all right," Donnie said.
That was what puzzled him. One night Munz's min-
ions had given him all the grief and pain he could
handle. The next night they'd given him Ida.

He thought of Elana, then of Grace. And he was
an agent on a case. Still maybe he was crazy not to
accept the gift.

But he knew that sometimes crazy and smart were
the same thing.

Ida cooked up a breakfast of toast, scrambled eggs,
and hash in the trailer's kitchen. They ate seated at
the tiny Formica-topped table that folded out of the
way when it wasn't in use. Donnie was still slightly
groggy, and his stomach still felt oddly tight, but
he was almost painfully hungry. In addition to Ida,
generous amounts of coffee and food went a long
way toward righting his world.

"Maybe you're doing the wrong job at the White
Flame," he said, washing down his final bite of toast
with coffee. "They should use your talents in the
kitchen."

"I enjoy cooking," Ida said, "but not for the kind of creeps who eat there."

"Speaking of creeps and meals," Donnie said, "I'd like to ask you for a favor. Next time Munz or any of his helpers eat in the White Flame, will you save their drinking glasses, unwashed and untouched as possible, and give them to me?"

"Sure. For fingerprints. But you forgot to mention Jason this time."

"This time?"

She was staring at him strangely. "You asked me last night to do you this favor, Donnie. The answer's still yes."

He leaned back in his chair and tried to remember but couldn't. The hours after the poker game, even parts of the game itself, simply weren't there. They were like missing puzzle pieces, some of them strategically removed to distort image and recollection.

He wondered just what effect *salvaje* had on people.

34

It was late morning when Donnie returned to Hutch's Drop Inn.

There was still a strange sensitivity in the pit of his stomach, but most of the effects of last night had worn off. Whenever he drove from shadow into sunlight, the sudden burst of brilliance through the windshield made his eyes ache even though he was wearing heavily tinted sunglasses.

As he turned the Cherokee off the road and drove it across the motel's gravel lot, he saw Hutch working in front of one of the end units. The scrawny old man was wearing baggy jeans and a stained T-shirt with a rip down one side. The cords and muscles in his skinny tan arms strained like stretched cables as he worked his old push broom.

Donnie parked the Jeep and watched Hutch lean the broom handle against the brick wall, then stoop and pick up a green garden hose. It had one of those nozzles that looked like a gun. Hutch held the nozzle with both hands, squeezed the trigger, and began playing a strong stream of water over the concrete walkway in front of the lower floor units. Donnie wondered what had prompted this kind of industrious behavior in Hutch.

Instead of going straight to his room, he walked over to where Hutch was working.

Hutch ignored him.

"Getting things ready for the seasonal rush?" Donnie asked, moving slightly to stand in the shade of the building.

"You bein' fuckin' sarcastic?" Hutch asked, still not looking at him. The powerful stream of water continued hissing over concrete, bouncing off the walk, and creating a mist that caught a rainbow.

"I guess I am," Donnie said. "It's because I'm surprised to see you sprucing up the motel. What's next, a bath?"

Now Hutch tore his gaze from the water and glared at him. "You might be a fuckin' guest, but I don't gotta take no shit off'n you. Says so right in the motel manager's manual."

"Word for word?"

"Close enough, way I remember it." Hutch turned most of his attention back to the hose, playing the stream of water over the walkway to inch a crescent of mud off into the shrubs. "I heard you was a big winner last night in a poker game."

"Came out ahead, anyway," Donnie said, not surprised Hutch knew about the game.

"You play cards with them three fellas, you won't stay ahead. 'Specially if you can't hold your liquor and gotta be shoveled up and dumped where some poor woman's gotta clean you up and set you straight. Guys like you need women to take care of 'em. Sure can't do it themselves."

"You ever been married, Hutch?"

Hutch spat into the hose's stream. "Fuckin' marriage! Only thing it's good for is it makes cheatin' fun. Way to deal with women is not get yourself all involved in the first place. They think they got some

kinda claim on your time an' everything you own.
Thing to do is get in an' out an' keep what's yours."

"Sound advice."

"It's free, anyway. Now get outa my fuckin' hair
so's I can work. Never know who's gonna check in.
Might be the fuckin' president."

"Of what?"

"Of the U.S. of A.!" Hutch's luminous eye sparked
like flint in the sunlight. "And why *wouldn't* he check
in here? He eats at fuckin' hamburger joints, don't
he?"

"Not every meal," Donnie pointed out. He thought
that while he was talking with Hutch, he might as
well ask: "You ever hear of *salvaje*?"

" 'Course," Hutch said, "it's Spanish for 'irritatin'
asshole.' "

The back of Donnie's neck itched as he walked
away, thinking that any second Hutch might direct
the stream of water at him.

Still wondering who Hutch might be expecting
who'd move him actually to do cleaning and mainte-
nance, Donnie locked the door to his room and
stretched out on the bed.

He was still tired, either from his late night or from
whatever substance had been used to drug him. And
it still bothered him that he could remember only
disjointed pieces of last night.

But he wasn't so bothered that he didn't drift off
to sleep.

He dreamed of giant mosquitoes buzzing and
snarling in the swamp, waiting impatiently for him
to venture outside his room so they could attack and
bleed him dry.

When he awakened it was dark, and he saw by
the luminous hands on his watch that it was almost midnight.

The room was still and hot. There was a fuzziness and sour taste in Donnie's mouth, and when he moved his thick tongue over his teeth they felt like mossy tombstones.

He glanced around at the gloomy but familiar forms of furniture in the dim room. The fear he'd felt during his nightmare had faded, but not completely.

Eventually he dozed off again, wondering if it had been giant mosquitoes he'd heard droning in his dreams, or the sound of an airboat in the swamp.

35

Light was seeping in through the closed drapes, and the phone was ringing, when Donnie opened his eyes again. Between rings, he could hear some kind of swamp bird nattering very near outside.

As he rolled over in bed and reached for the phone, he glanced at his watch: eight o'clock.

He pressed the receiver to his ear and heard Hutch's rasping voice. "You awake there?"

"I didn't ask for a goddam wake-up call," Donnie groaned.

"This ain't that. Got a message from a fella said he was your boss. Said there was somethin' wrong with the last test samples. He got busy just then and had to hang up. Said to wake you up about eight o'clock and tell you to call him. You been woke. Go back to fuckin' sleep, for all I care." Hutch hung up so hard the noise on the line made Donnie wince.

Wishing the shrill, annoying bird outside would shut up, he scooted his body around and sat on the edge of the bed, then replaced the receiver. Slumped forward with his elbows resting on his knees, he stared at the floor and tried to make himself wake up all the way.

Obviously it was Donavon who'd phoned and wanted Donnie to call him.

After a few minutes, Donnie managed to stand up. He drew a deep breath, stretched. He'd had more than enough sleep, and he knew that when he cleared the cobwebs from his mind he'd probably feel pretty good. Finally the drug he'd ingested at Hoppy's had worn off completely. His queasiness was gone, and despite the remnants of sleep, the room seemed steady.

He walked over to the window and rapped on it with his knuckle.

The bird became quiet, and Donnie saw a brief, fluttering shadow as it took flight.

Good. Fine. Maybe Donnie would be able to cope with the coming day.

When he'd showered and dressed, he left the room and walked across the lot to the Cherokee. Despite Hutch's efforts to clean and shape up the motel, the place seemed as crummy and deserted as ever. Other than Hutch's beat-up Volkswagen, Donnie's Jeep was the only vehicle on the lot.

He climbed in the Jeep and drove to Gas 'n' Snack, the combination gas station and convenience store whose public phone he'd used the last time he talked with Donavon. It had green-tinted windows and looked as deserted as Hutch's Drop Inn, but there was an old Ford with oversized tires parked near a corner of the building.

Donnie stood in the sun and punched out the number for Donavon, then leaned back against the warm metal of the Cherokee.

"Blondi tell you about Marishov being in Florida?" Donavon asked when the connection had been made and he was sure the caller was Donnie.

"Yeah. She did it in a way that made me know I was vulnerable to being sneaked up on."

"That sounds like her," Donavon said. "She tell you anything else?"

"That she hates the swamp and will never set foot in it again, even if you ask."

"Hmm. What else you got for me?"

"I figured *you* had something for *me*," Donnie said. "You're the one who called. Had me pulled out of a sound sleep at eight o'clock."

"I'm the boss. You go first."

"Why not? This morning was better than getting up for that Wayside Motel meeting."

"Your fellow agents," Donavon said.

"Not typical, thank God."

"People like you bother people like them, Donnie. That's because you're part of the system but you're not."

Not part of anything, Donnie found himself thinking. That was how it felt, anyway, being somebody else and then somebody else.

"Speak to me, Donnie."

He told Donavon about the poker game and what had happened afterward.

"I've played poker with you, and you always lose," Donavon said. "Those guys must be pathetic cardplayers. It sounds as if you're finally fitting in."

"I didn't notice anybody else getting drugged and dragged outa the place," Donnie told him.

"They mighta taken you someplace worse than they did."

"That possibility was on my mind when I passed out in Hoppy's bar."

"You sure you can trust Ida Clayton, Donnie?"

"As sure as I can be of anything in or around Belle Maurita. I talked to her about obtaining drinking glasses for possible fingerprints, and she agreed. I still can't figure why there's nothing in the computers on Munz, Pedro, or Pinscher, even without prints to feed into the system."

"It could be they were bad boys in another country," Donavon said. "We're checking that out now with Interpol."

So far, Donnie thought, everything in this conversation could as easily have been said at noon. "Why did you have the motel office phone me at eight a.m.?" he asked, not bothering to hide his irritation.

"You're a low-level EPA employee," Donavon said cheerily. "You're supposed to be up. I wanted to catch you before you ran outside to fish and collect test samples."

"I was planning on going out a little later this morning," Donnie said. "Now give me the real reason."

"Rafe wants to meet with you today. Can that be done?"

"Sure."

"There's a restaurant called the Lobster Claw on Highway 29, about ten miles north of Belle Maurita."

"I saw it driving in," Donnie said, remembering a small, flat-roofed building with an oversized faded sign featuring a huge lobster.

"Noon there okay for you?"

Donnie said it was.

"Rafe will be there," Donavon said. "I'll let him explain what's happening on the other side of Florida."

"You got somebody watching Grace Perez while he's gonna be with me?"

"She's being taken care of, Donnie. Don't worry, except for yourself."

Before Donnie had a chance to reply, Donavon broke the connection.

Donnie stood for a minute in the sun, then used the Bureau charge number to make a phone call to St. Louis.

She answered.

"Elana? Donnie." His throat was dry, making his voice husky.

"Where are you?" she asked, the old wariness in her voice.

"Can't say."

"It figures," she said with disappointment. "What do you want?"

"To talk to you. How are the girls?"

"Good."

"You?"

"What's the deal, Donnie? You're working—right?"

"Yeah."

"You calling from cover to pass the time 'cause you're lonely, just like when we were married?"

"We're still married."

"Only legally, Donnie. I spent enough time sleeping alone and wondering if, whoever you were at the moment, you were alive or dead. It's no fun being on the sharp edge of widowhood for weeks or months on end. Like it's no fun raising two girls alone."

"The classic cop's-wife predicament," he said bitterly.

"Sure it is. Only worse."

"I only wanted to talk, Elana. Like before."

"That's what I *don't* want, for it to be like before."

"It wasn't all bad."

"But we can't have some of it without getting all of it. You wouldn't take a normal agent's job, and I know you had your chances."

He didn't know how to reply. She was right about that. He watched a tiny lizard crawling over hot concrete in the direction of the highway, unaware of the ponderous, swiftly moving forces that could snuff it out in a second.

"Donnie?"

"Yeah?"

"You okay out there?"

The old gentleness was back in her voice now. What it meant, he knew, was that he was getting to her, doing it to her again. He'd made his choice, but here he was contacting her again from deep cover, clinging to a telephone lifeline to her safe, normal world she wanted him to rejoin. He had no right.

"I'm okay, Elana. Tell the girls I love them."

"They know you do, Donnie, but I'll tell them anyway."

He depressed the cradle lever with his thumb and stood holding it down.

The sun was getting hotter fast. Donnie's collar was sticking to his neck, and beads of perspiration were tracking down his forehead and cheeks. Blondi was right. Miserable climate! He replaced the receiver, then got in the Cherokee and drove it over to the pumps and filled the tank with gas.

When he went inside to pay, he also bought a shrink-wrapped cinnamon roll and a foam cup of black coffee.

Breakfast.

Damn Donavon for waking him up!

36

Lunch figured to be better.

Donnie sat at a corner table in the Lobster Claw and sipped a cold Budweiser while he waited for Rafe to appear. Though the building's weathered exterior looked small, the restaurant was surprisingly large inside and well appointed, with red carpet, a lot of light oak paneling, and chandeliers that looked as if they were fashioned from old ships' spoked wheels. There was a glass aquarium full of condemned lobsters near the entrance, their claws rubber-banded, waiting for the executioner. Donnie had looked over the menu and decided on a steak sandwich.

Diners were seated at half the tables. Many of the customers wore business clothes, but a few were in similar dark blue work clothes with name tags over the shirt pockets. There was a large water-processing plant nearby, and Donnie guessed most of them were employees on their lunch hour. He didn't see anyone he recognized from Belle Maurita.

Rafe came through the door and smiled and spoke to the hostess for a moment, then saw Donnie and walked toward him. He looked tan and healthy in brown slacks and a beige sport jacket with a green T-shirt beneath it. Several women glanced at him as he passed, a muscular, handsome man with wavy black hair and dark eyes. Donnie felt an involuntary resentment when he thought of Rafe spending so much time with Grace Perez.

Rafe shook hands with Donnie before sitting down. To the other diners this was going to look like an ordinary business lunch. And for Donnie and Rafe, that's exactly what it was. It was just their business often involved danger and death.

The two men exchanged small talk until the waitress had taken their orders and left, then Rafe leaned over the table and lowered his voice.

"Something maybe important, Donnie. A guy in Palmville, name of Harvey Gould, contacted Grace about two hundred acres of beachfront property her husband Luis had listed for sale before he died. Gould wanted details of a deal that was in progress at the time of Luis's death, so he could make a higher offer, and he said he'd pay a commission to Grace."

"She told you about this?"

"Sure," Rafe said. "She trusts me. You oughta see how her place is coming along. We got it almost ready for interior painting and wallpapering. She's doing some of the work herself. For therapy, she said. That woman is really something."

"The real estate deal," Donnie reminded Rafe, and took a sip of beer.

"I advised her to tell Gould she'd think over what he said. That's where it stands now. Meantime, I had Gould checked out. He's as advertised, a wealthy real estate investor specializing in commercial property. Got himself an office in Palmville. Also an entire floor of one of those big glass-paneled office buildings in downtown Fort Lauderdale."

Donnie finished his beer. "Maybe it's got nothing to do with anything," he said.

"Or something to do with Luis Perez's death. Or

with Agent Dunn's. Remember Dunn had Luis's name and phone number in one of her pockets."

The waitress, a hulking, ruddy woman who was an uncontrollable smiler and said her name was Madge, came to the table with a tall glass of iced tea for Rafe. She asked Donnie if he wanted another beer and he told her iced tea for him, too. She smiled at the coincidence and scribbled on her order pad.

When she was gone, Rafe said, "I need to know whether you want me to follow up on this. Maybe learn more about Gould and what the real estate deal was about."

"What about Grace Perez?"

"The job's going okay with the guys I hired. And if Donavon won't assign her a guardian angel, I can work Lily into the mix somehow to be her friend. It'd be natural if Lily wanted to ask her questions about her journalist neighbor who died the same night as Luis in the hurricane."

"Look into Gould some more," Donnie said, "but make sure Grace is covered."

"The other thing," Rafe said, "is this series of numbers the Bureau techs found in Agent Dunn's computer." He handed Donnie a slip of paper with what seemed to be a stream of unrelated numbers written across it.

Donnie studied the numbers for a few minutes. They had commas between them. Some of them were single-digit numbers, some double digit. None of them was higher than twenty-six.

"Anyone try matching these up with the alphabet?" Donnie asked.

"Oh, yeah. We've tried all sorts of things. My guess is you have to possess some kind of key to decipher them, like a book whose pages or chapters match the numbers. Only you have to know which book."

Donnie continued staring at the numbers, hoping some pattern would leap out at him. It didn't.

"Make any sense out of it?" Rafe asked.

"Not for now." Donnie refolded the paper and stuck it in his shirt pocket.

"Lily got a CD-ROM copy of everything on Agent Dunn's computer from the Bureau techs. She's still working on the string of numbers, trying to fit them in with something else that's on Dunn's disk drive."

"If she figures it out, have her call this number." Donnie wrote Ida Clayton's phone number on a napkin and handed it to Rafe. "It's safer than the phones at the motel. Lily can leave a message either with the woman who answers or on the machine. I'll get back to her."

Madge was coming toward them carrying a tray with their food on it. She was smiling at them as if they'd bonded and would be dear friends for the rest of their lives. Donnie wished food servers would get over that kind of need.

"Anything else?" he asked, while Madge was still out of earshot.

"Only that *salvaje* is starting to turn up more often in Miami. Local law figures the Mafia's involved, but they have no idea yet where the stuff's coming from."

Donnie nodded as Madge stopped near the table. She set the tray on some kind of folding support she'd been carrying, then began placing plates before them.

"Tell me, Donnie," Rafe said, "we're in a seafood restaurant, so how come you order a steak sandwich?"

"I identify with those lobsters," Donnie said, motioning with his head toward the glass tank near the door.

Rafe glanced in that direction. "You mean because they got their claws banded and can't fight?"

"No," Donnie said, holding up a hand with his thumb and forefinger an eighth of an inch apart, "because they're just this far away from being in hot water."

"Boiling water," Rafe pointed out. "That's what kills them, how they're cooked. I was told they give a little scream when they're dropped alive into the pot."

"Tell me about it," Donnie said, and asked Madge for some steak sauce.

37

When Donnie got back to the Drop Inn, Hutch wandered out of the office and stopped him on the way to his room. The recent physical exertion of cleaning up the motel seemed to have made him stiff and sore. His unique stooped gait was even more pronounced, and an expression of unbearable suffering darted across his scrunched-up face with every step.

"You got a message," he said, and handed Donnie a wrinkled pink form.

Donnie unfolded the form and saw sloppy printing in blue ink instructing him to call Ida at the White Flame.

"You got a busy social life for a guy who hasn't been in town long," Hutch said.

"How do you know it's not a business call?"

Hutch snorted.

"You don't listen in on your guests' phone conversations, do you, Hutch?"

The eerie glitter in Hutch's right eye almost broke into flame with his indignation. He staggered back a step, as if Donnie had stunned him with the mere question of him eavesdropping on a phone call. "You really think you got somethin' that fuckin' interestin' to say? I been wherever you been an' done what you done. I ain't gonna learn a fuckin' thing listenin' to your dumb-ass chatter with a waitress you been whammin'. I ain't no prevert nor no voyager."

Donnie was puzzled for a few seconds. "You mean 'pervert' and 'voyeur'?"

"Fuckin' right!"

"Never thought you were either one," Donnie said. He moved around Hutch's erect and indignant form and continued walking across the parking lot toward his room. The swimming pool smelled particularly foul today, as if there might be something dead in among the algae. The possibility made Donnie shiver.

"Hope you notice your bed's all made so's you could bounce a quarter off it, and the place is straightened up," Hutch said behind him. "Hope you don't forget to tip the fuckin' maid!"

Donnie knew who the "maid" was: an old man with a mismatched face, a luminous eye, and larceny in his soul. He wasn't angry or surprised by Hutch's goading. He'd figured from the beginning that Hutch was going to be sneaking around in his room. The old man might as well clean up the place while he was in there.

When Donnie called the White Flame's number, Blanche answered. She gave no indication that she recognized his voice when he asked for Ida.

As he waited for Ida to come to the phone, he hoped she'd take into account that their conversation might be eavesdropped on. He moved to his left and parted the drapes to look out the window. Hutch was nowhere in sight.

"Hello?"

Donnie identified himself and reminded her she'd left a message for him.

"I just wondered if you were coming into town for supper tonight," Ida said. There was a note of caution in her voice; she knew better than to talk freely.

"What's the special?" Donnie asked.

Ida laughed. "Aren't I special enough?"

"I'll be there about seven o'clock," Donnie said.

She hung up and he waited for another click on the line that indicated an extension or switchboard had been routed in.

If there was one, he didn't hear it. Maybe Hutch was behaving himself. Or maybe the motel was equipped with sophisticated listening equipment and it wasn't necessary for him to be on the line to eavesdrop.

Donnie had several hours before the drive into Belle Maurita. He changed into his fishing clothes, then dragged his waders, tackle box, and rod and reel out toward the parked Cherokee baking in the sun.

The office door opened and Hutch stepped out to toss half a cup of coffee into the shrubs. Sunlight caught the dark arc of liquid and seemed to hold it suspended in the air for a long time before it splashed into the greenery.

"Make your call?" Hutch asked, grinning crookedly at Donnie.

"I will later," Donnie said.

"Keep 'em fuckin' danglin', that's what I say," Hutch advised, and ducked back into the office and closed the door.

Donnie could feel the intense glowing eye trained on him from behind the dirty office window as he drove from the lot.

Things didn't go well. By four o'clock Donnie had caught a dozen fish.

Then he saw what was wrong. He'd attached a lure other than the Hopeful Hooker to his line. By this time, word had gotten around among the fish in the swamp that the Hopeful Hooker wasn't actually a distressed insect, and the brightly feathered, herky-jerky lure was left alone in its mechanical struggles through the water. That was how Donnie liked it. He wasn't actually here to catch anything.

He replaced the effective lure with the Hopeful Hooker, then continued fishing, smiling contentedly as he cast again and again toward an area where he knew there were no fish, but also where there was no thick underwater growth that might snag his line.

When he was sure no one was observing him, he released the fish he'd caught. Then he started back toward where he'd parked the Cherokee.

He stopped sloshing through the shallow water in his waders when he noticed the way the saw grass was parted. Looking more closely, he saw several bent or broken small branches.

Something large had moved through here, opening a wide path that was gradually disappearing as the swamp closed back in on itself.

Donnie followed the path, feeling the water move higher and higher on his waders. The drone of insects and the high-pitched chatter of birds was constant and seemed to be getting louder, as if they were protesting his intrusion.

He felt water slosh coolly over the top of the waders and spread on his hip. He'd followed the wide, almost indiscernible swath through the swamp as far as he could go on foot.

Standing still, he peered out along the path of whatever had passed into deeper water. Water too deep for him to continue along the faint trail marked by parted saw grass and disturbed leafy limbs.

Then he turned around and retraced his steps, thinking about his mosquito dream, with its faint buzz and snarl of what sounded very much like the airboats he'd been told couldn't operate in this lush area of the swamp.

38

_____

When Donnie sat down at a table in the White Flame that evening at seven, Ida spotted him from behind the counter and immediately came out and walked over to him.

"Pinscher and Munz's other two goons had breakfast here this morning." She smiled. "They all drank orange juice."

Donnie looked sharply up at her. "Do you—"

"—have the glasses? Sure I do. I slipped them into a paper sack, then set them aside in the kitchen."

Donnie wanted to stand up and hug her, but he knew she'd put herself in jeopardy for him, and any display of gratitude here in the White Flame would increase that danger.

"You better not give me the glasses here," he said. "Can you take them home with you when you get off work?"

"No problem. After my afternoon break, I came back with an oversized purse. The sack'll fit right inside it with room to spare. Anyway, Blanche trusts me, and the cook wouldn't give a damn if I was stealing glasses."

"When do you get off work?" Donnie asked.

"We close at nine tonight. Will you come to my place?"

"I'll be there," Donnie said.

The glasses should contain usable prints on Pinscher and Pedro. Carl was the only one Donnie might have prints on. He was the one who'd searched Donnie and confiscated his revolver, the only one who'd handled the gun. But Carl had already been identified. Pinscher and Pedro were the ones Donnie needed to know more about. And Curt Munz. Donnie wished Munz had eaten breakfast in the White Flame this morning.

Ida had her order pad out and was holding her pencil poised above it. "I'm not gonna ask," she said, smiling faintly as she looked down at Donnie.

"What I'm going to order, you mean?"

"What you really do instead of work for the EPA."

"I have hobbies," Donnie said.

"Sure. You want the special?"

"Yeah, why not?"

"You don't want to know why not," Ida said. She made a few short notes on her order pad and walked away.

Donnie didn't pay much attention to the special except to notice that it was some kind of meat patty covered with brown gravy and served with mashed potatoes and green beans. He barely tasted it as he used his knife and fork almost mechanically. His mind was on the late Luis Perez and an aborted real estate deal near Palmville.

And on nine o'clock.

After paying Ida for his supper and leaving an exorbitant tip, Donnie wandered down to Hoppy's and drank a beer while he waited for time to pass. Folks in Hoppy's either ignored him or made pleasant small talk with him. No one mentioned the poker game, or how he'd left Hoppy's afterward.

It was nine-fifteen when he left the bar this time,

and under his own control. Wally the bartender glanced at him as he was going out the door and nodded a nervous good-bye.

Cypress Avenue was pretty much deserted as he walked through the warm, gathering dusk toward Ida's trailer.

She didn't answer his knock.

He waited a full minute or more, then knocked again, louder. An uneasiness crept into his mind, then into his stomach. He shouldn't have gotten involved with Ida. Shouldn't have involved her in his business.

He knocked again, very hard, feeling the pain in his fist as he pounded rapidly on the aluminum door.

"You watch out or you're gonna put a dent in my house."

Donnie whirled to see Ida standing smiling at him. She was still wearing her waitress uniform, had one hip thrust out, and was carrying a large straw purse slung by a long strap over her shoulder.

"I thought you got off work at nine."

"I do," she told him. "We had customers hanging around. I got away a little late. Were you worried about me?"

"Sure I was."

"Good."

She stepped around him and unlocked the door, reached in and flipped a light switch, then swung the door out and stood aside to let him enter first. The scent of fried food still clung to her, mingled with her perfume.

When they were both inside, she closed the door, then leaned her back against it. "Maybe it's time for our relationship to be more than platonic," she said. "Maybe you should spend the night here even though you're not drugged."

"I better not," Donnie said.

"Oh? We got complications to deal with?"

" 'Fraid so." Not only did he still have the nagging conscience of a married man, and his professional reservations, he wanted to examine more closely the numbers on the paper Rafe had given him at the Lobster Claw, try to figure out what they might mean. And it bothered him somewhat that two nights ago Pinscher, Carl, and Pedro had *wanted* him to sleep here.

"I make allowances for complications," she said.

"I wish it were possible, Ida."

She looked at him with half a smile. "It is," she told him. "Just not tonight, apparently. You'll think about it later, though, and you'll regret not staying."

"I do already," he said. He felt tension tighten deep in him and realized he really did wish he were staying.

Ida didn't want him to leave immediately; maybe he'd change his mind if she delayed him. Still carrying her purse, she walked slowly and with a lot of hip movement toward the rear of the trailer, flipping light switches as she went.

She disappeared into her bedroom, and after a few minutes Donnie heard a faint beep and voices. He realized she was playing her answering machine and remembered he should tell her Lily might call.

He'd half expected her to come out of the bedroom wearing something calculated to make him change his mind about leaving, but he should have known better. She'd changed her attitude instead. Her motions and expression now suggested she could take him or leave him. That was her message. She didn't see him as an addiction, and she wouldn't mope after he left. She was kidding herself, Donnie thought. But maybe he was the one doing the kidding.

She reached into her purse and handed him a

small, crinkled brown grocery sack. He heard the faint clink of glass on glass as he accepted it.

"I meant to tell you," he said, "someone might call here for me. She might say she's a journalist, and if I'm not here, she'll ask if you'll have me call her. It's important."

"Personal or business?" Ida asked.

"Business."

"Then she really *is* a journalist?"

"Sure. But that has nothing to do with this."

"With us, you mean?"

"Us."

"She already called. I just erased her message. I figured she was some kinda crank who knew you'd spent the night here and she didn't like it and was trying to make trouble between us. We've got some extremists here in Belle Maurita."

"Do you ever," Donnie said, and pecked her good night on the cheek.

39

Gas 'n' Snack was still open when Donnie parked the Cherokee by the public phone in the corner of the parking lot, but there was only one other car in sight, the same old Ford that no doubt belonged to the clerk.

The parking lot with its convenience store and station was an island of light surrounded by the blackness of the swamp. Only a few stars in a cloudy sky broke the solid darkness, except when a car or truck swished past on the highway—headlight beams lancing into the night, then glowing red taillights disappearing like tracer bullets in the distance.

When Donnie punched out the number to get him through to Lily, she answered immediately.

"I thought you might have gone to bed," Donnie said. Even his voice sounded lost in the black void beyond the lot.

"Not hardly, at ten o'clock." Lily sounded hoarse and irritable. "I haven't been sleeping well lately. I'm attracting attention."

"Which means you're probably close to something."

"Whatever Agent Dunn was close to."

"The political corruption case," Donnie said. "C.J. told me it's starting to break."

"Maybe. And maybe that's why I have the feeling I'm being watched."

"Only a feeling?"

"At this point, yes."

"That could mean whoever's observing you is pretty good," Donnie said. He instantly regretted his words. He'd meant them as advice to be cautious. Instead, he might only be making her more uneasy.

But she didn't sound any more perturbed when she said, "The lab's figured something more from Agent Dunn's computer. Got the information from the pale yellow code on the Paintbrush feature of her Windows."

Donnie waited in the heat.

"They had to sort through a lot of paintings saved on the hard disk," Lily said. "And they aren't done yet. They don't even have the complete code broken, but they are sure of this. I won't go into detail now, but the information suggests Dunn didn't think *salvaje* had anything to do with the political corruption she was investigating."

"Was there anything on the corruption itself?"

"Along with misappropriation of funds, there's possible ballot tampering that helped to elect Governor Merchant."

"Jason Cohan's work?"

"Probably. The evidence is still being gathered and developed."

"Think Governor Merchant knew what was going on?"

"Nothing to suggest it at this point. But Cohan's one of his closest aides. And it's no secret he has his own political ambitions."

Donnie stood watching a tractor-trailer speed past on the highway, its tires whining and its diesel engine growling. He was thinking about what Lily's information meant. Probably whatever was going on in or around Belle Maurita had nothing to do with what was happening in Palmville. Yet there was the common denominator of Jason Cohan, and it was unlikely that Dunn was taken out because of the political case. C.J. was right: though politicians might have the balls to be able to kill, they also had an instinct for self-preservation and avoiding possible liability. Politics and organized crime were siblings but not twins.

And to Donnie, Agent Dunn's murder didn't smell much like a Mafia hit. But even without a *salvaje* connection there might be Russian Mafia involvement, rooted in the northeast. The Organizatsya killed more indiscriminately than the traditional Italian Mafia.

"There was something else found on Agent Dunn's computer," Lily said.

"About Iver LaBoyan, I'll bet."

"Right you are. I was wrong about Cohan being Jake. It appears LaBoyan was Jake and was Agent Dunn's source."

"He might have known about the money trail," Donnie said.

"That part of it's not clear yet. But Dunn did make a mistake and absently used LaBoyan's name once on Sidebar."

"Which is?"

"A software program that allows you to interrupt whatever else you're doing and make notes you can return to later. Notes tend to pile up if you don't delete them. The LaBoyan name isn't the only thing interesting that turned up on Sidebar. One of Dunn's notes mentioned Luis Perez phoning her the day before the hurricane, wanting to talk with her about picturesque Florida beachfront property because she was a journalist. He figured a published article would make the area more desirable and salable.

This note wasn't like LaBoyan's name; it was a page long. Dunn wouldn't have left it where it was found on her hard drive if it meant anything important. It was where anyone would have found it on an undamaged computer, so there's no reason to think Dunn wanted it concealed. And there's no indication Luis Perez suspected Dunn was anything other than a journalist."

Donnie was silent, watching swarms of moths circle and dart around one of the lot's overhead, faintly buzzing lights.

"If you're thinking about all this," Lily said, "I'll bet you've come to the same conclusion I have."

"You're the one who's already worked it out," Donnie said. "Tell me what you and I are thinking, Lily."

"A plausible explanation for Luis Perez's name being among Agent Dunn's effects means Dunn's murder might have been a mistake."

"Is that really what you believe?" Donnie asked. It was exactly the suspicion he'd been toying with as he stood there watching nocturnal insects flitting and burning away their lives.

"I'm leaning that way. The killers were going to use the hurricane as cover and diversion for their murder of Luis Perez, then they and everyone else were surprised by the intensity of the storm. Confused by the violence of rain and wind, they entered the wrong cabin and had no choice but to kill Marcia Dunn to eliminate her as a witness to their presence on the beach at that time. They might have had no idea who she was, only that she'd seen them, could identify them, and she was Luis Perez's neighbor."

"Then why was she so frightened before her murder?"

"She knew she had a particularly dangerous tiger

by the tail, but not that Perez was involved or that the tiger would come for him."

"All right so far," Donnie said.

"After leaving Dunn's cottage," Lily continued, "the killers made their way to the right cottage and killed their intended victim, Luis Perez, making it appear that, like Agent Dunn, he was the victim of Hurricane Blaze."

"What about Grace Perez?" Donnie asked.

"Maybe they planned on killing her, too, but lost track of her in the storm. They wouldn't have known she glimpsed them through the window before they came for Luis."

"She would have seen them when they came into the cottage."

"They probably didn't enter. I figure the storm destroyed the cottage before they reached it. In all the chaos afterward, they managed to find Luis Perez and do what they came for, then they couldn't find Grace. Or maybe they decided she wasn't important enough to kill." Lily waited for his reaction. When he didn't give her any, she said, "It makes sense, Donnie."

"It *could* make sense," he admitted. "It squares with Grace's account of what happened the night of the hurricane."

"And of course there's the possibility Grace was in on the plan to kill Luis."

"No," Donnie said, too quickly. "I'm sure her grief over his death is real."

"Rafe's sure, too," Lily said, "but the woman's got the knack of turning men's minds to mush."

"So do you, Lily."

"Donnie, Donnie . . ."

"You got an opinion?"

"No," Lily said. "I haven't seen enough of Grace Perez to form one. I will say there's nothing to suggest she was involved in anything illegal. But of course she was married to Luis."

"What do you think *he* was involved in?"

"Maybe nothing. Maybe the political angle. We've got a witness who claims to have seen him with Jason Cohan."

"But politics seldom lead to murder. Or so I've been told."

"That's true. But Jason Cohan must be involved in whatever's happening in Belle Maurita."

"I think we can count on it," Donnie said.

He heard what sounded like Lily yawning. "Maybe we should sleep on it."

"Before we do," Donnie said, "has there been any progress in figuring out the meaning of the string of numbers found on Agent Dunn's computer?"

"Not yet. And I don't think I'll come up with anything tonight, tired as I am."

"Get your sleep, Lily. And lock your door. You need to be careful. We know more than we did, but we still can't be sure what we're into. It hasn't clicked yet."

"Be careful yourself," Lily said. "The bad guys seem to be on your side of the state."

"Nobody's been murdered here yet," Donnie said.

But after hanging up, he remembered Ida's husband.

40

Donnie was worried that he might be too tired to figure out the mysterious string of numbers in Agent Dunn's computer. But he found himself wide awake as he lay in bed that night at Hutch's Drop Inn, his head propped on his pillow, the yellow shade on the lamp by the side of the bed tilted to compensate for the low-wattage bulb.

Staring at the sheet of paper in his hand, he wondered if the key to the numbers' meaning might be in the pale yellow writing found in the computer's Paintbrush software. It was a possibility, he decided. He'd call Lily tomorrow and suggest she look into it.

It was almost two a.m. when he noticed how often the numbers one through nine repeated themselves in various sequences, then appeared less frequently. Then the numbers ten, eleven, and twelve. He found himself dividing the numbers into pairs, then groups of three. As he scanned the paper from left to right, the pattern suddenly struck him. Though Dunn had made it less obvious by transposing some of the numbers representing months, it was possible—no, damned probable!—that each set of numbers indicated a date.

He felt like reaching for the phone and calling Lily immediately. But he realized if he woke her at this hour she'd probably be mad enough to drive to Belle Maurita and shoot him. Besides, she wouldn't be able to do anything with his theory until morning. All waking her would accomplish would be to anger her, interest her, and prevent her from sleeping the rest of the night.

He worked the light switch and tried to doze off, but his mind was still whirling with questions. If he was right and the numbers were in sets and represented dates, then what did the dates represent?

Finding out would be a job for Lily, he told himself, trying to switch off his mind as easily as he had the lamp.

He rolled onto his stomach, cradled his head in his arms, and lay listening to the shrill ratcheting of cicadas, and beneath their constant clatter, the lower, primitive thrum of the swamp.

It was a long time before he dropped into a fitful sleep.

He awoke at eight-fifteen, blinking into bright sunlight beaming between the closed drapes. Remembering last night, he reached for the phone. Then he withdrew his hand. He'd have to drive back to Gas 'n' Snack or use his scrambler, which was hidden outside in the Cherokee so Hutch wouldn't come across it in his room.

He decided on the scrambler; that might attract less suspicion than his frequent trips to the Gas 'n' Snack public phone. He looked again at his watch. It was still too early to call Lily in Palmville. He'd wait for a while, shower and dress first.

But Donnie didn't wait long enough. Lily had obviously been asleep at eight forty-five when she answered his call on the fourth ring.

He killed a few minutes, talking to her about other matters and making sure she was sufficiently awake, before he told her his theory about the string of numbers.

"Could be," she said when he was finished, her voice still heavy with sleep. "Jus' a moment."

While she was away from the phone, Donnie observed some kind of insect he'd never seen before, a small black beetle with stubby legs and yellow markings. It crawled up the wall and disappeared behind a drape.

Lily returned to the phone shortly and said, "I'm looking at my copy of the numbers, Donnie." She sounded all the way awake now, and alert. "Hmm . . . You damned well might be right."

He was glad to hear a measure of caution in her voice as well as excitement. She was stimulated by the possibility that they were closing in on a solution, not only to the numbers but to the entire case. She could feel it as he could, tugging at them like the outer edges of a whirlpool. But she didn't want to narrow the focus too quickly and exclude other possibilities.

"I'll get dressed and check on it, Donnie. Might have to use the library in Fort Lauderdale or Orlando."

"Let me know soon as possible if you figure it out," he told her.

"After me, you'll be the first to know," she assured him, before hanging up.

Donnie drive into the White Flame for breakfast, but instead of going through his fishing act afterward, he returned to the motel. It drove him crazy, waiting around for a phone call. And there was no guarantee Lily would soon glean meaning and information from the numbers even if they did represent dates.

The sun was particularly fierce today. The old air

conditioner in Donnie's motel room clinked and hummed and gurgled while it fought a losing battle with the rising heat. Lying on its back on the floor beneath the drapes, dead, was the black and yellow insect he'd noticed shortly after rising this morning. Probably another victim of the hot weather. Time seemed to be slowed by the heat and humidity the way people were, moving no further or faster than was absolutely necessary. Dogs wouldn't bother to chase cats, and if they did, cats wouldn't bother to run.

Lily didn't call all day.

No one called.

Hutch had eyed him suspiciously a few times, when Donnie had gone out to the Cherokee or walked to the edge of the swamp only to get out of the stifling, depressing room.

When dusk closed in, Donnie decided he'd better get his masquerade back on track and do his nightly fishing stint to make it seem he was seeking environmental instead of criminal evidence. Either way, he figured, he was trying to clean up pollution.

As he glanced around at the darkening swamp, he found himself thinking about Marishov. The Russian hit man was what he'd long feared—a professional set to catch a professional. Marishov's profession was slightly but significantly different from Donnie's, yet both men had to call on much of the same training and survival skills. In a way, the Russian was Donnie's opposite side of the coin, and the coin was in the air. Donnie knew there was a fifty percent chance it might land either way.

Not good odds when your life was at stake.

He was about to climb into the Jeep when a man's voice called his name.

41

Donnie reacted instantly, throwing himself sideways to put the Jeep between him and whoever had spoken.

But even as he did so, he knew that if the man in the shadows had been Marishov, he would have heard nothing. Ever again.

When he raised his head cautiously and peered over the Jeep's hood, he saw Jason Cohan standing in the faint illumination from the motel lights.

Cohan was dressed in an unbuttoned dark sport coat and tie, a white shirt with wide suspenders showing—Mr. GQ of the swamp. Donnie now noticed the red Range Rover parked beyond him on the road's gravel shoulder.

"Hey, sorry if I frightened you," Cohan said, smiling handsomely with large and perfect teeth. Donnie wondered, if Cohan ever met Blondi, which would be able to outbullshit the other? "I speak too loudly and suddenly sometimes."

"My mind was someplace else," Donnie explained, straightening up and walking around the Cherokee. He was perspiring heavily from exertion and from the sudden fright of thinking Marishov had found him and had the advantage. "Do we know each other?"

"I was wondering that myself," Cohan said.

Though still friendly, he didn't move closer for introductions. "I noticed you around town, and you looked familiar."

"I've been in the area awhile, testing for the EPA."

"The environmental organization?"

"Yeah, I'm a government employee. Are you one? Maybe that's where we met."

"No, never worked for any government."

Technically the truth, Donnie thought. "My name's Donnie Banner," he said.

"Oh? Are you interested in politics, Mr. Banner?"

"You mean because I work for the government?"

"For whatever reason."

"No. I'm registered, but to tell you the truth, most of the time I don't even know which party's in control. Doesn't make much difference to the EPA who wins elections. We got our same work to do."

"Then you don't have any idea who I am?"

"You?" Donnie looked confused, then alarmed. "I'm not insulting you because you're famous and I don't recognize you, am I?"

Cohan laughed. "Not at all."

He walked closer to Donnie, a much taller man than he'd seemed standing ten feet away, even with the fluffed-up hair. Donnie got a whiff of aftershave or cologne; a scent that didn't seem to belong in or around Belle Maurita.

When Cohan proffered his hand, Donnie shook it. It wasn't your ordinary politician's dead-fish handshake; there was strength in it.

Cohan continued gripping Donnie's hand as he spoke. He glanced at the equipment in the back of the Cherokee. "You fish for work or for play?"

"Strictly work," Donnie said. "It's the only way to collect samples for testing."

"You do the testing yourself?"

"Only preliminary tests. Mostly I send the fish and water samples to our lab."

"Then you have to fish and collect water samples from different parts of the swamp."

"That's right."

"So how's the environment around here?"

"Dangerous, like a lot of other places."

"Even more dangerous, I would think. Full of predators."

"I was thinking more in terms of pollutants," Donnie said.

"Microscopic predators or large ones," Cohan said with a smile. "It's only a matter of scale. I only wanted to get a closer look at you to make sure I didn't know you from someplace else. I'm satisfied now that I don't."

"Well, nice meeting you anyway," Donnie stammered.

Cohan finally released his hand, then gracefully backed away. "Have a pleasant evening, Mr. Banner. And good luck fishing."

Cohan's demeanor had suddenly become polite but dismissive, that of someone who was finished dealing with an inferior and had his mind on more important matters. But Donnie wondered if he'd really lost interest in him.

He didn't look back at Donnie as he got into the Range Rover and drove away.

Donnie stood watching the bouncing, wavering headlight beams until they disappeared in the night. Cohan hadn't been able to resist inquiring about him; Donnie had drawn his interest, then his conversation, the way the Hopeful Hooker attracted fish when it was working well. Yet their talk had been smooth and controlled by Cohan. He hadn't once mentioned his own name.

It didn't surprise Donnie that if Marishov was in

Florida searching for him, Cohan wouldn't have been informed or been briefed on Donnie's description. Like the Italian Mafia, the Russians played every hand close to the vest. Knowledge was power that could result in someone being killed if it was spread around carelessly. The Russian Mafia had adopted the ruthlessness and compartmentalization of the Communist party. What had worked so well and so long for the KGB would work for them, but it would be for monetary rather than political gain.

Donnie knew Cohan's curiosity had been only partly satisfied. He was sure Cohan hadn't figured him out yet, even if he suspected Donnie wasn't quite what he pretended. Donnie also knew that the suspicions surrounding him would soon result in some sort of action against him, if only to remove him as an uncertainty.

Then another, chilling possibility entered his mind. What if Cohan had wanted to get a good look at him so he could be sure who he was later and point him out? What if he was acting as finger man for Marishov?

Not likely, Donnie told himself. If Marishov was such a killer-craftsman, he wouldn't involve anyone else in his plans.

But there was no way to be sure. Or to do anything about the situation right now. Donnie couldn't forget about Marishov, but he had to concentrate on more immediate dangers.

The swamp was a treacherous place for a lot of reasons. He hoped that if Marishov did manage to find him before this operation was concluded, the Russian hit man wouldn't merely be standing over a grave.

42

When the sound of the Range Rover's engine had died down and only the insect din of the swamp occupied the night, Donnie climbed up into the Cherokee. He drove in the opposite direction Cohan had taken, toward Munz's compound. But he stopped and parked well short of the property's razor-wired boundary. While the swamp provided plenty of cover for him to conceal himself and observe what went on in the compound, he wasn't sure anything he'd learn would be worth the risk. Whoever had devised Munz's security knew his business.

Still, as he cast the Hopeful Hooker and waded through the shallow water, Donnie moved in the general direction of the compound. Eventually he could see a glimmer of light in the dark swamp.

Uneasily remembering the moths circling the burning lights of the Gas 'n' Snack parking lot, drawn to their deaths by the glow, Donnie moved closer.

He proceeded slowly, taking care to stay near dense foliage, making as little noise as possible as he shoved dark water before him and heard it ripple in his wake.

More of the compound came into view. Munz's house . . . one of the outbuildings. There were no vehicles in sight. No sign of movement inside the house.

A door slammed, making Donnie jump. Wishing he'd brought his night-vision binoculars, he moved to his left, straining to see who might have exited one of the buildings.

But no one came into view.

Donnie considered moving closer, maybe even trying to cross the razor wire. Then he stopped himself. Being caught a second time on or near Munz's property might prove fatal. He was pushing his luck needlessly, endangering not only himself, but the operation.

He began backing away, then heard something sloshing water in the blackness behind him.

Standing still, his heart hammering and a lump in his throat, he waited for another sound.

Minutes passed. Whatever had made the noise didn't make another. A swamp creature, Donnie told himself hopefully.

He started wading again through the dark water, making inevitable noise as widening patterns of ripples met saw grass, trees, and vines.

His breathing evened out and his heartbeat slowed only when he was a good hundred yards from Munz's property line. He began moving faster, not minding making noise now as he waded in the direction of the parked Cherokee.

A sudden loud snarl froze him.

Light played among the trees off to his left, and the snarl became a roar.

The engine and lights of an airboat—and close!

Donnie fought back his instinct to duck low and stayed precisely as he was. There was a chance whoever was in the boat wouldn't spot him if he remained perfectly still.

And if the beam of light flitting over the swamp didn't happen to fall directly on him.

For an instant he glimpsed a dark, boxy form through the trees as the roar of the airboat changed pitch, almost died, then continued as a throaty rumble.

"Despacio!" a man said.

Spanish, and Donnie couldn't translate it to English. He was sure it wasn't Pedro's voice he'd heard. And presumably the man was talking to someone who also spoke and understood Spanish.

The airboat's engine revved up to a steady roar again, then its dancing light disappeared. The sound of its engine moved away from Donnie.

He listened to the lessening roar for several minutes, until the swamp was again silent but for the droning of insects and the croaking of frogs.

Despacio. While the word's precise meaning was beyond Donnie, he thought it had sounded as if the man in the boat was cautioning whoever was piloting it. Donnie knew it must be tricky, jockeying the boat through the swamp at night. Branches could scrape the hull, or the airboat's occupants. Low-hanging limbs could practically behead someone in a boat moving fast at night. If he'd been urging caution, the Spanish-speaking man had given good advice.

Donnie waited at least five minutes before moving from where he stood.

He located the parked Cherokee without trouble, but he found himself checking the rearview mirror all the way back to the motel.

When he entered his room the phone was ringing.

Flicking the light switch, he hurried to lift the receiver.

Instead of speaking, he waited.

"Donnie?"

Ida.

"It's me," he said. He noticed it wasn't quite as warm in the room. With darkness, the air conditioner was catching up.

"I thought you'd want to know," Ida said, "that woman phoned again."

"Woman?"

"You know, the journalist. She wants you to call her."

Donnie was eager to break the connection and talk to Lily. "Thanks, Ida."

"I know you don't like using the phone at the motel, Donnie. Why don't you call her from here?"

"I don't think so this time, Ida." He used his shirt-sleeve to sop sweat from his forehead. "I've been having one hell of an evening."

"I think you don't want me to overhear your conversation with the so-called journalist."

She sounded miffed. He was surprised. "Ida, are you jealous?"

"You should know better than that," she said, and hung up hard.

She was right, Donnie thought. He should know better.

43

Tonight wasn't like last night. Donnie had no trouble falling asleep. He'd thought he was wide awake, and decided to occupy his mind and induce sleep by mulling over Agent Dunn's computerized numbers again. They weren't sheep, but he figured they'd do.

They did.

The next thing he knew he was waking from a deep and deliciously comfortable slumber, not quite sure why. Something must have disturbed him, some sound or sensation he couldn't discern as he fished around in memory. Like fishing with the Hopeful Hooker, he thought inanely, shifting position and trying to drift off again to sleep.

He slowly became aware of someone standing at the foot of the bed.

Marishov?

Jolted awake, Donnie started to roll to the side. Whoever was in his room might have a gun, might be aiming it at him right now. He was already planning what to do when he hit the floor. Be unpredictable. Use the darkness to—

"Donnie! Calm down, man!"

C.J.'s voice.

Donnie sat up on the edge of the mattress, letting out his breath. His adrenaline still hadn't acknowledged it was friend and not foe at the foot of the bed. The rough nap of the carpet scratched his bare toes. It was hot and damp in the room, as if the swamp had crowded in when C.J. opened the door.

C.J. walked over and switched on a lamp.

Donnie squinted, blinked, trying to get his eyes adjusted to what passed for light fighting its way through the yellowed shade.

"You're gonna ruin your vision if you're trying to read by that son of a bitch," C.J. said calmly.

Donnie clenched his eyes closed, opened them, and glanced down at his watch. Two a.m.!

His features still contorted from being pulled from sleep, then subjected to the sudden light, he stared up at C.J. "What the fuck are you doing here?"

"Tinker took a bullet in the arm early this evening," C.J. said gravely.

Donnie thought hard. Came up blank. "Who the hell's Tinker?"

"Steve Tinker. An agent Donavon called to come down from Georgia. He's been watching over Grace Perez while Rafe keeps tabs on real estate tycoon Harvey Gould."

Donnie stood up, then steadied himself. "Grace hurt?"

"Not a hair on her pretty head. Tinker's bicep was penetrated by the bullet, and it took part of the bone."

"Shit!" Donnie paced over the rough, worn carpet, shirtless in his Jockey shorts. "What about the shooter?"

"Got away. Tinker was stationed outside the Perez beach cottage when somebody fired through the window at Grace. It was just starting to get dark. Tinker caught a glimpse of the muzzle flash and returned fire. Got fired right back on. Wounded arm and all, he found cover, circled around, and advanced on the area where the shot had come from. When he got there, the shooter was gone."

"Any sign who it might have been?"

"All we know about him is he used a 9mm. There were two spent cartridges on the ground where he'd concealed himself in the bushes."

"Not very professional, failing to pick up his shells," Donnie said.

"Well, I hate to defend the man, but he was in a rush, what with Tinker playing Marines with him."

"How close did he come to Grace?"

"The bullet missed her by less than six inches. Blew the hell out of a vase on the mantel right near her head."

"She badly scared?"

"She's mostly pissed. And now she thinks there's something suspicious about her husband's death and wants to find out about it. More trouble."

Donnie sat back down on the edge of the mattress. "Why would anyone wanna kill Grace, if she's not involved in anything going on here in Belle Maurita?"

"Big if, Donnie."

Donnie gave him a dark look, and C.J. averted his eyes.

"Maybe we don't have this whole thing read right," C.J. said after a few seconds.

"*Despacio*," Donnie said.

"Huh?"

"Know what it means?"

"Some kinda Italian ice cream?"

"Nope. I think it's Spanish. At least the man I heard say it last night spoke with a Spanish accent."

"Why didn't you ask him what it meant?"

"He was in an airboat in the swamp, and I didn't want him or anybody else in the boat to see me."

C.J. tugged at an earlobe and made a face. "I was

told the swamp 'round here was too thick for air-boats to get around in."

"So was I," Donnie said.

C.J. shook his head. "I guess we shouldn't be surprised. The bad guys will lie. That's why they're bad guys."

Donnie knew C.J. was joking, but he also knew there was some truth to what he said. Sometimes it was easy to be distracted by the human qualities of the suspects in a case and forget what they might be capable of doing. The bad guys. It wasn't as if they had an evil extra something that made them easily identifiable; it was more that they usually had something missing, that scary void Blondi had mentioned. They were just like the rest of us, only without one or more of the checking mechanisms that made for morality and sometimes squeamishness. Some of them could kill and then enjoy a good meal. Maybe even kill *during* a good meal. Easy to misjudge folks who could seem ordinary but who were short some essential components. It was dangerous to forget that.

Donnie stood up and stepped into his pants. "I'm driving to Palmville."

"Right now?"

"It's a good time. Even if Hutch hears me leave, he won't know why or where I'm going."

"Why *are* you going?"

"I want to talk to Tinker."

"Might as well drop in on Grace Perez while you're in town," C.J. said.

"Good idea," Donnie said, playing along. "Glad you thought of it."

"Don't stand too close to her," C.J. said. "I'm about to head back east myself. Want to go with me in my car?"

"No, it'll be better if the Cherokee's missing.

Folks'll figure I'm away fishing or collecting water samples." Donnie knew that if Hutch realized he hadn't spent the entire night in his room, the old man would figure he was at Ida's. And of course Ida assumed Donnie was asleep at the motel. Neat, Donnie thought. Such a planner I am. "Take these with you and give them to Donavon," he said, handing C.J. the paper sack containing the glasses from the White Flame. "They might have prints on them that'll tell us what we need to know."

C.J. gripped the folded top of the sack and held it carefully. "I'll start back, then," he said. "I've gotta walk a ways to where I left my car. I didn't want to park too close; that geezer who runs this place is a nosy one. You can't trust him."

"Tell me about it," Donnie said.

He turned around to get his wallet and keys from the dresser and put them in his pockets.

When he turned back, C.J. was gone.

Donnie hadn't even heard the door open and close, but suddenly he was alone.

It was one of those times when he was struck by what odd people he dealt with and what a strange business he was in.

It scared him sometimes that he liked the people and he belonged in the business.

44

After checking into a motel a few miles west of Palmville, Donnie caught some sleep around sunrise, then woke up hungry a few hours later.

He found a Mexican restaurant that served breakfast and ordered *huevos rancheros*, sliced plantains, and coffee. He needed a clean if temporary break from Belle Maurita, and this cuisine was about as far as you could get from the White Flame's standard fare, so stomach be damned.

Driving in, he'd noticed progress had been made in the area's attempt to set things right again after Hurricane Blaze. There were fewer boarded-up windows, and fewer of the bright blue tarpaulins that were used temporarily to cover holes in roofs and walls. The streets were almost completely clear of litter, and most of the wind-felled trees or limbs had been segmented with power saws and hauled away. Of course, Donnie reminded himself, he was several miles inland from where Blaze had roared ashore full force.

When he was finished eating, he had a second cup of coffee, then went outside and called Donavon from the phone mounted on the restaurant's brick facade.

"Where are you calling from?" Donavon asked,

immediately picking up the sounds of traffic from the nearby highway. Much heavier traffic than could be heard anywhere around Belle Maurita.

"Restaurant called Rancho Ruiz, about two miles outside Palmville."

"I know the place."

"I just finished having breakfast there."

"Good Lord!"

"I want to talk with Tinker," Donnie said, "about last night's little adventure."

"Too late. He's already returned to Georgia. I got whatever you might need to know from him, though. It'd save time if you tell me what you already know."

Donnie told Donavon what C.J. had related to him about the attempt on Grace's life, about Tinker returning fire and scaring away the assailant.

"That's most of it," Donavon said. "The empty cartridges ejected by the shooter's weapon are at the lab. Techs might be able to get some idea as to what kinda gun was used. The way the ground was indented and the grass was flattened indicated the shooter was standing when he fired and hadn't been there long. Used a semiautomatic handgun, probably, and he didn't have time to recover the ejected shells in the dark with Tinker closing in on him."

"Any blood?"

"No. Looks like the shot only alerted the gunman and made him flee the scene."

"Marishov?"

"I don't think he'd have a reason to hit Grace."

"And I don't think he would have missed," Donnie said.

"We can't dismiss the possibility, though," Donavon said. "According to Blondi, he *is* in Florida."

"I wanted to thank Tinker."

"It can wait till after this is over, Donnie. He was only doing his job."

"Sometimes the job gets rougher than it should."

"You oughta know. Anybody ever thank you?"

"Not sincerely. Not even you."

Donavon gave a barking little laugh, but there was sadness in it. Both men knew theirs was the sort of thankless business where things got broken and people got killed. And as time passed, you found yourself more and more on the wrong side of the odds. If you were broken and not killed, maybe you could count yourself lucky.

"The Perez woman might get to be a problem," Donavon said. "She's determined to find out if there was anything suspicious about her husband's death. She drove into Fort Lauderdale and saw Harvey Gould."

"Maybe they were only talking business, the real estate proposal."

"Rafe says otherwise. Got the info from a secretary in Gould's office. He doesn't think your name was brought up, Donnie."

Donnie hoped Rafe was right. It could be fatal if Grace mentioned him to anyone involved in the Belle Maurita end of the operation and they figured out Donnie Blaine and Donnie Banner were the same man. And probing the wrong areas might be fatal to Grace even if she didn't mention Donnie. She'd already been shot at.

"Who've you got watching her now?" Donnie asked.

"Agent named Corcoran, from the same office as Tinker. He'd very much like to meet the guy who shot his buddy."

"We all would," Donnie said. "But it hardly ever happens. The world's not that neat."

"Corcoran's pretending to be an employee of Rafe's, digging around and doing work on underground gas or electric lines. Some kind of lie the Perez woman'll believe."

"I'm gonna be dropping by the cottage," Donnie said. "I don't want to get Corcoran stirred up."

"You won't if you act normal and you're driving your government Jeep. He knows about the vehicle and he's got a general idea what you look like."

Donnie stared at a string of traffic speeding past, everybody after the first car riding everybody else's bumper. Dangerous. "Why do you think somebody tried to kill Grace Perez?"

"No theories here," Donavon said. "Isn't that the sort of thing *you're* supposed to tell *me*?"

"That's the way the job's supposed to work," Donnie admitted.

After hanging up the phone, he watched the traffic for a while longer, enjoying the warmth of the morning sun and wondering why it was so much hotter in Belle Maurita. Swamp humidity, he guessed. He glanced down at the sleeve of the fresh shirt he'd put on this morning. It was nice to have creases in his clothes again.

His glance also took in his watch. It was almost ten o'clock, certainly not too early to phone Grace and make sure she was home, tell her he was on his way there.

Then he decided not to call first. Better to walk in unexpected on the real Grace, a woman he might not know.

Ignoring the phone, he put on his sunglasses and strode across the parking lot to where the Cherokee sat in the shade, not the real Donnie Blaine, looking for the real Grace.

45

Donnie saw no sign of Agent Corcoran as he drove along Beach Lane toward Grace's cottage. The road itself had been built up with trucked-in dirt and gravel and restored to its original condition, but the stretch of beach it led to still looked much as it had when Donnie had last seen it. The sand was still peppered with litter, and most of the buildings had been leveled or were obviously badly damaged. A few were in stages of repair. Grace's looked further along than the rest of them. The roof was complete and new, the exterior walls primed and ready for paint.

He parked the Cherokee and climbed out of its air-conditioning into the heat. Then he peeled off his sunglasses and looked around. Beyond the cottage, a man in work clothes was wandering the beach, probing the ground with some kind of instrument. As Donnie watched, he stopped walking, drew a metal rod from a cluster he held in his hand, and hammered it into the ground. The man glanced at Donnie, then continued with his work. Agent Corcoran, Donnie guessed.

The sunglasses dangling in his hand, Donnie strode to the cottage's front porch. Half its lumber was new and raw, still unpainted. He clomped up the replacement front steps, noticing how solid they felt beneath his soles, how tightly the mitered edges fit. It was fine craftsmanship. Rafe always had something to fall back on if he left the Bureau.

When Grace answered his knock, she seemed surprised to see him. Also glad. For a second an expression that suggested something like relief passed across her features. Donnie felt oddly like someone being greeted on arriving home.

Grace was wearing loosely fitted jeans and a yellow T-shirt. Her thick dark hair was pulled back and tied at the nape of her neck. Several wavy tendrils refused to submit and curled around her face. Her huge brown eyes were fixed on Donnie with such dark intensity that he averted his gaze, staring down at her dusty bare toes protruding from the straps of her sandals. Her feet were small, the length of her toes almost uniform so that there was a square look to them. Their nails were painted bright red, but the enamel was nicked and faded.

"I guess you've studied my feet long enough," she said in mock annoyance.

He looked back into her eyes and felt their pull. "Maybe I have a fetish."

She smiled. "Maybe more than one." Still smiling, she stepped back. "Come on in."

Her casual, flirtatious word play surprised him. Fresh grief had still had its inhibiting effect on her words and actions the last time he'd seen her. Possibly, as with Ida, anger had moved her beyond her deepest pain. Possibly she was using anger for that purpose.

He entered and looked around. A new air conditioner made the cottage comfortably cool. The interior had lost its feel of disaster. Furniture was precisely arranged and there were curtains or miniblinds on the windows. The blinds were all slanted so it would be difficult for anyone to see in. Behind the slats of one of them was a dark outline Donnie assumed was plywood or cardboard over the broken pane where the bullet had entered.

Grace apparently noticed his silent appraisal. "I can't hang anything on the walls yet," she said. "There's still a lot of hammering and vibration to come."

"The place looks great the way it is."

"Rafe is a find, Donnie. Thanks again for recommending him to me."

"Where is Rafe?" Donnie asked, remembering he was Donnie Blaine, cousin of Grace's late neighbor. He glanced opposite the window and saw where a bullet had been dug out of the wall a few inches above the mantel.

"He had to go someplace for a while on business. Another construction job." Grace took a step toward the kitchen. "Want some coffee? Anything?"

"No. Thanks, anyway."

She turned around and came all the way back to the center of the living room. A slight awkwardness seemed to have taken her over. "Are you going to be here in Palmville for a while?" she asked.

"Not very long." He searched her face for disappointment but saw none.

She motioned with a hand toward the sofa. When he'd sat down and tucked his sunglasses into his shirt pocket, she lowered herself into a chair facing him. The air conditioner decided it was cool enough in the cottage and clicked off. In the following silence, a gull could be heard screaming from the direction of the beach.

"Someone shot at me last night," Grace said.

Donnie pretended to be surprised. "You're sure?"

She pointed toward the hole above the mantel. "A

bullet came through a window and shattered a vase
only a few feet away from my head."

"You called the police, I hope."

"I didn't have to. There was a man outside the
cottage who chased away whoever tried to kill me.
He was with the FBI, I gathered. I still don't have
any explanation as to why he was there, or why anyone would try to kill me."

"Do you want me to try to find out?"

When she looked at him he knew she suspected,
wondered about him. "You said you weren't going
to be in town long."

"Maybe you could ask Rafe to find out about it
when he comes back," Donnie suggested. "He could
talk to the FBI, ask some questions."

"They'd be the same questions I already asked
without getting any answers."

He looked around as if a bit confused and still
trying to digest what she'd told him. "If someone
shot at you, how come you're still here?"

"I've been guaranteed by the police that the cottage is being watched. A Lieutenant Kozner came out
and assured me personally that I'd be safe."

Donnie knew what Kozner's assurance was worth.
It was actually the Bureau making it safe for Grace
to stay in the cottage. Reasonably safe, anyway.

"I have this, too. It was Luis's." She walked to a
small table, opened a drawer, and removed a long-
barreled revolver. It looked like a cheap Saturday
night special that might blow up in her hand.

"Do you know how to use it?"

"Well enough. I've fired it at tin cans. It's accurate,
and so am I."

Donnie didn't try talking her out of the gun. It
might save her life, and Grace wasn't the sort who'd
do something stupid with it. "You have *no* idea why
someone would try to kill you?" he asked.

She shook her head no and replaced the gun in the drawer. "And I don't know why the FBI happened to be in the vicinity."

He knew she wouldn't be fooled by Donnie Blaine much longer. What would she think of him when she found out the truth?

"Maybe it was somebody off in the distance shooting at something else," he suggested. "A stray bullet."

"No. When the FBI agent shot at the gunman, whoever it was shot back. The agent was wounded."

"Jesus!" Donnie said.

"I don't like the way this feels. A lot's going on I don't know about."

She *did* know about the Harvey Gould offer on the land her late husband had listed, but she didn't volunteer the information to Donnie. And she didn't mention having driven into Fort Lauderdale to see Gould after she'd been shot at. Was it that she didn't trust him, or simply didn't think it was any of his business?

"It sure sounds like there is," he said. "Could it have something to do with your husband?"

"I thought about that," she said, standing up and pacing. "Luis was in real estate, not organized crime. And believe me, he wasn't the kind of man who'd lead a double life. We didn't have any secrets from each other. At least, none that was important."

He believed her. Luis Perez, the straight citizen with a thriving business, married to a woman like this. That was enough of a life for anyone.

But even as he thought it, he knew he was being a fool. Grace was affecting his judgment, just as C.J. had warned about in Belle Maurita.

"It's possible Luis was innocent and unknowing," she said, "and somehow got accidentally involved.

I'm beginning to wonder about his death. If it was really what it seemed."

"The police say it was accidental. You oughta leave it to the authorities, Grace."

"I don't know if I can trust them to have done their job."

"Even so, it's not *your* job. Don't do anything that might put you in danger."

"I can be dangerous myself," she said, "instead of just a sitting target."

"I could understand you thinking that way if you were certain Luis's death was murder, but you don't know for sure."

"I forgot, you have to see proof. You're from Missouri, the Show Me state." She was smiling very slightly, appraising him with those dark, dark eyes.

He was sure now she didn't completely believe that. But she wasn't going to ask who he really was. Like Ida Clayton, she'd crossed the Rubicon; her grief and yearning now had more to do with life than with death.

Outside, the gull screamed again.

"We're Chinese now, you and I," Grace said, surprising him.

"What?"

"You've heard about that belief the Chinese are supposed to have that if you save someone's life you're then responsible for everything that person does in the future. Well, we saved each other's lives."

He leaned back into the soft sofa. "I hadn't thought of it that way."

She was staring down at him, her fingertips tucked into the hip pockets of her jeans. "I've thought of it that way a lot. Thought about you."

He sat looking at her, listening to the surf sighing outside on the beach. He could barely hear a rhythmic hammering sound, metal on metal. Probably

Corcoran driving a steel rod into the ground, pretending and looking as if he knew what he was doing. So much of life was role-playing, in or out of the Bureau, one role after another. Undercover. People had little choice.

"I thought I understood grief," she said, "but I didn't. It's complicated. Sometimes it's unbearably heavy."

He smiled up at Grace, meeting her gaze directly, aware of the trembling rise and fall of her breasts beneath the bright yellow material of her shirt. "Does your offer of coffee still stand?"

She nodded solemnly. They both understood her offer wasn't for coffee, and she was releasing herself from something, setting herself free if only momentarily.

"You know it does," she told him in a husky voice.

She came to him on the sofa and he held her, kissed her lips. Her arms wrapped around his neck, and one of her legs snaked up onto his lap. They held each other close and tight.

Saving each other's lives.

46

Donnie met Rafe by arrangement on the public beach south of Palmville. As he approached, he saw Rafe sitting on a stone bench facing the ocean. The wind had ruffled his dark hair and he was wearing elegant brown slacks and a white shirt without a collar. A gold bracelet and ring glinted in the bright sunlight. He didn't look much like a carpenter today, or a man who worked with his hands in any other occupation. Donnie wondered again at the deception and misdirection of the lives they led, how it had come to seem normal.

Though Rafe hadn't moved and was facing away from Donnie, when Donnie approached, he stood up and turned to greet him. The top two buttons on his shirt were unfastened to reveal a gold necklace glinting among dark chest hair. Rafe liked expensive clothes and jewelry and was fond of excess, and he was handsome and genial enough to bring it off.

The two men shook hands. Rafe's grip was firm and dry, and rough.

"You grew some calluses," Donnie said. "I know how. You're doing good work on Grace's cottage."

Rafe smiled. There was a toothpick stuck in the corner of his mouth. "A lot of the damage was cosmetic. And she's a fine lady who's had a bad time. The men work extra hard for her. So do I, I guess."

Donnie looked out toward the ocean. There were only a few people on the beach. Beyond them a man wearing gray swim trunks was floating in the ocean on a red raft that rode the swells as if on a gentle roller coaster. Several pleasure boats were anchored or drifting, far enough out to sea so that heat and dancing vapor made their white-on-blue images shimmer in the brightness of the sun.

"C.J. says that place where you are is a green hell-hole," Rafe said, observing Donnie admiring the scenery that was so unlike Belle Maurita.

"He's being generous. I suspect you'll see for yourself before long."

"If it's all the same to you," Rafe said, "I'd rather stay here with Grace."

"Do you think she knows more than she's saying about her husband's business?"

"No," Rafe said. He hadn't had to pause to consider. "Luis was one of those men who kept a high wall between business and family. We hold our women and children in such regard that we keep them in a world that's separate and safe. If you were Latin you'd understand."

"Is that a politically correct thing to say?" Donnie asked.

Rafe shrugged. "I don't know or give a fuck, amigo."

"What about Harvey Gould?"

"He doesn't care about political correctness either. Got himself a Latina secretary, treats her like shit. Got himself a black mistress, white wife. Treats them the same way. Equal opportunity jerk-off."

"Has he built a wall between business and the women close to him?"

"I don't know, but I doubt it. I'm getting to know

the secretary a little bit. We just happened to eat breakfast in the same restaurant and I struck up a conversation. This could lead someplace, Donnie. She has to be aware of what's going on in Gould's business, at least to some extent."

An elderly man and woman approached the bench, he wearing plaid shorts and white socks and shoes, she in a blue and green pastel outfit that was too tight. Both had expensive 35mm cameras slung about their necks and bouncing against their ample stomachs with each step.

Rafe casually turned and began walking along the beach, so his and Donnie's conversation could remain private. Donnie fell in beside him. They were far enough up the gradual slope from the sea that the ground was sandy but reasonably firm, so walking was easy.

"What it looks like so far," Rafe said, "is that Gould's a rich asshole, but businesswise he's exactly what he seems, a sharp commercial real estate investor. He thinks money can buy anything, and he's got enough of it to make his point. He owns plenty of commercial property, and a house on the Gold Coast that looks like it should belong to the royal family. It was damaged by Blaze, so he's staying in a corporate condo in town now, which makes my job easier."

"Who's the other bidder for the beachfront property Luis had listed?"

"Something called the Eagle Consortium. Probably an organization of wealthy investors."

"What do you think Gould has in mind for the property if he manages to get it?"

"My guess would be he wants to build a luxury hotel on it," Rafe said. "It's in a good location, about five miles north of Palmville. Lots of beach there, even after Blaze, and a great view of the ocean."

Donnie squinted out again at the bright sea. Nothing had changed. The man on the red raft lay motionless as the raft gently rose and fell. The white cabin cruisers hadn't moved. Gulls were still tracing circles high in the cloudless sky, as if the design of their dives and arcs meant something significant. Maybe it did.

"I need a translation from Spanish," Donnie said. "What's *despacio* mean?"

"Means 'slowly,' " Rafe said. "Wanna tell me why you need to know?"

"I overheard a man in an airboat say it in the swamp outside Belle Maurita."

"Sounds like he was telling whoever was handling the boat to take it easy and slow down, be careful."

"That was probably it," Donnie said. "It was dark."

They continued walking. Ahead of them Donnie saw three men picking through a pile of wreckage that had been bulldozed together on the beach. They were calling to each other and seemed to be joking, laughing, open about what they were doing. The debris was apparently public now and the city would appreciate people lugging it away so it wouldn't have to be hauled. The fine line between looting and scavenging.

"If Gould is straight and the real estate deal's irrelevant to our case, why do you suppose somebody took a shot at Grace?" Donnie asked.

"I've thought about it," Rafe said. "Maybe the shooter or whoever hired him doesn't know what's relevant or what she might know. Tried to play it safe by making her dead."

Donnie rubbed his chin, not liking the way things weren't adding up. "What would happen to the real estate deal if Grace died? Without her in the picture, would Gould have a better chance of getting the property?"

"I don't know," Rafe said.

"See if you can find out."

"Okay." Rafe stopped walking and looked over at Donnie. "But considering what almost happened to Grace Perez, I think I could do more good around her place. How much longer do you want me to stay on this guy Gould?"

"I don't know. Maybe another couple of days to make sure about him."

"I told you, he's an arrogant scumbag, but beyond that he's nothing more than a greedy and successful businessman."

"Maybe one who pays off politicians," Donnie suggested.

The ocean breeze kicked up hard and blew steadily for several seconds, making litter from Blaze scoot across the ground, then become airborne. Rafe combed back his hair with his fingers, sunlight glancing off his gold bracelet, then started walking again.

"There you might have something," he said.

After parting with Rafe, Donnie drove toward his lunch date with Lily. He not only wanted to talk to her about Agent Dunn's mysterious string of numbers, he wanted to touch base with her personally as he had recently with the others. They were exceptional people with rare skills, and meeting with them reaffirmed that he could count on them in what was soon to come. The time had arrived when he needed to feel the bond between them as well as know logically that it existed and was strong.

He understood the familiar coolness in the pit of his stomach, the heightening of his senses.

Long ago he'd learned the rest of the body was way ahead of the brain when it came to knowing something threatened its survival.

47

Donnie sat opposite Lily at a small white-enameled table near the taco stand where he'd bought them each burritos, cheese-covered French fries, and sodas. A fringed umbrella with a bottled water advertisement on it sprouted from the center of the table and shaded them. Nearby was a large trash receptacle around which bees droned. None of the bees ventured over to investigate the food on the table. They had everything they needed and saw no reason to start trouble. People should take a lesson.

Lily's red hair was mussed by the wind. She was wearing white slacks and a sea-green blouse that matched her eyes. In the soft but bright light she looked too young to be doing anything involving violent death. More like a college kid who'd come to Florida on vacation. Lily and Blondi. They should be surfing and giggling about boys.

"Do you really like this stuff?" she asked, pointing to her burrito. She'd just bitten one end off it and hot salsa was oozing out.

"Sure," Donnie said. "I love Mexican food."

"But this isn't really Mexican food. I've been to Mexico and I know."

He raised his eyebrows. "Cheese fries aren't Mexican?"

She ignored him and looked out at the nearby marina where damaged pleasure boats did their little bobbing dance at their moorings. Workers were making repairs on some of the boats, observed by half a dozen motionless, somber pelicans lining the dock.

"Any progress on figuring out the numbers from Agent Dunn's computer?" Donnie asked.

Lily turned back to look at him, studiously avoiding glancing down at her food. "Not yet. I'm sure you're right about grouping the numbers in sets that represent dates. My theory is they're publication dates. When we're finished here, I'm gonna drive to Fort Lauderdale and use their library to see what I can find out."

"How about using your computer? Can't you search the Internet for publications matching those dates?"

"I tried an Internet search," she said. "Mostly I wound up with horoscopes and celebrities' birth dates."

"Ain't technology wonderful!"

"Yeah. Like these burritos heated in that microwave."

Donnie chewed a bite of burrito and washed it down with Pepsi. He couldn't understand why Lily was complaining. She ate a couple of cheese fries. She seemed to like them well enough. "Want me to get you some more hot sauce?" he asked, motioning with his head toward the red and white stand where customers ordered at a small window. There were flames painted on the sides of the flimsy but neat stand.

She stared at him, green-eyed, freckled, puzzled, and Irish, and he told her never mind.

"Why do you think somebody shot at Grace Perez?" she asked.

"I was hoping you had it all figured out and you'd tell me."

"All I can come up with is the most likely explanation that somebody thinks she knows something and doesn't want her to share the information."

"That's how Rafe sees it," Donnie said. "Maybe the two of you are right. I don't know how to figure it."

"Her late husband was probably into something illegal, and whoever was in it with him doesn't know what he might have shared with her. Pillow talk can be dangerous, Donnie."

For an instant he wondered if Lily suspected anything between him and Grace and was cautioning him.

Then he decided she didn't. Because of who he was, what he'd done in his career, Donnie was given wide latitude in his investigations. Though his superiors would frown on it if they learned he'd slept with a woman involved in a case, it wasn't quite the taboo for him that it was for most undercover agents. But Donnie knew it wasn't a good idea, and sometimes it could jeopardize a case when it reached court.

He was usually more careful than he'd been during this investigation. He wasn't sure why he'd let his personal life become part of what was happening, didn't like to think he'd simply—

"Donnie?" Lily asked. "You still with me?"

"Still here," Donnie said, concentrating on the present. "Rafe is sure Luis Perez was a straight citizen," he said. "And he doesn't think Grace knew anything about her husband's business dealings. He told me Luis was the type who had his personal life walled off from everything else."

"You guys can be fooled by a woman like that," Lily said. She tried another bite of burrito, then pushed her plastic plate away in distaste and took a sip of soda through her straw. "It's fascinating to see reason overcome by biology."

"Maybe you're imagining that."

"Naw. Anyway, how would you know? What I'm talking about is sexual and Freudian in nature. What you don't even suspect is going on, because it's happening so deep inside your mind. The old id."

Donnie didn't want to talk about his id. Or about Grace. "You told me on the phone you thought you were being observed," he reminded Lily.

"Not now, though," she said. "I made sure I wasn't followed when I came here."

"I figured that," Donnie said. "Have you got any idea what you might have touched on that attracted attention and made somebody want to track your activities?"

"An idea, but nothing for sure. I think there's enough circumstantial evidence to build campaign financing fraud cases against a lot of state and local politicians. Remember I'm a journalist. My asking around about politics and money would be enough to make anyone involved uneasy."

"You might be getting close to hard evidence. Or to whatever else convinced somebody it was necessary to kill Marcia Dunn."

"That makes *me* uneasy," Lily said, "because it's only true if we're close to something much larger than campaign fund fraud. Hell, good attorneys can get that reduced to mismanagement. And if they can't, the client can blame the lawyers' bad advice for the crime and walk away with a rap on the knuckles instead of a prison sentence."

"There are usually better ways than murder to handle things if you've got an inventive mind," Donnie agreed.

"And lots of cash."

"What if you could link crooked political figures with the Mafia?"

"It wouldn't be a big story. The public accepts that people with power live together in the same small world. The kind of link you're talking about would have to be a photograph with a smoking gun in it. We should be so lucky."

A smoking gun and a body, Donnie thought. And maybe Marcia Dunn had been that *un*lucky.

A sudden breeze blustered in over the water, making the slack fabric of the table's umbrella snap taut like a sail. Donnie sipped soda and enjoyed the cool play of air on his face and bare arms. "What about Jason Cohan? How deeply is he involved in the political fraud?"

"Up to his handsome eyeballs. But that's not to say there's any proof."

Donnie knew the Bureau had to be sure before arresting anyone like Cohan. More often than not, guys like him simply sidestepped trouble and kept on operating.

"Cohan's tied in with whatever's going down in Belle Maurita," Donnie said. "So maybe there's a strong link between that and the political corruption."

"Maybe." She brushed a strand of hair from her eyes. "From what I hear, you've got a few of the other kind of missing links to deal with in Belle Maurita."

Donnie had finished his burrito. Now he eyed Lily's, lying on its red plastic plate with only a few bites out of it. "You going to eat that?" he asked.

"Are you kidding? It's yours." She slid the plate across the table so it was in front of him.

"I've got the feeling things are going to break soon," he said, "then people'll start talking to save their asses. We'll find out everything." He took a large bite of the burrito and chewed.

"The people who killed Agent Dunn and maybe Luis Perez aren't the sort who'll roll right over and expose their throats," Lily said. "There'll be a hell of a fight."

"I know. You ready for it when it comes?"

"I was born for it," Lily said without smiling.

Donnie ate a cheese fry and sat back in his unsteady white plastic chair, looking beyond Lily at the marina where the damaged pleasure boats were being repaired.

The pelicans lining the dock were now facing away from the boats and water, gazing morosely at him and Lily.

It was unnerving.

48

Before leaving town, Donnie checked in with Dona-von, who told him he was still awaiting a call on his extended search for information on Munz, Pinscher, and Pedro. Donavon said to phone him later from Belle Maurita, and there should be some word as to whether the search was successful.

After checking out of his motel, Donnie drove along the highway, then pulled off at the slight grade where Beach Lane branched toward the ocean.

He parked the Cherokee beneath palm trees disfigured by Blaze and gazed down at Grace Perez's cottage. There was no sign of Corcoran, but Donnie was sure he was around.

He thought about last night and Grace. And he thought about Ida Clayton. He smiled. If Ida knew about Grace, she probably wouldn't care. If Grace knew about Ida . . . different story, platonic relationship or not. Two widows. Maybe Lily was right about his id and something Freudian going on. Was it these women's proximity to death that on some level appealed to him? And did they sense in *him* a nearness to death that appealed to them? Maybe they were all like moths circling the same flame.

The cottage looked almost rebuilt, peaceful in the sun. Donnie thought if you cropped out the surrounding hurricane wreckage, the Chamber of Commerce could use a photo of the scene for its travel brochure.

A loud rapping on the window near his head startled him. He turned to see a large man with a tanned, weathered face and sandy hair peering into the Jeep at him.

Marishov?

Donnie tensed for action, then when he saw that the man was wearing work clothes, he recognized him. Corcoran.

Donnie lowered the window.

"I noticed you sitting here parked and wondered if I could help you with something," Corcoran said in a slow, friendly voice that didn't go with his wary blue eyes. His seamed features remained calm.

"I was just driving through and thought I'd stop and look over the hurricane damage," Donnie said. Apparently Corcoran saw a difference between parking next to the cottage and here, whatever he'd been told about Donnie. That was okay; Donnie wanted to see how the agent handled this.

"Driving through from where?" Corcoran asked.

"Miami. Headed for Atlanta."

"No kidding? I'm from Atlanta. What part of town you live in?"

Nicely done, Donnie thought. "Place called Buckhead."

Corcoran stepped back and his gaze danced over the Jeep. Buckhead was a wealthy area, and people there had four-wheel-drive vehicles as toys. Maybe Donnie was a rich guy with pull, one who could make trouble for Corcoran.

"Wasn't this Jeep parked down by the cottage yesterday evening?" Corcoran's voice was easy and casual to go with the almost uninterested expression that seemed stuck to his hard, broad face.

"This one or one like it," Donnie said. "Did you

notice the government seal on the door? There are lots of Jeeps like this running around Florida."

"What government agency you with?"

"The EPA."

"It figures," Corcoran said. "Hurricane like Blaze must play hell with the environment. But doesn't FEMA handle that kinda thing?"

Corcoran wouldn't let it go. Donnie was liking this guy more and more. That the Cherokee looked like the same vehicle didn't mean it was, or that it had the same driver. And when he was here earlier, Donnie had been too far away for Corcoran to know for sure he was the man who'd visited Grace.

Corcoran continued the charade but changed his role. He showed Donnie his badge and identified himself as an FBI agent. "We're keeping an eye on the beach in an effort to help the local police control looting," he said. "Would you please step out of the vehicle?"

Donnie didn't move, figuring he'd learned what he wanted and this had gone far enough. "Call Donavon," he said.

Corcoran frowned at him. "Donavon who?"

"Jules Donavon. Give him the license plate number of this Jeep."

"What are you trying to pass yourself off as?" Corcoran asked.

Donnie ignored the question. "You know who I am, or you would have been all over me the first time you saw me at the Perez cottage."

"I never saw you close-up," Corcoran said in his easy, confident tone, keeping his guard up. "Can't be too sure of things around here."

"Call Donavon and he'll give you an exact description of who I'm supposed to be."

"Put your hands on the ten and two o'clock position on the steering wheel," Corcoran said.

When Donnie had obeyed the instruction, Corcoran walked a slow circle around the Jeep. He glanced down for less than a second and had the license number memorized. Donnie liked that. Then Corcoran pulled a cell phone from beneath his shirt and punched out a number by feel, all the while with his gaze trained on Donnie.

He talked for a while into the phone without averting his eyes, then he listened.

The expression on his face changed, softened.

Tucking the cell phone back beneath his shirt, he strode toward Donnie.

"I'm sorry," he said, looking in through the rolled-down window. "I thought it was you, but I didn't know for sure. Had to play it careful."

"How it oughta be played," Donnie said. "Is everything going all right here?"

"Yeah. The lady doesn't seem scared, even after getting shot at."

"She has a gun of her own," Donnie said.

"I know. I'm not crazy about the idea, but I wouldn't try talking her out of it."

"Best if she doesn't know I stopped by to check on her."

Corcoran nodded. "You got it."

Donnie put the Cherokee's shift lever into drive. "Be her guardian angel," he said.

"My assignment," Corcoran told him as he stepped back so Donnie could drive away.

And not an easy one, Donnie thought. Corcoran's duty was to take a bullet if necessary in order to save the person he was assigned to protect. And Donnie knew that if it came down to it, the outwardly placid, friendly man would do exactly that.

As he stomped the Cherokee's accelerator and sped along the sunny, mud-stained highway, he made a mental note to remember Corcoran.

49

Donnie stopped for a late supper on the highway and got into Belle Maurita when it was dark.

He hadn't slept long or well during the past two nights, and he knew how exhausted he was. But even through his weariness he was plagued by his growing unease, his gut feeling that soon pieces were going to fit together snugly and images would be clear—and would be ugly. So before lying down in his room at the Drop Inn, he wedged his revolver between the mattress and box springs. If necessary, he could reach it in a hurry. Donnie Pistol.

He fell into a deeper, longer sleep than any he'd experienced since being drugged during the poker game at Hoppy's.

When he awoke with a sour taste in his mouth and a throbbing headache, it was almost ten-thirty.

Donnie decided it was too late for his regular morning fishing expedition. He took his time showering and dressing, slipping into khaki pants, a red pullover shirt, and Nike cross-trainers. Then he drove toward town for a late breakfast or early lunch, whatever the White Flame was serving.

The road to Belle Maurita seemed to get rougher each time he drove it, as if it would soon degenerate into simply another graveled, rutted side road on its way to nowhere other than being reclaimed by nature. But the Cherokee growled along over the bumps and cracks with gusto. The swamp was a stark contrast of lush greens and black shadows. Though it was a primal killing arena, it was also a place of mystery and seductive beauty. Only creatures that had been born to it knew its reality and never let down their guards.

Donnie didn't see Ida in the restaurant. Or hardly anyone else, for that matter. Only three other customers—a bearded man and two very overweight women—were in the White Flame, seated together at one of the back tables. Faint shadows from an overhead paddle fan danced over them as they sipped coffee and talked.

When Donnie sat down in one of the booths, Blanche Dumain waited on him. He asked where Ida was today.

"Called in sick this morning," Blanche said. "Made plenty of extra work for me an' Cookie at breakfast time."

"What's wrong with her?" Donnie asked.

"Didn't say. Like you didn't say what you wanna eat. Here for breakfast or lunch?"

"You serving both?"

"You betcha. This time of day we can change breakfast just a little bit, and we got us lunch. Eggs we already broke become omelets, pancakes become crepes, an' the bacon's good for BLTs."

"Some of those eggs could become quiche," Donnie suggested.

She looked at him in disbelief. "We ain't got much call around here for quiche. You're jokin', right?"

"Uh-huh."

He asked for a grilled cheese sandwich and a glass of iced tea.

*   *   *

When Donnie finished eating he walked down Cypress to Ida's trailer to see how she was feeling.

He knew when she came to the door that it wasn't good.

She was standing hunched over and in obvious pain. Her left eye was swollen, there was a gash on her forehead, bruises on her neck, and her nostrils were crested with blood. Her generous lips that usually looked slightly swollen were now incredibly puffed.

Donnie pushed his way inside and very gently held her. "What happened?"

"They came last night and beat on me," she said, her words dragging on her damaged lips.

"Did they . . . ?"

Ida looked up at him with reddened, moist eyes. "No, nothing like that. They wanted to get a point across."

Her speech was different in another way. He looked closer and saw that one of her front teeth had been broken in half to leave a jagged edge. "Who were they and what was their point?"

"You know who they were, Donnie."

"All three?"

"No, just Pinscher and Carl. They made it clear it was time for me to stop seeing you. I told them our relationship was strictly platonic. They laughed."

"Then they beat you?"

"Only Carl. Pinscher just watched and grinned. He liked watching a whole lot, I could tell." She held up her hands to show bruised and cut knuckles. "He 'specially liked it when I fought back. Carl mostly slapped my punches away or they bounced off his hard head. Then he hit me, choked me, and when I fell he started kicking me with those big boots of his with their pointed toes."

With steel under the leather, Donnie figured. Donavon had told him that was Carl's specialty, kicking people with his steel-toed boots.

"Did you see a doctor?" Donnie asked.

She nodded. "He told me I had cracked ribs and some bruised internal organs."

"Jesus! You oughta be in a hospital!"

"That's what the doc said. Maybe I'll check myself in over in Miami. Then maybe I'll stay in Miami."

"You'd leave Belle Maurita for good?"

"Yeah. They convinced me. Nothing's gonna change around here, Donnie. And they said if we didn't stop seeing each other, you were gonna be next. They said they'd take you into the swamp and lose you forever." She tried a smile but it hurt too much and she winced. "I know what forever means. After how Rod died, how do you think I'd feel if I knew you were dead in the swamp?"

"Ida—"

She put a cupped hand over his lips to quiet him. "I'm not only going because of you, Donnie. My staying here's become a waste of time. The corruption's so deep there's no way to get around or through it to the truth. Munz, the others, they're too strong. I know that now. In fact, I've known it for a long time but wouldn't admit it."

"Did you go to Chief Lattimer about what happened?"

She gave a hopeless little laugh that turned into a cough. "Yeah. He was real sympathetic, then he asked if there were any witnesses. Told me pressing charges would be useless, that Pinscher and Carl would have alibis all set up."

"The sad thing is, he's probably right," Donnie said. "He might even be part of their alibis."

She moved back away from him, a crooked, painful smile on her battered face. "Thanks for being you, Donnie."

"You don't have to leave Belle Maurita, Ida."

"Yeah, I do. And I will. I don't have much to take with me, and I've already got my car loaded."

He didn't know quite what to feel. Sympathy, rage, loss. All those things and more. The truth was he couldn't blame her for leaving. Maybe her timing was right.

"Where can I get in touch with you in Miami?" he asked.

She came to him and kissed him cautiously on the tip of his chin with her swollen lips. "I don't think you want to do that, Donnie. Those complications you mentioned. And we're sure to move beyond the platonic stage."

He wrapped her in his arms but didn't exert the slightest pressure. She felt small, light, so fragile. "Ah, Ida . . ."

She placed her palms on his shoulders and pushed gently away from him. "Ah, Donnie," she said with a resigned smile and without emotion. Almost mocking him. "Don't turn into a sop-headed romantic on me."

He shook his head. "I'm not too often accused of that."

"Only because you don't let people know you." She stared at him as if expecting him to say something. When he didn't, she said, "That's okay, Donnie, nobody's really who they say they are anyway." She reached out a hand and ran her fingertips over his cheek. "I sure hate melodramatic good-byes."

"That's something we have in common," he said, wondering if she had a lump in her throat as he did.

"Some platonic relationship," she said.

He nodded, unable to speak.

Time hung suspended the way it seems to do for things momentous and final, small things sometimes, when people sense direction and destiny being altered.

Then the trailer's air conditioner clicked on and the blower began to hum. Seconds and life started ticking away again.

Donnie had been holding his breath. He sighed. He reached out slowly and touched Ida's hair, then went to the door.

"Donnie . . ."

When he turned he saw that she was almost crying. But she wouldn't cry. Not Ida.

"It'd be a mistake," she said, "but if you still wanna look me up after some time has passed, Blanche'll know where I am."

He stood silently, held by her gaze, then he went out the door into the hot and glaring sun. A car or truck had passed recently and a layer of dust still hazed the air. It dulled his vision and he could feel the grit of it when he clenched his teeth.

Ida's battered face was a picture that wouldn't fade from his mind. Neither would the pained, defeated strains of her voice. His breathing was rapid, his heart was banging away, and there was a cold rage in his gut.

He knew what he wanted to do.

But he wondered if Donnie the EPA field agent would do it.

50

Yes, Donnie decided. The streetwise EPA field agent Donnie Banner would act on his rage.

Not as Donnie Brasco would, but he would act.

Within an hour after leaving Ida's trailer, he braked the Cherokee to a rocking halt outside the gate to Munz's compound. He climbed out of the Jeep, went to the razor-wire-topped gate, and tried to force it open, leaning his weight into it. The gate was in direct sunlight, and its steel surfaces were hot enough to burn Donnie's hands.

When the gate didn't budge, he stepped back, blowing on his palms.

"You don't wanna come on this side of the gate," a voice said in a Spanish accent.

Donnie turned to see Pedro standing in the shade of a cypress tree. He was holding one of the Ithaca 12-gauge shotguns he and the others carried. His thumb was hooked in his belt, and the Ithaca was slung in the crook of his arm and pointing at the ground. Donnie remembered the way Carl had blown the young alligator almost in half with one of the brutal lead slugs from his shotgun. Despite his seeming lethargy, Pedro could move just as fast. The shotgun could be raised, aimed, and fired at Donnie in an instant.

"I want to see Munz," Donnie said in a level voice.

Pedro's dark eyes were sad and sincere in his impassive face. "He's not here. Neither's Pinscher or Carl. I'm the only one."

"You shouldn't have beaten her up," Donnie said.

"I didn't. I thought it was a bad idea. Didn't make any difference to me if you and the bitch were knocking bones. What could it hurt?"

"Whose idea was it to give her a beating?"

Pedro shrugged, looking bored. "Who knows? Orders come down, we follow them."

"Down from where?"

Pedro smiled and shook his head. "You talk like the goddam IRS or them liberal social services spending all that tax money after the IRS steals it from the rest of us. Think you got a right to all the fuckin' answers. Well, you ain't even got a right to ask the questions."

"The order had to come from Munz."

"Then you should see Mr. Munz, talk to him. You seen yourself, he's a reasonable guy, didn't have your ass thrown in jail for trespassing. He'll listen to your complaint if he's got time. But you better calm down first. I was told to stay here because we knew you'd come around. Donnie Pistol's got himself a temper."

Donnie grabbed the gate again. Shook it.

"That's just what I mean," Pedro said. "Look at yourself, poor dumb fucker."

"I could drive my Jeep right through this damned gate," Donnie said.

"That'd be cool."

Donnie did some deep breathing and pretended to calm down from his pretended rage. It was difficult. All that pretending wasn't entirely make-believe.

Pedro regarded him impassively. "You come in here any way you want, Donnie Pistol. It won't make no difference to me. I'll shoot you in the head, put you deep in the swamp. Make you part of the envir-oh-ment. It don't take long. Part of you gets ate by this animal, part by another. You get shit out all over the place. Maybe show up in some of those tests like you make, huh?"

Donnie stared at Pedro.

Pedro stared back and smiled. "I don't care if you make trouble, bilateral fucker."

Donnie believed him.

"Tell Munz I'll be back to talk to him," Donnie said. He turned around and stomped toward the Jeep.

"You drive away and think about it," Pedro said behind him. "Is no bitch worth what's gonna happen to you if you come back here to make trouble for Mr. Munz."

Donnie didn't answer. He climbed into the Cherokee, slammed it into reverse, and gunned the engine. Gravel and dirt flew as he backed to a spot where he could turn the vehicle around without getting it stuck in the mud.

As he drove away, he glanced in the rearview mirror and through the dust saw Pedro standing motionless and grinning.

That was okay, Donnie figured, clenching his teeth in anger.

Donnie Banner was leaving.

Donnie Brasco would soon be coming back.

51

Before going to his motel room, Donnie drove up Highway 29 to Gas 'n' Snack and used the public phone to call Donavon. Standing in the hot sun, sweating and listening to the ringing on the other end of the line, he found himself getting furious again over what had been done to Ida.

When he finally got through to Donavon, he said, "They beat the shit out of her, scared her out of town."

"I guess you mean your friend Ida Clayton," Donavon said. "Calm down, Donnie. Who beat her?"

"Carl did the work with his boots. Pinscher watched and enjoyed."

"One reason they probably did it was to get a rise out of you, see how you'd react. You must have them puzzled. They suspect you're not who you claim to be, but they can't figure out who you are. They don't wanna kill you till they know for sure."

"They still don't know," Donnie said. "I drove out to Munz's place, but Pedro met me with a shotgun and said he was the only one there. I couldn't get inside."

"I guess Donnie the EPA guy would do that," Donavon said thoughtfully.

"I guess he did," Donnie said.

"Did Ida Clayton go where she'll be safe?"

"I think so."

Donavon breathed for a while into the phone. Then Donnie thought he heard paper rattling on the other end of the line, as if Donavon was frantically searching through his pockets for his notes. Donnie had seen him do it often and could picture it.

"Donnie, we got some information from Interpol on Munz, Pinscher, and Pedro."

Donnie stood up straighter in the hot sun. He no longer noticed the perspiration stinging the corners of his eyes, or the rivulets of sweat zigzagging down his ribs. "So tell me, Jules."

"Pedro is Jorge Castillo, a Cuban. He came to this country as a refugee six years ago, but when INS learned he had a record for burglary and assault, he was returned to Cuba."

"What about Munz?" Donnie asked impatiently.

"Raymond Munz, a German engineer who went to Cuba twenty years ago to help construct power plants, traveled back and forth between the two countries. Nine years ago he was charged in Germany with embezzlement. He paid the right people and was given asylum in Cuba. Since then, he has no police record but is known to have operated confidence games and handled stolen merchandise. Nothing violent. He's clever and mean, but he's small-time, Donnie."

Now Donnie was aware that he was sweating hard. He wiped perspiration from his eyes. "And Pinscher?"

"Also Cuban. His real name is Juan Picardia. He was educated at Orchinko University in Moscow. Has advanced degrees in psychology and chemistry and is bilingual. He was running a narcotics operation tied in with South American drug cartels, and he stayed in business and barely avoided imprisonment in Cuba by spreading money around in the right places. He's vicious, a killer."

"Only the last part sounds like the Pinscher I know," Donnie said. "Interpol must have made a mistake."

"It's always possible. Even *we* make mistakes."

"Tell me about it," Donnie said. "How does Interpol say the three of them got into the U.S.?"

"They didn't have them in this country at all. They were surprised. Far as Interpol knew, they were still in Cuba."

Donnie looked up at the sky so blue and bright it hurt his eyes. "I can't believe this."

"Mull it over, Donnie. In the meantime, Lily gave me a number where you can call her." Donavon passed on the number to Donnie, saying it once slowly and clearly and not repeating it. "She's made some progress figuring out that string of numbers that was on Agent Dunn's computer. Wants to talk with you about it."

"I'll talk to her soon as I hang up on you," Donnie said. He could hear the eagerness in his own voice.

"Before we can act, you've gotta make sense outa all this," Donavon said. "We need to know what to key on so we don't get misled."

"Chemistry," Donnie said. "You mentioned Pinscher has advanced knowledge of chemistry."

"I thought you'd perk up when you heard that."

"Or somebody Interpol thinks is Pinscher," Donnie amended. "Their description doesn't jive with the gorilla I know here in Belle Maurita."

"Maybe they've got two identities mixed up," Donavon said, "but don't you wonder who invented *salvaje*?"

Donnie tried to imagine Pinscher wearing a white coat and bending over a Bunsen burner. He said he wondered.

He hung up the phone still wondering.

52

When Donnie called Lily she answered immediately, as if she'd been anxiously waiting for her phone to ring.

"You were right," she said after Donnie had identified himself. "When you group them, the numbers on Agent Dunn's computer represent dates. I went with the idea they were publication dates and spent a lot of time viewing microfilm of various magazines and newspapers. I found a match this morning, then another. Once I had a few similar articles, I narrowed my search to their subject. There's no doubt about what the numbers refer to, but it still leaves us wondering why."

"All I've been doing lately is wondering," Donnie said.

"The dates match issues of *Miami Herald* news reports or editorials about a proposed referendum to legalize gambling in Florida."

Donnie was dumbfounded. "First we've got political corruption, then a drug operation, and now gambling."

"I don't know what to make of it, either. But one common thread is the Mafia. They're into all of the aforementioned in a big way. The gambling might be for laundering crooked political money. We could have something big there."

Plenty big enough for murder, Donnie thought. But nothing Lily had told him tripped his mental tumblers. If anything, the case had become more complex and baffling.

"Where's Governor Merchant stand on the gambling issue?" Donnie asked.

"According to what I've read, which right now seems like everything written on the subject, he hasn't taken a firm position. You know how politicians are—he's got his finger to the wind and wants to make sure he takes the popular stand."

"Anything about Jason Cohan in what you read?"

"Not that I can recall."

"Drugs, gambling, politics, the Mafia," Donnie said softly.

"Some unholy alliance," Lily said.

Which reminded Donnie. He related what he'd learned from Donavon about Munz, Pinscher, and Pedro.

"That clears up nothing," Lily said.

"Makes it murkier, in fact." He told her about Ida being beaten, and his trip to Munz's compound.

"Bastards!" Lily said. She held a particularly hard place in her heart for men who beat women. "Why would they want to do such a thing?"

"Donavon thinks they were trying to draw me out, see how I'd react."

"You reacted like any man with more guts than sense. You went out to Munz's place looking for revenge. Listen, Donnie, if they're to the point where they'd beat up a woman just to see your reaction, they're getting even more dangerous than they were. Probably the only reason they haven't simply killed you is they don't know exactly who or what you are and don't want to risk bringing lots of heat down on themselves."

"Probably," Donnie agreed. "If you come up with anything more, can I get in touch with you again at this number?"

"You should be able to. Or would you rather I called and left a message with your friend Ida? I'm assuming she's gonna be home for a while, after what happened."

"No," Donnie said. "That's out now. She's probably already left Belle Maurita. And don't leave a message at my motel, either. I'll get in touch with you later, but if you have something before then, get it to me through C.J."

"Okay," Lily said. "I'll still be looking through back issues of the *Miami Herald*, waiting for something to leap out at me and make everything understandable."

"Glance over your shoulder now and then," Donnie told her. "You're probably sitting right where Agent Dunn sat not long before she was killed."

"Sobering thought," Lily said, sounding not at all afraid.

"Sobering world," Donnie said, and hung up.

Dusk was starting to close in on the swamp that stretched in every direction from where Donnie stood. The automatic lights above the parking lot had flickered on. Headlights glowed on every third or fourth car that passed on the highway. The collective scream of insects was getting louder, and mosquitoes were out in force and thirsting for blood.

Donnie walked over to the grocery side of Gas 'n' Snack and bought a six-pack of lime-flavored bottled water. He sipped from one of the bottles as he drove to Hutch's Drop Inn, mulling over what Donavon and Lily had told him, finding no new meaning in any of it, but a lot more to wonder and worry over.

Whichever wise soul had defined life as a predicament, Donnie agreed with him.

In his room at the motel, Donnie lay in bed with his head propped on his pillow. Everything was so complicated it seemed impossible to make sense of it.

But he knew it wasn't impossible. He often had this feeling shortly before the picture became clear. The question was one of time. Donavon had the kind of operation going that would hold together only so long before one of the bad guys figured it out. Donnie was sure that was going to happen soon. Lily was right; the blatant way Pinscher and Carl had assaulted Ida Clayton meant his own time was running out.

It had grown dark in the room since he'd taken off his shirt, shoes, and socks and stretched out on the bed. The air conditioner wasn't winning its fight with the heat this evening, so he decided to strip down to his shorts. He got out of bed and padded barefoot to the closet, unbuttoning and unzipping his pants as he walked.

He stopped and stood still when his right foot stepped on something hard and metallic.

Donnie bent over and picked up a metal disk, then looked at it closely in the faint yellow light.

It was the bronze Aztec calendar he'd found on the closet shelf and slipped into a pocket of a different pair of pants days ago. It must have fallen out when he was undressing for bed or changing clothes.

As he stood staring at the Aztec calendar on the medallion, he heard again the cautioning Spanish voice: *Despacia.*

And suddenly Donnie understood. All of the elements meshed: Marcia Dunn's death. Iver LaBoyan. The razor-wired compound. The snarl of airboats in the swamp at night. The *Miami Herald* news items on the proposed gambling referendum. The poker game and his drugged drink and then the night with Ida. Hutch uncharacteristically cleaning up the motel the next morning. The attempt on Grace's life. Rod Clayton's ugly and mysterious death. Harvey Gould's interest in the beachfront property north of Palmville. And Luis Perez's death the night of the hurricane.

Fragments of a whole.

Clicking into place.

Grace, in more danger than she knew.

Probably there was no imminent danger, with Corcoran on watch. Yet the other agent, Tinker, had been shot and might easily have been killed. Grace would have been next.

Donnie was sure Luis Perez had been murdered because of what he knew and might have been about to share with a neighbor he thought was a journalist. Despite the wall Rafe had assured Donnie would have been built around Luis's business affairs, Grace might know something of what her husband had known.

Which would be too much to allow her to live.

Donnie slipped his shirt, socks, and shoes back on, tucked his revolver into his belt at the small of his back, and left the room. He jogged across the lot to where the Cherokee was parked, then scampered into the vehicle and started the engine.

The Jeep's tires made a loud grating noise on the gravel as he jockeyed it out of the motel lot and accelerated onto the highway.

Behind him, Hutch turned away from the office window and picked up the phone.

53

Donnie stopped only once on the drive to Palmville, at a small restaurant to buy a cup of black coffee to go. He had to stay awake at the wheel, keep the dark road from hypnotizing him, and it would be wise to have caffeine in him to keep him alert for whatever might happen before he'd have another chance to sleep.

Logic told him there was probably no reason to rush back to Palmville, that tomorrow would be soon enough and he should still be fast asleep in his motel room in Belle Maurita.

Instinct told him to drive faster.

On the turnoff to Beach Lane, he slowed his speed. He'd decided to park the Cherokee in the same spot he had the last time he was here, when Corcoran had approached and talked to him. It might be smart to observe the Perez cottage for a few minutes before blundering up to it and losing any advantage of surprise or needlessly frightening Grace, who was probably sleeping soundly and safely.

He killed the Jeep's lights and coasted onto the road's gravel shoulder, then steered for the deep, jagged shadow of the hurricane-maimed palm trees that had earlier concealed him from anyone down on the beach.

He had to brake hard and fast to keep from running into the dark sedan that was parked among the trees.

The car was situated to provide the driver a view of the cottage. And the driver appeared to be sitting and staring in that direction, so preoccupied that he hadn't heard the Jeep's approach.

Donnie had removed the bulbs in the Jeep's interior lighting, so it remained dark when he eased open the driver-side door and squeezed out. He stood still for a moment, staring at the black or dark blue sedan and the back of the driver's head. Then, his revolver held close against his right thigh, he moved silently toward the driver at an angle so the man would have to turn his head sharply to the left in order to catch a glimpse of him.

Since the sedan's engine and air conditioner weren't running, the windows were cranked all the way down to admit the ocean breeze. Which meant the driver could hear what was happening outside the car.

Donnie's right shoe crunched glass or a seashell beneath its sole. He couldn't be sure if he'd been heard, so he took the final three steps to the car in a smooth rush and held the revolver inches from the driver's head.

"Don't so much as twitch," he said in a tight voice. He thumbed back the gun's hammer so the man could hear the soft metallic clicking of the action.

The driver remained motionless.

Donnie edged around toward the front of the man. "Place your hands on the steering wheel where I can see them. Do it now."

The man didn't obey, leaving his hands resting casually in his lap.

With a start, Donnie recognized him. Corcoran. *Corcoran with a neat round hole in his forehead!*

The bullet's exit wound wasn't so neat. Now Donnie could see the dark splattering of blood on the car's light upholstery. Corcoran was staring intently straight ahead at the cottage, at the ocean, not seeing any of it.

Donnie reached out his free hand and felt the side of the dead agent's neck.

It was still warm.

Quickly Donnie moved away into the darkness.

Fear and a subdued, racing excitement kicked in along with his training. Alert now to every sound or movement around him, he kept the cocked revolver at the ready in his right hand as he made his way through the warm, moon-touched night.

Toward Grace's cottage.

54

Donnie had been approaching the cottage obliquely to lessen the chance he'd be seen through a window. But as he got nearer, he heard voices from down on the beach.

He angled to the south and saw three figures standing by the Perezes' damaged boat dock that extended as a pier into the sea.

When he heard what sounded like Grace's voice, he crouched low and moved toward the surf so he could use a pile of discarded lumber on the beach for cover and get closer to the figures without being seen.

As soon as he was positioned behind the stack of used lumber, he peered through a space between crossed boards and saw that there were three people standing near the dock: two men, and a woman who had to be Grace.

"There's a fast way and a slow way," the taller of the two men said in a lazy drawl, and Donnie recognized Carl's voice. The second man was too small to be Pinscher. Pedro, maybe.

Fast way and a slow way to do what? Donnie wondered.

He found out immediately.

Carl placed a leg behind Grace's calf and shoved

her to the ground. As she started to get up, he kicked
her in the thigh. Her leg went limp and she fell back.
He took careful aim and kicked her other thigh. Donnie saw one of her arms snake out and try to grab
his leg, but Carl laughed, backpedaled, then darted
forward and began kicking her harder and with
amazing rapidity, in the sides, on the arms. Then
he danced away and stood about five feet from her
motionless form. It all happened so suddenly Donnie
hadn't had a chance to react.

"Save her head for last," Pedro suggested. He
thought they were alone with Grace and wanted to
make this last as long as possible.

Carl nodded and raised a hand, as if he was out
of breath and didn't want to speak right now. Sadism
could be wearing. He got down on one knee to tie
one of his boot laces that had come undone during
the assault.

"Look out there!" Pedro yelled, and he leaped
toward Grace and grabbed something from her, then
flung it away into darkness. "Bitch had a gun."

"Waited too long to try an' use it," Carl said, still
working on his boot lace as if nothing had happened.

Donnie braced his right forearm on a length of
moldy lumber and took careful aim with his revolver. He wanted to shoot Carl, but Pedro was
nearer, standing, and was the better target.

He squeezed off a shot and heard Pedro yelp.

Donnie already had Carl's position diagrammed in
his mind. He moved the revolver to the right less
than an inch and squeezed the trigger again.

A bullet *whacked* into the lumber pile, and splinters
flew from a board near his right ear as his shots
were answered. Donnie dropped to the ground and
changed position. Muzzle flashes must have drawn
the return fire.

When he inched to the edge of the lumber pile and

peered back toward the dock, he saw movement on the damaged pier. Then a boat motor sputtered and roared.

He hadn't counted on them having come by boat. As he stood up, he saw the dark form of a small runabout speeding away from the dock, leaving a white *V* of churned water in the moonlight as it bucked over the waves. It was out of pistol range within seconds.

Donnie couldn't be sure if one or both men had gotten into the boat. Maybe Pedro was lying in shadow on the beach, dead or wounded.

Grace was still down and hadn't changed position.

Donnie had to take the chance he might be fired on. He broke from behind the stack of lumber and ran toward where she lay.

It took only half a dozen steps before he saw even in the faint light that she was alone. No other body lay near where she was curled in the fetal position by the dock.

When Donnie reached her he bent over her. She was breathing rapidly and sobbing in pain.

"They were going to kill me," she moaned in disbelief. Donnie knew the reaction. It seemed unbelievable and tremendously insulting that another human being would want to stamp the life out of you. Much more personal than you could believe until you were an intended victim.

"They're gone," he told her. "You're okay now, Grace."

"Donnie?"

"It's me."

"They were the same two men I saw outside the cottage the night of the hurricane."

"I know." He leaned closer and kissed her forehead, cool and dry in the night. "Lie still. I'll get help."

As he straightened up, he saw blood splatters, black against the ground in the moonlight. Maybe Grace's blood, maybe Pedro's. Possibly even Carl's. Donnie had no way of knowing if his second shot had found its target.

"You're not going nowheres, hoss," a drawling voice said.

Donnie whirled and saw Carl step out of the darkness. He was carrying one of the Ithaca shotguns and had it aimed squarely at Donnie's midsection. So it was only Pedro who'd sped away in the boat.

"Best toss that pistol out some ways from you," he said.

Donnie obeyed.

Then he heard shoes scuffing over sand, and another figure emerged from the night.

Jason Cohan.

While Carl was dressed for murder, in a dark T-shirt, jeans, and his pointed steel-toed boots, Cohan was dressed to kill but not take part in the action. He was obviously only going to observe the night's planned wet work and make sure it was done right. His tailored suit was dark but his shirt was white, with a diagonally striped tie. The shine on his black shoes gleamed in the dim moonlight.

"You got into something bigger than you thought, Mr. EPA man," Cohan said.

"Like hell he's from the EPA," Carl drawled. "Johnny Pistol, he's some kinda secret agent man. Gonna die now, along with sweet stuff, there." He moved the barrel of the shotgun in Grace's direction, then back toward Donnie. "You an' me gonna take a walk to the end of that pier. Get far enough out so the tide carries you away. Some shark gonna chew you up and shit you out. Have sweet stuff for dessert."

"Real estate," Donnie said.

Carl blinked. "Huh?"

"Pardon?" Cohan said.

"The murders of Luis Perez and his neighbor had nothing to do with drug smuggling. Real estate was the prize."

Cohan smiled. It made him look a little like a young Robert Goulet. "That's right. Munz said you were dangerous and bright. So you should understand the murders were necessary. Nothing more than business."

"But you I'm gonna also kill for pleasure," Carl drawled at Donnie.

"Our dead friend up there in the car," Cohan said casually, as if referring to a mutual slight acquaintance, "he had FBI identification on him. Are you FBI, too?"

"I fish and analyze water," Donnie said. "But you plan on killing three people here tonight, and you already killed two others. What makes a piece of land so valuable?"

Donnie recognized the look on Cohan's face. Gloating. Ego gone wild and with a compulsion to advertise. Cohan couldn't stop himself from bragging any more than an alcoholic could resist a longed-for drink, especially if he was bragging to a man who wasn't going to tell anyone what he'd said.

He tried to stop smiling but couldn't quite control his facial muscles. "There's a secret consortium of high-ranking Cuban officials in league with the Mafia and Central American drug cartels. With my help, they're laying the groundwork for controlling future gambling in Florida after the inevitable normalization of relations between the U.S. and Cuba."

"The Eagle Consortium," Donnie said.

"Exactly. And they know precisely where they want to build, on the land brokered by Luis Perez and sought now for similar reasons by Harvey Gould."

"And the consortium needs corrupt Florida officials to make it work."

"Like-minded cooperative souls," Cohan corrected. "The consortium needs influential people on its side to get a gambling referendum on the ballot and get it passed, and they're in the process of gaining leverage on those people in whatever way possible. You can see how monumental this is. Our projections indicate that once Cuba's an open country, and with the consortium preventing casinos from operating there, Florida will be the gaming capital of the Latin world. So the stakes in the game you inadvertently became part of are immense."

"So's your gamble," Donnie said.

"But it's a gamble we're going to win, because we'll do whatever's necessary. Luis Perez figured out what was happening and had to be killed. And he was heard phoning the journalist Marcia Graham, who also had to be killed in order to keep her from spreading information about the operation. Only Hurricane Blaze, then the presence of the handyman Rafe, delayed Grace Perez's execution."

Grace raised herself up on one elbow. "Luis told me nothing," she groaned.

Carl casually slammed her in the head with the stock of his shotgun, and she fell back.

Then he pointed the gun at Donnie. "Time to take a walk, Donnie Pistol. We're goin' out to the end of the pier. Soon it'll all be over an' the tide and the fishes'll have you."

"Just do what we came for," Cohan told Carl. He was crisp and businesslike now, his few minutes of self-indulgence past. Time was money again. Everything was money. "Him first, then her. I'll keep an eye on her."

Carl sneered. "She's hurtin' bad. She ain't goin' nowheres on them legs."

"I'll watch her anyway," Cohan said.

Carl jabbed Donnie hard in the ribs with the shotgun barrel. "You heard, Donnie Pistol. Now we gonna walk the walk."

He prodded with the shotgun again.

Donnie glanced down at Grace, who was lying facing away from him with her hands pressed to the sides of her head.

Then he walked ahead of Carl, out onto the swaying, damaged pier that creaked with every step.

An unsteady last mile for the condemned.

55

Donnie felt the splintered boards give and sway beneath him as he walked slowly toward the end of the pier. Ahead of him the vast Atlantic lay dark as eternity. He tasted the old-metal acid of fear, and a coldness spread in his stomach that made it almost impossible to walk. He had to fight it! Had to hope!

He tried to keep his body loose and ready as he gradually slowed his pace. He had his eye on a broken section of railing and had to time it so his last desperate chance was possible. And at that he'd have to rely on luck. Carl would have to cooperate, and Carl wasn't an amateur.

But Carl assumed he, Donnie, was an amateur. He might not be an EPA field agent as he claimed, but Carl wouldn't suspect who he actually was, or what skills he possessed. So maybe seven would come up on the dice, four aces would be dealt, the fifty-to-one shot would win by a nose. Maybe Carl would get careless. For an instant.

As they approached the broken railing, Donnie slowed almost to a stop, as if he were having difficulty keeping his balance on the swaying dock. He tensed his body without changing its outward bearing.

And Carl cooperated.

He impatiently prodded Donnie in the small of the back with the shotgun barrel to speed him up. Donnie knew precisely where the barrel was, and it was in so close that if he moved fast enough he might knock it to the side before Carl had a chance to react and squeeze the trigger.

That was the theory, how the move was taught.

Donnie abruptly jerked his body and his arm around, feeling his forearm strike the shotgun barrel. The gun roared. He didn't know if he'd been shot.

But he was grappling now with Carl, shoving him toward the broken rail. Donnie only had time to realize he'd swept the shotgun barrel far enough to the side as he'd spun away, and the deadly slug had missed him, before he felt the railing give way. He sucked in air as, locked together, he and Carl dropped from the dock into deep water.

On impact with the sea, they separated. Then Donnie felt one of Carl's hands grab his wrist. Carl's other hand gripped the same arm, farther up. So Carl had dropped the gun. Donnie wrenched his arm free, and the two men sank near each other into darkness. Donnie pressed his legs together and pushed upward with both hands, accelerating his descent. He'd been prepared for the drop and had taken a deep breath. Carl had reacted instinctively to the plunge from the dock and shouted in surprise, leaving little air in his lungs.

Donnie groped around over his head with both hands and found one of Carl's ankles. He knew he should be able to outlast Carl underwater.

Carl realized the strategy instantly and began kicking at Donnie's hand with his free leg. That gave Donnie a chance to grab the pants cuff of that leg and hang on.

Now Carl was struggling desperately, running out of oxygen. Donnie held both of Carl's ankles locked beneath his left arm, felt the laces of the steel-toed boots with his right hand, and worked to untie them. He recalled his mistake of swimming with his boots on when he'd pursued Grace into the ocean. He would have drowned if Grace hadn't changed her mind about dying and saved him.

But Carl had Donnie to help him instead of Grace. And Donnie wasn't in a helpful mood.

Carl tried to jackknife his lean body and get at Donnie with his hands. Donnie took time out from trying to untie the boots and paddled downward again with his free hand, making reaching him impossible. He didn't want Carl to break loose and get his head above water even for a few seconds to draw a breath.

Finally he managed to untie both boots, then he looped the loose laces from left and right boots together in a knot and yanked them tight.

Tying someone's shoelaces together was an old practical joke, but not this time. Donnie held on to the laces firmly with one hand and forced himself and the writhing Carl deeper with the other, working his legs in reverse froglike kicks.

Carl was writhing so powerfully now that Donnie had to stop paddling and hold on to the soaked laces with both hands, feeling them dig painfully into his fingers. He felt himself running out of oxygen and knew Carl had to feel the same heavy pain in his chest, the same unresponsiveness in his muscles. Only more so, Donnie prayed. More so.

Donnie simply held on to the laces now and conserved his air, letting his body swing back and forth with the rhythm of Carl's agonized writhing, acting the sea anchor to whatever buoyancy Carl might muster.

Carl's fierce struggle to rise worked, but not fast enough.

When they were still several feet beneath the surface, the struggle ceased and his body became still and limp. Donnie looked up and saw an arc of bubbles trail like a bright string of pearls from Carl's slack mouth and drift toward the moonlit world above the sea.

Donnie released his grip on the knotted laces and let Carl's body drift away.

Then he paddled and kicked hard, straight upward.

When his head and shoulders broke the surface, he gasped, pulling precious air deep into his lungs, and rolled onto his back. His right hand, still stinging from where the laces had dug into its flesh, made contact with the slick, deep-textured curvature of one of the dock's stanchions. He used its solidity to push himself toward shore, staying below the dock and moving from one wooden pillar to the next.

When he finally pulled himself onto the beach, he saw Grace sitting up, still holding her head with both hands.

Cohan was gone. As if he'd never been there. Donnie knew the wily pol would say exactly that, that he was somewhere else on this warm Florida night. And probably he'd be able to prove it with a concocted alibi.

Half crawling, half walking, Donnie made his way over to Grace.

"S'okay," he said, slumping down beside her. He threw back his head and drew air into his lungs.

For several minutes the rasping hiss of his fight for oxygen, and the slap and rush of the surf, were the only sounds.

Again he thought about the last time he and Grace had slumped in pain on the beach, miraculously together on firm ground. Sweetly and wonderfully alive only as people could be after a recent game with death.

"Where's the other one?" Grace asked.

"Dead. Drowned. Dumb-fuck went swimming with his boots on."

Donnie was breathing okay now. The sibilant *shushing* of the surf had the night to itself.

"God, I hurt!" Grace moaned.

Donnie lowered his head and looked over at her. She was pressing her palms against her temples, staring down at her crossed legs.

"Don't try to move, Grace. I'm going up to the cottage and call for help."

"The other man ran. Just disappeared like a ghost in the dark."

"I know."

"The scumbag!"

Donnie was glad to know she still had fight in her. He worked his body into a stooped position, then managed to get to his feet. "You'll be okay, Grace . . . It's over."

But as he stumbled up the beach toward the cottage's lighted windows and felt himself regaining strength, he knew it wasn't over.

It wasn't nearly over.

56

Donnie's first phone call in the cottage was to 911 to summon help for Grace.

His second was to Donavon.

Donnie followed the ambulance that carried Grace to Johnson Memorial Hospital. Donavon had used his influence and she didn't have long to wait before being wheeled to an examination room.

For half an hour Donnie sat in a cool vinyl chair and watched doctors and nurses come and go with their brisk strides and preoccupied expressions. Once he stood up and went to the curtained examination cubicle where Grace's injuries from the beating were being assessed. He caught a glimpse of bright blood and a web of glistening thread against flesh before a dark-haired nurse noticed him and shooed him away.

Only when he'd learned the extent of Grace's injuries, and that they weren't life-threatening, did he leave the hospital and drive fast toward Belle Maurita.

The rendezvous point was Hutch's Drop Inn. When Donnie pulled into the parking lot at 2:10 A.M., everything appeared normal except that there were three cars parked at wide intervals before doors to downstairs rooms. A rush of business for Hutch's.

Donnie parked the Cherokee near the door to his own room and climbed out. But instead of entering the room, he walked across the dark, deserted lot to the office, marveling at the lack of indication of what he knew was true. Only the three cars. But those who hadn't been guests at the motel wouldn't see anything unusual in that.

The night was quiet except for the insect drone of the surrounding swamp and his own crunching footsteps. The motel didn't look any more like the staging area for an FBI operation than it did a jumping-off point for illegal immigrants.

When he tried the office door he found it unlocked. He entered and stood before the old mahogany counter. The office seemed as deserted as the parking lot. The low coffee table off to the side of the registration desk had the same ancient *Popular Science* on it that had been there when Donnie first arrived in Belle Maurita. He remembered the promise on the cover that inside were easy-to-follow plans to build a hi-fi record player. On the wall was the same 1967 calendar with the pinup who'd tried her hand at casting only to hook and somehow remove the top of her sun suit. It was still June. The pinup was still sexily distraught, pursing her lips and looking off to the side for help.

The door behind the desk opened, but Hutch didn't emerge. Donavon did. He was dressed in black except for the orange "FBI" lettered on the back of his bulletproof vest.

"Hutch give you any trouble?" Donnie asked.

Donavon smiled. "Nope. He threw a fit like a two-year-old at first, then he went along quietly. He's in a holdover cell in the Belle Maurita police station, along with Chief Lattimer."

Donnie was impressed. "You tied Lattimer into things in a hurry."

"Hutch did it for us," Donavon said. "Old bastard dangled enough bait to get the promise of a deal if he ratted out some of his cohorts and described the operation. Members of the consortium and their henchmen are smuggled into the country near Belle Maurita. That's Munz's job."

"With Hutch's help," Donnie said, recalling the Spanish medallion he'd found on the back of the closet shelf, the Spanish spoken in the airboat that night in the swamp.

"This motel's the staging area for the trip north," Donavon said. "The illegals are from Central America and Mexico, and sometimes from Havana. Ships bring them from Cape Catoche in Mexico to rendezvous points in the Ten Thousand Islands off the Florida coast, then they're transferred to airboats and transported through the Everglades to Belle Maurita. From that point, they're driven north into other areas of Florida or east to Miami, where the Mafia provides phony identities, helps to get them assimilated into society, and they work to build and fortify the foundation for their future gambling empire."

"Hutch give you any other names?"

"No, but he will. Lattimer was only the first, as a gesture of good faith, Hutch said. He won't give us any more till he's conferred with his attorney."

"The others won't be so easy," Donnie said.

"We're ready for them. Your team's concealed in motel rooms, along with a SWAT team from the Bureau's Miami office."

"SWAT team been briefed?"

"While they were on their way here. They look good, as if they know their business and like it."

"I hope they like it tonight," Donnie said.

"Since you were delayed, I laid out the operation. We're going to block the road out of Munz's compound, then go in quietly. We should be able to catch them asleep."

"Imaginative," Donnie said.

"It'll work, and we won't have to use planes and tanks." Donavon bent down, straightened up, and laid a shoulder-fired Heckler and Koch MP5 automatic weapon with extra clips on the counter. Then he tossed Donnie a package containing black clothing and an FBI-marked vest like the one he was wearing. "Soon as you change clothes, I'll pick up the phone and we can roll."

"Who do you have to call?" Donnie asked.

"Florida Highway Patrol. They're supplying a chopper to light the area after we've gotten in and signaled them. It's gotta be in the air already to get there fast, in case something goes wrong and there's a pursuit."

"Something'll go wrong," Donnie said. "It's that kinda party, and we're hitting too fast to know much about it other than what I've told you."

"We've already located the razor wire and cut through it," Donavon said.

"There's bound to be other security. Maybe even a sentry."

"Sentries we can deal with. And if an alarm sounds, we go in double-fast."

"Some plan."

"It's what time permits. And the SWAT guys want to keep it simple. They say it's the best way, in swampy terrain like this at night."

Donnie knew the Miami people were right. Also knew that someone was probably going to get hurt or killed in a very short while.

As he was pressing on his vest's Velcro fasteners, Donavon was picking up the phone.

57

Donnie drove the Cherokee with Donavon up front in the passenger seat, Rafe, C.J., and Lily in back.

"The plan's to get in close," Donavon was saying. "The SWAT team will fire a diversionary device into the main house, then we'll all go in fast. You and your team will approach from the rear and enter that way."

Donnie knew the diversionary device would be a flash-bang grenade that made tremendous noise but didn't do much damage. They were used to disorient and momentarily paralyze an apartment's or house's occupants so that in those few valuable seconds SWAT team members could storm in without being fired on. Usually.

When they were less than a quarter of a mile from the wire-topped steel gate, Donavon raised his hand, and Donnie braked the Cherokee slowly to a halt on the road's soft shoulder. The two vehicles behind it also pulled to the side and stopped. They'd been driving with their lights out. Now Donavon didn't want engine noise to reach the compound and announce their arrival.

When everyone had gotten out of their vehicles, a tall SWAT guy walked over to where Donnie and Donavon stood.

Donavon introduced him to Donnie as Hearn, the commander of the SWAT team, and they shook hands.

"Your people ready?" Hearn asked Donavon. He was about forty, with finely chiseled features and hooded blue eyes, and looked like he should be playing Patton in a movie.

"You bet," Donavon said. "Just give us a few minutes head start so we can get in position."

Donnie looked at Donavon, but he didn't look back.

"Okay, let's do it," Hearn said, sounding enthusiastic.

He turned around and swaggered back to where his people waited. There were about ten of them. They wore dark uniforms with helmets and were bulked up with gear and FBI-lettered bulletproof vests like the ones worn by Donavon and Donnie's team. Their baggy pants were tucked into their boot tops paratroop fashion. They carried their stubby MP5 automatic weapons as casually as if they'd been introduced to them while infants in their cribs. They looked dangerous.

Donnie said to Donavon, "It would be convenient if you briefed me."

"I was getting around to it," Donavon said. "Rafe can lead you to where the razor wire's breached. You circle around and go in with your team, rush the house when the flash-bang grenade goes boom."

Donnie looked at his three team members, all in black outfits not unlike the SWAT team's. Rafe and Lily had lampblack smeared on their faces. It made them look as dangerous as the SWAT team, and a little crazy. That was pretty much the way it was, Donnie thought.

He cradled his automatic weapon. "Lead on," he

said to Rafe, who was grinning like a maniac, up for anything.

"Do it right," Donavon urged as the E.O. Squad spread out and faded into the dark swamp.

Rafe said nothing as he slogged through the knee-deep water. He knew precisely where he was going, all right. Donnie figured Donavon had sent him to scout the area and locate the wire as soon as the squad had arrived in Belle Maurita.

When they were close to the compound, Rafe slowed, then stood still. He looked at Donnie in the moonlight and motioned with his arm. Donnie took the lead as the squad waded through the breach in the razor wire.

Donnie knew the way now. He motioned for everyone to stay low and be as silent as possible, then he led them toward the back of the main house, which he knew would soon be visible through the trees. He picked up the pace a bit. They had to be in position, not only waiting but ready in every way, prepared to kill or to die, when the SWAT team fired its flash-bang grenade and there would be sudden hell.

A hundred feet from the rear of the house, Donnie stopped the advance. He pointed at C.J., then toward a window. C.J. ducked low and moved silently up to it, then pressed himself close to the wall alongside it. The ground was built up slightly there, but because of the house being up on pillars, the window-sill was about even with his chest. Donnie pointed to a second window, and Lily made her way to it, almost invisible except for the bright orange "FBI" on her back. There was a rear door to the house. Donnie waved his hand, and he and Rafe moved toward the wood steps leading up to a small porch. As soon as the grenade shattered the dark silence of the swamp, the E.O. Squad would burst into the house from the rear while the SWAT unit stormed in through the front.

Donnie felt his heart whamming away inside the snug vest as he waited. A mosquito lit on the back of his hand, but he ignored it. The only thing on his mind now was what was about to happen. The trick was to have the scenario laid out in your mind, follow it, but be ready to change it instantly as the situation demanded. He was intent. He was ready.

The barking explosion from inside the house made the ground shake and sent a charge of pain through Donnie's ears. Then he could hear the SWAT team yelling to further confuse the house's occupants as the front door was battered down and men and weaponry poured in.

Donnie was already up the back-porch stairs, feeling Rafe close behind him. When Donnie kicked the door open, Rafe flashed past him and was inside.

Automatic weapons fire sounded, picked up, and became deafening. This wasn't good, but it was no surprise.

Donnie was in what looked like a dark kitchen. He spun in a circle, weapon aimed straight ahead like a compass needle in a magnetic field, clearing the room to make sure he was alone. Then he made for the next room, keeping in mind that Rafe was ahead of him.

There was another burst of gunfire. More yelling. In Spanish. The acrid stench of discharged rounds and the diversionary device was heavy in the air.

Donnie tensed himself to burst into the next dim room.

"Me, Donnie!" a voice said behind him. A hand touched his shoulder lightly. "It's Lily."

Donnie nodded without looking back. Then he went.

There was a body on the Oriental carpet in this

room. A man wearing only white shorts. Five feet away from the man a shotgun lay on the floor. Donnie stooped, felt no pulse in the man's neck, and moved on.

A door crashed open to his left, bouncing off the wall, and a figure in white shorts and a sleeveless undershirt bolted out screaming and spinning in tight circles as he fired an automatic weapon. Donnie hit the carpet and returned fire. Heard Lily do the same. The man from the closet crumpled and went down fast and hard, as if he'd been running on electricity and his switch had been thrown. Donnie pumped more rounds into him, doing no favors and taking no chances.

"You okay?" he asked Lily.

"Hit in the arm," she said through clenched teeth. He could tell she was in tremendous pain.

"Pull out," Donnie told her. His voice was higher than normal.

"Fuck you," she said.

She tried to rush past him, a 9mm in her left hand.

"Me first," he told her, blocking her way.

They were about to clear the next room when there were half a dozen shots from a handgun or rifle.

Then silence.

"All right!" a frightened voice shouted. "Be cool now!"

Donnie couldn't be sure if it was a SWAT unit member or one of the bad guys.

"Goddam arms behind you!" another voice said.

And lights began to flick on in the front of the house.

Donnie and Lily cautiously advanced. Donnie became aware of a fluttering roar overhead. The Highway Patrol chopper. Outside the house the grounds were suddenly bathed in brilliant light. There were

more shots. Everyone in the house flinched and
ducked low before realizing the gunfire was outside.

Then one of the SWAT unit guys glanced out a
window and nodded grimly.

"She's been hit," Donnie said, holding Lily and
looking at the nasty hole in her left forearm.

"Just now?" the man at the window asked.

"Earlier."

Now Lily stared down at the bullet wound.
"Couldn't have hit the damned vest," she said.

"Mighta gone through it," a SWAT guy with blood
on his uniform told her. "We got help for her out
here." And he gently took Lily from Donnie and led
her out through the front door.

"You okay?" Rafe asked in a breathless voice, suddenly appearing beside Donnie.

"Haven't explored all my parts," Donnie said, "but
I think so."

"Me, too. Charmed life."

Donnie saw Hearn across the room and walked
toward him. When he passed the doorway to an ad-
joining room and glanced in, he saw a shaken Munz
standing in his underwear with his wrists cuffed behind him.

"That one's Munz," he said to Hearn, pointing into
the room.

The two of them went in together. Munz looked
at Donnie, then looked away. The expression on his
fleshy face was one of pained tolerance, as if he were
merely irritated that his sleep had been disturbed.

"Says he wants an attorney," a young SWAT member guarding Munz said.

"Gonna need one bad," Hearn said. He looked
over at Donnie. "They tell me the entire house is
clear now. Let's see what we got."

Overhead, the sound of the helicopter faded. Apparently no one in the house had escaped to flee into the swamp.

Donnie and Hearn did a walk-through of the house. The man in the kitchen was dead. So was the one who'd burst from the closet and shot Lily. A Latin man with a long ponytail sat slumped against a wall, shot at least twice and bleeding heavily, while a SWAT unit member stood nearby with his bulky automatic weapon trained on him.

"Five's what we came up with," Hearn said. "Two dead, two wounded—assuming the one outside's still alive—and Munz, who wasn't hit."

"Something's wrong," Donnie said. "There's no Pinscher. And the other one, Pedro, would have had time to get back here just like I did if he's not hurt too bad."

"They must be up to mischief someplace else tonight," Hearn said. "Like over where you just came from in Palmville."

It made some sense, Donnie thought. Certainly as far as Pedro was concerned. And Pinscher could well be with him.

"Think we can get Munz to tell us where they are?"

Hearn shook his head. "You know those kingpin assholes. He's probably got some high-priced lawyer waiting by a phone twenty-four hours a day, ready to file an appeal even before he gets convicted." He looked more closely at Donnie with his hooded eyes. "I understand you guys are some kinda extra-special unit."

Donnie told him that was right.

"I can't let you touch Munz or the wounded one," Hearn said, "much as I'd like to."

Donnie smiled, knowing what Hearn was thinking. "We're not that kind of extra-special," he said.

Hearn returned the smile. "Good. You'd never know it to look at you."

A sweaty, redheaded SWAT team member without a helmet came in and said, "The outbuildings are cleared, sir. And the man down outside is dead."

"Thanks, Andy." Hearn moved toward the front of the house. "Let's go out and see if the casualty's one of your missing bad guys," he said to Donnie.

But the dead man sprawled on his back near the storage building was plump and blond, wearing only pants and boots.

Donnie looked down at him and shook his head no. "Four men and Munz," Donnie said. "Munz is the only one of them I ever saw here."

"Maybe the others are only here when Munz's regular protectors are gone," Hearn suggested. "A big tamale like Munz wouldn't sleep well if he wasn't guarded."

True enough, Donnie thought. It might also explain how they'd so easily surprised the house's occupants. They were playing the second team.

Hearn wandered off, and Donnie caught a glimpse of luminous orange lettering on the back of a vest and saw Rafe looking around at the edge of the swamp beyond the storage building. Donnie went to join him.

As he approached, Rafe turned around to face him.

Only it wasn't Rafe.

The figure dressed in black with the bulletproof vest and FBI lettering on his back was Pedro.

And Donnie understood why the helicopter reported that no one had left the scene. The chopper's light would have picked up the luminous orange FBI lettering and counted Pedro, and probably Pinscher, among the good guys.

Pedro was holding his big Ithaca shotgun aimed at Donnie. He looked okay except for a blood-soaked bandana wrapped around his head where Donnie's shot in Palmville had clipped him.

"You guys think of everything," Donnie said.

Pedro spat off to the side, turning his head but not averting his eyes. "You don't know the half of it, Donnie Pistol. But we're gonna take a walk in the swamp and I'm gonna show you the rest."

Pedro waved the shotgun barrel as an instruction to Donnie to walk in front of him.

As they moved into the dark swamp, Donnie glanced back once at Pedro and beyond him at the lighted house and activity of the SWAT team tying loose ends after the operation. The night insects that had ceased making noise when the gunfire started were screaming their primitive, desperate messages again. Men's voices from outside the house drifted on the night, getting fainter.

Pedro gave Donnie a slow smile. In charge again. In total command. The Bilateral Commission squarely in his sights.

The blackness of the swamp enveloped them.

58

They'd walked a short distance when Donnie heard movement off to his left, and Pinscher stepped out from behind the knotted root system of a mangrove tree.

He was wearing dark clothes and an FBI bullet-proof vest like Donnie's and Pedro's. Also like Pedro, he was carrying a 12-gauge shotgun. Surprisingly, he didn't look particularly upset by the night's events.

"I ain't at all shocked to see you, Donnie Pistol," he said.

Donnie stared at him. He understood why Ida had noticed Cohan talking with Pinscher and not Munz. Why Munz had seemed so afraid of Pinscher. Interpol had it right.

"You can ease up on the yokel talk," Donnie told him. "I know who and what you are."

Pinscher smiled. "I knew you'd get to it eventually. Also assumed you were FBI. So we were prepared for what happened tonight."

"You're the one in charge of this end of the gambling consortium operation. Munz is only a figurehead."

"Exactly. His job was to draw attention away from me while I played my role of thug and acted freely." Pinscher's voice had changed in inflection but not in tone. Yet he seemed suddenly more refined, almost like someone else. An intelligent twin brother talking to Donnie. "So Munz and I were both acting. It worked well, didn't it?"

"He's also your cutoff," Donnie said.

"Right again, Donnie Pistol. He was to be a diversion if there was a raid on the compound. And that's precisely how it worked. The authorities think they have the big fish, so they're not overwrought about trying to catch up with me or Pedro."

Donnie nodded toward Pedro. "I suppose he's a Rhodes scholar."

Pinscher laughed, not his usual sadistic guffaw but a soft chuckle.

"Fuck you, Donnie Pistol," Pedro said sullenly.

"Pedro's much as he appears," Pinscher said. "A very capable but limited professional. Not unlike yourself."

Pedro smiled at Donnie.

"He's only being nice to you," Donnie said.

Pinscher moved closer. "It's time for us to take a walk now. I want to introduce you to someone you should meet."

He moved to Donnie's right and back a few steps, so he could trail him slightly. Pedro got behind Donnie and shoved him in the direction they were going to walk.

Toward the road.

When they reached the parked vehicles, Pinscher held his shotgun on Donnie while Pedro fished the keys from Donnie's pants pocket.

They climbed into the Cherokee, Pedro behind the steering wheel, Donnie in the passenger seat beside him. Pinscher sat in back, ready to send a poacher's slug through the seat and through Donnie if anything irregular happened.

Pedro crammed the Cherokee into reverse, got it

turned around, and they drove for a few miles before veering right on a narrow cutoff barely visible until you were almost upon it.

After driving another half mile over rough and rutted road, almost getting stuck a few times in low spots, Pedro parked the Cherokee at the edge of a clearing in the swamp.

Pedro got out of the Cherokee first, then held his shotgun on Donnie while Donnie and Pinscher climbed out.

"Get that FBI vest off you," Pedro said.

Donnie obeyed.

As the vest hit the ground, a man walked from shadow into moonlight. He was medium height, slender but with a gymnast's build, wearing jeans and a black T-shirt. His hair was cropped close and his face and arms were smeared with lampblack so that he was almost invisible in the dark swamp. In his right hand was a Russian AK-47 automatic weapon.

"Mr. Marishov, I presume," Donnie said, around the lump of terror in his throat.

Marishov's blackened features smiled, pale eyes and white teeth catching the moonlight. "Composure in the face of death," he said. "That's admirable even if it changes nothing."

He raised the AK-47 to firing position.

59

The automatic weapon spat a muted, staccato burst, and Pinscher and Pedro dropped facedown, dead before they had time to be surprised. Pinscher twitched once, and his hand trembled then was still.

"They knew me by another name," Marishov explained with a thin smile. "You killed them with a word."

"You killed them with a gun," Donnie said. "You're responsible."

"A moralist? In our line of work?"

"We're not in the same line of work."

"Not anymore," Marishov said.

And he moved the AK-47's barrel toward Donnie.

Donnie was beyond fear now, in a lonely place of sadness and surrender.

The shots chattered through the swamp.

Marishov's automatic weapon spun and dropped from his hands and he darted to the side like a deft shadow.

Donnie, alive again and acting on instinct a million years old, bolted for the cover of the swamp.

More automatic weapon fire, then the deeper booming of one of the big shotguns Marishov must have picked up from where Pinscher and Pedro had dropped them. The louder shot caused roosting night birds to flap startled into the dark sky.

Another single deafening shot, as something whizzed through the brush near Donnie, who was still trying to figure out what was happening.

Then he heard the grind and roar of the Cherokee starting, and he made his way back through shallow water and thick saw grass so he could peer toward the clearing.

The Jeep was pulling away, picking up speed.

A slight figure was standing at the edge of the trees, futilely aiming a stubby automatic weapon that apparently was jammed.

As the Jeep rocked and roared away without lights, the figure sprinted toward the two dead bodies and scooped up the remaining shotgun.

Another deafening shot hit nothing but caused more night bids to take wing in the following silence.

As Donnie walked into the clearing, Blondi turned toward him.

"Let's get that fucker!" she said.

She began running through the swamp, her long blond braids bouncing and swinging. Donnie stayed a few steps behind her, vines clutching at his ankles, branches scratching his face and arms. They could still hear the rumbling of the Cherokee's laboring engine. Blondi seemed to know where they were going.

There was another loud shot, but in the distance.

"C'mon!" Blondi muttered under her breath as they ran through the night. She was swinging the shotgun in her right hand like a machette to clear a path. *"C'mon, c'mon, c'mon!"* Donnie didn't know if she was urging him or herself to go faster.

When they reached the flat, dry surface of a road, she stopped, and he staggered up to stand alongside her. They were both breathing hard enough to be heard even over the screaming of the dark swamp. There was a pain under Donnie's right ribs, pulling him sideways, and he could barely swallow. The dust of the Jeep's recent passing still hung in the air, coating his sweating face and arms and leaving grit on his teeth.

A small Suzuki four-wheel-drive vehicle sat at the side of the road. Even in the faint light, it was obvious that its left front tire was flat and shredded.

The last shot they'd heard, Donnie realized. Marishov disabling the Suzuki so he couldn't be pursued.

"That thing got a cell phone in it?" Donnie asked.

Blondi looked at him and grinned, then ran to the chunky little vehicle and yanked open the door.

Then she turned back toward him with a disappointed look on her young, pale features.

"It used to have one," she said.

"He thinks well under pressure, doesn't he?"

"Admirable," she said, slamming the Suzuki's door.

"That's what he said about me a little while ago. 'Admirable.'"

"Well, you two can admire each other while I puke. I almost had the fucker!"

"You saved my life," Donnie said. "How'd you get here?"

"Followed Marishov. I picked up his trail in Fort Lauderdale, tracked him here, lost him, found him, followed him into the swamp."

"Just in time," Donnie said.

"That's a Sinatra song," she told him.

"I wish I knew how to thank you."

"Change that tire," she said.

60

"**M**unz will tell everything he knows to save his neck," Donavon told Donnie.

He and Donnie had finished breakfast and were sitting over coffee at a back table in the White Flame. It had taken a while to sort through the results of last night's operation. Agents were in fact still searching the compound and Hutch's Drop Inn.

It was almost ten o'clock, so there were only a few other customers in the restaurant, and no one within earshot of Donnie and Donavon.

A young woman who looked nothing like Ida had waited on them, spilling the cream when she placed it on the table, learning the job and still awkward.

"What about Cohan?" Donnie asked.

Donavon smiled and shook his head. "He was at a charity event in Panama City the night Grace Perez was beaten and you drowned Carl. Witnesses will swear to it."

"Will prosecutors be able to tie him in with the Mafia and gambling consortium?"

"Doubtful," Donavon said. "But it's also doubtful a gambling referendum will pass in Florida unless there are safeguards against corruption. And the Cuban government will be hard on its budding capitalists. The best bet to get Cohan might be in the political contributions scam, but he's probably covered himself there, too. He'll probably be running for governor someday."

"Then watch out," Donnie said.

"Then we might have to come back here." Donavon sipped his coffee, then held the cup out and regarded it. "Is this a local brand? It tastes like swamp water."

"I've tested the water," Donnie said. "It's okay." He wished Donavon would stay on the subject. It was like him after an operation to unwind by putting it out of his mind and talking about trivialities. Everyone dealt with the letdown differently. Donnie couldn't turn loose of things that easily. Sometimes not easily at all.

"The Bureau techs finally got the yellow Paintbrush code broken down," Donavon said. "What Pinscher told you is the way it was—he was top man in Belle Maurita from the beginning."

"Was 'Jake' Iver LaBoyan?"

"That's something we'll probably never know for sure. But LaBoyan was with Immigration before he changed jobs, so he might have had the goods to expose the operation. I'm satisfied he was Agent Dunn's source."

So was Donnie. "That Blondi's quite an operation," he said. "Did she do anything that might blow her cover?"

"No," Donavon said. "And Marishov didn't get a good look at her during the shootout in the swamp. So she's still somebody else, back in Miami, doing what you used to do."

"I hope she doesn't have to do it as long."

"Don't worry too much about her. She's trained and tough, like Lily."

"How is Lily?"

"She's gonna be okay, but it'll take her six months

to regain full range of motion in her arm." Donavon looked around. "I wonder sometimes how places like this, in these little towns, stay in business. You know, my first wife and I used to talk about opening a restaurant."

Come back, Donnie thought.

Donavon sipped his coffee again and made a face as if he were about to spit. "What about our civilian woman, Grace?"

"Doctor says she'll be fine. She has a concussion, three broken ribs, external and internal bruises."

"Doesn't sound fine."

"It'll take a while, like with Lily."

Donavon finished his coffee and slid his chair back away from the table. "Time for me to get busy. I'll be putting together the paperwork on this operation for the next two weeks, while you get time off to relax somewhere and recharge your batteries."

"At least you didn't get shot at," Donnie said.

Donavon smiled as he stood up. "There is that. There's also Marishov, Donnie. Your Jeep was found in the swamp with gas in the tank, so he's no doubt got other transportation and made it out of the area. He'll take time to regroup, but someday he'll come for you again."

"I don't need reminding."

Donavon ignored the check the new waitress had laid in a puddle of cream on the table. "Let me know where you light, Donnie. I might need to talk with you about details."

"Okay, Jules."

Donavon paused. "You and the rest of the squad, you did a helluva job."

"Thanks, Jules."

Donnie sat for a while after Donavon had left, sipping a second cup of coffee. Then he paid for breakfast at the cash register and told Blanche Dumain good-bye. She came around from behind the counter, hugged him, and handed him a folded slip of paper. He knew what was on it.

He got in the rental Chevrolet the Bureau had given him to replace the Cherokee, then drove through Belle Maurita for what he hoped was the last time. The few people on the sun-drenched sidewalks gawked at him with open suspicion, as they had when he'd first arrived. They hadn't trusted a stranger. They'd been right about him.

Donnie drove north on Highway 29, then east over the Everglades Parkway to the Florida Turnpike. He pulled onto the shoulder just before the interchange and sat in the car with the engine idling, watching heat waves dance above the baking steel hood.

He had a decision to make.

He could turn north, toward Palmville.

Or south, toward Miami.

Whichever road he chose, it would lead to a woman trying to piece together a new life he might be a part of someday. Or to a man seeking to kill him while, like Donnie, living as someone other than himself.

Different worlds. Different people who were becoming someone else, changing . . .

Who were they?

Who was he?